The shining splendor of our logo of this book reflects the glitt Look for the Zebra Lovegr romance. It's a trademark tha and reading entertainment.

HIS WICKED, WICKED WAYS

"Will you have your wicked way with me?" murmured Rafe. "Right here, right now . . . in my bed."

She laughed at his cockiness. Many names described this rugged man before her, few of them beautiful. Liar, lover, betrayer. Matador, revolutionist. Murderer. She ought to run screaming. Ought to.

It might be crazy and foolish, but Margaret wanted her wicked way with him, wanted it with every fiber of her being. *Just don't trust him. Don't trust anything he says or does.*

He took Margaret's hand, leading her to the massive bed. Bringing her hands behind his waist, his lips to her brow, he let his warm breath caress her skin as he asked, "Will a simple siesta be enough for you?"

She shivered, enthralled. Bending back from the waist, she watched his reaction as she replied, "Rest is my last desire. You are my first."

MARTHA HIX

WILD SIERRA ROGUE

ZEBRA BOOKS
KENSINGTON PUBLISHING CORP.

ZEBRA BOOKS are published by

Kensington Publishing Corp.
475 Park Avenue South
New York, NY 10016 .

First Printing: August, 1993

Printed in the United States of America

For Roy's girls . . .
Tina, Jackie, Stacy, Tiffany
and — ohmagosh! — our very own triplets

Part One

. . . The Journey

They followed in the footsteps
of those
before them—
Columbus . . . De Léon . . . Quixote

One

San Antonio, Texas
October 1897
in the calm of afternoon.

Hell waited to pop. Somehow he knew it waited. While he bathed to get ready for the big blond stuff of his insatiable lusts, Rafael Delgado tried to shake the portentous unease settling heavier than his noon meal. Once before he'd had this feeling. When fate had turned on him. When the black of night and his own crimes had broken his spirit. When he'd quit being the Magnificent Eagle of Mexico.

You're nothing. Except for your appeal to women, you've lost it all. And now—something bad is going to happen.

Ridiculous.

Rafe snickered at foreboding, stepped from the copper tub, and rubbed a towel along his hard hairy thighs. "You gobbled down too much chicken-fried steak," he assured himself, "that's all."

He had no worries, if he kept the past buried.

9

Burying old miseries had become a skill carefully honed, such as when he'd wielded a *muleta* in the bullring, in his younger days. Or as he now saw to the breeding of fatlings for those arenas of Mexico. Or as he caressed womanly curves.

The thought of such curves urged him into taking one more glance at his bedroom. Perfect. A lair. The bed fit for royalty, made with new satin sheets and scattered with petals from some of the last roses of the year. All it lacked? The delectable and delicious Mrs. Boyd.

Rafe favored females tall and fair. Looking up to women like Dolores Boyd did something good to him. One lucky hombre described Rafe, so why count fortune's teeth? "Hurry, beautiful Dolores. This is for you." He patted the front of his britches, wrestled with buttoning them, and sang. "Tonight, tonight, tonight. Your eyes of blue, your hair of gold, your ruby lips . . . I will behold." Gazing from left to right and back again into the mirror hanging above his bureau, he combed his short-cropped hair away from his temples. "Yum, Do-lor-es. I will be true—"

Suddenly, the comb dropped. He scowled at his image, aggrieved and heartsick. Now he knew. Omen, thy name was reality. A gray hair poked through the raven-black ones.

"Look at you. Scarred and gray. Old. You're losing it, hombre." He plucked the offender from his scalp. "Ouch!"

Rubbing his head, he cursed any and everything that popped to mind. The strangest thought sur-

10

faced. He had a mental image of a McLoughlin triplet. Dark hair, blue eyes, and lips like cherry wine . . .

Damn. Just what he needed. A reminder of yet another failure.

Determined to get a grip, he sucked in his stomach and tucked in his butt, before he took a side view. *You still have what it takes to please the ladies.*

No bull's horn, in Rafe's glory days, had ever gouged his flesh. His muscles remained superbly toned and distinct in relief, despite thirty-nine years of abuse. Darkened by outdoor work, along with a trickle of the stock of Moctezuma, his face wasn't a source of shame, even though the sun had begun to plough lines from the corners of his eyes. And, of course, a jagged scar cut into the right side of his mouth. Yet many a lover had enjoyed running her fingertip along this flaw. For such a lovely, he must tend his grooming, must make himself worthy.

The mirror reflected a woman entering the bedroom. He winked rakishly and blew a kiss to his cook, while he selected the pomade jar from amid the chaos of his toiletries.

"A visitor waits outside," Ida Frances Jones announced.

"She's early. See her in." Rafe glazed the left side of his head. "Is the champagne chilled?"

Rafe, not getting a reply, set the brilliantine on the bureau and wheeled around. Drying her hands with a dishtowel, the stout and motherly Ida Frances met his quizzing stare with flattened lips.

Obviously the visitor wasn't the most recent apple of Rafe's eye.

He groaned.

"She told Ida Frances she's in a hurry for you," the cook said in third-person delivery. Solemn as the father of Mexican independence, the sainted Hidalgo, she steepled her fingertips beneath her chin. "Poor dear, so many ladies require so much of you."

True. Rumors ran rife hereabouts: he could serve many mistresses in a night's stand. Perhaps so. But with a few exceptions, he was a one-woman man — one woman at a time. For a week or two, sometimes a month. While he hated disappointing as much as one of his lady friends, Dolores took precedence. Hence, he queried with hesitation, "Which one is she?"

"A new one. Someone named McLoughlin sent her. Ida Frances believes she said Gil McLoughlin."

Rafe scowled again. Now he knew why he'd had a hunch of trouble. Neither fried meat nor a gray hair had been the cause. Trouble bore a Scottish surname. "Get rid of her!"

Simultaneous to his exclamation, two pointed ears and a tiny head popped from the nest of Rafe's house slipper. A pair of black eyes much too big for her face rounded at her master's shout; the small canine body, fawn in color, began to shake. One ear flopped inward. Frita yipped.

All the doting and adoring master, Rafe rushed over to scoop the elderly Frita into his palm. Her upper lip folding back in what he took for a smile, the Chihuahua dog sighed and leaned in to his fingers.

Idly noting that Ida Frances hadn't moved, Rafe cooed, "Forgive me, little confection, for disturbing your siesta. Ah, yes, kiss Papá. There's a good Frita. There's a good girl. Yes, my sugar. So forgiving of a mean old Papá. So pretty. So sweet." *Such bad breath.*

She raked the pad of his thumb with her tiny tongue. While he stroked her chest—he enjoyed stroking all sorts of female chests—she gazed up, worshipful.

"Papá's baby. Brought all the way from our home in Mexico, from Santa Alicia." Despite having earned a king's ransom for his prowess in the arena, Rafe and his pet left with the clothes on his back, the collar on her neck, and barely enough gold to secure title to this ranch.

"You should get yourself a wife and a houseful of babies. You would make a good father." To make him sound as sterling as Ida Frances found him, she added, "And husband."

He tucked the now placated Frita back in his shoe. "Ah, my darling cook, my devoted friend, I thank you. But a family would be cheated, having me at its head."

In a dozen ways he would cheat a wife, were he to take one. He wasn't the Anglo ideal of ice-cream socials and quiet evenings by the hearth, nor did he measure up to any respectable Hispanic standards. He wasn't sure what he was anymore.

Once, crowds parted when *El Aguila Magnífico*—the Magnificent Eagle, the greatest matador in the

13

western hemisphere—strode among them. Once, respect came from his skill with the *muleta* and from his family name. Once, he'd been feared and revered for predatory deeds against that name. Once was nevermore. It had been eight long, trying years, since fate exiled him from the sweet bosom of his mother country.

Near the start of those years, Rafe had thought he'd found peace in the Lone Star State, yet betrayal—*Forget it!* Rafe asked, "Did she say what she wants? In particular."

"She, uh, didn't get specific." Ida Frances cleared her throat. "Oh, I forgot. She's *daughter* to Gil McLoughlin."

"Olga?" Time tripped. Disoriented, Rafe blurted, "Charity?"

Immediately, he knew without confirmation that these were wrong guesses. He slapped his hand on his chest, feigning an attack of ill health not too far from the truth, given that the last of the McLoughlin triplets—despite her resemblance to her exquisite sisters—was enough to turn even an iron stomach.

He said, "Don't tell me it's Margaret—*La Bruja*."

A question formed in the cook's broad face, asking why he referred to the broom, which meant the witch in Spanish. Ida Frances asked, "This fits her?"

"Right." His lip curled. "She's living proof beauty can be but skin deep."

"Beauty?" Ida Frances sounded baffled.

"Yes, she has the requisites. But I've always thought she's in dire need of a good—" He cleared

14

his throat. "To my way of thinking, Margaret McLoughlin starches her drawers."

He reached for a flagon of men's cologne, then splashed a goodly portion on his cheeks and armpits. His hand froze. Was he primping for *La Bruja?* Quickly, he replaced the stopper.

Frita crawled out of his shoe, shook herself, then, tail drooping, toddled on rickety legs through the miniature trapdoor leading to the patio. A nature call, Rafe suspected as his cook asked, "Why does the lady's name sound familiar?"

"You've probably read about the McLoughlins in the *Express* or the *Light*. The broom's father is Secretary of State under McKinley." Rafe took a fresh shirt from a drawer and twisted the subject. "Have you heard of the Four Aces Ranch in Fredericksburg?"

"Ah, the Four Aces and McLoughlin. Now your cook makes a connection. The McLoughlins own it."

"Yes. But they live in Washington and Havana and Madrid. Or wherever else whim carries them."

"You know the family well?" he heard.

He shrugged into the shirt and buttoned it over the golden crucifix nestled on the dense mat of his chest. "You might say I know more than I want to."

"Tell Ida Frances more. Don't leave her guessing. You know she can't stand riddles."

Rafe strode to the bed, collecting his guitar from its corner perch as he went, and settled onto the coverlet to strum a few chords of *"España Cañi"* before leaving his explanations at a bare minimum.

15

"In '89 the triplet Charity was charged with smuggling Texas silver into Mexico. I saved her good name. But she repaid me by telling Margaret about my 'misdeeds.' "

In turn the witch filled the most demure of the triplets with tales of his carnal excesses—all true, why try to deny? Actually, his debauchery roused the prudish Olga's interest, he recalled with a bittersweet smile converting to a scowl. Years had past since he'd thought of the Spanish countess of American descent. And that was just as well.

The cook bent a curious eye. "Ida Frances's worked for you since 1895, but she doesn't remember a mention of *La Bruja*."

"I haven't seen her in four or five years."

Regardless, some word had reached him. Talk of a lengthy stay in an obscure place. Such gossip usually led to rumors of a bastard birth, but Margaret McLoughlin, given her disposition, would turn off even the most desperate of hombres. She had to be a virgin.

"I know the McLoughlins from the Scotsman to his Hessian wife Lisette, and on to the oldest living McLoughlin, Maisie," Rafe said, getting back to his explanations. "It goes without saying I know the three daughters." Especially the Countess of Granada. "Have you read about the Wild Hawks of the West show? The triplet Charity stars in it."

"But what about the one you call Broom?"

He recalled what he knew and what he'd learned secondhand. "She's spoiled, useless as a house cat. When she should have learned flower arranging and

16

the proper way to treat an hombre, she had her nose stuck in tomes." He paused, then embellished, "No doubt she studied witchery and spell-casting."

"I suppose a young lady from such an illustrious family can do as she pleases." The cook brushed a crumb from her apron. "Ida Frances never guessed you were close to such a family."

"I'm not. I've never dined at their table, nor called on the household, nor shared a cigar with the patriarch." He'd never even met the only son, Angus. "They have no use for this lowly Mexican bull breeder," Rafe said bitterly, stiffly. "Except for dirty work."

Loyal to the top of her braids, Ida Frances got one of those mama-cat looks protective women were so good at. "You are a fine and splendid man. The most exalted matador in all the world. No one should treat you with disrespect."

Rafe laughed. "It's been almost a decade since anyone tossed a rose into the ring for me."

"Ida Frances will send the visitor away."

"Wait. Don't ask me why—I don't know!—but I'll see her." Rafe rubbed his scarred mouth and glanced at the closed shutters leading to the patio. "Show her out there."

Aiming to get Margaret McLoughlin's goat, he would keep her waiting. He shucked his shirt, relaxed in the bed where he'd entertain Dolores, and set his fingers to *"España Cañi"* again.

Music, faint yet hauntingly moving, drifted from

17

Rafael Delgado's residence of whitewashed adobe and red-tile roof.

Aggravated at everything and especially at the situation which jerked her from the brownstone in Manhattan she called home, Margaret McLoughlin followed the Eagle's fusby servant woman around the dwelling's perimeter. The strains of guitar grew louder as they approached the rear.

Margaret hadn't been asked in. It might have been nice, being spared the sun—she'd forgotten how sweltering a Texas afternoon in October could be. But no. The host hadn't invited her inside. A gracious gesture on his part might have shown some refinement. Amazingly, Rafe *did* have class and breeding in his lineage, but Margaret saw him as a throwback to a darker age, of a stripe most often seen on a wanted poster.

His domestic fiddled with a rusty hasp to open a weathered and creaking gate leading into a courtyard. The moon-faced woman cast a surly nod her way. "Mr. Delgado will be with you in a little bit."

Intent on getting the upper hand with Rafe—she figured he was the guitarist nearby—Margaret raised her voice. "Did you not give your employer my message? Tell him to be quick about it. I'm in a hurry."

"The great Eagle is a busy man," was the woman's contemptuous reply. She took her leave.

Could he have earned such loyalty? Margaret wondered, doubting it. Anyway, who gave a care? She had enough on her mind without mulling Rafael Delgado's character—he, whose greatest claims to fame were seducing vulnerable women and out-witting dumb animals.

She glanced in the music's direction, seeing closed shutters. She dreaded confronting Rafe. Always, she'd gotten the impression he saw the worst in Olga when he looked at Margaret. "Why worry?" she said *sotto voce*. "Any physical resemblance is now just in passing."

Weary from the arduous trip south, as well as from her general state of ill health, she searched for a place to sit down and make a few observations. She'd pictured his home being a veritable museum to his matador days, but there was nothing in sight relating to that faded renown. Amazing.

The patio of terra cotta tile was built in the court-yard manner, a small fountain in the center. Climbing rosebushes grew on a trio of trellises. Two hide-covered chairs circled a wrought iron table, but the setting didn't invite her invasion.

The table had been set with stemmed goblets, a bowl of fruit, and a bucket of champagne. Black silk material, probably some sort of thin robe, lay across the back of a chair. In front of it, a single rose rested atop a china plate. No doubt about it, the offing held seduction. Forced or otherwise.

Rafe never changed.

Just as she shook her head in disgust, something moved on the flagstones. Fawn-colored, small. A rat!

Margaret shrieked, backed away. The beastie quivered and quaked, began to cower. Heart beating twice as fast as the guitar tempo, Margaret mur-

19

mured, "That's not a rat. It's a dog." Her father once described this breed indigenous to northern Mexico. "And you've scared the little thing half to death."

Yes, and don't you know Rafe got a thrill from your shriek. She crouched down to extend a hand. "Little doggie, can we be friends?"

The mite tottered forward. And, surprisingly, she crawled into the cup of Margaret's hand. "Why, you're old!"

Margaret scratched the muzzle gone white with age. She couldn't picture Rafe Delgado as master to an ancient canine, especially a tiny one. Brutes like Rafe tied in with beasts, such as Alsatians or wolfhounds. They kept piranhas in their fishbowls. They stood up to two-ton bulls. A delicate dog such as this commanded a gentle hand.

"Little one, I'm not going to start giving Rafe undue credit." Margaret stood and held his pet at her heart. "I've known him eight years. He's a degenerate and a satyr and a bum. And then there are his bizarre political activities. Or, *were.*"

The one word best describing him was too awful and horrible even to whisper to a dog, though Margaret did shudder. Trying to get a look in the closed windows while pacing up and down the flagstones, she groused, "Where is he?"

Rafe didn't deign an appearance.

"I ought to abandon this project. If only I hadn't made Papa several promises." Margaret didn't renege on promises. "But if he knew the whole ugly truth, he wouldn't put so much faith in Rafe," she

20

confided to the pint-sized dog now licking the cushion of her thumb. "I'd *love* to fill Papa's ears, but I promised Olga not to tell her awful secret. Which doesn't mean I am thrilled at asking for help. My father is convinced, you see, no one knows the Copper Canyon better than Rafe."

Margaret didn't dispute Rafe's knowledge of that area of the globe. Yet . . . "Haring off to Mexico, especially with him, ranks one peg ahead of prancing nude through Central Park."

Hare off she must in these times of political intrigue. Both President McKinley and Gil McLoughlin, wishing to save the lives of American boys, stood firm against the popular hue and cry of *"¡Cuba libre!"* With Papa embroiled in affairs of state—and with communication impossible into a spa rumored to be the Fountain of Youth—the family business of collecting a vagabond Lisette had fallen to Margaret's reluctant shoulders.

"I've got to make a quick trip out of it," she said.

Much awaited her return home. Her neat and well-ordered life, in a big city like no other on earth. A professorship, at long last. A tear spilled as she cuddled the Chihuahua under her chin. "And my two precious babies."

She must return with all haste. *What if I can't?* She froze at the mere thought. After all these years of fits and starts, she had to make something of herself this time around. It might be her last chance.

"You're being ridiculous. You have plenty enough time to take care of family business. The rest will

21

take care of itself."

After being set to her paws, the Chihuahua lapped from a dish of water, licked her whiskers, and vanished through a trapdoor. Margaret tapped a toe, her irritation building as she whiled away more minutes, waiting for Rafe.

It was hard to believe she'd once thought the has-been matador terribly intriguing.

Two

Rafe scratched his chest while ambling on bare feet to the patio to face *La Bruja*. Her back to him, Ida Frances's rosebushes framing her tall form, Margaret evidently hadn't heard his approach, for she continued to sniff the blossoms.

She wore bustle and corset beneath a drab skirt of brown and plain white blouse with puffed sleeves. Whereas her mother and sisters were big-boned and filled out nicely, Margaret had become anything but the latter. Even viewed from the rear, her appearance shocked Rafe. He remembered her as shapely, near plump. There was a frailness to her now, as if she needed to be fattened on beans and tortillas and the fruits of amour.

Fruits of amour?

He couldn't imagine Margaret relishing so much as a nibble of passion.

One glance beyond the patio walls told him the autumn sun would set in an hour or so. *Merdo*. He'd been keeping Margaret waiting, when he needed to get rid of her. And fast.

"I know you're here, Rafe." The last red rose of the Indian summer at her nose, she inhaled and hummed a note of sensory approval. "Are you surprised to see me?"

For a moment he stood struck dumb. In his memory he'd recalled her voice as a series of braying snorts. It was nothing like that, nor did it have Olga's little-girl quality. There was a full-bodied richness to Margaret's husky voice, showing intelligence and strength.

He remembered her strength.

Always, strong women put him off.

Still giving him her back, she asked, "Have you no courtesy welcome for me?"

"I don't live by courtesies."

"My, how thoughtless of me, overlooking your ill-manners." She smoothed hair not as richly hued nor as lustrous as he remembered it. The *café noir* was now just brown.

He snickered. "I see you're still wearing your hair in a bun. Like a schoolmarm."

"I am a school—" She turned. Her mouth dropped at the sight of his gold-adorned, shirtless chest. Then, like an old woman's, her lips puckered into disapproval; she favored her great-grandmother Maisie at this moment. "No decency . . ."

Whereas Rafe had been shocked, he turned speechless. Maybe he'd expected to find her features unchanged, or perhaps he'd been looking for a suggestion of Spain's loveliest countess. What he got was the awful truth.

Margaret's complexion used to be peaches and cream, but it had faded to a waxy gray with her skin stretched across sharp bones. What happened to her once glorious radiance? All right, a semblance of her beauty remained, but Margaret looked at least a dozen years above her twenty-eight.

Hard feelings vanished. With typical gallantry toward a needy damsel, Rafe wanted to make everything right for her. Stepping closer, forcing a smile, he started to speak; she beat him to it, saying, "Speaking of hair, yours looks funny." She smirked, not a pretty sight. "It's all greased down on one side, and fluffy on the other. Sleep in a puddle of pomade, did you?"

No wonder the witch was skinny—she'd been living on sour grapes. Keeping a good distance from her, he rubbed some of the hair cream to the right side of his head. "State your business. I'm a busy man."

"Yes, of course, you're otherwise engaged." With a blue-veined hand, she fiddled with the sole item of beauty connected to *La Bruja,* a cameo brooch. "At your toilette, to be sure."

"It wouldn't hurt you to pay more attention to *your*self."

Mixing English and Spanish—both she and Rafe were fluent in the other's mother tongue—she said pointedly, "Unlike some people, I pride myself on being above vanity."

"You don't say, *Santa* Margarita. Nice ring to saint. But saints are kind, I've been taught. Your disposition might honey up if you left corsets to the well-padded." With true sentiment, he added, "Those stays must be gouging your ribs."

She yanked at something, mostly likely the corset

hem. "Ever the charmer, aren't you?"

It was always this way with them. Mutual dislike, mutual antagonism. Which was an awkward scenario for an hombre used to charming and being charmed by the ladies. Unappreciative women gave him the shivers. Thankfully they were few and far between. But what should he do about this one? Extend an olive branch?

A long time back she'd written a book. Rafe had a grudging respect for anyone diligent enough to put something like that together. Him, he got restless just reading one. "I've heard good things about *Columbus and Isabella*."

"*Christopher Columbus and the Catholic Kings*," she corrected, then waxed enthusiastic. "You know, 1492 was a pivotal year in history . . ."

On went the oration. A yawn threatened Rafe. Long-dead Moors, Jews, and Inquisitors had nothing to do with the business of bull-breeding, or of loving the ladies. Margaret did capture his attention, though, when woe blanketed her gaze.

"Anyway"—she sniffed—"it's 'Mortimer' McLoughlin's book, not mine. Not really. Not only was I forbidden from using my own name, it missed being printed during the quatercentenary of the Great Discovery. Thanks to the court action against my plagiarist, the book wasn't published until 1893."

"More's the pity." Rafe started to ask why her nabob father hadn't used his influence in the matter, but decided to leave well enough alone. He grinned, teasing, "So what brings you to my humble abode—praise for the landholder?"

Annoyed. She got annoyed, especially when he gave his shoulders a roll and his biceps a flex. Her teeth clenching and unclenching, she said, "Praise for the landholder? You never change do you, Rafe? Ever vain and pompous."

"Do you really expect me to answer that?"

"*I* expect nothing. To *me* you don't exist."

"Which is why you're here to praise me . . . ?"

"Maybe I should laud you. Let's see now."

They stood glaring straight at each other. Although he'd challenged her, it aggravated him no end when she tapped her fingernail on an incisor and looked him up and down, as if he'd been swinging from a butcher's hook for days on end.

She said, "No visible deformities or epidermal eruptions. No bucked or overlong or missing teeth. Plenty of hair atop your head, as well as on that chest of yours. Ears that don't wave in the breeze. And—correct me if I'm wrong—but from looking at those muscles you so love to flaunt, I'd say a lady wouldn't need to hire a woodchopper, were you in her employ."

¡Maldición! He longed to rattle the harridan's teeth—like his uncle Arturo did the life from the slaves who worked his silver mines.

Continuing to damn him, she pointed out, "There is one thing I admire in you, Rafael Delgado. I'm glad you're short. I wouldn't like looking up to you."

His vanity slashed, Rafe ordered himself to consider the source. He knew why she hated him. It wasn't his height, which was a couple of inches above hers, and, besides, he was tall for a *mexi-*

27

cano, anyway. She hated him because of Olga.

Olga was also the main reason he had no use for the McLoughlins.

If it killed him, he would fire the parting shot. His voice rife with innuendo, he pointed out, "Big things come in small packages, *mujer.*"

Bustle bobbing, Margaret stomped over to the table. Her forefinger and thumb picked up the Chinese kimono he'd purchased as a gift for the *lovely* and *amenable* Dolores of a hundred charms. As if it were beyond loathsome, Margaret made a big to-do as she dropped the silken mass to the table. Finished, she went into the gyrations women endured to seat themselves.

She skewered him with blue eyes. And they were the sad eyes of an unhappy, unfulfilled woman.

The McLoughlin triplets may have been identical (at least they'd started out alike), but he noticed for the first time that their eyes were different shades of blue. Charity's snapped with a turquoise tint. And Olga's were pale, weak. Warning himself off the subject of *her,* he honed in on her sister again. Fringed with thick ebony lashes, Margaret's eyes were as blue as the summer sky of his home state. To Rafe, nothing was prettier than the summer sky of Chihuahua.

Dios, when Margaret McLoughlin started looking attractive, he'd definitely been too long without a woman.

"Why did you come here?" he asked, weary of sparring.

She poked stray, wavy hairs back into the tight, dark bun at the crown of her head. "I'll make this as brief as possible. I want to hire you. You're to escort me and my bro—" She coughed. "Me and my fiancé to—"

"Fiancé? *You've* got a man?" Rafe had never figured her for a housewife. This was a woman of purpose, a person out to set the world afire, as he'd been when he first entered the *plaza de toros*. What had happened to her ambitions?

She took him wrong, took insult. "Yes, I have a man. A very fine-looking *young* man. Tall. Very tall. A Teutonic god, he's been called. You're old enough to be his father, I do believe. You *are* forty-five, aren't you?"

Forty-five did it. His temper boiling like the water required for cocoa, he shouted, "*¡Estoy como agua pa' chocolate!*"

"You needn't shout. *My* ears work fine."

Witch! Her *novio* must be a blind, deaf, and moronic Hun. On the whole, no able hombre would pick *La Bruja* for his own. Oh really? Rafe himself had had his eye on her, back in the beginning—back before she treated him to a large serving of her personality: colder than ice, romantic as a saddle sore, meaner than *el toro* with a *garrocha* stuck in his shoulder thews.

Keeping his voice even, Rafe asked, "What *exactly* do you want of me?"

"Help."

"Tell me something I don't know already."

"My mother is at a health retreat in Mexico. It's supposed to be the Fountain of Youth."

The daughter, in his estimation, was the one in need of a miracle.

"My father wants her home. I expect you to guide me and Tex Jones to her."

"Tex Jones?"

"My intended, of course. We must leave as soon as you can get your house in order."

This sounded more like a demand than a job offer, which sat worse than greasy meat. "Anything I've done lately to make you think I'd desert my ranch to step to your tune?"

"You'll do it. You'll do it because you like money and I'm willing to pay you; though you ought to do it for nothing, since you're indebted to my father."

The woman was loco in the head. If anyone was indebted in this situation, it was Gil McLoughlin to Rafael Delgado. There was the matter of a debt of honor. A debt unpaid. Back in '89, back in Chihuahua, McLoughlin had promised to arm the revolution, if Rafe came to Texas and testified in Charity McLoughlin's behalf. Rafe kept his end of the bargain. And several times in the ensuing years McLoughlin had called on his good nature. For some strange reason, Rafe had never been able to say no. There was no time like the present for a change.

"For Pete's sake, don't just stand there frowning at me. Say something," she demanded.

"Since I am a snake in the grass, why do you insist on hiring me?"

"My father won't have it any other way."

Rafe lit a cheroot, tossed the match away, and as smoke curled from his mouth, he fashioned an *O* that undulated heavenward. "Ah, yes. Rafe to the rescue of a McLoughlin woman. Again."

"My mother isn't in trouble, not unless some fanatic gets to her, which I doubt. She's discretion itself. Of course, we McLoughlins can't be too careful, what with the Fourth Estate dwelling on our links to Spain."

"And with Mexico being a powder keg of sympathy to the Cubans."

"Exactly."

That she and her father assumed he would line up at their sides — well, it chafed at a raw wound. There was a lot not to like in the moneyed McLoughlins. A rancher turned lawmaker turned statesman, Margaret's father defended Spain against Cuba, while Rafe likened the island's struggles to those of Mexico in the early part of this century.

Like his own family — the Delgados of Chihuahua — Gil McLoughlin and his dynasty represented factions Rafe had left his profession to renounce and fight against. Wealth. Inequity. Class distinctions.

Margaret jumped to stand and march up and down the patio, as if she were a Prussian general designing the charts of war. "Now, after we collect Mother, we'll head for Tampico. She, Tex, and I will catch a boat from there. You'll be free to do as you please."

"Wait just a minute. Who's to make sure I get back safe and sound?" Rafe goaded. "I've grown soft over the years. I'm no longer the great eagle of Mexico. I'm just another Mexican, who's taken up the ways and language of a Texan."

"You've still got an accent."

Obviously he wasn't getting his point across. He

31

shortened the distance between them. "I'm not referring to the inflection of my voice. I'm trying to tell you—you can't count on my name for protection."

"I want a guide, not a bodyguard."

"Really? Who's to say you won't get your throat slit in Mexico? Who's to say your Teutonic god will get back alive? And who's to say I won't be the one to slit your throats?" He tightened his grip. "I am an outlaw. And you know it."

"You won't murder us." She shoved his fingers away. Her shoulders squaring, she seemed alive with bravery and challenge.

For the very first time, he kind of fancied her daring. Kind of. Had his advancing age turned his brain to mush? "Be careful giving your trust, Margaret McLoughlin. You might get hurt."

A moment passed as she assessed him, then a half chuckle lifted her meager bosom. "I appreciate the warning, but I've been to hell and back already." A dash of melancholy laced her rich voice. "Tempting death is the least of my worries."

Admiring her courage too much for comfort, Rafe asked, "Does your father realize . . . Does he know about the trouble I left in Chihuahua?"

"Yes. Of course. He knows you all too well. Of course, he doesn't know the whole truth about you and Olga, and let's *not* get into *that*. Anyway, my father isn't one to make snap decisions."

Margaret started to take a deep breath, but she coughed instead. The deep croup alarmed Rafe, but he told himself not to make too much of it. She'd probably suffered no more than a recent chest cold, maybe even a bout of lung fever. She might look bad, but she didn't look as bad as his sister had . . . when Maria Carmen fought a losing battle against consumption.

Swallowing, Margaret took a restorative breath and braced herself by holding on to the back of a chair. "As for the method to his madness, Papa figures you'll shield us against your kind."

"A dangerous tactic, I'd say. But you'll go along with whatever he wants, won't you? You follow blindly in his stead."

"With my eyes wide open, I do my duty to *family*. A close family, in my opinion, is the most precious jewel ever mined."

He knew she meant it. And, suddenly, without warning, he envied her devotion. With the exception of his priestly brother, Rafe's family — *Jesucristo,* he couldn't picture them anymore — loved one another by the points of daggers and swords and repeater rifles.

"Funny, I find it, your father sending a delicate" — oh, he was proud of not saying *sickly-looking* — "daughter after his *mujer*. Why doesn't he go after his woman himself?"

"Papa can't leave Washington just now. He's busy with the affairs of state — you know we may end up in war over Cuba."

"You've got a brother and two sisters."

"Angus manages the Four Aces. And I thought you knew that my sisters live in Europe. But Olga and Leonardo are traveling — Well, that's not important right now. I am the one called on. And I do my duty to family."

He knew she spoke the truth. Of all the

33

McLoughlin daughters, Margaret was the fixer. She wouldn't quit until the job was done, even though she might gripe the whole way. For the second time today, Rafe let down his guard. "What would your father do without us?"

"No telling." A grin softening her ravaged face, she lifted her palms in a gesture of acceptance. "Good old Rafe and Margaret to the rescue."

They shared a laugh, and it felt good to Rafe. He didn't wish to study on why. Since she'd mentioned the Gulf of Mexico port of Tampico, curiosity forced him to ask, "Where exactly is this Fountain of Youth?"

"It's called Eden Roc. It's near *El Ojo de la Barranca,* in—"

"The Eye of the Canyon. In Chihuahua state." His good feeling vanished, Rafe felt his throat closing. And it had nothing to do with his having heard of Eden Roc. The slightest movement impossible, he murmured, "I know the area well."

"Then you know it's a very isolated place, several days' journey from Chihuahua city. I believe the area around Eden Roc is inhabited mostly by Tarahumara Indians."

The Tarahumara. Rafe could almost hear their drums and chants, could almost taste their potent beer and voluptuous virgins. What a wonderful time he and Hernán, as youths, had one summer there. As men, they had taken Rafe's young brother to a nearby village's notorious whorehouse to make a man out of Xzobal. How Rafe and Hernán had laughed when the boy who became a priest ran screaming from Señora Pilar's spate of instructions.

Hernándo! Rafe had to clench his teeth, else he'd scream out his dead cousin's name.

Turning on his heel, he went to a table of bottles, selecting tequila. Dust blown from the glasses, he poured two shots, then went over to hand Margaret one. She set hers aside. He quaffed his. "I do not wish to return to Chihuahua."

"You'll be well paid."

He started to say she'd be better off staying well away from Eden Roc—the old man who owned it being loco as a Yaqui on peyote, according to the Tarahumara—but he heard something in the distance; a quick look over the patio wall confirmed his suspicions. Dolores and her buggy approached. What was he going to do about *La Bruja?*

"Margarita," he said, pronouncing her name in Spanish and waving a hand, "I don't want the money, I—"

"Good. Then you'll do it as a favor to my father."

He'd forgotten her miserly bent; she could pinch a peso until the eagle gave up the serpent. Another time he might have found humor in that. "Now, now, let's not get ahead of ourselves," he said. "I didn't say I wouldn't want compensation for services rendered."

He crossed to her chair and took her arm. "You've got to get out of here."

"Must you always be rude?"

"Yes. Always. Now go." He picked up her handbag, thrust it into her hand, and started leading her to the door. "Nice to see you again," he lied. "Give your papá my regards."

"I am not leaving till you promise to take me to

35

Mexico!"

"I'm not promising anything."

Margaret got an eyeful of the approaching buggy. "I *promise* I won't leave until you say yes."

Three

Returning to Chihuahua could cost his life.

A bead of sweat rolled down his back and into the waistband of his britches; though more than half of October had passed, the weather remained warm and sultry, even on an early morning such as this. Rafe paced the railroad platform and made a point of ignoring the McLoughlin spinster and her future husband, though it proved difficult, since she was hectoring a porter over proper care of her numerous steamer trunks.

While it was amazing such a woman of simplicity could outdo the most equipped of travelers, Rafe didn't mull the contents of her stores, the narrowness of her brown traveling suit, nor did he dwell on his own situation.

He concentrated on the mundane. Fog tumbled into the smoke that bellowed from the locomotive. Hawking his wares, a ragged paperboy held aloft the San Antonio *Light*. A taco vendor pushed his cart between the crush of men, women, and children waiting to catch the westbound Southern Pacific.

Margaret marched over to the station master; her mouth began to ratchet.

"Lady, I don't have nothing to do with the routes," Rafe heard the man reply.

She could have been an opera singer, so voluminous was her voice when she said, "But this is the epitome of inconvenience. It is a straight trip to Chihuahua, if we head for Piedras Negras."

"Ma'am, as I told you, there's trouble with rebels between Piedras Negras and Chihuahua city, and the president of the Southern Pacific has done decided we'll take our passengers to El Paso. You can catch the Meskan train outta Juarez. And, madam, that be all I intend to say on the matter."

Rafe didn't listen to Margaret's protest.

"All aboard!"

At the conductor's summons, Rafe doffed his Stetson to wipe his brow. Now that it was time to leave, he thought about what the journey would bring. After eight years of vowing never to set foot in his home state without the armature of war backing him, Rafe Delgado—revolutionary and murderer—was about to start the return journey to hell. But he'd go with nothing but a Colt Peacemaker, and a gun belt studded with bullets.

What about when you return to San Antonio? If he returned. Maybe he'd take Ida Frances's advice and find some nice little wife, then get some children. A certain peace accompanied that thought. *Bring out the walking sticks and liniment.*

A strawberry blonde, luscious and ripe as any strawberry in a field of June, sidled up to Rafe and patted her ample bosom. "My goodness, it's warm, isn't it, sir?"

"Indeed it is, señorita." On instinct, his mouth curved into a smile around the half-smoked cheroot. Taking a long look at this big blonde reminded Rafe of the Amazonian morsel he'd been forced to turn away, thanks to the witch. He stepped to the side, making a gesture not unlike when he'd flourished the *muleta*. "May I help you aboard?"

"By all means."

He held her fingers and guided her elbow as she took the first step. Something poked his side at the same moment a thank you gushed into his ears. He turned his head, catching sight of an umbrella; he felt its tip wedging between his ribs.

Dios, what was the matter with the witch? If he didn't know better, Rafe would have guessed Margarita was jealous. "Remove that poker, or you and your man will be traveling to Chihuahua by the seat of your broomstick."

Iced blue eyes chipped into the slate of his. Her mouth pinched like that of a woman wearing tight shoes, she huffed, "I didn't hire you to further your love life."

No, she hadn't. And he hadn't wanted to guide Margaret and her man to Eden Roc, not even for the obscene amount of money he'd demanded in a ploy to get her to cease and desist. He felt no overriding responsibility toward them or their quest. It wasn't as if she'd worked for the money.

Two nights ago, when she stood in his home and argued, he'd realized something. Her request had

39

been a sign, a divine signal for him to return . . . and somehow honor Hernán's memory.

Then, even if it cost his life, he would have a purpose beyond stud.

"I know what you want, *bruja*." He slapped at the umbrella. "Help aboard. You've got your own hombre for that."

"Obviously you misunderstand. I said—Oh, *never mind!*" The umbrella tip receded. Swiveling on the ball of her buttoned shoes, Margaret stomped up and into the car. "And don't call me an old hag."

"Bruja has two definitions."

"Don't call me witch, either. Miss McLoughlin will do."

"You don't say . . . *Margaret.*"

She gave an ooh of aggravation before disappearing past the conductor. Her man shrugged at Rafe, then followed, and Rafe took another puff from the thin cigar before tossing it onto the rails. Something about Tex Jones struck him as peculiar, and his feeling had nothing to do with jealousy over realizing Margaret's fiancé wasn't in jeopardy of going gray.

An hour ago, Rafe—a few minutes late by Margaret's timepiece; early by his own standards—had met the happy couple at the San Antonio rail station. During those sixty minutes, Rafe had noticed something besides the wet behind a couple of ears. The ox of a straw-haired hombre hadn't cast so much as a yearning gaze at his woman.

Well, who gave a damn? Rafe climbed aboard. Ambling down the aisle, he saw the lovebirds sitting on facing seats. And Tex Jones had his eye on the strawberry blonde. It shouldn't have mattered to Rafe, Jones's inattention to his bride-to-be. To Rafe, she was nothing but a witch and a *chingaquedita,* the last a vulgar term for an irritating female. But any woman, no matter how unpleasant, ought to have her man's undivided attention.

Blondes. They ought to be burned at the stake. Men were fools for them, Margaret bemoaned inwardly, as Tex took his turn ogling that floozy and acting touched in the head. Rafe had already done his stumbling over her. The worst part of the situation? Over the past two days Margaret had been unable to stop herself from recalling the sight of Rafe's bare chest. Or of that golden cross snuggled in those jet black swirls of chest hair. Or of that hard flat stomach. Sin looked like heaven . . .

He wasn't a burly or strapping man, Rafe. Though his shoulders were muscular and broad, there was a litheness to him, typical of those in his former profession. It took agility to get out of the way of more than a ton of fire-snorting beef on the hoof.

"Ain't she purty," came a whisper.

"If you don't put your tongue back in your mouth," Margaret threatened Tex in her own whisper, "I'm going to snip it with my embroidery scissors."

Tex nodded absently. "That's nice."

Oh dear. She did have a job ahead of her! Rafe

Delgado might be a lot of things, but he wasn't an imbecile, and if a certain fair-haired young man didn't behave himself, Rafe would suspect Tex Jones was more, or perhaps less, than he was supposed to be.

And Rafe kept an eye on the man who might be hers. Garbed in leather and suede and enough cheap cologne to suffocate a Longhorn bull, Rafe strode toward her. What he lacked in height he made up for in presence and nimbleness, which must have been handy in the bullring. Once, Charity had commented on Rafe's catlike grace; Margaret had laughed until her stomach ached at the prosaic reference. She was no longer laughing. And it pleased her they met on equal ground when standing.

Margaret liked looking men dead in the eye. She preferred to look down at them.

Rafe leaned toward her. "You're staring."

Her line of sight flew downward, but it bounced like a ball. Knowing his character, she knew any woman would have her hands full, trying to keep the upper hand with Rafael Delgado.

He took a seat across the aisle, parallel to Tex Jones. Before unbuckling his gun belt and placing it on a handy empty seat, Rafe raised a tanned, callused hand to run a forefinger down the scar lashing into the corner of his sardonic mouth. That Argentine gaze had question written in it.

He defined inquisitive.

If there was anything to be thankful for, it was that she'd eschewed bustles and corsets for the trip's duration, so she didn't suffer fashion's dictate. Once upon a time she would have worried about embarrassing jiggles, but that had been once upon a time . . . when she had something to jiggle. Giving the devil his due, Margaret admitted inwardly that Rafe's comment on her corset had been the deciding factor in her decision.

Again she glanced at Rafe, who stared at her. He had a way about him. When he centered on a person, his attentions were solely and squarely *there*. His stare was at times flattering and disarming. In this case, the latter.

He rolled a slender cigar from one side of his intriguing mouth to the other. Intriguing? *Mercy sakes, have I lost my marbles?* Just because that scar made her wonder just how it had come about . . . Just because his mouth moved sensuously with every expression he made . . . Just because his anything-but-thin lips were sketched with a fine line of fair skin contrasting to his Mediterranean skin tone, didn't mean she was fascinated by the villain.

Did it?

Surely the naive and smitten fool of 1889 was no more.

He took the Havana from between his teeth, removed a tad of tobacco from his bottom lip, and made a small sound of spitting. "You two been engaged long?"

"Not too very."

One winged black eyebrow hiking, Rafe moved his thumb in a rhythmic motion. "If I had my guitar, I'd play you a serenade to a long life of love."

"How very thoughtful."

43

"I think so." His eyes crinkled in mild amusement. "Say, I understood you were living up in New York City. How'd y'all meet?" He took another puff. "Ice-cream social? WCTU gathering? Sing-Sing?"

She squirmed. "We've known each other for ages."

"Longer than you've known me?"

"Yes, now that you mention it."

"Isn't life a strange thing? Next you'll be telling me you changed his diapers." Rafe moved his scrutiny to Tex. "What line of work are you in, Jones?" After a moment, he asked Margaret, "Is he deaf?"

"As a post," she lied.

On a whistle of steam, the train chugged out of the station. Tex excused himself to "see the conductor." While he took a too-slow walk past the frothy object of his interest, Rafe leaned across the aisle. "I sure am glad he's gone. And I sure am glad the seats around us are vacant. I've been wanting to tell you something."

"Oh? What?"

"I looked up Teutonic gods."

"It's never too late for an education."

Rafe extended his legs — it was impossible not to notice the fitness of that pair of limbs — and he rested one booted ankle over the other. A click of tongue. A shake of head. "You know, it seems to me . . . Whoever called your hombre a young Siegfried, musta been well into a bottle of mescal."

"I beg your pardon?"

"Don't get me wrong, Margaret — oh, you wanted me to call you *Miss*. Don't get me wrong, Miss, I

44

don't do a lot of studying on other men—that's kind of sissy, don't you think? But to my way of adding up two and two, your hombre appears to be fresh off the farm. You'd call an hombre like that 'hayseed' in English, right?"

"He is a man of the land. *Ranch* land."

"*Bueno*. That's my language. But you know Spanish. You McLoughlins are big on Spain. *Viva España*. And all that. Well, that's neither here nor there." His aristocratically chiseled nose twitching, Rafe studied his hand as he rubbed a knee. "Kind of young, isn't he? How does 'callow youth' strike you? Whatcha gonna do with an hombre like that, Miss Margaret McLoughlin?"

"Marry him."

"You reckon he'll be able to do you any good?"

"Rafe," she hissed, going red, "don't be crude."

"Crude?" All innocence, Rafe rounded his eyes. "I was just wondering if Jones will be able to make you a living."

Liar. You know exactly what you meant. And it was dirty. "My living is not your concern."

Rafe nodded. "I'll just shut my trap." A moment passed. "Just one more thing. Did your papá—never mind."

A middle-aged couple left their seats, moved down the aisle to sit behind him. Tex started back toward Margaret, but before he arrived, Rafe leaned to whisper, "Did your papá buy that hombre for you? If so, I think ole Gil got cheated."

Ooh, to slap that smug grin off his face . . . !

She wanted to go home.

45

She yearned to return to the life only just begun. Thanks to her gender, then to the loss of health, professional recognition had long eluded her. Come January, though, she would begin a professorship at Brandington College, New York City; this being her first year in the classroom, she needed to make preparations. And her babies—

Tears burned the back of Margaret's eyes.

Save your tears for something you have control over, she ordered herself.

Tex took his place opposite her. Her heart racing for a reason she pegged on the nerves of lying—not to mention being subjected to Rafe's bullying—she asked Tex with fake sweetness, "Dearest, may I interest you in a game of checkers?"

A moment passed before she repeated her question. Tex paid no attention, but Rafe certainly did. This in mind, she unpacked her knitting and *tried* to disregard the insult wreaked upon her pride by Angus Jones McLoughlin's neglect of duty.

When she'd arrived at the Four Aces Ranch to rendezvous with her brother—who hadn't allowed anyone except for their mother to call him Angus in half a dozen years—she'd said to him, "It will be better if others see us as an engaged couple rather than siblings." After the horrible hurt of Frederick von Nimzhausen and his thievery of her dissertation—as well as her naivete—so many years ago, she was touchy about attention. "I don't want men getting any ideas I'm available."

"Yep, Sis, I understand. Why, those Meskin fellers, they'd woo even a nanny goat just for the fun of it."

"You needn't put it that way, Tex."

Be that as it may, then and now she knew attention would never come from Rafael Cuauhtémoc Delgado Aguilar, previously known as the Eagle of Mexico, late of Santa Alicia, State of Chihuahua. The world's greatest matador, once. Yet, as she traveled toward Mexico with the has-been, she gave the situation another thought. She could have been taking a certain pleasure in allowing him to think she'd landed a young and handsome and *adoring* swain for her very own.

The plan would fail before it began, if Tex didn't play his part to perfection.

"Tex . . . dearest, do fetch me a lemonade."

He waved a hand of dismissal. "Naw. Ain't interested."

"Don't say ain't. You've been spend—" *Gracious, shut up. You treat him as a vexing kid brother, and the whole world will think you're a fishwife or worse—a sister.* But the fact remained: Tex had been spending too much time with the cowboys at the family ranch in Fredericksburg; his English was atrocious and his charm nonexistent, both of which were unpardonable for the adult son of one of Texas's most prominent families.

Margaret fell to remembrances. It was a balmy morning, three weeks ago, in her brownstone. The little ones napping in their brass bassinets, the sounds of New Yorkers on Fifth Avenue filtering upward, and the lilt of her cook Bridget's singing brogue coming from the kitchen, Margaret had just finished reading an article in the *Times* about a twelve-week-old strike in the coal mines, being resolved with promises of eight-hour days and other concessions. She began to skim a story about the silver mines that honeycombed northern Mexico.

Then Maisie McLoughlin arrived.

Amazingly fit and hearty at ninety-eight, Margaret's great-grandmother carried a letter from Gil McLoughlin. After the import of it sunk in, Margaret wailed, "But I don't want to go to Mexico."

"Me, I would be thinking a trip t' paradise a nice enough proposition. Did I tell ye aboot the time when Charity and I were taking the waters at Bad Homburg—"

"This was just before you got caught cheating Bismarck himself at the Wild West show, wasn't it?" Margaret couldn't help but interrupt.

"Let's no be talking aboot that, lass." Maisie patted her shoulder. "I would be thinking Mexico of interest t' ye. Ye are a scholar in Spanish studies."

"Mexico has nothing to do with Spain. Not anymore. Anyway, I've heard and read quite enough on the halls of Moctezuma. It's a political nightmare. A hotbed. The devil's own den."

It was peopled by pitiable women, ragged children, and Latin males obsessed with advancing their love lives, or with deposing the country's first decent president, Porfirio Díaz. Or with both. None of which was any concern to Margaret McLoughlin.

She had her own situation to consider. "Maisie, I

cannot leave my babies to Bridget's care. She's new. I barely know her. And from what I can tell, beyond her cooking skills, all she seems to know is some song about taking Kathleen back home."

"Ye have me t' turn t', lass. I'll take care of wee Deniece." Concern set into a century of facial gullies. "The lad, though, he might be too much for the strength of me."

"Lunch!"

Both women turned to rosy-cheeked Bridget. Within a few minutes an acceptable working arrangement had been finalized, utilizing the Irish cook's brawn and Maisie McLoughlin's brain to handle Margaret's precious bundles from heaven.

She had vowed to make it back in record time.

Margaret yanked herself back to the present, peering out the train window.

Texas, miles and miles of Texas greeted her. Not a pretty sight, this part of the state. She glanced at Tex. The blonde did something. He grinned in her direction, his eyes giving every impression of a lovesick calf's. Where was Margaret's parasol when she needed it? Heck, even a broom handle would do.

The train rumbled down the tracks, well into the desert, skirting the muddy depths that divided two countries. In Mexico, they called it the Bravo. Over here it was the Rio Grande—the grand river.

Rafe tried to siesta, but Margaret's yammering at her hombre kept him as well as the other passengers owl-eyed. What a *bruja*. And to think he'd felt sorry

49

for her this very morning. Of course, Rafe knew the problem. Jones and the blonde.

Natalie Nash, she called herself when Rafe had returned from the water closet and she asked him to have a seat beside her. He'd declined, for unexplainable reasons.

"Leave him alone," Rafe growled as Margaret lit into Tex about picking his teeth with the point of his knife.

"I'll thank you to mind your own business, Rafe Delgado."

He uncrossed his arms to thumb the brim of his Stetson up a notch on his brow. The heel of one hand propped on a knee, he leaned across the aisle. Taking in the disapproval in Margaret's skeletal face, he said, "You are my business."

"I'd like to know how you came up with that," she hissed.

"You hired me, and until we get to Tampico, take note. I give the orders and you follow them. ¿Comprende?"

"You are certainly toplofty for a hired hand."

Tex smirked. Margaret thumped his ankle with the side of her buttoned shoes. And Rafe was on the verge of laughing. He had the craziest notion to kiss those rigid lips soft.

It couldn't be because she reminded him of Olga. No two identical triplets were ever less alike than Margaret and Olga, since Olga knew how to make a man of five-ten feel ten feet tall.

(Yes, but when the countess chose her born-to-the-purple husband over Rafe, *la condesa* cut him down to size.)

Answering Margaret's remark, he said mockingly, "Toplofty? Why, Miss Margaret McLoughlin, you're mighty insightful." At her raised brow, he fell to a growl. "Remember this. Every outfit has a leader. And I'm the *toplofty* chief of this one."

"Here, here," said a man seated behind Rafe.

"Elwood, hush."

Thereafter, the clickety-clack of the wheels gave forth the only sounds as everyone, goggle-eyed, watched and waited for either Rafe or Margaret to make the next move. Natalie Nash moved. She crossed her legs and raised her hems a couple of crucial inches. Tex cleared his throat.

Rafe, amazed his *cojónes* weren't responding to Natalie's open invitation, cast a glance to his right. *Damn you, hombre, why don't you pay attention to Margarita? Can't you tell you're embarrassing her?* Warning himself off her love life, Rafe demanded, "Jones, if you've got a problem with Margarita taking orders from another man, speak up."

Tex, sturdy and built for hard work, or at least giving this impression, raised and shook his palms as well as his head. "No problem. But I never knew nobody to get Maggie to act meek."

"You've met him now."

Margaret swelled up like a toad. "Of all the nerve!"

"*Bruja,* I've got enough nerve to fill this train."

Tex picked up a newspaper and hid his face behind it.

Margaret looked ready to bawl in outrage. "To

think I left my career and my two sweet little babies for this—"

"You've got children?" Rafe croaked, put off his course. The air got thin, quickly. Her mysterious stay at some nebulous place began to take a curdled form.

She blushed pink, to the roots of her dark hair. The expression gave her an almost girlish look, a certain vibrancy and vulnerability which touched a chord in a man long jaded by life, love, and the pursuit of both.

She mumbled, "They, um, they're . . . Deniece and Denephew—"

"They're cats," Tex supplied from behind the San Antonio *Light*. "Persians. Spoiled, useless cats. They couldn't catch a mouse if you had one hooked to a fishing pole."

Tex laughed. So did Elwood. Rafe did not join in. He had no desire to make sport of Margaret's soft spot. Besides, he'd left his own pet behind, so he knew a person could miss an animal's presence. *Frita,* mi niña, *I wish you were in my pocket right now, going home with me to Chihuahua.*

"Let's . . ." Margaret, her blush deepening to sangria's scarlet, laced her gloved fingers. "Let's play the quiet game."

Strangely pleased she wasn't someone's mother, Rafe wondered *where* she'd been during her mysterious absence. And he couldn't help feeling sorry for her. Frita might be important to him, but he had women to occupy his time. Less than fit, the bloom of youth gone, and betrothed to an hombre of roving eye, Margaret lived a life brightened by mere cats. He sensed, though, she didn't want his pity.

"I don't like playing games," he said seriously. "Jones respects the chain of command. What about you? Do you agree I'm the *jefe?* Or do I leave the train at the next stop?"

Rafe got the impression she didn't require that he wait for the train to pull into Sanderson. And if the wheels cut him in half when he jumped, she'd shout for joy. Yet her answer held a meek quality. "All right. You give the orders."

Her heart wasn't in the capitulation, Rafe knew. No matter. It would be before it was all said and done. *Holy Mother, is this what I even want, the bother of her?*

Four

Even though Margaret was eager to make a quick trip out of the journey to Eden Roc, she needed a break from a particular Latin male. Lady Luck smiled when afternoon waned. The train lurched to an unexpected and swaying stop, that sent hats and bandboxes flying and passengers squealing in fright.

Workmen left the caboose to check the problem, and a few minutes later the engineer sent word: the brakes couldn't be fixed until morning. Therefore, passengers would be accommodated in Alpine, at the Hotel Edelweiss. The locomotive, thankfully, had passed the city limits of the west Texas town.

"It's just a short walk to the hotel, folks."

The passengers debarked. Tex, behaving for the first time today, offered an arm as Margaret marched toward the hotel. Dust clogged the air, and the stench of cattle was enough to curl even a daughter of Texas's toes, so she fanned her hand in front of her face and wished to heck she was back in the civility of New York City.

Something thumped and squeezed in her chest,

when she recalled how Dean Ira Ayckbourn of Brandington College had reacted to her announcement of "business in Mexico." The dean showed a paucity of patience, threatening her with those dreaded words, "If you aren't in the classroom on the morning of January third . . ."

The beady-eyed dean had no compassion whatsoever.

If the truth were known, though, Margaret's sour disposition had little to do with Brandington College or with homesickness. The cause pointed to that strawberry blonde and the Latin peacock who supported her dainty hand, while they swayed and promenaded toward the Edelweiss, chatting and chirping as they went. Vacuous magpies, they.

It was all Margaret could do not to make an appropriate face, the kind most often seen in a schoolyard. Rafe brought out the very worst in her, leaving her powerless to govern so much as a particle of wits. Even if her faculties were in place, though, she wouldn't have appreciated her hired man's neglect. But what good had it done, complaining to the rogue himself? Not a half hour earlier, Margaret had a private word with Rafe on the subject, and what did he do? Asked if she were jealous, patted her hip, and winked an amorous eye. *Satyr!*

The blonde swatted an area in the vicinity of Rafe's well-hewn biceps brachium. "Now, Mr. Delgado, aren't you the awfulest thing?"

It seemed a rhetorical query, though Margaret could have filled her ears. Meanwhile, her brother muttered an expletive.

"Hush. She's much too old for you, anyway," Margaret whispered, now feeling the distance between train and hotel in her tightening chest and atrophied leg muscles.

"I wish you'd quit thinking of me as a kid, Maggie. I'm twenty-two, you know."

"I know you're grown," she replied, taking in puffs of hard-won oxygen. "Even if you haven't been acting it today. Anyway, that strumpet is my age if she's a day." An exaggeration to be sure. Tex's age was more like it. Margaret then said, "She's not nearly as pretty as our sisters."

"I'd argue with you on that, Sis."

They reached the main section of town. A man wearing a garter on his arm burst from a saloon and pitched a bucket of slop to the street. Wagons, buckboards, and riders passed over the puddle. Women with bonnets on their heads and baskets on their arms strolled along the boardwalks and greeted acquaintances in pleasant exchanges, while their children played and their menfolk smoked and gabbed amongst themselves.

"A typical frontier town," Margaret murmured to no one in particular.

"You'd know the West, Sis, since you spent a couple years in San Angelo."

"That was as far west as I got." Those were two interminable years under Dr. Woodward's care. Forcing a laugh, she went on. "I know for certain neither this town nor that hotel resembles anything in the Alps."

"Guess I'll take your word for it. When I was across the seas last year, I didn't get no further east than Gay Paree."

"Somehow, little brother, I cannot imagine you in Gay Paree."

As the sun set over the hills, Margaret granted Alpine one thing. The tangerine and aquamarine sky was breathtaking. She made this observation a few minutes after registering, while staring out her second-floor window.

Her brother, having deserted his own room, had propped himself up in her bed, a forearm supporting his neck; three pillows, his back. "Maggie . . . I'm kinda worried about Mutti."

Mutti — German for Mama. This was what Tex called their German mother, but Margaret preferred English and French name tags. She asked, "Why are you worried? If anyone can handle herself in a difficult situation, it's our mother. She did, you know, cook her way to Kansas while carrying triplets."

"Yep. But that was near on thirty years ago. It's not like her to go off alone to that Eden Roc place. Do you think her dander's up over something?"

Worried all of a sudden, Margaret tugged the side of her lip between her teeth. "Now that you mention it, she's not one to take off alone to isolated places for long periods of time. Did I tell you Papa says she doesn't plan to return till after Easter?"

"You told me." Tex's jaw jutted. "And I'm telling you, something stinks."

By now Margaret was having a word with herself. One with her sibling seemed in order. "Let's not create our own problems. Our mother is just fine. We do have something to worry about, though. About Ra—"

"You've been pricklier than a porcupine here lately," Texas observed, his interruption joined with a brotherly frown. "I know you ain't too happy about taking time to fetch me from the ranch and getting on with our trip into Old Mexico, but did I do something in partic'lar to set you off?"

"Oh, no, honey. No! Well, except for . . ." Her rebuke could wait. She left her post to walk to the bed. Tall and broad-shouldered, Tex was incredibly handsome, and until today, she'd thought he could do no wrong. She told him so.

"That's mighty nice of you to say, Sis. But you've still got an aggravated look in the set of your jaw. It's time you lightened up. It ain't good for you, being crabby. You know you were sick for so long—"

Unwilling to discuss her health, she said quickly, "I'll try to do better." Tousling his flaxen-colored hair, she teased as well as complimented. "You know, Texie, except for your single-mindedness about the ladies, you are a fine young man."

Her "ladies" perked him up, and his blue eyes danced. "Ain't she lovely, that Natalie?"

"Don't say ain't." Margaret wasn't stupid enough to ask who Natalie might be. "Tex, Rafe is suspicious already. If you don't stop flirting with her, he'll get wise."

"It was a dumb idea of yours, this engagement act." A frown raked his face. "Anyhow, it gives me the shivers, Maggie, trying to act attentive toward my own sister."

"I am more than weary of the charade myself. Today was awful in the extreme, thank *you* very much." She sighed, her shoulders drooping. "But the ruse will serve purposes. No man will bother me, and—"

"I think you're making too much of that angle." Tex picked an apple from the basket on the bedside table, then polished it on his trousers leg. "You're too skinny and old for most fellers."

That hurt. Almost as deeply as it hurt when Rafe made fun. Rafe aside, it shouldn't bother her, Tex's remark. Getting her career off the ground mattered. Ever since she'd planned a future sans baby's breath and certain refrains from "Lohengrin," Margaret had wanted to be judged on abilities, not looks.

Something good had resulted from her years of struggle for scholarly recognition—and from her fight for life. The curse of beauty plagued her no more. Yet she shot back, "There's always the odd bird who might get ideas. If you'll recall, I am identical to my two gorgeous triplet sisters." *You don't resemble them, not anymore, and you're glad for it. Remember?* "I can't be all bad." She finished on a weak note, "Can I?"

"You've got a nice face, Sis." Tex cocked his head from one side to the other. "It's sort of comely . . . when you're not frowning. But you ought to eat more, put some weight on. Buy new clothes—none of them in brown. And do something with your hair."

"I am what I am."

"That ain't no reason not to try something different. Try that Gibson girl look."

"Like Natalie?"

"Now that you mention her . . ." He grinned.

Margaret gritted her teeth, but the action turned to grinding when her brother surmised, "You might even get ole Rafe interested in you, if you was to gussy yourself up."

"*He* would be my last reason for making myself over."

Tex took a big, crunching bite of the apple. Studying the core closely, he said, "I think you're wrong there, Maggie. I think ole Rafe is the reason you've been touchy as an old cook. I'd bet a dollar to a doughnut, it wouldn't take much for you to get downright silly over that feller."

Margaret prayed this wasn't true. But what about in the beginning?

"Sis, I didn't mean no offense. Sis? What's wrong?"

"Nothing. Everything. I . . . I was thinking about the first time I laid eyes on Rafael Delgado."

"Was he wearing his matador getup?" Tex sniggered, not paying any attention to her negative answer. "I bet he looked plumb silly, decked out in sequins and a mouse-ear cap."

For the strangest reason, Margaret didn't like her brother making fun of Rafe. "That's enough."

"Now, now, don't get testy. Testier." Tex imparted one of his winning smiles. "I know the two of you don't have no use for each other, but tell me about when y'all first met, Maggie. You know Papa had shuffled me off to school, 'cause Charity had got herself in another fix. So, I don't know nothing, or very little, about what all went on."

Margaret had spent a good bit of her growing-up years reading to Tex, or spinning "once upon a time" and ghost tales. Though an adult, he still wanted her storytelling. Never in all these years had she agreed to tell him anything about Rafe Delgado. Now, though, she felt the need to talk.

Why mention that the wild and impetuous Charity went on trial back in December of '89 for smuggling Texas silver across the Rio Grande? It was a tense, anxious time for the McLoughlin clan; no one could back her claim of innocence. They weren't without hope, though. If found, the Eagle might be able to save her from the gallows. Then, amazingly and on a technicality, Charity managed to get herself freed, but no one breathed easier, not with tarnish still on her halo.

"Papa had traveled to Chihuahua to find Rafe," Margaret told Tex. "But he came back empty-handed. Imagine our joy when Rafe showed up and swore our sister knew nothing—until it was too late—about the smuggling ring she'd gotten involved in."

"I know about that, Sis. Tell me what you thought when you first saw ole Rafe."

Emotions—good and bad, indifferent and spirited—surged through her. She closed her eyes. And smiled. "Confident . . . defiant . . . invincible, Rafe strode forward. I suppose it was somewhat like when he used to enter the arena." Her legs going weak, she sat down. "But he wasn't Rafael, *el matador magnífico*. He was every bit the Mexican rebel. Bandoliers strapped his chest. Head to toe, he was dressed in black. Dust coated his leather vest and britches. His sombrero—it was silver-studded, I seem to recall. His spurs were pinging. His step was as confident as the look on his incredible face."

"Did he say anything to you?"

"Not right away. Not until we had gathered at the hotel to celebrate Charity's vindication." Margaret's chin trembled, but she chuckled dryly to cover her blatant show of emotion. "He just sort of glided across the room and halted in front of me. He lifted his fingertips to my jaw, and said, 'I would steal you away to Chihuahua. Will you like that, *bella amorcito?*'"

Tex's eyes turned speculative. "I wonder if some o' that gliding and sweet-talking would work with Natalie?"

Margaret couldn't answer, so caught up in the past was she. Quite simply, Rafe took her breath away. She wasn't alone in this. His blatant masculinity, his raw virility had drawn women from all directions. Three ladies had swooned in Judge Osgood Peterson's courtroom. Maisie acted as if she were twenty instead of ninety. And Margaret—sensible, level-headed, studious Margaret—did her own swaying. Immediately, she started wondering about Chihuahua.

He might not have the sophistication of a Frederick von Nimzhausen, nor was he as tall as her kinsmen, nor was he handsome in the classical sense; but Rafe Delgado, on that day in December, seemed to have no flaws.

And now, during this Indian summer evening, Margaret laughed and rolled her eyes. "I wasn't too discriminating at the time." Since, she hadn't given

Chihuahua two thoughts.

"I'd say you're a majority of one, Maggie. 'Pears to me the ladies find him as pretty as a speckled pup."

She laughed once more, this time at the comparison. "I grant he has a fascinating edge. He exudes something. Like some sort of love potion. Rather disgusting, in my opinion."

Uninterested in Rafe's appeal to women, Tex said, "I wonder why he never went back to Old Mexico."

Knowing the answer all too well—he wasn't one to leave a bird's nest on the ground!—she decided a change of subject was in order. "Tex, there is no such word as hisself."

She reached for the pitcher and poured a glass of water, but she couldn't wash Rafe from her thoughts. All those years ago he'd shown no interest, not after his initial notice, even though she'd made herself available enough. What a ninny she'd been. She'd talked and acted like an idiot most of the time, saying and doing the wrong things over and over, only to start all over again.

In those days, the awful truth according to Charity hadn't overly bothered her. From gossip about his participation in sexual orgies, Charity and her then-lawyer Hawk linked him to the Gonzáles silver-smuggling ring. Well, Rafe knew about the operation, but he'd somehow kept his hand out of it.

In the wash of Rafe's appearance in Texas came more gossip, little of it complimentary. Outside of his public persona, he was a shadowy figure in Mexico, known for amorous excesses and accused of crimes against the wealthy, including his own family.

And still Margaret didn't find him loathsome. Her loathing came later. After . . . Olga.

When the Countess of Granada arrived from Spain too late to lend moral support to Charity, she became dazzled by Rafe's notoriety from his bullfighting days. And he fell for her. Obviously he liked his women prim, married, and on the simpleton side. *Margaret McLoughlin, shame on you, decrying your poor afflicted sister.*

"Is that all you've got to say, Sis?"

"I really have said enough."

She wouldn't mention the evening—in the shadows of the Alamo—when she'd allowed Rafe to think she was his adored. Nor did she mention what happened the next night, when Olga—her clothes torn, her lips bloodied—had run crying to Margaret with a horrible tale of assault.

"Sis . . ." Tex abandoned the apple. "You okay?"

"Yes! And you were right a while ago. Rafe is the reason I'm touchy as an old cook."

Margaret jumped up and marched across the room to tug pins from her hair. She set a brush to the mass, and as she yanked, she wanted to shout, *I don't want any part of Rafe Delgado!* To be attracted to her sister's attacker was just too offensive to consider.

Five

"Delicious. Simply delicious. Do help yourself to a bite, Señor Delgado. I think you'll love it."

Her eyes the hue of milk chocolate, her voice as sweet as any Margaret McLoughlin had ever heard, Natalie Nash offered apple strudel, but the come-hither invitation meant something altogether more enticing. After all Tex's fawning over the buxom Miss Nash, her breathy dinnertime attentions were reserved for Rafe and Rafe alone.

"I do have a sweet tooth." Wearing a finely cut suit of clothes, not to mention deceptive innocence in his eyes, Rafe continued to accept worship as if he were a veritable pasha of the East. And, surprisingly, that worship had come to him without so much as a mention to his fame of bygone days.

They sat at a candle-lit table for six in the Edelweiss's dining room, Margaret next to Tex, who had made a point to seat Natalie at his right. Rafe sat opposite Margaret. Rounding out the sextet . . . a middle-aged couple from the train, Mr. and Mrs. Elwood Ashkettle of Beaumont, Texas. The Ashkettles—or at least the distaff side of them—provided a rapt audience for The Great Casanova Come Alive In West Texas.

"Such a handsome man as you, you ought to have some nice lady baking goodies for you." Her old-fashioned sausage curls bobbed like mad loose springs as Sally Belle Ashkettle spoke, giving Natalie a chase for the blue ribbon when it came to cooing and oohing at every word Rafe had to utter, mutter, or blurt.

Margaret jabbed a fork into her own piece of apple strudel, previously untouched, afterward uneaten. She took a dark look at the black lock of hair falling over his forehead. *What's the matter, Rafe? Lose your comb?*

All of a sudden, Margaret felt a hairpin shifting. Darn. She thought she'd mastered this back-combed style. Her mud-brown wavy hair, she supposed, was just too heavy or too long, or both, for the Gibson girl roll. Yes, she had tried a new hair fashion, had even added a bit of hair cream for artificial highlights. It didn't have anything to do with Rafe, the reason Margaret experimented. She did it for Tex, didn't she? Anyway, she could have been wearing a wimple for all Tex or Rafe noticed, so intent was their scrutiny of Natalie Sloe Eyes.

As well, Mr. Ashkettle seemed to have trouble keeping his mind on finishing his meal; he was likewise engaged.

A female diner—she appeared to be on the sweet side of twenty—sashayed by their table and just happened to brush against Rafe. "Oh, my goodness gracious, sir. Do pardon me." Was it an accident

66

that her handkerchief drifted to the floor, compelling the Great One himself to lend assistance?

Other women paid court. If Margaret had eaten her dinner, it would be coming back up. Besides herself, was there a female in this room who wasn't under his spell? Doubtful. Of course, they didn't know him as she did. No one except for the principals and Margaret knew what Olga had suffered, that Rafe had nearly wrecked her marriage to one of Spain's lesser ranked yet eminently influential royals, Leonardo of the Houses of Hapsburg and Borbón.

Margaret took another look at the dining room. Natalie wouldn't be shocked to know about Rafe. And that redhead two tables over, she didn't look as if anything would shock her.

What was it that called for all this adulation? Ordering herself to be unbiased and unprejudiced, Margaret set her fork down to take an assessing look at Rafael Delgado. His facial features were acceptable if not laudable, his scarred mouth giving him a rather sinister mien. Margaret, whose tastes used to run to pipes and tweeds, had never found rakish scars cause for collapse, not even during the madcap period of her infatuation with him.

Watch it, Margaret — think unbiased.

Except for not being bowlegged like a lot of cowboys, his physique was no better, or no worse than a hundred hands who had worked the Four Aces Ranch over the years.

Rafe was no youth. *Who'd want one?*

His curling black hair, clipped short and brushed back from his temples, didn't contrast with the tanned, olive skin. Swarthy and somewhat Moorish-looking described this son of Mexico. The Delgados and their collateral lines must have hailed from Andalusia, if she was any judge of Spanish descent, which she was, given her years of study in the Iberian discipline. Yet those piercing eyes hinted at an ancestor from the north of Spain, Castile or Soria or maybe even the Basque region.

Did Mesoamerican blood flow through Rafe? she wondered. Again she studied the subject, answering her question with a silent, "Don't be preposterous."

According to Great-grandmother Maisie (she always looked for blue blood, even claimed a link to the fabled Scottish kings Duncan and Robert the Bruce), the Delgados had arrived in Mexico with Cortés, and owned land exceeding the size of Vermont, New Hampshire, and Connecticut put together. They rode in gold coaches and had their finger in all aspects of commerce, agriculture, and mining. To keep the line pure, their marriages were arranged with as much care as that given to royalty. The Delgados were as close to royalty as Mexico got.

But Rafe's middle name was Cuauhtémoc, the same as the last Aztec emperor. Interesting. Conceivably, it wouldn't be so awful, being in Mexico, Margaret decided. It would provide the perfect opportunity to see how Spanish blood had spread in the aftermath of Cortés's sixteenth-century conquest.

"Margaret, you're being uncommonly quiet this evening." Rafe ignored his harem and sipped port. "Don't you wish to say anything?"

Candlelight, golden and soft, accentuated the dark shadowing of a jawline incapable of being close-shaved, but she'd drop her drawers to him as well as to the morning traffic at Grand Central Station before remarking on his appeal. "I've nothing to say."

"But you were staring, Margarita." He leaned toward her, cocked his head slightly. "And from your expression . . . Are you dyspeptic?"

More than a tad. "I'm fit as a fiddle."

"You won't stay that way if you don't eat. And you didn't eat your dinner. Do you want something different? Waiter!"

"No! Please no." Her eyes going to and fixing on her own dessert, Margaret cut a piece and forced it into her mouth.

"Pay her no never mind," said Sally Belle Ashkettle. "She's one of those shy types. Unsociable. They like to be left alone."

Margaret took no offense, since she didn't care what the woman thought, but Tex growled. And Rafe chuckled, a deep sound. "Señora Ashkettle," he said, "you are quite wrong. Señorita McLoughlin is not shy. I promise you."

"How gallant, sir. I myself have always admired gallantry." Sally Belle smiled, then shoveled a heaping forkful of apple pastry into her thick-lipped mouth. Her lip rouge had smeared during the first course, some of it having ended up on her chins, both of which bobbed as she chewed. "What kind of woman are you partial to, sir? Did I mention that I made my debut in—"

"Pum'kin, you made that debut thirty years ago,"

69

her husband cut in. "Pass the butter."

"Elwood, you are ever so rude." From the motions of her body as well as the lamentable Elwood's, Sally Belle kicked her spouse beneath the table. Not missing a beat, she said in a shrill, affected voice, reeking of ambitions above her background and circumstance, "You speak English ever so nicely, Mr. Delgado. Have you lived in these United States a long time, if you please?"

"Eight years this December."

"Do you have a family?"

"No, señora. No wife, no children. I do have a poor little mother in Chihuahua city. And my one brother—well, Xzobal is a man of God."

The grand inquisitor, Tomás de Torquemada in bouncing sausage curls, kept her beady eyes pinned on Rafe. "What made you leave Mexico, pray?"

He picked up his wineglass, twirling the contents. A momentary, almost imperceptible shadow flicked in his eyes. No one seemed to notice that flicker, save for Margaret, though who couldn't notice his pearly flash of teeth accompanied a smile that moored to Sally Belle's simpering grin?

"The ladies are more lovely in Texas," claimed he.

To Margaret's way of thinking, Sally Belle had nothing on him when it came to an affected voice. Gone was the western inflection and verbiage, which he seemed to be able to turn on and off at whim. His enunciation took on a certain Don Juanish quality under circumstances such as these, not to mention that accent getting thicker and richer with each passing moment. Add "fake" to his list of failings, she decided even before he said, "It was for the lovelies such as you, Señora Ashkettle, that I left my country."

Sally Belle giggled like an imbecile.

There ought to be a law against men like Rafe. Really?

Actually, even knowing he spoke lies, many women would respond to such blather. Most men didn't even bother to lie. Thus, it would be easy to fall prey to such a rascal. Poor Olga. No wonder the dimwit had been gullible enough to allow liberties that led to attack. *Remember when you yourself stepped into his arms? You allowed him more than a few liberties. If you hadn't been interrupted, he would have done more than stroke your private places with his fingers.* She squirmed on the chair, recalling how it felt to learn the excitement of truly living.

". . . In Texas, pretty lady."

Margaret missed the first of his latest to Sally Belle, but her anger rose, most of it directed inwardly for being such a nincompoop back then. Besides, enough was enough of his twaddle.

"Oh, please." This was strung into several syllables that drew everyone at the table's attention. "Why don't you tell these nice people the real reason you stayed in Texas? The pickings were better here. Such as a certain benevolent gentleman providing stock for your ranch. Correct?"

"Maggie! You promised to behave."

Rafe's smile vanished. His nostrils flared. His eyes shot silver; it was hot molten metal that blistered Margaret, yet his voice was cool as tin in a February snowstorm. "Margaret, for shame, making up sto-

71

ries like that. If you don't watch out, people will think you escaped from some lunatic asylum." A strange expression, akin to a realization, flashed on his face. "Is that where you were?"

"Most certainly not! And I stand by my words about you."

"That's your prerogative. But if I said too much about that generous hombre, I'd be forced to mention how I came to know him. I'm sure these *nice people* don't want to hear about a female smuggler's escapades."

"Oooh, I do!"

This came from the world's most seasoned debutante. Natalie and Mr. Ashkettle seemed wholly in agreement. Appearing on the edge of despair as he ogled the object of his unrequited affection, Tex swallowed and exhaled. And Margaret could have bitten her tongue. What was the matter with her, broaching a subject that lent itself to an airing of Charity's dirty laundry?

Anyway, what good had it done?

It showed that you can be as impolite as that Ashkettle woman.

Margaret breathed in relief when Tex changed the subject, asking Natalie, "Where are you headed?"

"Home."

"Where's that?"

"South of the border." Natalie didn't so much as glance Angus Jones McLoughlin's way. Anew, like hot glaze on rum cake, her gaze melted into Rafe, who looked as if he could use a cooling off. His furious glare remained squarely on Margaret.

Her remark was uncalled-for. *The libertine de-*

72

served it. She ought to apologize. *Don't grovel.*

Tex leaned toward Natalie and commented on her remark. "By golly, ain't it a small world? We're on our way to Mexico, too. We'll leave the train in El Paso to catch the southbound Mexican North West out of Juarez. Any chance you're making our connection?"

She waited a moment—to give Rafe a chance to comment? When he remained mum, she answered, "None that I know of."

"But I thought you said you're going into Mexico."

"Please don't let my plans concern you, Mr. Jones."

"Call me Tex. And Miss Nash—" Grinning, Tex took a big sip of coffee. "Nash sure does ring a bell. Why, I'll swanee. You any kin to Isaiah Nash down Chihuahua way?"

She swung her gaze to Tex. Annoyance spilled across her dazzling features. "What if I am?"

"Isaiah Nash is proprietor of Eden Roc. My moth—" He shot a quick glance at Margaret. "My soon-to-be mother-in-law is staying at that health retreat."

"I imagine she'll enjoy herself immensely."

While Natalie may have said this, Margaret suspected an undercurrent ran through the words. What if something was amiss down there? Mother could be in trouble!

The mysterious siren dabbed her lips with a napkin. "If you'll excuse me, I believe I'll call it a night."

All three men rose. All three stumbled over their

boots to see Natalie to the staircase leading to her room. How many years had it been since a man stumbled and fumbled to escort Margaret anywhere? Lord, it couldn't have been a decade, could it? What silly, ridiculous thoughts. She could find her own way into or out of any given situation, and didn't need some salivating buffoon leading the way.

Sally Belle spoke. "Would that we could be as lovely and young as Miss Nash . . . wouldn't you agree, Miss McLoughlin? But then, you already have luck on your side. You've landed a fiancé young enough to be your son."

Stunned and hurt, Margaret wanted to cry. But she wouldn't. Instead, she said, "Why don't you give your mouth a rest, Mrs. Ashkettle? Why don't we *both?*"

Like Natalie, she'd had enough for an evening. Margaret rushed from the table, but didn't return to her room.

Six

Under a netting of stars, Margaret walked along Alpine's main thoroughfare, no other human in sight. Not bothering to bark, a fat black dog rolled in the mud surrounding a trough. A distant catfight moaned and wailed like the west Texas wind, and the solitary horse hitched to the post in front of a saloon made the sounds of restlessness. Clutching her arms against the cool of the desert night, Margaret walked with her head lowered. She never thought it would come to this, but she didn't like being unattractive and old-looking.

If Sally Belle Ashkettle saw her as peer to Tex's mother for Pete's sake, then others would be looking at her with the same eye. Maybe she ought to try to get herself together. How did Rafe see her? *Idiot, he no doubt can't stand the sight of you, after the way you dressed him down in public.*

Warning herself not to get softhearted toward him, she wondered about her mother. Was Lisette safe in Eden Roc?

Heavens, there were so many things to worry about.

"I hope you're pleased with yourself."

Rafe. She cringed at his quietly spoken admonishment, then turned to eye him. Noting that they were on the porch in front of the Land Office, she took a retreating step from the anger that radiated like heat from a red-hot stove. Her heart pounded. It wasn't from feminine weakness to an attractive man. With Rafe scowling at her—that was murder in his eyes!—she more than regretted opening her big mouth, back there in the dining room.

Rather than speak, she moved to the bench lining the porch and took a seat.

"I was wrong about you. Here I've been suffering under the impression that you wanted nothing more than the intellectual life, when all the while you've lived to make me miserable." Rafe tossed his Stetson to the bench alongside Margaret, and stood still. "You delight in trying to unman me."

"It does have its rewards."

He moved in front of her, looming. His shirt, she couldn't help but notice, was unbuttoned at the throat. The gold of his neck chain and crucifix stood out against the dark of his hairy chest, pulling her attention. Her mouth went dry—nerves, of course.

His cologne bath had faded, and the lingering scent—rather musky, somewhat woodsy—had its charm. Charm? Good God.

"What would you gain from seeing me castrated?" he asked.

"Satisfaction. I hate you."

"Strong words."

"Move back," she ordered. "You make me nervous, hulking like some primate straight off a boat from the Dark Continent."

He didn't kowtow. Bending at the knee, he crouched down on booted heels to hover so closely that his breath spilled over her face. Thankfully it wasn't offensive. For some strange reason, she didn't find his presence repugnant at all, which left her confused and bewildered. Where was her strength of character? Gone. Her mother would be brokenhearted to know her daughter had fallen so far from manners, graciousness, and a clear head.

Lisette McLoughlin was a long way from Alpine, Texas, and Margaret couldn't fathom why Rafe got under her skin. But he always had, and it was getting worse.

"Do you really think I've given you good reason to hate me?" he asked. "Just because I once loved your sister."

When was rape called *love?* Margaret could have lashed out, reminding him of his offenses against Olga. But the victim herself had explained the whole of the horror: Margaret had heard enough on the subject. Anyway, what he'd done to Olga, he'd probably done to dozens of other women, married or not.

Margaret elevated her nose. "I hate you, because you're a degenerate. I've heard you participated in alcohol-sodden org—"

"I don't deny it."

"And you're a satyr."

"You could say that."

77

"And you're a bum!"

"It's no crime to be poor." He straightened. The night, the porch shadowed his features. Nothing hid disgust. "I wish you could hear yourself." His was a near murmur. "I wonder if it would bother you, hearing yourself. Your voice reeks with too much money and not enough affection. Affection from anyone or for anyone. Except for a pair of Persian cats."

Fearing he spoke the truth, she lashed out, "You're still a bum. And that has nothing to do with being rich or poor. You took advantage of Papa."

"A lie."

"How do you explain him turning over prime cattle? Those crossbreeds were Papa's pride and joy!" As far as ranching concerned him anymore. "He wouldn't have parted with that stock without a darn good reason, something like being cheated out of them."

"If that's what he told you, you ought to call him down for lying."

"Gil McLoughlin will lie when pigs fly."

Rafe muttered something about pigheaded females. "If you want the truth about the money situation between me and your papá, listen closely, because I'm only going to tell you once. He reneged on a promise. When things got ugly about it, he sent a couple of breeders and an elderly bull as a peace offering. I took the deal. I had my reasons, which I won't reveal, since they're none of your damned business."

This didn't sound like her father, not at all; she

said so.

"Then you don't know him. That cattle aside, I still consider Gil McLoughlin in debt. He promised to buy guns and ammunition for my people, if I would testify in your sister's behalf. He didn't pay."

"He shouldn't have to pay for the truth." She'd done some reading on the subject of Mexico, and putting everything into perspective, she said, "He doesn't believe in civil disobedience. That's what you meant to cause. Against the legal and peaceable government of President Porfirio Díaz."

"Not the government. I knew I could do only so much. I was out to stop the Arturianos—those who follow my uncle Arturo Delgado." Rafe paused. "But let's talk about this 'legal and peaceable' you speak of. It's fair if you're as rich as Margaret McLoughlin. It's hell if you're one of the peons who sweats blood to fill a rich woman's money bucket."

Why was Rafe trying to shame her, when . . . "You, a successful matador and a *Delgado* to boot, would shame me over money? Then again, your family cut you off."

"I know about being poor. I saw the hell of being under the yoke of a rich man. That's how I came to want revolution in Mexico."

She paused for emphasis. "If you're such a martyr to the cause, where have you been since December of 1889? Correct me if I'm wrong, but haven't you left your buddies to catch as catch can?"

He flinched. "Margaret, enough. I don't want to get into this with you."

Why should she show mercy? "Olga told me all about you." She gasped for breath. "You played at

79

being the revolutionary, Rafe Delgado."

"I *play* at nothing. Except affairs of the heart." Again, he straightened, but didn't stand. His glare unmistakable, he said slowly, "You know *nothing* of how it is with the Delgados. Or with Mexico and her ruling party. Or with *me*." He wiped the back of his hand across his mouth. "But I know something damned well. I know I almost pity you."

His stinging remark evoked memories. Always, someone felt sorry for her, either for having so many problems in her career, or on her lack of a wedding ring, or over her health and appearance. She would *die,* though, before she'd allow Rafe to know her sufferings. "Pity me? I don't need pity."

"No? To my way of seeing things—since you've gotten to be the meanest *bruja* I've ever met in my life—you're not getting what you need from that hombre your papá bought you . . . possibly with *my* gun money."

"No one bought Tex," she came back hotly, truthfully.

She started to argue about that meanest-witch business, but he said, "If he's with you of his own free will—may the Lady of Guadalupe have mercy on the poor devil. Because you two don't act like you want to spend the rest of your lives together."

This would be the perfect opportunity for the truth, but Margaret wasn't about to spill it. "Just because I reserve my affection for private moments, doesn't mean I don't love Tex Jones with all my heart."

Rafe said nothing, but the intensity of his gaze made her uneasy. She fidgeted. Then a crooked finger lifted her chin, forcing her to face that intense gaze.

"I hope you'll be happy with what little you're both willing to settle for," Rafe said quietly.

Taken aback at the lack of tension in his voice, amazed that he would offer good wishes, she didn't know what to say.

He saved the awkward moment. "You're through with Jones, Margarita. Come morning, he'll be on his way back to San Antonio. Or back to whatever rock he crawled out from under."

"No, Rafe, no. He's going with us." She took a breath. "That's not your decision to make."

"I'm the chief — *el jefe* — remember? You agreed to this. Now — shall I tell Jones he's on his way? Or will you do it?"

The air between them vibrated with tension.

"I'll tell him no such thing. Neither will you!"

Rafe closed his fingers around a hand swatting his shoulder. *"Cariño,* listen to us. We argue too much."

"We've always argued. And what do you mean, calling me an endearment?"

He laughed softly. "I'm a lover not a fighter . . . at least with *las mujeres.* And you are a woman not to be ignored."

Directing her hand to his mouth, he centered a hot kiss on the palm. A shiver of something nice wound through Margaret, at the same moment he answered, "Would it be giving you an advantage, admitting you affect me in ways that I don't want affected?"

Rafe saying she impressed him? Something was wrong here. She shook her head to make certain her ear canals were indeed clear. His hand slid over her throat and upward, combing into her hair; she trembled at his touch. With a deft motion he freed the pins; Her hair spilled over his fingers and across her shoulders. When he spoke, the irritation in his voice had vanished. Smoky was its quality. "Your hair looked lovely at dinner. I could hardly eat for wondering what it felt like, all this. It's beyond my wildest fantasy. I like your hair unbound. You're a very provocative woman, Margarita."

"Th-thank you." Ordinarily she would have dissected each word, but even though she knew he lied about her lackluster hair, nary a rejoinder came to mind. Liking the way he'd given a Spanish twist to her commonplace name, liking his compliments and somehow drugged into wanting to believe them, she felt the beginnings of a blush. Definitely, she felt a strange warming in her veins. And Rafe . . . oh, my goodness. He had never seemed so handsome nor appealing.

"Why am I interesting all of a sudden?" she managed to ask after gathering the minimum of reason.

"You've always interested me. When I fell for Olga, it was because I mistook her for you."

"Oh, dear. I never imagined . . ."

The inside of his thighs settled at the outside of hers, as he angled toward her. She felt the arch manliness of him, and the impact scattered any iota of those freshly gathered wits. He took her hands, guiding them around his narrow waist. Then he slanted his lips over hers, brushing them with a feathered touch.

She liked the feel of his warm muscular back, as

well. Slowly, slowly, slowly, her palms moved up and down that back. And his hands caressed her hips, then moved to her shoulders. When he kissed the curve of her throat, something strange happened, something as foreign as the country they traveled to. Tiny sparks burst within her, arrowing from her heart to her tummy—the magnetism of the sexes. This was what Charity had spoken dreamily of. This was what Olga had cried over. This refreshed her memory of that night in old San Antonio. How could a man so wrong seem so right?

"You need loving," he whispered against her ear. "You need it bad. But not here. Let's go back to the hotel."

Hotel got her attention. "Rafe . . . I can't believe you're saying these things to *me*."

"If Jones were doing his job, I wouldn't have to." Rafe broke away. Despite the dark of evening, she caught the hard glint in his metallic eyes. He reached for his hat and stretched to his full height, which gave him the dominance advantage. "Dump Jones. You need a real man."

Thinking straight for the first time in several minutes, she lanced into his remarks. "Is that what you call a libertine who ra-ravages married women? A real man?"

He chuckled sourly. "That's what the married ladies call me."

Rafe stood and wheeled around, leaving her standing on the Land Office porch. Leaving her with the oddest sensations. She had thrown out serious charges. He'd insulted her. He'd mocked her. He'd put her in her place. He'd made her realize something dramatic. For some ungodly reason, she wished to hear more of Rafe's sweet talk.

"Admit it," she said under her breath. "You're as silly and simpering as Sally Belle Ashkettle. And that simpleton Olga. But you're worse. You're love-starved."

No!

All she wanted and needed was that professorship.

"Maybe not."

Good God.

Was Rafe honest when he'd said he mistook me for Olga?

Natalie Nash was on pins and needles to see Rafe Delgado again, tonight, and it wasn't necessarily to run her tongue along the source of that formidable bulge at the fly of his britches. If her suspicions about his identity were well grounded, she ought to be warning him of dangers ahead. Where was he? Earlier—it was now two hours after dinner—she'd gone by his room and knocked several times. In her own room, she muttered, "Damn."

"Did you say something, Miss Natalie?"

"I did not."

Dabbing a lamb's-wool puff that stirred a cloud of scented talcum powder through the air and onto her porcelain-white bust, Natalie sat in her dressing gown at the making-up table and watched Tex Jones from the corner of her eye. The scent of his bay rum filled the hotel room. His hair parted down the middle, he sat on the edge of the bed with his knees spread and his laced fingers dropped between them. He was well dressed for a cowboy. He meant no doubt to make a good impression.

"Guess I ought to be going," he said sans conviction.

In her throat she made a little noise of agreement, but he dawdled. A few minutes earlier she'd answered his knock, hoping it was Rafe Delgado calling. How was she going to get rid of Tex Jones without causing a scene? She yawned, hoping he'd be bright enough to understand.

"Sure am thirsty." He eyed the bottle of bourbon she'd gotten from the desk clerk.

Obviously he wasn't going to leave like a gentleman. On a frown she took another look at him. He was a lot more than passably attractive, given his Nordic features, frame, and coloring, but she didn't care much for cowboys. While she was in no position to be choosy, she liked a better class of man; more particularly, a man of means.

Or a man like a particular smoky-eyed Latino.

Rich or poor, Rafe Delgado had what it took to turn any woman into no more than a bowl of pudding. If a hundred people milled around, he would stand out in that throng, what with his virile good looks and the-world-is-my-bedroom sensuality. When he had looked Natalie in the eye, it was love he made to her. Sweet, wild, hotter-than-sin love.

But was he the celebrated *El Aguila* of the ring, the notorious Eagle of the rifle? She should have met the Eagle; their paths should have crossed when Arturo had courted her, but somehow she'd never seen him in person. Of course, there were posters to

85

his homage, but five years had passed since she'd seen one, and she hadn't paid that much attention to begin with.

Natalie's ample bust heaved as she considered her uninvited companion. Since Tex wasn't budging, how could she get something out of him? Mulling this, she invited him to help himself to the liquor. He tossed down a shot; she started to speak, but he beat her to it.

"Miss Natalie, you're prob'bly wondering why I knocked on your door," he said, his voice clear and sharp. "It's like this. My mother, er, in-law is down at Eden Roc, and I got the impression at dinner . . . well, that things might not be right down there. Now, I don't mean to put you on the spot, ma'am, but I don't want anything happening to Lisette McLoughlin."

"You've nothing to worry about," Natalie replied, vaguely recognizing the name.

"Then why do you get a funny look in your face ever' time I mention the place?"

Natalie Nash—failed actress and falsely accused embezzler returning to Mexico with an arrest warrant biting at her ankles—owed this young man nothing. But she wasn't without compassion; she responded to the honest concern in Tex's plea.

"I promise you, your Lisette McLoughlin will be fine at Eden Roc. It's a cosseted refuge. Isaiah invites but a select few to share his paradise." He'd allowed no guests in the beginning. "Guests are treated as royalty."

"Phew. Boy howdy, am I glad to hear that."

She studied the cowpoke. "You seem truly concerned for the lady. She must be special to you."

"That she is. That she is."

Natalie picked up her hairbrush. Running the bristles through long strands of peroxide blonde, she said, "Your lady Lisette. I've heard this name. She is of Washington, isn't she? Isn't she wife to a highly placed government official?"

"Yes, ma'am."

Which meant Tex's fiancée was daughter to a whole bunch of money. What brought the cowpoke and the wealthy spinster together? A more unlikely pair, Natalie had never met. Tex was lariats, campfires, and muscles as refined as a racehorse—or perhaps Loki, longboats, and North Sea gales—while his fiancée seemed a colorless female too long on the vine.

Natalie pitied the worry and anxiety she'd seen in Margaret McLoughlin's pinched face. Several times Natalie had had the urge to offer friendship, to offer a kind word, or at least conversation. But she was a man's woman, and knew nothing of how to talk with those of her own gender.

Anyway, Margaret McLoughlin was rich enough to buy a husband and have her choice in the doing. So why did she choose a cowboy who picked his teeth with a knife and spoke too slow and too cattle-trail for the drawing room? Why did she settle for a man who would sit on another woman's bed?

Natalie said to Tex, "I wish you happiness in your upcoming marriage, but don't you think Miss McLoughlin might be embarrassed to find out you've come to my room?"

"I reckon she'd be more than embarrassed." He

licked his lips and ran spread fingers through his hair, the latter action leaving the mass of it sticking straight up. "Don't get the wrong idea about me calling on you. I mean you no disrespect. Don't mean Maggie none, either. What I'm wanting is, well, you see, I've gotta find out about that Eden Roc place. I'm all het up, worried about Lisette."

Natalie's low opinion rose. This was a good man, kind and caring, this cornpone Tex Jones. And while he and his intended were a strange pair, Natalie decided he had potential.

She set her hairbrush aside. "At dinner, you asked if I'm related to Isaiah Nash. I am. I'm his daughter."

"Thought that might be the case." Tex poured another whisky. "I'd sure appreciate it, ma'am, if you'll tell me about Eden Roc. And about your pa. I know a few things. He was a mine owner in the Virginias. He went to Old Mexico to do business, but didn't invest in silver mines. He bought property in the middle of a bunch of deep canyons in the Sierra Madres. And he's been pretty much of a hermit ever since."

For twenty-five years. "You heard right."

"What's so special about Eden Roc?" Tex asked.

"Ponce de Leon searched for it. But Isaiah found the Fountain of Youth."

Skeptical, Tex shook his head. "Ain't no such thing."

"On the contrary. Eden Roc is a site of . . . special powers. The water. The caves." Incredibly, Natalie found herself missing the damned retreat. "There are many wonders to behold."

88

She recalled her friends among the Tarahumara Indians living closeby. The poor Tarahumara. They seemed immune to the restorative powers of Eden Roc, for they aged at a swift speed. Her first love, a Tara brave, had grown old before her very eyes. It hurt to think of Netoc.

"I've always hated Eden Roc," she said honestly. "Isaiah bought the property when I was a motherless fifteen. He took me from the things a young girl longs for. Her peers. The familiar." Her eyes burned as she recalled how it felt to be uprooted at a tender age. "And the opportunity to be courted."

"Sorry to hear that, Miss Natalie. But I guess you did leave."

"I did. It took several tries," she said, a bitter taste rising. "Isaiah would have kept me there forever, but I had to get away. The bright lights of the theater beckoned me. Or at least, I thought they did. As it happened, I'm not an actress."

"I'm right sorry, Miss Natalie. You're sure pretty enough to be anything you please."

"You're a dear to say that."

"Are you . . . are you going back to Eden Roc?" he asked.

She came to her senses. What was she doing, confessing everything? She must not tell Tex Jones anything about her plans, which hinged on Arturo Delgado marrying her and giving her the protection of his name and considerable influence.

Hinged?

Of course, he'd marry her.

Arturo adored her. For five years he'd been waiting for her. Arturo would save her from the law.

Answering her telegram, he would meet her at the depot in El Paso. Once they crossed the border, left U.S. jurisdiction, and his ring adorned her finger, she could breathe easier. No one defied the Arturianos. Not even the United States government.

"Miss Natalie, you all right?"

She nodded. Yes, she'd be fine. But what about that other fugitive from justice? She had to make certain Rafe and Arturo's Rafael were one and the same. Since Tex knew him . . . "Tell me about Rafe Delgado."

A scowl moved across Tex's remarkably handsome face. "What's he got to do with anything?"

"I know a man by his last name in Chihuahua. Arturo Delgado. Surely you've heard of him, he's one of Mexico's most prominent men. He has a nephew named Rafael, who lives in San Antonio. This Rafael was a matador. Is this too much of a coincidence?"

"My sister said—Aw, damn."

"Your *sister?* Wait a second. Aren't you engaged to Miss McLoughlin?"

"I, uh, I didn't say my sister is Maggie." His face turning red, Tex got to his feet. "I—I'd better be skedaddling outta here, let you get some rest."

"Not so fast." She went to him, using the heel of her hand to push him back to the bed. And she saw Tex in a whole new light. This cornpone was *son* to a fortune. What if . . . ? *Natalie, you're forty years old. He's a boy and you need a man. A man like Arturo.* "Mr. Jones—Tex—surely you aren't making a long journey into Mexico with a stranger."

"Rafe's an okay feller."

If he was Arturo's Rafael—this had to be the case—"okay" might not be true. According to Arturo, his nephew was not only a troublemaker and an outlaw, he was a killer. Of his own cousin. Arturo's son, Hernań. If this Rafe was that Rafael, he'd be smart to stay away from Mexico. Arturo was living for revenge's sweet day.

Wait. If she warned Rafe, she'd be betraying Arturo. There really was no contest. Arturo—and her own freedom!—came first. Best she remove herself from the Rafe situation with all haste. Best she stay over in Alpine a day or so.

Seven

"You got any tequila?"

The barkeep, a smallish hombre with a handlebar mustache growing below paltry strands of dun brown hair combed over his bald spot, answered in the negative, so Rafe ordered a beer. It had been thirsty work, trying to find a hayseed to send packing.

The beer came sliding down the bar top on the crest of the announcement, "Two bits."

Thankful for the quiet of the near-empty saloon—the one down the street had a soprano in red satin and all the drinkers—Rafe forked over the money, hitched his booted foot on the brass rail, and leaned his elbows on the bar. Normally he wouldn't mess with his hair, but tonight Rafe raked fingers through it. He finished one tankard, then asked for another, which he made short order of. Loco. He'd gone loco. What was the matter with him, making sweet nothings with *La Bruja?* The woman was a witch, dried-up hag and all.

Damn. He was getting hard again, thinking about

her. Skinny she might be, but there was a willowy quality to her, a grace that held his attention. And he couldn't ignore her expressive eyes. Little hid in those big, big eyes.

If only she'd rest up, fatten up, do a bit of relaxing, Margarita might bloom again. If Eden Roc lived up to its reputation, she ought to benefit from it. Damn. Double damn. *¡Merdo!* Why in the name of all the fiends in hell should he be trying to reclaim a lost cause? He didn't even like her, *por el amor de Dios.* Besides, women didn't degrade him like she did, not and get his lusts up. So why was she any different?

Did it have to do with her incredible straightforwardness? Or was it because she was so damned much braver than he was? She wouldn't have allowed eight years to go by, with a cousin unavenged.

"Ya look a mite troubled, buddy." Rag in hand, the bartender wiped dry a glass and held it up to the light for inspection purposes. "Got woman troubles?"

"Me? Never!" Rafe took a comb from his suit coat and gave his hair a grooming. "I never have woman troubles." Oh, yeah? What about Olga? "I am *muy hombre.* All the women say so."

"Then what are you doing here?"

Rafe said nothing. He kept his own counsel. Always had. He ought to just get out of here. But. As mankind had done since the first bazaar had purveyed spirits to the woebegone, Rafe confessed all, opened up like a book with a broken spine, spilling his pages to the bartender. "I have had woman troubles."

"What happened?"

"She chose her husband over me."

"Happens all the time."

"I suppose." Rafe rubbed his scarred mouth. "A strange one, that Olga. Prim and modest. But night after night she came to me." She held herself back on each of these occasions, offering intimacy yet allowing her inhibitions to rein in base desires. "One night was different." By the Alamo and on the banks of the San Antonio River, she wore perfume of violets. A band played in the distance. There wasn't a cloud in the midnight sky . . . when she got hot and warm, got to be a real tigress in his arms. "I never forgot that night."

Despite the bad ending to their affair, he persisted in remembering that night as special above all others. There was an honesty to her, the way she acted and reacted, that he'd never found before. It was as if she truly loved him, and wasn't simply sampling forbidden fruit. If he lived to see his great-great-grandchildren, he would never quit regretting that distinctly special night had been intruded upon.

He lit a cheroot only to take no more than a puff from it. "I decided I was in love with her. I wanted to spend the rest of my miserable life with her."

"Yours is an age-old tale, buddy."

"I imagine. But things changed the next night. She informed me she wouldn't divorce her husband."

"Divorce? Man alive—that's serious."

Rafe took a reflective swallow of beer, his thoughts retreating to a cold winter night. Riding in the carriage he'd borrowed to impress her, she'd said the words that had lanced his spirit. She wouldn't give up being a countess. "Oh, Rafael, I'm so sorry — I wouldn't hurt you for anything, you are so sweet and dear — but I can't ask Leonardo for a divorce. It just isn't done, not in royal families. And it would hurt him even more if he knew I left him for a — now, please don't take offense — for a man without rank."

The countess returned to Granada, to her high-born husband. "That was the last time I ever saw her."

Funny, how that didn't hurt as it once had. "After I put some time behind me, I was glad she spurned me. Even if she'd gotten a divorce, we were too different for the everlasting love sort of thing."

What he didn't confess was the contents of Olga's letter, received after she sailed for Spain. "You and I are going to be parents." Swearing she had acted in haste and promising she would return to him, she instilled false hope. For Olga and their expected child, he'd stayed in Texas and beggared himself to Gil McLoughlin. For nothing he had let his people down. He'd let Hernán's memory go unavenged. She never even bothered to send word whether the baby was a boy or a girl. "She's nothing but a fickle-hearted woman of empty promises."

"Life's nothing but a bouquet of fickle-hearted females. How 'bout another beer?"

Rafe glanced up, nodding. It was then he caught sight of the painting that hung on the wall behind the bar. The scantily dressed, overblown woman was typical decor for this sort of cantina. *I wonder what Margarita looks like, naked?*

Holy Mother, what was he going to do with her? "There's this woman . . . I can't stand the sight of her, yet I can't get my mind off her. She's got a *novio,* but he doesn't treat her right. I've been looking for him."

"This lady, is she kin to you?"

"No."

"Work for you?"

"No."

"You in love with her?"

"Hell, no!"

The barkeep hooked the rag over his shoulder and parked a forearm on the bar, leaning forward. "You just want to bed her."

"I do. I got it up tonight, wanting her. Damn good thing, too, since there's this *chiquita* on the train who's wanting her tonsils tickled, but I've been soft as mashed potatoes around her. I was beginning to get worried."

"You've got the lovesick blues, man."

Rafe waved a palm in denial. "It's not that bad. I want to spread the *bruja*'s legs is all. I don't know what the hell is wrong with me. She's mean as a rabid dog, and looks like one, too. Well, she's not that bad." Once, she'd been heavenly beautiful. What were looks, anyway? A lot of his women weren't raving beauties, and once he thought about it, he preferred them that way. "When I told Margarita she needed good loving, I meant it. I even volunteered to help her out."

"What did she do after you said that?"

"Same old thing. Insulted me."

"If I was you, I'd find that other gal. Do your

96

business with her. Just pretend she's the ornery one."

Rafe laughed. "No. Those two aren't mixable."

Natalie reeked of passion. Margarita, well, if that dry, amateurish kiss she'd given him was any benchmark, she never even thought about copulation, much less engaged in it. Still and all . . . Being a master at lovemaking, Rafe felt confident he could rouse the passions in the harpy from New York City.

First, though, he needed to get shut of Tex Jones.

He left the bar, made his way back to the Edelweiss by way of the town's other saloon. Jones wasn't to be found. Intending to check the hombre's room one more time, Rafe headed for that section of the hotel.

He heard a male voice coming from Natalie's quarters. *"Merdo,"* Rafe muttered and neared the door, "that's Jones."

The bastard.

It wasn't enough, trifling in the same hotel where Margarita slept, Jones wasn't even trying to be discreet about it. Rafe pounded on the door. "Open up!"

Natalie, frocked in a dressing gown, answered the summons. "Well, hello —"

"Jones."

Without further ado Rafe pushed past her, charged forth, and crossed the room in nothing flat. This is where a sensible hombre would have engaged in a stern reprimand, but Rafe's marbles were scattering to kingdom come.

He grabbed Jones by the shirt lapel, and even

though he was outweighed by a bunch of pounds, Rafe hauled the slack-mouthed, wide-eyed Jones from the edge of the bed and to his feet. "Damn you to hell for doing 'Rita this way!"

He drew back his fist and slammed it up into Jones's face. He caught his jaw. Natalie screamed. Jones landed on a chair that collapsed with a bang, his shoulder crashing against the bed's foot rail. He spat blood and shook his head, but Rafe advanced. The moment Jones got to his feet, Rafe drew back his fist again.

"Stop!" That was Natalie. She started bawling.

Jones did his own screaming; he shouted, "D-don't. You've gotta—" Again Rafe's blow connected. "Listen." Jones spewed blood. "She's my—"

"Take your hands off him!" Margarita. That was Margarita. "Rafe, don't you dare hurt my baby brother!"

At this same moment Rafe's knuckles smashed into Jones again, this time in the gut, which caused his quarry to double over. Rafe's brow wrinkled. *Her brother?* Rafe went still. And when he did, Jones decked him—hit him with all his superior weight and height and force. Rafe, his jaw and head in misery, fell hard on the floor.

From far, far away, he heard Natalie say, "He was standing up for you, Miss McLoughlin."

"Oh, my goodness."

"Tex, Tex honey, you poor thing," Natalie wept. "Let me help you."

Brushing her skirts out of the way, Margarita bent over Rafe. She had the strangest look on her face, as if she really was concerned. "Oh, Rafe. Whatever

98

got into you? So sweet of you. But look at you, all beat up." She wiped his bloody jaw with the hem of her skirt. "Whatever am I going to do with you?"

Right then, he didn't care. The lying, conniving—Black closed in on him.

Eighteen hours passed from the time Rafe had charged into Natalie's room, but Margaret still found it difficult to believe he would go to such lengths. Difficult, perhaps, but she could barely contain her grins. Shameful grins. Here she was, wanting to smile over Rafe, when a despicably brutal yet wholly noble deed had been perpetrated against her kid brother.

And Tex had been thwarted in his quest for Natalie.

When the westbound train had *finally* pulled out of Alpine, hours past schedule, it lost one passenger. Miss Natalie Nash refused to go on, and Tex had pouted over the loss, even now, as the train rumbled on toward El Paso and into the night.

As it was, he'd taken himself—all bruises and injured dignity—to a seat well away from Margaret and Rafe, his wounds probably hurting more inside than outside. Poor Tex, he ought to have the right to court Natalie. It was with the hope of Natalie surfacing at Eden Roc (coupled with his concerns over their mother) that had kept him from turning back.

Margaret felt sorry for the romantic fool.

Sally Belle Ashkettle left her seat, walked toward the water closet. As she passed Margaret, she jerked her nose up. If not for the compassion and the jar of salve she'd offered Tex and Rafe, Margaret still would have hurt over the woman's snide remark about her age.

Margaret glanced across the aisle to get a covert look at Rafe. Her champion. Bless his knightly heart.

She wanted to acknowledge his act — she shouldn't go so far as *thanking* him for beating her brother to a bloody pulp, should she? Since he'd been indisposed to let her form so much as a syllable to him, apologetic or not, between the fisticuffs and the present, she settled for taking a good look. His black Stetson pulled low on his brow, he napped with his chin dropped to his collarbone. His boots crossed, he'd hitched a heel on the rail. With those muscular legs stretched out like that, it was impossible not to notice the very manly lines of him, especially in the crotch area.

Crotch area — good grief!

What was she doing, ogling him like that? Never had it been her way to gaze upon a man's privates. Well, there was that one time with Frederick, in the newborn days of this decade, when she'd returned to New York from Charity's trial. On the heels of having Rafe shatter all her romantic illusions by raping her sister, she'd set out to talk her former professor — former confidant! — out of stealing her dissertation and having it published under his name. *Frederick, you crumb.*

Whatever the case, she had allowed von Nimzhausen too many liberties. The seduction scene had come to a grinding halt, when she laughed at

100

the white cotton of his voluminous drawers and the pink flamingo legs beneath. Under her breath, she said for the thousandth time, "Thank God for those drawers."

Rafe groaned in his sleep, then fidgeted. The bruise on his jaw had turned black and angry, the darkness highlighting the white scar above it. *How did he get that scar?* Thinking of scars all the while he lay injured—gracious. Where was her compassion?

Poor Rafe. Poor Tex. *Poor me.*

Margaret pressed her knees together and laced her fingers. Everything had gotten complicated. Getting Mama back to Papa wasn't going to be simple, nor swift, if these last few days were any bellwether.

Again she glanced at Rafe. Her knight in black Stetson. *I bet he never raped Olga! Olga probably made everything up to save her marriage. Who could blame her?* Devotion to her triplet fought with that voice of reason, leaving Margaret in a quandary.

Did he?

Didn't he?

All she could be positive about was, she'd been awfully hateful to Rafe. Yet with valiant intentions he took up for her, and like David with Goliath, he went after a taller opponent. This bespoke an ingrained goodness, a strength of character flagrant in fiction, but rarely witnessed in real life.

She at least owed Rafe an explanation. Could she say it? Could she admit that she, a drab if there ever was one, had been vain enough to think she needed protection from men, mostly from Rafe himself?

Oh, he had kissed her, but that was to make a point. His passions weren't for her.

A tiny tug of emotion pulled at her heart.

Yet Margaret couldn't help feeling a vitality that refreshed her blood, bones, muscles, and soul. As a survivor of a terrible sickness, she rejoiced in the privilege of vitality.

"Cupcakes. Anybody wanna cupcake?"

The vendor's announcement roused Rafe. Or it could have been Margaret's voice, or the rattling of her change purse as she answered in the affirmative. Feeling hungrier than she had in ages, she bought two pastries plus a string of jerked beef, and handed one cupcake across the aisle.

"Keep it," Rafe groused, as she bit into the other icing-covered cake. He turned his head.

"Rafe . . . I know you're a bit upset, but—"

"I'm more than a bit upset."

His cupcake in hand, she stood and crossed the aisle to take the empty seat facing him, but he turned his attention to something on the other side of the window. The dark of night?

"I've apologized to Tex a dozen times. And I want you to know how sorry I am about . . . about, well, you know what I'm talking about. Oh, Rafe, I had no idea you'd fly to my defense."

"That's right. You always figured me for a no-good, so why would you think I could act chivalrous?"

His boyish pout caused her to sigh in frustration and set the foodstuff aside. "Would it help if I apologize for deceiving you?"

"No."

"My mother swears that sweets make for sweet." She smiled—an unfamiliar expression. "I bet this cupcake would make your mood all better. Want to try it?"

"No."

"Would you like for me to get back in my old seat?"

"Yes."

Scowling at the hard set of his battered jaw, she exhaled. "If that's the way you feel about everything, why don't we consider our contract null and void? You can catch the return train, once we get to El Paso."

"If I do, I'm keeping the money you paid me."

Her Scottish thriftiness and Teutonic respect for money reared. "You will not."

"Not much you can do about it, is there, *bruja?*"

"You would like to think not!"

She realized something, and it hit her quite suddenly, right in the face. It was stimulating, arguing with Rafe. The nasty, hateful sort of pitched battles of the past weren't fulfilling, but small skirmishes did have their charm. She announced, "You'll either repay me, or you'll live up to your end of the bargain."

They argued for a good half hour, until Sally Belle Ashkettle complained to the conductor, and he threatened to put Rafe and Margaret off the train.

The train pulled into El Paso in the hour before daybreak. Every bone in his face aching, Rafe gathered his belongings and stomped down the aisle,

103

past yawning and stretching passengers, plus Tex and his broom of a sister. Repay her—huh! Like her father, she owed *him*.

Making a fool out of him, letting him think she was engaged to her own brother—he ought to wring her scrawny neck. Last night, after they had argued over money and were forced outside to the undulating connections between the cars, she admitted her reasons. They made Rafe damned furious. *¡Estoy como aqua pa' chocolate!* Damned furious. The witch had thought he would rape her, had even hinted he might have touched Olga in anger.

Holy hell, rape Margarita!

Rafe Delgado didn't rape women. Never had, never would. And to tell the truth, he'd never been in a situation even to give it consideration. Yet he'd refused to give Margarita the satisfaction of a defense against such absurd charges. Nonetheless, he had assured her in lengthy terms that he had absolutely no interest in her, even if she tore her clothes off and begged him to ease the misery of her voluptuous lusts.

"Have no fear," she said snootily. "I would sooner bare my bosom to Jack the Ripper, than to the likes of you."

"What a nasty thing to say, even for a witch. That Ripper is a monster."

That was last night. Today Rafe remained in bad temper. Witch. Broom! Harridan. Virago. He hated arguing, had had enough of it for a lifetime, thanks to the perdition of Chihuahua in late 1889, but arguing was all Rafe and Margarita seemed to do. Angry he might be with her, yet he would carry on to Chihuahua state with the McLoughlins, only because he was headed there anyway, thanks to that divine signal pointing southward. Once they reached the city of Chihuahua, though, he was history.

Why? Things could get ugly, once Arturo discovered the prodigal nephew returned, but Rafe had known this all along. To the point, Rafe had had his fill of the McLoughlins. For years they had been the death of him; this latest insult was the final blow.

As he descended the steps, he flipped a coin to the nearest porter. "You need to help the skinny lady behind me. She's got a *lot* of luggage in the baggage car."

"*Sí,* señor."

Rafe tossed his valise across his shoulder and hastened down the platform. Tex's voice slowed but didn't stop his forward pace. "Rafe, can I buy you a cuppa coffee?"

"Not thirsty."

"A shot of whiskey?"

"I told you, I'm not thirsty."

"Wanna just hold up for a dad-blame minute?"

Turning to Margarita's brother, Rafe saw that the young hombre looked like the bowels of hell on a Saturday night; he had to feel even worse than Rafe, and that was more than awful. "What do you want, Jones? Uh, *McLoughlin.*"

Passengers, including *La Bruja* and her not inconsiderable pile of possessions, passed by before Tex replied, "You've gotta forgive Maggie. She didn't mean no harm, playing like we was sweet on each other. You see, Rafe, she's kinda funny, my Maggie. She didn't like setting herself up to get hurt."

"You've lost me. I don't know what you're talking about."

"She's scared of men. Well, I mean she's scared of getting tangled up with one, so she does whatever she can to make sure that don't happen."

"Why? She have a taste for women?"

"Naw, not Maggie. She ain't got no taste for nothing."

"Why?"

Tex spat a wad of tobacco onto the ground. " 'Cause she tied in with a feller up New York way, and got herself hurt real bad. That was a long time back. Myself, I wanted to go after him with a rope, but—"

"Wouldn't be that Frederick hombre, would it? The one who stole her manuscript."

"Yep. That's him."

Rafe's first instinct turned out to be sympathy. Since he knew about being betrayed, he understood what she'd gone through. But his sympathy didn't last long. All sorts of scenarios tumbled in his brain. He grinned. She *might* have experience in passion. His loins stirred once again, his insulted pride taking a back seat to lechery. Bedding the *virago* between here and Chihuahua city had possibilities, especially if she did some good old-fashioned begging before he allowed her nine inches of heaven.

Well, eight inches.

"Any chance your sister is a fallen woman?" He'd never had a taste for virgins. Yet, oddly, he had a contradictory urge to be the first man to sample from the font of her womanly delights. *You are one*

106

mixed-up hombre, Delgado.

"I don't rightly know what all she's done or ain't done, but I can vouch for one thing. She'd rather be an old maid than let down her hair with the fellers. That's why she's got a real tart tongue."

Rafe took a cheroot from his coat pocket, extended it to Tex; the offer declined, he stuck it between his teeth and lit the end. Staring at the ground, Rafe swung the valise slowly from his shoulder, dropping it. Like Margarita, he knew what it was like to hurt. He knew it well.

The latter part of 1889 was hell turned heavenly . . . turned hell. He'd wanted to right Delgado wrongs—and there were many wrongs, including a bad, bad situation at the Santa Alicia silver mine. A contingent of Yaqui Indians had been given as gift to Tío Arturo. Rafe and his cousin Hernán—and to a certain extent, Rafe's half brother, the newly frocked Father Xzobal Paz—had opposed slavery in any form.

While this was going on, Gil McLoughlin asked Rafe to testify in his daughter's behalf. Uninterested in saving the rich *gringa* from herself, he'd sent her Texan papá packing.

McLoughlin had barely left the hacienda before Xzobal Paz brought news to El Aguilera Real. The slaves had arrived. Rafe and his followers had ridden to the Santa Alicia, had meant to make certain the slaves would receive fair treatment. The entrance to the Santa Alicia was lined with hired guns. Arturianos. They fired on Rafe and his men. And they fired back. A man stepped out of the office. Hernán walked into the line of fire.

Hernándo, my cousin! We didn't mean to hurt you! I . . .

Rafe squinted at the rising sun. That's what Olga had been to him—the rising sun. The day breaking into the abyss of night. Gentle, patient, easy to be around—Olga had been the beauty of Margarita without the threat to his masculinity.

"Rafe? You all right, old buddy?"

He gave a curt nod to Tex Jones. Correction. Tex McLoughlin. "How is your—?" A fist tightened in Rafe's chest; a vision of loveliness and serenity formed in his mind, as he finished asking the question that he couldn't pose to Margarita. "How is your sister?"

"Ain't you heard nothing about Charity? She's right famous. She and Hawk, well, that Wild West show they got together has done real good. And Ole Hawk, he took to Europe like a duck does to water. They're happy as a cuppla ducks in water." He laughed at his own slim attempt at humor. " 'Course, they got 'em some younguns now. Twins. A boy and a girl. And another babe expected."

"I, uh, that's nice, but I didn't mean Char—"

"Rafe, I sure do thank you for helping our Charity, back when she was in trouble." Tex offered a hand for shaking. "I didn't get to thank you then, but I wanna now."

That out of the way—both men winced when their skinned knuckles made contact—Rafe got insistent. "How is your sister *Olga?*"

Suspicion worked its way into Tex's open-as-a-book expression. "That's a funny look you've got on your face for a feller just making small talk about

108

my sister. How well do you know Olga?"

From the funny look in *Tex McLoughlin's* face, another trial by fists might be in the cards. Enough of that, Rafe decided. "We got to be . . . friends, when she arrived from Spain to be with Charity at the trial." As events played out, the trial was over in record time, even before Olga could arrive. Charity had gone free, had taken off with her man for Europe. Apparently the two sisters had passed on the Atlantic.

"Olga's a married woman," her brother stated, disapproval evident. "Leonardo's a right nice feller."

Rafe didn't repeat his question on her well-being. It was better not to know.

Picking up his valise, he stepped around Olga's brother and started again for the depot. Maybe Olga was the reason Rafe flew to Margarita's defense. Could it be that he still harbored feelings for the brunette beauty? Again and again—after he'd realized she wasn't coming back to Texas—he'd told himself his feelings for her were nil. His present interest spelled curiosity, pure and simple. Olga wasn't the reason he'd wanted to help her sister.

His actions had been for Margaret alone. She was the one female who didn't want him, and that had a powerful allure.

How would he handle her?

His gaze traveled to a wagon and the tall, thin woman standing beside it. A grin curved Rafe's mouth. "I'm going to make a sweet little pussycat out of that hissing she-cat," he promised himself. "She's going to be purring in my arms between here and the city of Chihuahua."

109

Whistling, he waved to her. Yes, Margarita was his intention . . . and Olga was simply a four-letter word.

Eight

Deep in Mexico, between Texas and the Gulf of California, amongst the series of canyons that gouged deep and wide into the high plateaus of the Sierra Madre mountain range, Tarahumaran drums echoed mournfully to greet the morning, while a light rain pattered against the roof of a cabaña built in the Eden Roc compound. These sounds and the fingers of dawn beaming through a window to the east awakened the brown-haired male occupant.

As a representative of the Spanish government, he had duties to perform for the Queen Regent and her son Alfonso XIII, the only boy to be born a king. Thanks to the rabble of the United States becoming more and more sympathetic to the Cuban insurgents, the border between Mexico and the United States must be covered.

Unfortunately, the local *patrón,* known colloquially as *El Grandero Rico*—the richest baron among the rich—wasn't enthused about cooperating. Soon the master spy would sidestep Arturo Delgado by traveling to the Federal District, where he would call on the President.

Business, though, placed second in the Spaniard's desires.

In his prime, handsome, mustachioed—and having been forced into celibacy for the past four months—he reached for the beloved American female who slept on the next pillow, her flannel nightgown buttoned to her chin. "Wake up, my darling," he murmured timidly, fearing rejection. Only with her was he timorous. "Will you permit me to touch you?"

She shook her head. "No. Sick." Following a practiced path, she jumped out of bed and dashed for the slop jar that waited nearby, emptying her stomach, but not before tying a dressing gown around her growing middle. Ever modest, even after twelve years of marriage, she didn't allow her husband to glimpse anything that might be construed as nude or nearly so. But he was accustomed to her delicate sensibilities.

He said, "The babe . . . I'm sorry my son makes you sick."

Her fingers gathering a wad of nightgown beneath her throat, she leveled her eyes straight at him. "Are you staring at me?" She blushed. "If you are, please don't. You know it makes me uncomfortable."

"No, I'm not staring at you," he lied, taking his fill of sable-dark hair and an oval face more exquisite than any work of art displayed in the Prado Museum of Madrid.

He looked at the small mound of her stomach, knowing she hated the idea of bearing another child, almost as much as she disliked being touched by his gaze. Or his hands. But he loved her, which was almost enough to make a fulfilling marriage. He felt certain that once the new babe came, she'd forget the last one.

And he worried. Did she know the truth about that infant?

Surely not.

And he had more crucial concerns. They were waylaid here in the wilds of Mexico. Getting out wouldn't be easy. In the interim, he had agents to supervise. "We should have stayed in Mexico City, where you were properly attended by physicians."

But no. She had insisted on visiting her mother. He had, as usual, humored her, because he had much, much to make up for. If she knew the extent of his corruption, he would lose her, and the mere concept racked him with shivers. "My dearest wife, we should leave—"

Olga's shaking hand brushed dark, dark hair away from her temple, before groping for the thick spectacles that no longer helped her eyesight. "Please leave me be, Leonardo. Be assured I don't wish to hurt your feelings. But I just want to be alone."

"Is it too much for a husband to ask the comfort of his wife's arms?"

She turned away. "Must you be indelicate?"

His patience snapped. The Spanish nobleman, cousin to kings, threw the covers aside and jerked on his unmentionables. Always, he'd done all the trying in their marriage. She'd never been able to return his love, nor would she verily *try* to fake the

113

tiniest shred of affection. She ought to try harder. After all, hadn't he taken her back after her *perfidia* in Texas?

You think me a tonto—*a fool as blind as you!* Not for a moment had he believed her story of rape, and still didn't, even after all these years. It would serve his countess right if he accepted the Swedish massaging woman's invitations. Or perhaps he should visit the whorehouse in the village of Areponapuchi.

But what would that prove?

Except for one cardinal sin committed upon his wife's first child—for which he would regret for an eternity—Leonardo de Hapsburg y Borbón, Count of Granada, deserved better than what he was getting.

"Back to bed, Olga," he ordered, engaging a new tactic. *"¡Andele!"*

"It's time to get dressed. I feel it in the warmth in the air, and—"

"Back to bed." He advanced on his cowering wife.

Tapping her toe impatiently, Margaret stood beside the buckboard while the wagoner loaded her baggage for the quick trip between El Paso and its sister city of Juarez. Tex walked toward her; he was alone, the majority of the train passengers having departed the platform several minutes ago.

Where was Rafe?

Did he procrastinate as punishment for their tiff over money? Surely not. Rafe didn't know the word punctual, much less ascribe to the principle, that was all. An inner voice asked, "So you're now the authority on Rafael Delgado?"

She wasn't. And she didn't know what to make of him, indeed, but she was becoming more and more certain that Olga had lied.

At that moment Margaret saw him. His Stetson sat at a rakish angle; his wide shoulders accentuated the narrowness of hips supporting a gun belt. The power of his thighs outlined by the jaunty yet infinitely controlled lift to his step, he headed in her direction. She started toward him, meaning to impart a piece of her mind about his tarrying. But he stopped short. He took a backward step.

Something's wrong.

Margaret followed his line of sight, glancing to the right and seeing a cluster of men. Three of them circled a nattily dressed gentleman emitting the aura of money and lots of it. As for his companions, well, except for the de-rigueur-for-Texas holsters buckled at their ready, they didn't look menacing; and they seemed to be chatting amiably in Spanish, so why was Rafe continuing to move to the rear?

Feinting to the left, he ducked between two railroad cars, disappearing from sight. Where the heck was he going? Surely he wasn't—He wouldn't— Why, that rascal.

He was ditching her!

She turned to Tex, who yammered with the driver. "Take charge of my steamers," she ordered, and plucked a derringer from the reticule that she tossed into the buckboard. "Get them to the station in Juarez. I'll meet you there."

"But, Maggie—"

115

"Don't argue, Angus Jones McLoughlin." Pistol in her right hand, she waved it. "Get gone to Juarez, and now!"

She picked up her skirts, damning the bulk of them, and ran after the artful dodger. The quartet of men moved in her direction, the gentleman asking if he could offer assistance, but she'd have none of that. This was between her and Rafe.

As if he were within hearing, she muttered, "Who do you think you are? You didn't win the argument. And I won't have you cheating."

She'd show him that he couldn't dash off, McLoughlin money in his bank account, and not pay the price. Up ahead she saw him crossing another set of tracks, heading south, for the river, it appeared. Slowing her pace, she aimed and fired. Naturally, he was out of range. And he didn't look back. He kept running.

So did she.

And she was surprised she could run this fast—she couldn't recall the last time she'd had the strength to run. Envisioning McLoughlin money collecting interest in his bank account had a powerfully stimulating effect, she decided. Self-congratulations vanished quickly, when her legs began to wobble and her chest to clamp. Trying to suck air in, she slowed but didn't stop.

Rafe descended an incline, kicking up dust as he went.

She gathered puny strength. "Stop!" she shouted from the hilltop and pointed the derringer. Less than a stone's throw separated them. "Stop, or I'll shoot again."

116

He stopped, turned. Even though she felt faint, she could see him shaking his head in disbelief. Whether it was from getting caught—or from the ridiculous picture she must have made, her traveling suit in disarray and her hair falling into her eyes—or from any idiot knowing she couldn't fire this derringer again without reloading, she had no idea.

"Madre de Dios, am I glad it's you." Arms going akimbo, he called, "Come on down here. And hurry."

"Rogue! You'd deceive me, would act as if I've shown up merely for teas and crumpets." It was time to show him the person *now* in charge. In his language, *el jefe.* "You get back up here, Rafe Delgado." Doggone it, could he hear her squeaking voice? "Right this instant."

"Can't. Gotta run." He jerked his head in the train's direction, frantically motioning her downward. "They're after me. And it didn't help, your calling attention with gunfire. Let's go, *cariño.* Now."

Well, what could she do but obey? Already he was on the run again. She followed, needing to clutch her aching side, but unable to, else she would be forced to stop. He ground to a halt behind a dilapidated shack, scattering a couple of nested Rhode Island Red hens. When she faced Rafe, Margaret lifted her gun arm. *Maybe he won't notice it's a single-shot weapon.*

"Dios, put that damned useless thing away. You and pointed objects. I swear I'm going to break you of pointing them at me, I swear I will."

"You dare to speak of my habits, when you have

117

just tried to run out on your duties?" *Don't faint. Whatever you do, don't faint.* She leaned against the shack's wall, thankful for its support. She jabbed the barrel flat to his washboard-hard belly.

His click of tongue and sigh of exasperation accompanied a grin laden with sensuality, all of which took away the anxious look in his shadowed, bruised face. "If that derringer were loaded, *bruja*, you could do my women a great disservice, should your forefinger get a little itchy."

Concern jumping into his gaze, he asked, "You're pale. Are you all right?"

As she nodded a reply, Rafe took the derringer from her clammy grip, stuffed it behind his gun belt. "Margarita, you're wrong about me. I wasn't running out on you. Did you see those men up there? The one in charge is my Uncle Arturo. He means to have me shot. I won't be a sitting duck for bullets."

Shot? Bullets? The respectable Arturo Delgado would fall to such violence against a relative? All this seemed to be coming at her in ebbs and surges of clarity, as if she were in some supernatural warp of movement. With her head pounding, her stomach roiling, and with her lungs gone immobile, she couldn't think straight. "You . . . you'd b-better explain."

"Later." Rafe grabbed her arm. "Right now, we've got to get away from here."

Unable to show the bossiness that had propelled her to him, she coughed. Deeply. "Where — we — g-going?"

"Mexico, of course." Rafe stopped dragging her

along. "What's the matter with you? I thought so. You *are* sick. Aw, hell. Aw, *chinga!*"

He caught her as she fell unconscious.

It was probably no more than a quarter hour before Margaret came to, and when she did, she was resting on a patch of bald earth under the shade of a weathered shed, her head in Rafe's lap. A ripe odor assailed her; it wasn't Rafe. She heard the rush of water from the river that served as a dividing point between two nations. "Which side are we on?"

"The Mexican."

"How did we get here?" she asked weakly, and noticed that the bottoms of his britches' legs were damp.

"I carried you. And, *gringa,* you are heavier than you look," he added with a tease in his tone. He brushed a wayward hair from her temple and held a tin cup — where the devil had he found a cup of potable water? — to her lips. As she downed the refreshing drink, he inquired, "Feeling better?" At her confirmation, he brushed a leaf from her cheek. "You scared the hell out of me. Why didn't you tell me you're sick?"

"I'm not!"

Cantankerous about her health, she jerked her head from its cozy cradle and dusted her sleeves as, a tad recovered, she sat up. It was then that she got her first good look at the land of the Eagle and Serpent. "Good God."

Mexico was no garden of temporal delights.

First of all, the shed turned out to be an out-

119

house. The sun-baked dirt surrounding it was littered with garbage, a horribly thin mongrel compet-
ing with a couple of equally thin hens for the
scraps. Two buzzards lurked in a sick excuse for a
mesquite tree. And from next to the skeleton of an
old donkey cart, a trio of curious, grimy Indian
tykes—the boy picking his nose—watched Rafe and
Margaret.

Her heart went out to the children. "You'd think
their mother would at least keep them clean. Poor
little things."

"They look healthy enough," Rafe said, affront in
his tone as well as in his face.

Margaret started to take another sip from the
cup. "Heavenly days, where *did* you get this?" And
who guaranteed it was potable? Revolted, Margaret
whispered, "Whatever got into my mother that she
would love this wretched country?"

"For a learned woman you can sure say some
stupid things. Surely you don't imagine Eden Roc as
anything like a peasant's meager abode."

"Cleanliness is a cheap commodity." Margaret,
who had designed an elaborate water works at the
Four Aces Ranch, envisioned several improvements
that could be made right here. "I've heard—and
now I've seen!—your country lacks even the basics
of sanitation."

Rafe dusted the brim of his Stetson. "Wretched it
may be, but it's got lovely parts, just like any other
place. Likewise, poverty isn't confined to Mexico.
It's all over the United States, too. The Mc-
Loughlins just haven't seen it."

"I'm sorry. I didn't realize you were so touchy.

Believe me, I meant no personal insult."

" 'Sorry' has surely worked its way into your vocabulary."

"Don't get testy." She got to her feet, and sympathies limited to the urchins, she waved at them, then ordered Rafe, "We've got to find my brother. Let's go."

The sun warmed her head and shoulders as she marched down a path leading to a dirt road; she didn't feel too wonderful, but another fainting spell wasn't imminent. Before long, the driver of a hay wagon offered a ride downtown, which she accepted; Rafe caught up with her. He helped her aboard, then hopped up himself. They bounced along for a mile or so with no conversation between them. Rafe rested a wrist on his bent knees, stuck a piece of hay between his teeth. As if overwarm, he rolled up one shirt sleeve, then another. Margaret couldn't help but notice the sheer masculinity of his arms and hands. Over and above the coarse black hairs and the network of raised veins, they showed strength as well as calluses.

She started to comment on those calluses, to mention that he must have taken a large part of the workaday responsibility on his ranch, but he spoke from profile. "Margarita, ever since you showed up at my *vacáda,* I've been wondering about your health. You're just not as . . . robust as you used to be. What happened, *querida?* What is wrong with you?"

"What about your uncle? I wish you'd tell me why he wants you shot. I think you owe me, as your employer, an explanation."

"I asked first. What's wrong with you?"

She took a quick glance at Rafe. The bruise on his jaw had turned black. One thumb hooked behind his gun belt, he had a worried look to him. When he repeated his question, she said, "You ran my legs off, that's what is the matter. Ladies do *not* exert themselves—it's bad form."

"No, Margarita. There's something more here. So stop being defensive and tell me." He bent his index finger and nudged her gaze to his. Understanding and compassion softened the silver irises of his eyes, along with the aristocratic planes of his face. "Margarita," he said in little more than a whisper, "I used to have a sister. Like you, María Carmen wasn't strong."

"What do you mean, *used to have?* Is she dead?" His nod was subtle as he crossed himself.

"I . . . I'm sorry, Rafe. Sincerely I am." Twice she patted his knee in a gesture of commiseration. "I lost a brother, but we were small children at the time, so I can't promise I know what you're going through, but . . ." A panicked feeling set in, as she tried to imagine what it would be like to lose her sisters or Tex. "It must have been awful for you."

Not even for brotherly grief would Rafe be put off his interrogation; he took her hand and forced her to face him. "You're consumptive, aren't you?"

"I am not! Never. No. Not me." The sky fell. The earth imploded. Margaret fought hard to escape the truth that was herself. "I'm never sick."

Shying from his scrutiny, hating that he could see through her, she squeezed her eyes closed and let her chin fall to her wizened chest. It had been a long,

long time since her last night sweat and bloody cough. A whole year had passed since she was released from the sanatorium. A whole year. And yet . . .

"Lord, help me, you were right, Rafe."

Despising her cadaverous body, yet not totally ungrateful that it hadn't completely quit on her, she buried her face in her bony hands and gave way to self-pity. Sometimes, like now, she found herself plain scared. Would she have the strength to meet the challenges of her goals and ambitions?

"We'd better find a doctor," Rafe said.

"No, no. The doctors swear I'm over it." She surrendered to self-pity and the shame of her illness. "But it's still obvious. I'll never be myself again. Oh, God."

"Enough of that talk. We're headed for a fountain of miracles, remember?"

"If only I had my mother's faith in the place . . ."

"Put your faith in it. You're going to be fine. *Fine.*" He rubbed her temple with the pads of two fingers, brushing his thumb on her forehead. His touch felt as gentle as a mother with her newborn. "Margarita, *querida,* don't be ashamed of being sick."

"What do you know, Rafael Delgado? You haven't had people run from you, lest they breathe your contaminated air. Me and my kind, we are virtual lepers."

He chuckled, winked. "Well, sweet of my heart, I've had some experience along those lines. You McLoughlins haven't been much on *my* breathing *your* rarified air."

Heartened that he hadn't shown pity—surprised he was so wrong about her family—she gaped at Rafael Delgado. Who was this dark, tender man? For years she'd been certain of his ignoble ways and lack of sensitivity, or at least she would have sworn so. Could it be she'd spent years suffering under misconceptions?

Not quite ready to believe she'd been so very, very wrong, she confined her comments to absolutes. "Don't want you to breathe their air? Wherever did you get such a ridiculous idea? Every time I see Charity, she goes on and on about you—as if you were the greatest man in the world, besides her husband and our papa, that is."

"I *am* the greatest man in the world. At least at rescuing McLoughlin women."

Margaret rolled her eyes. "My parents think you hung the moon. My great-grandmother—do you remember Maisie McLoughlin? She thinks you're, well, she thinks highly of you."

"How is the crusty old thing?"

The fondness in his tone surprised Margaret. She assured him the formidable Scotswoman remained invincible, to which he commented, "A crafty one, your *abuela.*"

"That she is." Margaret picked straw from her traveling suit. "And Olga . . ." *Should I broach the subject?* "Olga loved you very much."

Margaret almost didn't want to witness his reaction.

Nine

The hay wagon came to a wobbling halt at the same moment she mentioned her triplet sister's name, and Margaret's relief at the interruption flowed wider than the neighboring Rio Grande. Although she'd broached the subject, she didn't feel comfortable conversing with Rafe about Olga. Margaret feared . . . well, what if some nuance gave him away, shouting his guilt?

He tossed the driver a coin, jumped from the wagon, and helped Margaret to the busy street. "I know a good restaurant near here. Let's have breakfast."

From the tense look on his face, it was obvious Rafe wasn't eager to discuss Olga, either. And food, Margaret decided, was a capital, if not a bland enough idea.

Asking time and again if she were feeling all right, he took her hand and led her southward. Commenting at length, Margaret made observation after observation to Rafe. The general aroma left something to be desired in Juarez, a town that teemed with brown-faced people, all seemingly in no rush to get anywhere, such as the alm-seeking beggars lounging against walls and around the monument-decked plaza. As for monuments, Mexicans seemed to have an it's-Sunday-let's-erect-a-statue passion.

"Do you suppose that harks back to the days of idolatry?" she asked, dwelling on the stark difference between Mexico and her mother country.

"I never gave it much thought."

"I'd say this place is to Spain what the West is to New York," she theorized.

He hurried on to point out that it was a colorful and rather festive place, Juarez. Banners and flags waved in brilliance from all sorts of places, including an open-air shoe-shine stand. Vivid paint must have been in high demand over the years, being that the buildings—all crowded close together—were veritable Easter eggs of colors.

Margaret, long a watcher of people and animals, concentrated on them. Though an ocean separated the countries, this place carried a resemblance to the medinas and bazaars of the Moorish world.

Merchants unresponsive to No! in several languages hawked brightly colored clothes, knick-knacks of dubious use, and lengthy leather whips, while ragged peddlers sold food and colorful fresh fruit drinks. Up and down the dirt street, burros packed goods on their scrawny backs, while fine horses carried the bejeweled to their respective fates. Chickens and goats roamed freely and ecstatically wild, children played in the open ditches, and painted prostitutes plied their trade from open door-ways.

It came as no surprise when Rafe drew a lot of attention from those professional women. Even the less vocal, higher classed females cast many a covert stare at Rafe and his unmistakable strut. Each and every of those women shot Margaret envious glares.

After a few minutes Rafe and Margaret turned easterly and entered a less crowded avenue. Trees grew here, and the buildings, decorated with wrought iron, were whitewashed and spaced farther apart than on the previous street. A fine coach passed the couple. This part of town was in fact beautiful, "Rather like provincial Spain," she commented.

"I told you Mexico isn't all poverty," he said smugly.

"I don't believe I argued the point."

He gestured to a one-story building with open windows and pots of cactus growing at its entrance. "May I present Carmelita's?" He sketched a bow. "Herein lies the best food in Juarez. Or it used to be, when I was last here."

The regret when he voiced the addendum gave Margaret pause. And she wondered, probably for the first time, what his life had been like in the days before Texas. What did he leave behind?

She entered Carmelita's. The wall decor came at her, figuratively. Lithographs, faded and yellowed, graced each of the walls; those posters announced corridas of years past. "That's you, Rafe," she said. "You're on all of them."

He laughed. "I especially like this one."

She added her own laugh. The poster he pointed to had been embellished by an artist of sorts. The corners of Rafe's eyes had been blackened, giving him a cross-eyed appearance. She said, "I didn't think you had much of a sense of humor about your appearance."

"I don't. Usually. Let's eat. The food is delicious."

The meal did prove savory, the establishment scrupulously clean, and the plump, gray-haired proprietress friendly as a cocker spaniel pup. By the time Margaret had finished the plate of eggs and tortillas, not to mention a whole pot of rich and delicious Mexican hot chocolate, her eyelids were drooping like a basset hound's.

"She's had a tiring journey," Rafe explained when Carmelita came over to cluck and hover. "A few minutes rest and she'll be fine."

"Ah, *sí*. The señorita can siesta on my little bed. You find something to do, *El Aguila*. Come back later."

Before Margaret could say a word, Carmelita hustled her into the back of the restaurant, and led her to a narrow cot with crisp white sheets. The bed looked more than inviting, the trip having indeed caught up with her.

The proprietress scurried about, closing the window shutters. "You will find water and towels to freshen with on that table." Carmelita indicated a commode of rough walnut standing above an enameled chamber pot. "My wrapper will go around you three times"—she pulled back the sheets—"but it is clean, and you will be comfortable."

128

Margaret nodded, half asleep, and mumbled a thank you.

"At mass tomorrow I will give a prayer of thanksgiving to our Lady of Guadalupe." Carmelita, seriousness at its zenith, bent her head and raised templed hands. "For many years I have prayed that the Eagle would return."

"I figured from the posters that you admire him. Highly."

"I do." Tears glistened. "And he is here. He will save our nation."

Her brow quirking, Margaret cocked her head. Rafe save Mexico? The only thing he'd save was Lisette McLoughlin. "How can a matador, an *ex*-matador, save a nation?"

"Did you not know that he left the arena to devote his energies to the needs of the people?"

Never had she put much stock in those rumors of rebellion, and he didn't strike Margaret as a magnanimous soul. Moreover, he'd said his argument had been confined to his uncle. In her state of exhaustion, wherever the truth of him was centered, she wasn't interested in giving anything too much thought.

She barely heard Carmelita say, "Did you know a Spanish spy has been arrested here in Mexico?"

It was all she could do to get out of her traveling suit and serviceable underthings, drag a wet rag over her face and other parts, and don the soft, sun-smelling wrapper. She fell upon the cot, dragging the sheet under her chin and closing her eyes.

* * *

She awoke languorously, as if she had taken too much of Dr. Woodward's cough elixir. A piquant aroma—a melange of cooking smells liberally laced with chiles—wafted to her. Opening one eye, she saw that a squat candle burned on the table next to the cot. From the doorway leading into the restaurant, Margaret heard the clink of dishes and silverware, the whir of several voices, and the strains of trumpet and guitars in symphony with a drumbeat, not unlike that heard from the tall tapering drums of the Dark Continent.

And she saw Rafe.

Rafe. In a chair pulled next to the bed, he sat with an ankle crossed on a knee. *"Buenos noches."* Good evening.

Rafe. All smoky devouring eyes . . . and finely honed physique. His American dress had been abandoned for more traditional gear that Margaret knew had overtones of Spain, and he looked magnificent. A *faja* as red as blood sashing his waist, he wore a white shirt and dark britches, tight britches. Lastly, soft boots of black kid encased calves in no way resembling those of a pink flamingo.

Oh, Rafe. His scent was leather and smoke. He sipped from a snifter of something that was probably brandy. With his ruffled shirt unbuttoned to the middle of his chest, it was impossible not to notice the golden crucifix. Margaret had the sudden urge to furrow her fingers through the crisp black hair surrounding the cross. *Close your mouth, lest you'll drool.*

She yanked the covers up another inch under her chin. "What time is it?"

130

"Supper time."

"We must get out of here. Tex will be waiting."

Rafe shook his head. "No need to rush. He knows where we are. He's rented a hotel room, so we'll meet him tomor—"

"Hotel room? He doesn't need a hotel. Oh. I see. We've missed today's train, haven't we?"

Rafe set the snifter on the table. "Actually, we're not taking the train to Chihuahua city. Young Siegfried and I bought a wagon and team this afternoon."

Young Siegfried. Was Rafe ever going to let her live down that Teutonic god remark? The man was a born tease! But this wasn't the time for teasing. "Excuse me? You've opted for a slow method of transport, when the train would get us there in practically no time?"

"I can't chance running into any of my uncle's men. The Arturianos."

"Why? What is wrong between you and Arturo Delgado?"

"Shhhh." Candlelight casting his face into interesting relief, Rafe leaned forward to press his forefinger against her lips. "You have been taxed by the trip, and we have a longer one ahead of us. Tonight we relax. And enjoy ourselves."

"How can we do that?" she asked and brushed his touch away. "You know we're not compatible."

On an odd twist of lips, he replied, "I suppose we can act as if we don't know each other."

The funniest feeling came over Margaret, rather an envy. Olga had received his attentions and affections—before their final fateful night at least, and

131

the jury was still out on that specific event — but Rafe didn't bother with his celebrated charm when it came to Olga's witch of a triplet sister.

She recalled something Tex had said. *Meskin fellers would even woo a nanny goat.* To improve her chances, maybe she ought to look into growing a beard and stalking clotheslines for sustenance. *But Rafe said he mistook Olga for you, in the beginning.*

Sweet talk. Pure gibberish. But wasn't that what she sought, blandishments? Truth be known, she wanted to find out for herself just what was so exceptional about Rafael Delgado.

Struggling for life in Manoah Woodward's sanatorium for the consumptive, Margaret had prayed to walk in the sunshine once more. And not to die a virgin. Up to now no one had stirred her senses. But with Rafe . . . Her passion for him had simmered just below the surface for ages. Okay, he might be as worthless as a wooden nickel. So be it.

Going to her grave without knowing a man intimately didn't hold much appeal. Furthermore, her fainting spell had been a reminder of Dr. Woodward's prognosis. In not so many words, he'd told her not to bother socking acorns away for an old age.

She squeezed her eyes shut, turning her head to the wall. This action wasn't for romantic woolgathering, though. Neither foolish nor simpleminded enough to delude herself into thinking Rafe would ever have a romantic interest in her, she knew if he was now showing interest, it was suspect. He'd had eight years, after all, to notice Margaret for Margaret.

But, dang it, heaven was just a sin away. And whether heaven or hell was in the offing for the ever-after, she wanted her last chance at heaven on earth.

"Margarita? Are you all right? What is the matter?"

Facing him, she opened her eyes to the beauty of him.

"I bought you a new set of clothes." He reached for a pile of gaily, gaudily printed garments. "A skirt, a blouse. A petticoat. You've got new slippers, too. Sandals, they are."

"I can't wear that. They aren't me."

"What *is* you?"

"I'm not one to wear vivid colors. They'll give the wrong impression. I don't like calling attention to myself."

He held the skirt at his shoulder and stroked the material, as Margaret had stroked her adored babies. He said, "You'll call more attention by wearing Victorian browns."

All she could argue was, "You didn't have to go to such expense."

"You're wrong." He chucked her chin lightly. "We've got the whole evening ahead of us, and I'm the one looking at you."

There you go, Margaret. There's your reason. Don Juan gets down to the basics. He wants you spruced up for the sake of his eyesight. Why did that have to hurt?

He rose, put the chair away, and strode to the doorway. His fingers on the fastener, he said,

133

"Freshen up, *cariño*. I'll be waiting for you in the dining room."

Collect your wits. So you're not his ideal. Why should he want a chalky-faced scarecrow? Don't let him get the better of you.

Rafe was getting the better of her. It was a pastime for him—like a game of solitaire, just something to kill time—his attentions. Yet Margaret had difficulty keeping him in the proper perspective, for this was a night of a thousand sighs.

Every time she looked at him, she sighed.

Under a cap of starlight, in the cloak of evocative music and two dozen posters featuring *El Aguila Magnífico,* they dined in the open-air courtyard, off-side to a cage of parrots. At first it seemed as if the eatery's business was slow, but Margaret learned that Carmelita, assuming lovers were in her midst and in honor of the adored *El Aguila,* had rejected all comers for dinner. Except for the supposed lovers.

A waiter, the epitome of discretion, served a main course of baked *cabrito,* young goat. With the meat came Spanish rice, refried beans, a piquant tomato-onion-and-cilantro relish called *pico de gallo* plus piles of corn tortillas. They washed down this repast with glass after glass of chilled sangria. And all the while the music played . . .

Attentive as Don Juan in the flesh, Rafe stared into Margaret's eyes. "Mexico becomes you."

She sighed. "Th-thank you."

She lowered her gaze to comb his broad chest,

134

and she had a mirthful thought. What would it be like to study for an advanced degree in the difference between a golden cross and the texture of pitch-black chest hair?

Some nagging, shrill little voice — her conscience — kept shouting at her. Why couldn't she find the wherewithal to get down to business? Her baby brother was somewhere in this foreign city, probably scared for his sister — while she wasn't moving so much as a hair to put him at ease. Half-dressed — decked out in revealing soft cottons and negligible foundations — she ate and drank . . . and ignored shrill little voices.

Contemplating that intriguing scar at the corner of Rafe's mouth, she spilled a goodly amount of sangria.

"Something wrong?" Rafe inquired and sopped up the mess.

"Wrong . . . wrong . . . something wrong? Chirp." A green wing flapped. "Chirp. *Besame culo.*"

Margaret and Rafe both laughed at the bird's profanity. "I don't imagine he knows what part of his anatomy he's proposing we kiss," she said, faking a casual air. "But he, she, it is a beautiful bird."

Fingers warm, callused, smoothed across her cheek. Rafe's gaze didn't waver from Margaret. "Yes, a beautiful bird."

She swallowed. Such a glib tongue had he, even to woo a nanny goat . . . or perhaps a colorless and lovelorn imitation of the beautiful and serene Lady Hapsburg. *How does he feel about her, after all these years?* To cover her discomfiture, Margaret said, "About my brother, shouldn't we pay up and get on to meet him? I'm sure he's lonely, and—"

"Margarita, lonely? A young hombre in a town like Juarez? Tex is not lonely."

Recalling those tarts who'd issued catcalls to Rafe, Margaret took a quick look around to make certain no one could eavesdrop. They were alone, save for the occupied musicians. "Tex may be an adult, but he's green, Rafe. Green as grass. I shudder to think of him being corrupted by women of the night."

Rafe threw back his head, laughing in his easy fashion. "Silly sweet, you are too old for such innocence. Hombres his age are already corrupted."

"You can't know that for sure." Margaret blushed. "Anyway, I don't think of him along such lines. He's my kid brother, he's in my care, and I don't want anything to happen to him. This is a vulgar city, so I think we should take our leave."

"No."

"No?"

"Right. No. And don't worry about the jades of Juarez amusing your young lion." Rafe winked. "Your brother swears he's glad for the delay, and I have no reason to doubt his sincerity. Understand, he wishes to meet the train in El Paso tomorrow. Need I say he seeks Miss Nash?"

"Well, I think we should go by the hotel and make certain he's all right."

"He is all right."

"You're playing an evil game with me, Rafe, and I want you to stop it at once. Now. Where can I find Tex?"

"I'll tell you. Later."

"Oooh, you can be exasperating." She squared her shoulders. "On the train you told me you don't enjoy games, yet you are playing me for a mouse in the cat's paw."

"If you'll remember, I qualified my remark. In affairs of the heart, I love a challenge."

Affairs of the heart — bah! It was tempting, the urge to argue, but it would be futile. She figured he, a master in the tournament of amusements, loved nothing more than contests of any sort, and he was better at them than she.

Resting her chin on laced fingers, she eyed the musicians. "I can't peg the music. It isn't quite the sound of the mariachi." *It's too lush, too sensual, too provocative. Too much in the wild style of Rafe.* "It's somewhat akin to the flamenco of the gypsies, yet it doesn't mimic the sounds of Spain, not precisely, although it does have a flavor of the bolero. Would you agree this has North Africa — black and Moorish Africa — and the melange that is the Americas to it?"

Rafe bent across the table to trace his finger down her cheek . . . and she trembled. "Must you always figure everything out? Can't you ever let anything be, and live for the moment?"

She studied him, trying to assess the name of this new game. Recreation for an idle hand, perhaps? Rather than answer, she said, "Help me, Rafe. You're a musician. What is this music?"

"How do you know I'm a musician?"

"Don't . . . don't be absurd. It's well known that you are a guitarist." *Olga told me so.*

He hooked an ankle with one of hers, and his palm smoothed over her shoulder, before his thumb flicked her breast ever so lightly, ever so exciting. "Tell me what you know about me."

Her heart pounded when his thumb made another foray at her breast. "Y-you're a dangerous man," she managed to answer. *What do you mean to do with me?*

"I am not dangerous. I am a simple Mexican bull breeder."

"And the pope is just a Catholic."

Rafe chuckled and relaxed back in his chair, bringing the wine goblet to his infinitely kissable lips, and the look that he gave her was one that pulled—pulled? No! Yanked—her into the flare of his incendiary gaze. "You are the dangerous one, *querida*. Brave, unwilling to give in. That's where your beauty lies, in your spirit."

"Of course. And Yorkshire shoats lay golden eggs. If you're not dangerous, explain about your uncle. Or explain *all this*." She gestured around the restaurant. "A businesswoman turns away clientele, and that same woman lights candles to thank Mexico's patron saint for your return. Carmelita says you gave up the bullring for a more noble cause. Did she tell the truth?"

"She did. The *suerte de matár* began to sicken me with its violence. I likened it to the violence and brutality wreaked upon the luckless of this country."

"You amaze me."

"Is that good or bad?" he asked, and leaned forward to trace his fingertip along her jaw.

"Good," she answered, not certain whether she

meant his history or his touch, for her face tingled where he stoked. "You must have been an impressive rebel in your heyday, Rafe."

His chest puffing, he smoothed his hair back. "I was."

"I'd like to hear all about it."

"Let's not discuss bygone days."

"Let's do. I'm thinking—"

"Shhh." He took her hand in his. "Quit thinking, little witch. You overtax your brain with all your suppositions and theories." His knee settled against hers. "Dance with me."

Gracious, his was a tempting offer, but Margaret was no vision of suppleness and form on the dance floor. In fact, Frederick the Crumb, after leading her in a polka at the German Club in San Antonio, had made snide allusions to Hugo's Quasimodo gamboling on the *Ile de la Cité*. "I don't dance."

With his thumb Rafe wiped a line of condensation down from his glass. "At all?"

"Not to this. It is much too vigorous for me."

"You have been in Spain. Did you not dance the flamenco, *querida?*"

"The flamenco is for gypsies."

"Let yourself be a *gitana* tonight." His lips twitched as he studied each of her features in turn. In a voice soft, quiet, attentive, he asked, "How are you feeling?"

"Fine." Thinking of golden earrings and the flaring skirts of gypsy dancers, she took a sip of the icy sangria. She wasn't prepared to make a fool of herself, but the idea of spinning around the dance floor did have its charms. "I'm quite recovered, thank you. My long nap was what the doctor ordered."

"That is good. For you *will* dance with me."

The drums went rap, tap, rap . . . deep and low. Rafe stood, offered a hand that she waved away.

"Do you deny me because you haven't settled your mind about this music?" Not giving her time for a reply, he said, "It is the sound of a place you should know well. It is the sound of Cuba. Have you not been there?"

"No." The McLoughlin interests were wide in Spain's misbehaving child in the Caribbean. Plus, Papa and Mama owned a sugar plantation and rum distillery outside Havana. They used to visit the island frequently. And Cuba was the center of her father's political crisis, but . . . "No, I haven't."

"I'm surprised. But Cuba is far away. And tonight . . . we shall dance."

"I said no."

Unlike the merchants of this city, Rafe understood the word no. He moved a couple of footsteps toward the musicians, presenting his back and centering his attention on the bandstand. One wide shoulder stirred, in time with the music. The stark white of his shirt, the blood red sash at his waist, those tight black britches — this attire seemed perfect for a lithe body such as his. But what was he about? Did he intend to dance for her?

She watched, mesmerized, as his body moved ever so lightly to the primitive beat, then made a half turn. In profile, a lock of hair having fallen to his brow, he squinted at the stars before dropping his chin as if in thought. One foot tapped in rhythm, and he became as one with the music. Lithe of motion, hypnotic in effect, he must have looked like this when he'd lured the *toros* to him.

He lifted and swung his chin, extending a hand in silent invitation. She didn't move. "Come to me, *querida*."

Something invisible pulled her, something such as a moth to the flame. On her feet Margaret went into the Eagle's arms—and they were warm, strong, encircling. Yet she remained jumpy. "I have two left feet. I don't know what to do."

"Just follow my lead," was his creamy reply. "Dancing is an expression of letting go one's reserve. Soar with me, *paloma*."

Unable to argue giving over control—not particularly wanting it at this point, for she had tumbled headlong into dementia—she let him twine his fingers with hers. Gyrating his hips and lifting their joined hands high, he threw back his head and emitted a groan as earthy as the music. She stepped closer, and when she did, she felt the heat of his body, the raw power of it, the invitation of a journeyman lover.

Rafe's gaze never leaving her, he released Margaret's fingers and began to dance around her, his muscled form moving expertly, erotically. "Follow your desires, *amorcito*. Do as your feelings demand."

Her weight rocked from one foot to the other. As if they had minds of their own, her feet vibrated in step with the sounds. Her nervousness vanished as the mood of the evening enveloped her.

Utterly agile, ever nimble, Rafe inched closer, his

chest touching hers. Excitement flashed through her. Drunk on the dance, on him, she rolled her shoulder to his. "This must be what it feels like to fly," she murmured thickly.

"*Sí, sí, mi paloma*." The tip of his tongue touched her earlobe. "Fly high, *paloma*. Fly free."

He was taunting her, daring her, beseeching her. She loved it. Suddenly the music switched rhythms, but neither she nor Rafe missed a step, and her body curved to his. He growled deep in his throat, and ground his hips against her pelvis. The difference between them, the feel of their heated bodies in contact . . . oh, my! All of a sudden one of his arms braced her waist, the opposite hand twining with her fingers anew. Around and around he twirled her, their toes tapping, their fingers snapping, their hearts beating fast. In tune with each other.

" '*España Cañi,*' " she murmured when he whirled her around.

"*Sí, querida. 'España Cañi.'* The procession for the bullfighters."

She had heard this song in Ronda, a town built high on an olive-dotted precipice in the Sierra Nevadas of Andalusia. It was a village famed for its bullring, and home to the late Francisco Romero, the first matador of great fame. In Ronda, as well as when Rafe had played these strains on his guitar, she'd never known this clarion call to blood sport could also become a song of seduction. Not until now. The song lured her, pulled her to Rafe—to his eyes and lips and body movements. She trembled, her flesh heated to the scorching point, as he made love to her without ever touching her intimately.

The trumpet lifted. The musicians brought the music to a crescendo, and began to gather and pack their instruments. And Rafe pulled Margaret even closer.

"Te quiero, Mah-gah-reeta. *Hoy."*

For whatever reason, and she didn't wish to study on it, he wanted her. Now. She wanted him . . . now. And the musicians departed. So had Carmelita and the waiter. Margaret and Rafe were alone.

Ten

Margaret smiled into his eyes. "I want you, too."

Rafe carried her into the small darkened room where she had napped the day away, then laid her on the cot. She rolled to her side, making room, and he stretched out next to her. Her greedy fingers went to his chest, her every action a celebration. She hummed low in her throat at how the flesh-toasted cross felt in relation to chest hair soft as a sigh.

It was the same as she remembered it . . . from long ago. "So very, very nice."

"I'm pleased you approve," he said silkily. "The cross was a gift from my sister. María Carmen."

Of course, Margaret didn't correct him.

He dispensed with her hairpins, murmuring, "That's better."

Their lips met, their arms winding round each other, and her fingers now furrowed through the thick hair at Rafe's nape. Trailing kisses to her ear, he whispered, "I have gone loco for the need of you."

144

Her passions climbed to an even higher level, as he continued kissing and caressing her. The scent of him filled her senses richly, deliciously, with overtones of sandalwood cologne, not at all cheap. Her head lolled backward as he sipped from her throat and drew the drawstrings of her blouse below her breasts.

"They . . . they aren't much," she said worriedly, as he eased back to gaze upon the muted sight of her. "Not like they used to be." *Not like Olga's.*

"For me," he said, echoing a reference he'd made about himself, back at his ranch, "big things come in small packages, *querida.*"

His head dipped to take a crest into his mouth; her fingers tangled in his hair, she pressed him to her. He suckled and laved and caressed, laved and suckled and stroked, giving each breast its share of attention. Both peaks grew hard as pebbles. Her woman-place became heavy, aching for surcease. Never, not even in her wildest dreams — not even in her recollections of the night his hands had sought her hidden places and she'd encouraged him onward — had she imagined the preamble to coitus could be this . . . stimulating.

A low growl issued from Rafe's throat as he groaned, "You're amazing. I thought you'd be an icicle. But you are hot as the most blistering day of July. I like the surprises of you."

His praise thrilled her, left her feeling as if she were the world's most special woman, which was a wonderful feeling for a woman long ignored and much too insecure about her appeal. Her qualms vanished. Enraptured, she kissed him, but he took the aggressive role, his tongue slipping into her mouth.

"I'm going to undress you," he whispered when he dragged his mouth away; his toes traced her ankle.

"Yes, do."

"And you will do the same for me?" he asked.

Strip him? Cowardice and inexperience reared, now that she was on the brink of experiencing the Big Secret, yet she whispered in return, "With pleasure."

"I wish to kiss you. Everywhere. But first . . ." He took her hand and guided it to the warmed silk of his trousers; he made her fingers fasten around the abundance of him. "Know your power, *cariño*. This is what you do to me."

"Oh, my." In the shadow of the Alamo she'd wanted to explore his flesh as he explored hers, but she'd gotten no further than his chest when a constable had shouted them apart. There was no one to stop them tonight. "You are finely made."

A world of wonders fit him. He was rigid and hard—so very hard, like a brick. Hot, hot like a kiln. And he was large, very large. She ached to have him in her, yet her curiosity begged appeasing. "Do you hurt?"

"Very much." He nuzzled her neck. "You will make it better."

Ever inquisitive, she found herself much in awe of how the male appendage functioned. Olga, when newly wed, had been a wellspring of information about sex, but the intricacies of physiology were sadly lacking. When Margaret tried to get to the bottom of a list of questions, Sister Ninny had

146

gotten all flustered and Victorian-acting. Charity, too, had expounded on the beauties of passion, but, like Olga, she was no scholar and didn't reckon on matters in a studious fashion. Passion was one thing, a fertile mind another. "I wonder how it gets hard like this."

"It is you, *amorcito*. Just being around you does it."

"Rafe, you're exaggerating. I've been in your company numerous times, and I would have noticed if you'd gotten this way. Only the blind would miss it." Blind. *Don't think about Olga's affliction.* "Aren't you going to say something?"

"Margarita . . . not now. Later."

"But, Rafe—"

"Shhh. Be quiet."

"I will not."

"Mujer. I am trying to make love to you." His hand smoothed over her hip. "Hush, or you'll spoil the mood."

"All I asked is how your you-know-what got hard. If you don't know, please don't worry about appearing stupid. I share your ignorance."

No longer thrilled with her surprises, he uttered a string of curses while rearing back from her. "If you want to know how one goes soft, observe!"

She's gone. Lost to me. Life ain't fair.

The wind lowed like a mournful steer. A tumbleweed rolled end over end to crash against the train depot wall. That hot desert zephyr then burst, blowing Tex McLoughlin's Stetson off his head, all ten gallons of it landing on the steel tracks that glinted in the unrelenting sun. These were the tracks where the westbound train had departed ten minutes ago. Natalie Nash had not been aboard, either on arrival or at departure.

A piece of newspaper whirled across Tex's path. He glanced upward and to the right, to the parched and serrated peaks of Mount Cristo Rey, then to the left, in the direction of the flatter foreign land across the river. It seemed to reflect his emptiness, the loneliness of the desert.

A carriage pulled out, taking a quartet of men away. Apparently, they too had waited in vain for an arriving passenger. Tex had seen them here yesterday; today the one in charge had said in Spanish, "She betrayed me. Once more the bitch has let me down. She'll never do it again."

The world was full of woebegone men, Tex decided, and glanced up the tracks, toward Alpine. "I shouldn't've listened to Maggie," Tex said, grieving to the only other being in sight, a black-and-tan mutt who'd taken up with him this morning. "I should've stayed put in Alpine. And done what I wanted to, not what I was expected to do."

For all his twenty-two years, Angus Jones McLoughlin had been the dutiful scion carrying the required baton. Gil and Lisette McLoughlin's surviving son would raise cattle and younguns on the Four Aces Ranch. This was how it was done in Texas. A man wouldn't even have to be too clever in the doing, since most ranches were money-making propositions already, the Four Aces a gold mine beyond compare; and even if it wasn't, the family fortune

148

had been invested and reinvested. Wholly in lucrative enterprises.

So . . . at the proper time and with some retiring little woman at his side, Tex would branch out into politics, following in his father's footsteps. That's what you did, when you were a Texan with money in the bank and cattle on the hoof. He'd always felt he wasn't cut out for the highfalutin sort of life, though. He was a country boy and common cowpoke by choice. For Miss Natalie, though, he would change into anything she wanted, if she wanted.

"Money or nothing else don't matter," he lamented to the cur. "She's gone, gone, gone."

And all he had to remember her by was a heart full of pain and one small kiss, given just before the train had pulled out of Alpine. Though he barely knew the blonde beauty, he was positive no other woman would ever do for him. Tex was a man who knew his mind.

After spitting a particle of dust from his tongue, Tex reached down to give the mutt a scratch on the ear and to grasp his hat. "Duty calls. I've got to find my sister. And fetch our mother."

He ambled toward the mount he'd rented from an El Paso livery, saying to the wayward wind, "Maybe I'll get lucky and Natalie will show up at Eden Roc."

His luck, to his way of thinking, had never been that good.

The trip by wagon into the Chihuahuan Desert and toward the Sierra Madres couldn't be considered anything but a trial. While Rafe was glad to be back in Mexico, his mood was as black and sour as a grizzly bear disturbed in winter.

His aggravation wasn't necessarily because the wagon was too bogged down with Margarita's heavy steamer trunks, or because Tex McLoughlin had done nothing but pout like an offended schoolboy. It was because his sister sat next to Rafe on the spring seat and chattered like a damned monkey. She acted as if nothing had happened at Carmelita's, but Rafe had not forgotten, not for a moment. Losing his potency brought him great shame. It had never happened before.

"She might have had me under some magnifying glass," he told himself for the tenth time in four days. Since Carmelita's, he'd made no further attempts at lovemaking, not even when she flirted with him at the quaint inns — *mésons* — where they took quarters. Had he gotten too old for the feats of a Don Juan? If that first gray hair he'd yanked from his scalp was an indicator, walking sticks and liniment were on the horizon.

Worthless to the ladies, what could he do with the rest of his miserable life? What was his purpose? Paying respect to Hernán's sacrifice, that was his purpose.

How to accomplish it, that was the question.

On the fifth morning of their journey to Eden Roc, about three hours after they had left the village of Moctezuma, Rafe drove the wagon onward, Margarita beside him, her brother snoring from a makeshift bed atop the trunks. Thank God for those snores. Rafe didn't know how much more of Young Siegfried's bellyaching he could take. *And if I never hear the name Natalie Nash again, it will be too soon.*

"Would you like one of these?" Margarita asked and offered a tin of cookie crumbs.

"No," was his cross and terse reply.

The skinny witch—buttoned to the throat in her usual garb of brown gabardine—hadn't stopped eating since Juarez. At the rate she was going, she'd reach the city of Chihuahua and the two hundred-pound mark at the same time. At least she'd gotten some color back in her complexion. And she'd done a lot less wheezing and coughing.

"My goodness," she commented and dabbed her mouth with a handkerchief, "the terrain does provide intriguing sights. Roadrunners, cactus, white sand. And more roadrunners, cactus, and white sand. On occasion, and with cause for celebration, we find wide fissures in the earth. Arroyos."

"We're not down here for the landscape." He did, however, for lack of anything better to do, launch into a catalog of the city of Chihuahua's attractions.

Evidently unimpressed with the travelogue, she replied, "Yes, but I really do think we should have taken the train. It's much more expedient."

"I've lost count of the times you've told me that."

Her single-mindedness never ceased to amaze him. Nor was he unaware of her acute curiosity. When she said, "You never have told me *exactly* why you're running from your uncle," Rafe rolled his eyes.

151

"Because I—"

Unanticipated, the wagon gave a sudden lurch to the left; traces and harnesses pinged, horses whickering and screaming at the unexpected movement. Baggage slipped. Tex gave a shout. The cookie tin as well as Margarita's bonnet went flying, though she grabbed the tin as if her very existence depended on it. Rafe somehow got the team stopped and the brakes set. He twisted around and gave a look downward, confirming what he suspected. "We've lost a wheel."

He and Tex hopped to the ground, Rafe giving Margarita assistance. An inspection of the total situation provided bleak news. Several spokes had splintered, were broken. There were no tools to repair it, since Margarita's collection of steamer trunks had prevented bringing them along. The weight of her possessions had no doubt put too much strain on the wheel. *There'd better be gold in those damned trunks.*

"I'll saddle one of these nags and go for help," Tex offered.

"Do it. Keep to a southerly path, and just before you reach that next squat range of hills, you'll run into the village of El Sueco." To ease everyone's mind, Rafe added, "We're not too far from Chihuahua city."

Rafe started to hoist himself to the wagonbed. "I'll get the wagon unloaded and jacked up."

Margarita dabbed her forehead with her handkerchief. "None of us is doing anything until we've had a bit of refreshment. Rafe, get my green tru—"

"Refreshment?" Rafe snapped and put his foot

152

back on the ground. *"Por el amor de Dios,* we're in trouble, woman! It's at least a four-hour trip to the nearest village. We're not taking time out for tea and bonbons."

She rolled her eyes and waved a hand. "Oh, you. Don't be such a crab. I've got some wonderful Swiss chocolates that I've been saving for a special occasion, and . . ." She grinned at her brother, who had gotten his saddle from the wagonbed. "Dr. Pepper."

"Well, shuckums, Sis, why didn't ya just say so?" Tex dropped the saddle. "Where're they at?"

"The green trunk."

Young Siegfried leapt upon the wagon and hoisted the trunk as if he were hoisting a basket of feathers, setting it on the ground as if it were a casket of rubies and diamonds. Or perhaps his adored Natalie. Since Rafe had nearly broken his back putting that trunk into the wagon, it was all he could do not to stomp off. It was no fun getting old. And weak. *You're not so old, Delgado. He's just younger and bigger.*

Right.

On her knees, Margarita opened the treasure chest, revealing row upon row of carefully packed, well-insulated bottles that gleamed in the sunlight and were filled with dark brown liquid. She gushed, "I knew these soda pops would come in handy."

"Come again?" Rafe asked and feared the reply. "What are soda pops?"

"Soft drinks. Beverages. Libations."

Speechless, flat-out poleaxed—that was Rafe. Somehow he managed to choke out, "You packed fancy *drinks?* Drinks! *Mujer,* we are not on a Nile

153

cruise." He slapped his forehead with the heel of his palm. "I dread finding out what you've got in the others."

"Oh, stop making a scene." After removing two sealed tops, she handed a bottle to Tex and then to Rafe. "Enjoy."

The bottle felt cool, almost cold to the touch. By the time Rafe had brought his to his lips, Tex had guzzled one bottle and was asking for another. Rafe took a swallow. Bubbles of something went up his nose, and that something popped and snapped. He coughed. And like to choked. But, oddly, the liquid was sweet and delicious. He wiped his mouth with the back of a hand, asking, "What is this?"

"Carbonated water and Dr. Pepper syrup. It's bottled in north Texas, in a village called Dublin. I telegraphed the bottling plant before I left New York, and had them ship these cases to the Four Aces." He started to put the bottle lip to his mouth, but she cautioned, "Take it easy until you get used to it. Sip . . . and you'll enjoy the bite."

Tex, a veteran drinker of Dublin's finest, didn't have to take precautions. He guzzled six bottles before he set out for help with the wheel. As he rode away, Margarita seemed to be walking on air, so pleased was she at providing cool soda pops in the desert of northern Mexico. In her excitement she ate half the box of chocolates. As she perused yet another selection—while Rafe was stacking the last of the trunks on the ground—he couldn't help but chuckle.

"What are you laughing at?" she inquired and sucked the center of one candy into her mouth.

"You. You've taken on quite a zest for snacks."

She rifled through the box. "I'm surprised you noticed, you've been so cross."

"I notice everything about you."

And right now . . . he forgot all about being testy. He wouldn't mind if she devoured him like she'd done that bonbon. His eyes melted down her, from her dark hair to her chocolate-smeared lips to the breasts that he had tasted in Juarez. A familiar stirring in his groin roused his smile. Ah, ha. He *was* still a man. He made the sign of the cross. "Come here, Margarita. Come here and let me kiss you."

Her eyes widened in surprise, a grin playing at her lips. Never breaking her gaze, she reached to the side and set the box of candy on the driver's seat. She took a step in his direction. Then froze.

"Look out," she warned. "Behind you."

He heard hoofbeats and the sound of men. Immediately figuring his vengeful uncle and the Arturianos were on his tail, Rafe drew his Peacemaker and whirled around. Riding over the crest of a sand dune came three riders, one on a palomino and the remaining two on proud pintos. Good horseflesh, Rafe assessed. Who cared about the grade of the horses?

"Shoot 'em! Shoot their mounts from under them!" Hopping up and down, Margarita jabbed a finger in the air. "Rafael Delgado, don't just stand there—aim and fire!"

He knew not to shoot first and ask questions later; he'd done that one too many times. He also knew not to order Margarita to take cover under the disabled wagon; it might fall on her. "Get behind those trunks," he ordered. "Stay low."

Stalwart as a standard bearer, she stood tall and straight and dauntless. She was either brave or crazy. Or both.

The riders rode closer. Their rifles were drawn. One—obviously the leader, even though he looked years younger than his hard-bitten *compadres*—rode the magnificent palomino and sat regally upon a Spanish saddle. They were not of the Delgado gang.

This, Rafe knew for sure. He recognized the leader, who ordered, "Throw down your gun."

Complying, Rafe heard the soundless knock of opportunity.

Eleven

Unlike other of Samuel Colt's Peacemakers—precision firearms that had won the West—this one bit the dust, literally and figuratively.

In view of Rafe's cowardice in the face of highway robbers, Margaret seethed. Tex gone, she and Rafe stranded, and now a trio of suspicious-looking, bandolier-wearing Mexicans had them cornered. And disarmed. Dad gum it! If only she could get to her derringer—*Don't be simpleminded*. What good would that ridiculous toy do them?

And why, pray tell, did Rafe wear a gun belt, if he had no intention of putting it to practical use?

Worry she might, but as a creature of habit, she made a quick assessment. The one in charge—a stocky young man with a dark walrus mustache and mahogany curling hair clipped above his ears—had to be a son of Spain. The other two, well, Mesoamerican screamed from their russet skin tones, prominent cheekbones, and poker-straight hair.

"*Buenos dias,*" called Spain's son.

A specific benevolence drifted from his tone. He

157

motioned for his companions to hold their fire, after which he doffed his silver-studded sombrero, letting it hang by its strings down his back. He gave a saddled bow toward Margaret. "Good day to you, pretty toothpick. I see you have trouble."

"Yes," she answered in Spanish, warily, "but my bro—"

Rafe interrupted. "Yes, we have trouble with the wagon wheel. You will help my wife and me?"

His wife? He shot her one of those murderous, don't-correct-me looks, very like a spouse's. That was all he'd done since Carmelita's, given her dirty looks. Between him and the lovelorn Tex, she'd had it to the gills with sulking men.

His arms half-raised, Rafe ambled toward the riders. "Allow me to introduce myself. I am Rafael Delgado."

"*The* Rafael Delgado of Chihuahua?" the head man reacted.

"I used to be."

The rider to the leader's right spoke up, admiration working its way into his Indian-penny frown to display a gold tooth. "Then you are the Eagle."

"I've been called that."

The smallest of the trio spoke as all three holstered their firearms. "Mexico has missed you, *El Aguila Magnífico. Bienvenido.* Welcome home."

Heavenly days.

They might as well have salaamed, so awed were they; Margaret noticed and knew instinctively that they weren't paying homage to some faded matador. It was the outlaw they respected. Not a comforting thought.

"What do you call your woman?" the top dog asked.

"I am Margaret," she answered, not appreciating being discussed as if she weren't there.

"Mucho gusto, Señora Delgado."

"Equalmente," Margaret returned, and didn't bother to keep the snideness out of her I'm-pleased-to-meet-you-too.

He pointed to the left, then the right. "These are my men. This is Javier. And this is Pedro." Smiling widely, showing lots of strong teeth, the introducer pointed to his own chest, which was crossed by bandoliers. "I call myself Francisco Villa."

"I have heard of you, Pancho Villa." Rafe took a step in Villa's direction. "Earlier this year, when I delivered a prize-winning bull to Nuevo Laredo, I saw you there, from the distance. At the corrida."

"But how could I have missed such an esteemed personage as *El Aguila Magnífico?"*

The very picture of humility and modesty, His Excellency the Most Magnificent of Fowls became invested with a puffed chest and a broad smirk. Margaret rolled her eyes.

Villa took a step in the Eagle's direction. "Thank the Blessed Virgin, you are returned. Your people have been crying for you to fight *el pinche gobierno."*

"No, no. My fighting days are over. The fornicating government does need to be unseated, but it will be for younger men such as you, to fight for our people's rights."

"Not Pancho Villa." Villa laughed. "I care only for robbing the rich and helping the poor. As *El*

159

Aguila Magnífico once did."

"I am flattered to be remembered." Rafe parked an elbow on the floorboard, leaning in a relaxed pose against the wagon. "But you are the talk of our border towns. It is said the highwayman has, shall we say, become very concerned for the great unnumbered."

As the two men continued to fawn, Villa's associates cried, "Long live Villa! Long live *El Aguila!* Long live Mexico! Down with Porfirio Díaz and his cronies at the Jockey Club! Down with the hated *patróns!* Down with Don Arturo—the slave driver of Santa Alicia!"

Even Margaret knew that Mexicans of modest means pegged everything amiss on the Porfirianos, or to a lesser degree on the land-owning *patróns* such as Rafe's uncle. Even clerks and flunkies took their share of abuse. Really, to a politician's daughter, this kind of talk could get to be a yawning bore.

After the accolades died to a roar, Villa smiled at Margaret. "You come with us to our little house. My hombres will come back and repair your wagon wheel. Manaña."

"Many thank you's," Rafe said. "We happily accept."

I'll just bet he'll fix our wagon. Margaret could have thrashed Rafe for falling in with these strangers. And what about Tex? "May I have a private word with you, *viejo?*"

The riders laughed at the appellation, but she intended to call Rafe a worse nickname than old husband, if he didn't do something beside play sheep following the leader. She marched to the far side of the crippled wagon, her supposed husband in her trail. She rounded on him, whispering, "What do you mean, 'we happily accept'? Who are those men?"

"Outlaws."

"That puts me at ease."

"Villa can help us. If we work it right."

"We? *We?* I'd like to know how you came up with a plural in connection to those desperados. Speaking of which, why didn't you shoot them when you had the chance?"

"Margarita, I refuse to kill at your command."

"Well, isn't this a fine how-d'ya-do? We could both be lying on the ground, dead, for all—"

"Stop it. You aren't dead. You aren't hurt. You aren't even inconvenienced by Villa and his men. And don't forget . . . your own father trusted your fate to me. So, do us both a favor and quit your hectoring."

"No one said Papa is perfect," she returned, and grudgingly accepted—in her thoughts—that Gil McLoughlin hadn't been wrong. So far. "I think it's downright yellow to leave our fates to the Fates."

A muscle ticked in Rafe's jaw, then above his eye. His tone low, he replied, "It's too bad you aren't a man. Blood thirst such as yours could earn you more fame than writing books. You could head armies. Whip slaves into workers. Enter the corrida."

"I do have my strengths," she said, refusing to be insulted. She posed another question. "But what about Tex? What about—?"

She had several what-abouts, none of which got

answered. Rafe did an about-face, left her to stew, and returned to his new buddies. The one called Pedro gave over his fine mount to the stranded travelers, then jumped upon the bare back of the remaining workhorse. The entire party set out, leaving the steamer trunks behind.

Taking some comfort in their southerly course, Margaret left a trail of crumbs for Tex to follow—the cookie tin first, then pieces of her attire. By the time the band reached a secluded adobe dwelling in the lee of a conical hill, Margaret was on the verge of giving up her shoes.

"I will *not!*" The picture of indignation in the waning sunlight, Margarita squared her shoulders and stamped her foot, which disturbed a hen from picking through the measly grass in front of Villa's adobe hideout. "I refuse to wring that chicken's neck. And if you think I'm doing any cooking, you've got another think coming."

"But, pretty toothpick," cajoled the lead bandit, "you are a woman. We do not have a chef to make a feast. And it is supper time. Me and my men and your own man"—Villa grabbed his belly—"we are so hun-gree." Pedro and Javier, who were milling about like trained ducks waiting for a dinner cracker, both laughed. "Would you please do the cooking?"

"Mr. Villa," she said sternly, "I don't detect any crippling new diseases keeping you gentlemen from feeding yourself as you did before you found us. And where—may I be so bold as to ask?—are your manners? My h-husband"—she choked but recovered quickly—"and I are your guests."

"*Sí, doña*. But you are still a *mujer,* and women take care of *hombres*."

Combing his hair, then propping a shoulder against the hideout's outer wall, Rafe watched Margarita have it out with Villa. Her face had taken on the pink of indignation, and her bosom heaved with the same emotion. *She's attractive like that.*

From the famed bandit's expression, he likewise enjoyed her indignation. She thrived on indignation and fusses. Rafe figured to let her and Villa keep arguing. It was harmless enough. Unless they got more excited about each other than in the subject matter, in which case Rafe would step in. Quickly.

Depending on the theory of honor among thieves, Rafe intended to make friends with Villa and his *bandidos*. The going could get tough between here and the city of Chihuahua without allies. Besides, a couple of ideas had been forming. Until a few minutes ago, when they had ridden here from the abandoned wagon, he and Pancho Villa discussed the miserable conditions at the Santa Alicia silver mine.

A shiver lanced Rafe. As if it were yesterday, he saw the mine. He saw Hernán fall dead. If only he could call back that night—Impossible. He'd had all these years to know Hernán would be alive, if not for Tío Arturo. *You aren't without guilt in the death.* Rafe wouldn't be dragged down by inner voices. He'd settled his mind—he'd make something of his cousin's sacrifice. That was enough—wasn't it?—since Hernán had stood on Rafe's side of right. His cousin would want it this way.

"Do you have a problem with your ears?" Margarita quizzed Villa and pulled Rafe out of his plans. "I said I won't cook. And I won't. Case closed."

Rafe chuckled, wondering the extent of Margarita's cooking skills. From Olga, he knew their mother had served as trail cook on a cattle drive to Kansas back in '69, so the daughter ought to have the mother's talent. That's the way they did it in Mexico, passed on traditions, and after his years in Texas, Rafe knew *norteamericana* mothers were not that different from their southerly neighbors in traditional respects.

". . . Well, you are way wrong, Mr. Villa."

Villa turned to Rafe. "Why did you marry a *mujer* who cannot cook?"

He shrugged. "I was drunk."

The Villanistas got a laugh. Margarita, sparks popping from her blue eyes, did not laugh. She flounced off—as if the devil himself gave the marching orders. Rafe wasn't worried. She'd be back. This was, after all, the desert. And she was, after all, a hothouse flower in need of creature comforts. Such as Dr. Pepper.

"Your wife, she is spoiled." Villa lit a cigar and threw the match down. "But she is pretty. Very pretty."

Rafe smiled. Yes, she was pretty, very pretty. While not the picture of her old self, she beat the average woman for looks. And she was spoiled. And she was bright. And she was learned. And a wanton pulsed beneath her schoolmarm veneer.

His eyelids dropping to half mast, he smiled and recalled the way she'd looked in the peasant clothing he'd bought her. She might be too thin; so what?

She was more than womanly enough. And all those chocolates and such that she'd been scoffing down, well, extra food was sure to make some soft padding. So, who cared if she couldn't cook?

Culinary talents might not matter, yet Rafe got the oddest feeling all of a sudden.

Disappointment.

He'd never figured Margarita for unadventurous stuffings. Back a long time ago, when he'd had ideas to sweep her off her youthful feet and get between her long Texas legs, he'd gotten intimidated by her gumption. She was the kind to go head to head with the likes of Tío Arturo and the entirety of his henchmen—and do it with no more than derringer and a daggerlike tongue. Being in the shadow of such valor would have reflected badly on Rafe's virility. Now, though, he rather wanted a *mujer* with the stuff of a warrior.

Why he'd had a change of heart, he had no idea. Maybe these were the wages of getting older.

Margaret was fit to be tied.

Thank you, Rafael Delgado, for sticking up for me with that Villa villain. Was it her fault she'd been born neither curious nor impoverished enough to conquer the cookstove? Lisette had never encouraged her daughters thusly. "I've done enough cooking for all my daughters," she'd said, when her triplets were little and could still gather as a set at her sweet-smelling bosom. "You girls stay out of the kitchen."

Presently, the sun sank toward the western horizon; the air took a dip in temperature. And Margaret, having left bits of her suit jacket here and there for Tex until it was no more, wanted to hug her arms against the chill—or perhaps to try to relive those tender moments with her mother. Too angry for anything besides stomping, though, she charged forth in a meandering path, seething and wishing she'd never left New York City. *Where do you think you're going?*

Where had she been?

In all her twenty-eight years, she'd never supported herself. The few dimes in royalties she'd earned from her book hadn't covered research expenses. She knew her father, feeling sorry for her, had sent errand boys out to buy the unsold copies, which meant she couldn't even take pride in accomplishment when that inflated check had arrived.

In the domestic area she had nothing to recommend herself. She neither cooked nor cleaned. Of course, ladies of her station didn't cook or clean, though they did study the art of making a home. When she should have been learning such graces, Margaret had been untangling her tongue around foreign languages, or reading about adventures and adventurers, or dreaming of discovering some heretofore unknown tidbit of history that would set the world afire.

A lot of good any of that did her now, in the middle of her own adventure. Why was it not written that past explorers had to know their way around a skillet as well as a compass?

Okay, but where do you think you're going from here?

Since her trail led to this spot, she couldn't go traipsing off, the portrait of outrage unavenged, and leave her brother a cold trail. She didn't have as much as a handkerchief to rip for markers.

"Margaret," she muttered, "you are at a distinct disadvantage."

Her next move? She'd rather dine on a buzzard than eat any crow whatsoever, but she'd have to turn around. A good hundred yards separated her from the shack. Rafe and the other men continued to mill around in front of the place, she saw. She took a deep breath and blew it out. Hunger panged.

A buzzard dipped to a low figure eight, sizing her up as a prospect for tomorrow's nourishment.

Ugh.

She'd simply have to go back, be honest, and beg the men's indulgence.

No!

Again she whirled around.

"Where is your pride?" she asked herself. "Your blood isn't that of craven ancestors."

She was a McLoughlin, the get of such heroes as Robert the Bruce and King Duncan. The black Celts of the Highlands flowed in her veins, too, including that of the invincible Maisie McLoughlin. A son of that land of Scots, her father had arrived in the United States in meager circumstances, then served his adopted country in the Civil War. Afterward, with sheer grit and determination, and by the sweat of his brow, he'd become what he was today.

Furthermore, Margaret was the child of Lisette Keller, an immigrant acquainted with hard times. The Kellers knew about beating the odds. They had

167

scratched out a living in crowded Nassau-Hesse before they undertook a harrowing trip across the
Atlantic in the bowels of a hell ship, Lisette losing
her mother on the ocean. Arrived on the shores of
Texas, the Kellers triumphed over the arid soils to
stake their claim to freedom.

Margaret herself had examined every nook and
cranny in Spain and the far reaches to acquaint
herself with Columbus and the Catholic kings,
which was not to mention her triumphs over ill
health and professional injustices.

She could darn well prepare a chicken.

Not long before dusk, Margaret gained a new
respect for masters of culinary arts. Cooking was
work. Thankfully the men, including Rafe, had disappeared; she took relief in not having witnesses to
her calamitous efforts. The area in front of Villa's
shack looked as if someone had sliced open a pillow
and scattered the contents to the breeze. Margaret
was covered with feathers and worse, but the cursed
chicken and a double handful of rice were assembled to toss into the fat pot of boiling water hooked
over a cookfire.

Feeling pleased with herself, she blew a hank of
hair out of her eyes, as well as a bit of white fluff
from the tip of her nose. "And I got most of the
feathers plucked, too."

"Most of the feathers?"

She wheeled around, catching sight of a sardonic
mouth, and raised a hand of restraint. "Just get
away from me. I'm not speaking with any Benedict

168

Arnolds." She noticed Rafe held a guitar at his side. "Pray tell, are you planning a dinner serenade for your new chums?"

"If I serenade anyone, *bruja,* it will be you." His nostrils twitched. "What's for supper?"

She began a snide remark, but quelled it when she saw something never before seen. She would be stripped naked in front of the Villa gang, if the look in Rafe's eyes wasn't admiration!

"I'd like to help you," he said earnestly.

"You're about seven million chicken feathers too late." She laughed and batted at yet another piece of down that floated to her nose. "But if you've got a suggestion or two, I'm listening."

"I rummaged around inside." He motioned to the hideout. "Came up with a few things that might add flavor to your . . " He leaned to the left to look at the readied ingredients. *"Arroz con pollo."*

"What kind of flavor?"

"Mexican, of course. Be right back. Start the chicken."

He set the guitar aside, then entered the adobe shelter, leaving her to smile and wonder at the wonders of Rafe. As well, she took a moment to straighten her hair, dust her clothes, and wash her face and hands. Rafe returned with a knife, a cutting board, and a mortar and pestle in one hand; in the other, a wreck pan. The pan was filled with a cornucopia for the kitchener, that would have put the stores of her trunks to shame.

St. Nicholas, it seemed, had come to Chihuahua.

Santa's bounty included chiles both fresh and shriveled, thyme, sage, oregano, onions, and a small bowlful of dried tomatoes; naturally, Rafe had to tell Margaret what was what in most cases. Thereafter, he patiently chopped, pulverized, and explained, then allowed her to add the ingredients to her witch's brew. A delicious aroma wafted.

"What will we serve as a beverage?" she asked, complacent at their bonhomie.

"Dr. Pepper is out." Rafe jacked up a light-hearted brow. "But I have a good substitute. Boil some water in that kettle over there, and we'll make laurel tea."

"Laurel tea?"

"Yes. The Tarahumara Indians of the Copper Canyon swear by it. And, what luck, our friends had a tin of leaves in their cupboard."

"Aren't we fortunate?" With childlike enthusiasm she filled the kettle and hooked it on a cleek next to the chicken concoction. "My, this cooking business is fun."

"You are quite a woman, *bruja de dulce*. Quite a woman." Ladling a spoonful from the pot, he blew on it. "Take a taste. See if it's pleasing."

Actually, she was pleased at his praise, along with being called a sweet witch. Was this why that spoonful of flavored chicken and rice tasted more scrumptious than the most exquisite dish served along La Gran Via of Madrid? No. It was because the accomplishment was hers. Hers and Rafe's.

Several minutes passed as they set the table. Done, Rafe took her hand. "Margarita . . ." His every feature turned intense and solemn in the flagging sunlight. "Villa thinks we are newlyweds. He offered to turn his *casa* over to us. That means he

170

and his men will be sleeping outside." A black brow elevated. "Are you going to pitch a fit at bedtime?"

She ought to. She ought to be screaming right now, asking why he perpetuated the marriage charade. She ought to be begging him to help her find Tex, although, instinctively, she felt her brother was in safety's embrace.

Wanting what she'd wanted for ages, she leveled her eyes with Rafe's and answered in a firm voice, "No. I won't protest."

An hour later, Pedro belched and said, "Señora Delgado, you are a wonderful cook." Javier rubbed his stomach, his eyes rolling in ecstasy to the back of his head. Both Villa and Rafe added expansive praise for the chicken and rice, and not one word about the occasional feather.

She drew herself even taller than her five-eight. This afternoon she wouldn't have given a hoot about pleasing these Villanista ruffians, but in pleasing them, she pleased herself. The most satisfying part? Rafe's pride in her. Not so long ago, if anyone had accused her of wanting to please him, she would have bawled them out.

"If you grow tired of your wife, amigo," said Villa, "I will take her for one of my brides."

"I must disappoint you, señor. She is mine. Forever. An hombre could never grow tired of a wife like 'Rita. Or bored with her. Never in a million years."

Rafe seemed the epitome of sincere. A tiny voice warned her not to be gullible—any decent husband

171

would praise his wife, for goodness sake—but Margaret wasn't listening. She wanted to bask in all this glory. Her grin was as bright as the light of a crystal chandelier.

Rafe picked up the borrowed guitar, adjusted the strings, then strummed the beginnings of a beautiful tune. His silver gaze reflecting in the moonlight above, he dispensed a weighty look Margaret's way. It seemed as if they were the only two people on earth, his expression conveying want and need as ripe as her own. The tune he played was about love and romance and how nothing was finer in this world than a man and a woman together. Together in the deep of the night.

She smiled, looking forward to the privacy of Villa's abandoned bedroom.

Twelve

Was this night never going to end?

The chicken had been reduced to a small pile of bones, hours ago. The moon hovered high in the star-sprinkled sky. A fire roared in the pit; the men lounged around it. The melodious tone of Rafe's sere-nading guitar sharpened her senses. Her eyes kept wandering to the hideout, to its promise of privacy.

Margaret, sitting at the outdoor table, faked yawn after yawn, until they were coming on their own, yet these Mexicans didn't take a hint. The best part of the situation? The meaningful gazes Rafe sent her. Fre-quently.

When Rafe excused himself for a nature call, he leaned to give Margaret a kiss on the cheek along with a gruff, "Later, *querida*."

She glanced up at his slate-silver gaze, at the sen-sual curve to his lips, and she grinned. "Oh, my, yes."

He winked and made for the bushes.

Meanwhile, Javier and Pedro were passing a bottle of something horrid back and forth. Pulque, they called it. One taste of the milky white stuff was

173

enough to turn Margaret off it for eternity. Thankfully neither of Villa's men seemed inclined toward intellectual dialogue. They were in their own realm, making fun of the world in general and Mexico City's citizens in particular. "Chilangos" was the mocking term. Chile-eaters. Wasn't that the pot calling the kettle black?

Villa stood and walked over to fill her wineglass. Now that she had given in to cooking, he played the munificent host. "Pretty toothpick, has your husband told you about his noble deeds of yesteryears?"

"No, Señor Villa, Rafe is much too modest"—wasn't that laughable?—"to brag."

"But surely you have heard—"

"I'm afraid I've been at a disadvantage. I haven't gotten much word of Rafe as he was in Mexico, in the bygone days." She smiled encouragement at the brigand. "I wouldn't be offended if you told me some of his exploits."

"I was but a *muchacho,* wet behind the ears, when he was our country's great hope."

Even though the light fell dim, thanks to evening shade, it was unmistakable, the hero worship in Villa's dark eyes. A mad thought struck, leaving her with the oddest feeling, rather a second sight. She visualized many thousands, if not millions of people giving *their* worship to this Pancho Villa.

Well, she knew it was a deranged thought.

Villa answered her query. "The Eagle was born rich as a king, yet from the time of his first cry as a babe, he gave all that he had to the less fortunate."

"Go on."

"It is said he was in swaddling clothes when he first

174

transformed into the great bird of Zeus. The eagle is the symbol of Mexico, I assume you know. It is said he flew from his golden bassinet and soared over poverty's reaches. In his claws were grains from the Delgado silos. He rained wheat on the hungry villages."

Oh, yes. Of course. Right. *Tell me another.*

Villa sounded very like something she'd become acquainted with since crossing the Rio Grande. Mexicans were great ones for the exaggerated yarn. But fact was fact. Pancho Villa and his men revered *El Aguila Magnífico,* as Carmelita had. The question in Margaret's mind was, what had turned a member of the moneyed Delgado family into a revolutionary?

Actually, she wondered, too, about something else. What was going through his mind and heart, now that he was back in Mexico? Doing her own embellishing, she revealed, "My father said Rafe once had an army at his disposal."

Actually, Papa had said a cadre of sorry-looking, under-armed so-and-so's had lounged around Rafe's hacienda, close to the village of Santa Alicia.

"*Sí,* he had an army. Like me, they robbed from the rich and gave to the poor. And when the defeated Yaqui Indians were given over as slaves to work the mines, *El Aguila* stood up to the Arturianos. The balladeers will always sing to his valor."

Impressive. "Tell me about this country."

"It is no fun to be a Mexican of low birth," said Villa. "Most of our people live in servitude and eternal arrears to their *patrón*. Arturo Delgado could be emperor, so far-reaching are the powers Porfirio Díaz gave him. The Federales might as well be Arturianos

175

alone. *Señor Grandero Rico* has them in his pocket. Our Eagle knew this is not fair, not right, and goes against all human dignity."

While she made no comment — she wasn't versed in the plight of the Yaqui Indians — she, naturally, had an opinion. Rafe, courageous and brave, had been no complainer sitting on his tush. He'd shown the courage to act. And he'd had the wisdom not to take her advice and shoot these men who'd come to their aid.

". . . And it was such a sad day, when Hernándo Delgado died." Villa shook his head in sorrow. "He was *El Aguila's* most trusted colonel, you see."

"Hernándo *Delgado?*"

"Yes, Delgado. He and the Eagle were cousins. Hernándo worshipped your husband. So much so that he rose up against his own father, Arturo Delgado."

The pieces of the puzzle started to come together for her.

"A terrible accident happened," Villa sighed. "Hernándo took a bullet during an abortive raid against the Santa Alicia silver mine. *El Grandero Rico* blames the magnificent Eagle. He claims your husband's was the killing bullet. Don Arturo seeks revenge against his own nephew."

Poor Rafe. How awful, to have such a terrible tragedy happen in his family. No wonder he shied from guns. And the revenge —

"Ah, here is your husband. He will tell you about it."

Villa's confidences weighed on her mind, but Rafe, smiling warmly in her direction, didn't appear in the confessional mood. Once she thought about it, she

176

realized he wasn't the kind of man to do a lot of talking about the pains of life that hurt the most.

Villa's sidekicks began to sing an off-key version of *"Jesusita de Chihuahua."* Javier and Pedro, she observed when the song tapered off, were more than merely drunk. *"Viva Mexico!"* was their chorus, obviously a favorite ode, though tributes to Rafe, Villa, and a hoped-for revolution went along with florid praise for mothers, motherhood, and the smoothness of tequila. They moved on to slurred remarks against the President, his supporters, and foreigners wielding too much power in Mexico, namely Americans. She began to get ill at ease.

"Spain has planted spies in our home state," Villa announced. "They use us for their Cuban gains."

Javier lurched to unsteady feet. "The bell for freedom tolls in Cuba." It was almost a sob.

"Down with the Spanish and the lovers of Spain!" Pedro shook his fist. *"Cuba libre!"*

Now they trod on family ground.

When Villa added his like opinion, she started getting hot under the collar.

Then Rafe agreed with the idiots, and Margaret exploded. "Not one of you knows what you're talking about." She jumped to her feet, the chair wobbling behind her. "Why should Spain turn over Cuba to a bunch of ridiculous rebels? I've been told the majority of the islanders are lazy and shiftless, that they want to be hand-fed from the plates of their betters."

"Are you making a joke?" asked Villa. "You joke about 'betters.' "

"Absolutely not. I feel—"

"¡Margarita, *silencio!*" Rafe set the guitar down.

"I will not hold my tongue. I've read about your country. And my father serves the United States, so I feel I'm in a better position to gauge the political situation, in a worldly and general scope, than a bunch of outlaws. Robbing from the rich won't settle Mexico's problems."

Villa's men looked on the verge of murder. Villa had a shocked expression. Rafe clenched and unclenched his fists. Margaret kept talking. "You ought to be thankful for President Porfirio Díaz. For the first time since you demanded independence from Spain—and that was almost ninety years ago!—Mexico is experiencing peace and prosperity."

"Do you know that many of Mexico's children have never tasted meat?" Rafe asked in the voice of restrained fury.

His question took her aback. Yet a good debater didn't quail. Furthermore, he no doubt exaggerated. He, himself, had called her attention to the well-being of those Indian tykes in Juarez. "There are two schools of thought on the meat issue," she said. "Many authorities believe meat bad for the digestion."

"One authority being the ace of the Jockey Club," Villa said with a cynical chuckle, and looked at the other men for acknowledgment. "The mestizo Porfirio Díaz has turned on his own."

His men were not chuckling. Shouting imprecations, Pedro leaped from his place in front of the fire. Javier, the bigger of the two, lunged at Margaret, his knife raised.

Her fearful side demanded she scream and cower. Her brave front took over. "Put that thing away."

178

Metal glinted in front of her eyes. She flinched.

In a flash Rafe knocked the knife to the ground. All hell broke loose, Pedro pouncing at him and Javier diving to retake his possession, but Villa stopped the fray, demanding, "Enough!"

Margaret shook. Why had she felt it necessary to lower herself to their level? The drunks retreated, thankfully. Rafe shot her a look of aggravation. Great God in heaven, here she was in the middle of nowhere with Mexican desperadoes, any one of whom would slit her throat. If she made it alive to Eden Roc, she was going to give her mother a large piece of her mind for taking a holiday in this wretched country.

Be honest, Margaret McLoughlin. You go too far with wretched. For all his crankiness and aloofness of late, Rafe had given many glowing descriptions of this land of Moctezuma, and she found beauty in it all, thanks to his clear love for his native land.

He stepped toward her. "Margarita, back off."

Villa shook his head in disgust. *"El Aguila,* why did you marry such a woman?"

Rafe put a protective arm around her. "Please excuse my wife. She is of a rich family, and doesn't understand the plight of the poor." His fingers cut into her upper arm. "Apologize, so these good men will know you meant no insult."

Since she wished to see Manhattan again, and not from the interior of a pine box, she forced down another serving of crow. And, to tell the truth, she was feeling somewhat awful about that meat remark.

Margaret glanced from one man to the next. She saw pride and determination. They would fight for their beliefs. Would Rafe be among the combatants?

Images of blood and fallen bodies swam before her eyes, causing her stomach to lurch with dread. *And what about a more serious threat? Rafe's uncle would have vengeance.* She lectured herself to keep such worries under control. "I apologize. This is your land. You know it better than I."

Remarkably, Javier offered an apology, too. "Forgive me for my rash temper," he said in a surprisingly sober voice. "But, lady, *mi doña,* I do not apologize for flying to the defense of poor people."

"We are God's forgotten." Pedro stood tall. "But the people of Mexico will rise to fight for freedom."

Villa suggested, "Shall we cut the evening short?"

Everyone agreed.

As the bandits made preparations for beds under the full moon, Margaret didn't worry that her life might be at stake, that Javier would slink in under the dead of night to slit her throat. Rafe would protect her, come what may.

Protect her. And more. She craved the succor of his arms . . . and trembled with expectation. If there was anything to give thanks for, Rafe was it. Twice he'd flown to her defense, even if he didn't appear too keen on his stance at the moment. What woman wouldn't be both flattered and gladdened?

"Margarita?" Her gaze climbed to Rafe's troubled visage, and he asked, "Are you so callous that you have no regard for the plight of innocent children?"

"Rafe, must you make me feel guilty?"

"Someone needs to."

"Well, I think you overstated the situation."

He took a backward step. "Don't blind yourself, Margaret McLoughlin. This isn't a perfect world."

Everything in his voice spoke to her heart, and she stared at the darkened ground. "I've spent my life studying various subjects. But maybe I have a lot left to learn."

"That you recognize this is to your credit."

She coerced her eyes to his. "I can't understand what I don't know. I recognize little children shouldn't suffer, whatever the state around them. But I stand by what I said on other scores."

"Which proves you have a *lot* to learn." Rafe grimaced, took her hand, then exhaled. "No more arguing, okay? Let's go to bed."

Thirteen

Rafe's was an excellent suggestion, going to bed, Margaret thought, though he could act more enthusiastic. *You ask too much. Okay, these stinkers may have riled you, but you do ask too much, Margaret McLoughlin.* Tonight, she wanted . . . much.

His hand going to the small of her back, she inhaled around the anticipation forgotten during the fracas with the Villanistas, and followed him toward the one-room *casita*.

"Wait, *El Aguila*. If you do not mind, I would like a private word with you." Pancho Villa tossed his bedroll to the ground and brandished a flask. "Join me in a drink?"

Oh, no. She groaned.

"I won't be but a few minutes," Rafe promised in a whisper.

While Javier and Pedro snuggled down in their makeshift beds, Margaret entered the house. Already a kerosene lamp burned on the table next to an iron bed of wide proportions. Guns and ammunition were stacked in corners; vests and britches hung on pegs.

The bedclothes appeared clean. Margaret stripped out of what was left of her well-used traveling suit. She panicked. What did a woman wear to lose her virginity?

Heavenly days, was she up to all this? Her nerves jumped like Mexican jumping beans. *Be sensible. The rest of the night is for you and Rafe. Don't waste it.* Again she wondered what a virgin wore to offer herself up. Even if she'd had her trunks, she supposed nothing appropriate lurked in the confines.

Should she strip naked? That seemed too brazen, even for this woman who decided to behave as wantonly as any Jezebel who hawked her wares on the streets of Juarez. She shucked everything save for her pantaloons and camisole. Her topknot unpinned, she brushed her hair for more than the required hundred strokes.

"Where is Rafe?" she mumbled after putting the brush back in her valise.

More time passed. She stretched out in bed and pulled the sheets up. Crickets sang from outdoors. From the distance she heard a coyote bay. While she heard no voices, she knew conversation progressed. What could Villa say to Rafe that was so interesting?

"The church turned its back on Father Xzobal when he was given the death penalty."

The hand holding a glass of pulque, which Rafe had been bringing to his lips, froze midway to his mouth. He couldn't breathe. His head swam. He let go the cigar Villa had given him. During the past half hour, as the bandit had spoken of this and that, Rafe

183

had given perfunctory answers, for his thoughts had been on Margarita and the dangers of her speaking too much of her opinionated mind. Mostly, though, he'd been thinking about bedding her.

She now dwindled from Rafe's thoughts.

For years he'd yearned to see his younger, only brother. Certainly, he'd had no idea of finding the gentle Xzobal in trouble. *Mother of God, don't let Xzobal be martyred, like Hernándo.* Akin to many of his Mexican brethren, Rafe believed violent death an honorable estate. Yet a brother was family.

It took his all to ask, "Is he dead?"

"No. I saved him. He is well."

"Thank the Holy Mother." Suddenly drained, yet ebullient, Rafe crossed himself before he grabbed hold of the corral fence to steady himself. "What does he want? How can I help him?"

"What all *chihuahueños* should want—what you and I have yearned for. The removal of the richling Arturo Delgado."

"Yes, but how can I help my brother?"

"That is for you to decide."

"True." Brow furrowed, Rafe voiced his curiosity. "What happened that he fell from ecclesiastical grace?"

"Ach, what do you think? Since the days of Benito Juarez, the church has been running scared in Mexico. The archbishop shies from controversy. Father Xzobal organized a walkout at the Santa Alicia silver mine. The picketers were fired on. When the smoke cleared, most of the strikers were either dead or wounded. Father Xzobal, despite his injuries, managed to flee. Your uncle, the mine owner, demanded his own nephew's arrest and execution."

Rafe exhaled harshly as Villa added, "The Federales found the good Father Xzobal a week later. They hauled him to the prison in Chihuahua city. The church, by law, refused to support your pious brother. There was no hope of saving him from the firing squad. Until we helped him escape."

Rafe broke into a cold sweat. He hadn't set foot in his home state since December of '89, yet he knew his uncle's way of thinking. It wasn't a pretty thought. He licked his too-dry lips before saying, "Let's clear up a misconception. Xzobal isn't Tío Arturo's nephew. Xzobal is my mother's son, not my father's. My uncle seeks vengeance against *me*. He blames me for Hernándo's death. It's me he's truly after. Xzobal is but an excuse."

"He does blame you. Arturo Delgado shouts the loudest for your death."

"Have charges been filed against me?"

"El Grandero Rico says vengeance will be his. And his alone. He is out for blood."

Rafe laughed without mirth. It hurt, knowing one of his own *familia* would have him dead. Of course, he'd had years to become used to it. But the most hurtful part was remembering his boyhood, when he and Xzobal and Hernán had played together — engaging in games of war, cards, and acting out the roles of Dumas's musketeers. Tío Arturo, never far away, had been the adult to cheer them on.

"The Eagle will soar above his tragedies," said Villa.

Rafe didn't doubt future success. He was returned. And that had been the biggest step in conquering the unconquerable. What he needed was a plan. He swallowed pulque, the nectar from hell charring a path to his stomach. "I saw my uncle in El Paso."

"Ah, *sí*. He went to reclaim his woman."

"How do you know this?"

Villa smiled, wide and slow, and blew out a puff of cigar smoke. "One of my *mamacitas* works for the exalted señor. She tells me everything."

"Is it for curiosity's sake, your interest?"

"Oh, no, *El Aguila*. Oh, no. I watch the activities of your uncle, so that I might rob him."

Giving a dry laugh, Rafe mentioned, "He's away from his interests now. Why haven't you moved?"

Villa lifted his hand to point at the midnight sky. "An eagle flying overhead bade me pause. And now I know why. I was to wait for *El Aguila Magnífico*. You will ride with me and my boys against *Don* Arturo."

All afternoon, all evening, Rafe had figured Pancho Villa could help him. Not inclined to this particular suggestion, though, he frowned. "Tell me where my brother hides."

Silence.

"Don't just stand there, hombre." It was all Rafe could do not to grab Pancho Villa by the ear. "Where is Xzobal?"

"Near Santa Alicia."

"We must hurry there. At first light."

Villa took a puff from his cigar. "If you're willing to meet my price . . . that has nothing to do with money. First, we will rob the offices of the Santa Alicia. Mañana."

"Arturo *is* greedy." Rafe took a contemplative swig of hell's nectar. "Robbery might impress him as no peaceful strike did. But it would take more than one robbery to bring him down."

"It is a start."

Yes, it would be a start. The idea began to grow on Rafe, then wilted. "Count me out. For now. Once I've taken care of my brother, then you and I will talk."

"El Aguila, if you do not ride with me, and *now."* Villa threatened sharply, craftily, "I will not tell you exactly how to find Father Xzobal."

"The eagle doesn't rule the skies by quailing at threats, even from other birds of prey." Rafe took a message-laden step forward and patted the carved-irony grip of his Peacemaker. "This Eagle needs no help in finding what he seeks."

Rafe wheeled around, making for the hideout. He felt compelled to find his brother — immediately — and make certain Xzobal was gotten to safety. This would kill two birds with one stone. Xzobal would be out of jeopardy. And that would spoil Tío Arturo's hoped-for revenge: both Rafe and his brother would thwart him.

Grand plans, but they left out one crucial detail. What would, could, and should Rafe do about Margarita? Courageous, fearless Margarita. Aggravating highbrow Margarita. In the wake of El Paso, he'd been of a mind to abandon her in the core of Chihuahua, and they were within a few hours of the city, but he now wondered if he had the strength to turn his back on her.

This was something he needed to sleep on.

Sleep?

His ideas had in no way included sleep. Should he bed her, though, when he wasn't certain what he

187

would do in morning's light? Sweat popped on his brow. It would take a stronger man than Rafe Delgado to do the right thing. He could try, though. *Do whatever it takes.*

Make her angry. Rouse her temper. Insult her. Whatever it took.

He could start by staying away from her and her bed. Right. And what would he say to Villa, once the separation of "husband" and "wife" came to notice?

In a sumptuous hotel room in the city of Juarez, Natalie Nash sat alone and cried. Yes, Arturo had been waiting for her at the train station in El Paso. Yes, he'd gotten her across the border and arranged for the amply suitable accommodations. But the widower had refused to marry her.

"When I marry again," he had said as they stood beside the untouched bed, "it will be to a young woman. A woman who can give me sons to replace Hernándo."

She stared. Stared at sixty years of Latin perfection. He neither looked nor acted old. His straight hair—the rich brown of sable—had been clubbed back neatly from his unlined face. He was almost as handsome as his nephew. Further, Arturo's body many times had been taken for one of a man less than half his age, thanks to the curative powers of Eden Roc.

It was natural that he would want to start a new family.

"I'll give you sons," Natalie said.

Arturo looked at her as if she had just dragged herself through excrement. "You have the dew of youth in your face and between your legs. But you are forty years old."

She wasn't going to allow his insult to hurt her, nor would she point out that he could have fathered a daughter of forty. "There's still time for children."

"May I be brutally honest with you? When I marry again, it will be to a young woman from a fine Mexican family."

"There is nothing wrong with my bloodlines. The Nashes are of high society. And my father is rich and respected."

"It's not the same. You are the melange of *norteamerica*. A land of curs. I want the purity of Spain," Arturo exhaled. "I refuse to make the mistake my brother made when he married Rafael's lowborn mother. I will not marry beneath my station."

Dear God. Natalie realized that Arturo was serious. Panic and desperation grabbed her, yet she called up bits and pieces of strategy, discarding one after the other, before she said, "Your ideal of the perfect lady — would she be a loyal helpmate? What guarantees would your ideal give you? In the name of having your best interest at heart, that is."

"You have a strange look in your eyes, Natalie." He dusted the sleeves of his cashmere coat. "And it doesn't flatter you, falling to the machinations typical of your gender."

"I've missed your guiding presence."

"You should have thought about that before you left me for the high life."

"Yes, I left," she replied, then took the biggest gamble of her life. "When I was *returning* to you, I saw —" She paused for emphasis. "I have seen your

189

evil nephew. He's left the protection of San Antonio."
Interest and fury replaced the indifference in Arturo's
chiseled face, and it was all she could do not to grin
like a Cheshire cat. She buffed her nails. "I know
where you can find Rafael."

Arturo cut the distance between them and grabbed
her by the hair. "Tell me everything you know."

She did.

Arturo, obviously, felt no obligation or gratitude.
After he'd listened to everything she had to say—
damn him to hell!—he left anyway.

That was four days ago.

She laughed, laughed here in that same hotel room.
Hers would be the last laugh. When she had realized
the situation wasn't going her way, she sent Arturo on
a wild-goose chase to the Federal District. "Rafael is
headed for the city of Mexico."

Natalie still hadn't come up with an answer to her
own dilemma. She couldn't stay holed up in this
hotel. She was fast running out of money, and the
desk clerk had been demanding cash or trade. "I don't
want to stay here in Mexico," she mumbled. "Not for
another moment."

But where could she go? She feared the authorities
would nab her, should she cross the border. "You
could go home."

Oh, God, no. Not back to Eden Roc and her father.
She couldn't take Isaiah and his crackpot ideas. Anything but that. Through her avowals, something
popped to mind. Tex Jones—Tex *McLoughlin*—was
on his way to Eden Roc.

While she wasn't keen on facing Isaiah again, she
could tolerate him for a few days. She was willing to

190

make a lot of sacrifices for the end results. Her first smile in days lifted her rouged lips. It wouldn't take much to vamp Tex McLoughlin. All she had to do was find the hayseed. His name would protect her from the long arms of the law.

"He doesn't have a chance."

Secretary of State McLoughlin was the second most powerful man in America, and if she had his family clout at her back, she could return to Chicago—and beat the trumped-up charges against her. She smiled. Yes, Tex McLoughlin—like Eden Roc never could—would cure her ills.

Fourteen

Rafe.

Finally.

Relief washed over Margaret.

"I thought you were never going to get finished chatting with Pancho Villa." Hers was a partial tease, uttered in the room lit by the moonbeams spilling in two high windows and by the kerosene lamp. "I'd begun to wonder if you'd abandoned me."

His silence became a palpable thing. Shucking his vest and shirt, Rafe kept his back turned. His impressive shoulders drew her attention, yet she closed her eyes, confused at his problem. Finally, the sound of him crossing the tiny bedroom, sitting down on the crackling mattress of ticking-covered straw, then jerking his boots from his feet, served as an answer.

When he stood to pull his britches off, she spoke. "Did I touch a chord, Rafe?" Her shoulders pressed to the mattress. "Were you planning to abandon our task? Are you?" She paused. "I guess you're still mad, because I spoke my mind about Cuba."

"And about Mexico. And about hungry little children."

"I admitted I have a lot to learn. What more can I say?"

"Try nothing."

She tried. Seeking to mollify, she couldn't just sit mute. "I've been thinking." She hadn't, but — "I think I've come up with a plan for feeding those little ones, if what you say is true about their plight. When I was in Spain, I —"

"¡Silencio!" He yanked the top sheet up and stretched out on the bed. He didn't touch her. In the dim light she saw he rested his neck on his wrist, his line of sight centering on the ceiling. His was not a relaxed pose; tension radiated like spokes of the blistering sun. "Just don't say one more word about Spain or the Spanish," he ordered. "Not one damned word. Understand?"

"Pouting is not one of your more attractive features."

For a moment she feared he would charge out of bed as well as from her life, so angry was his string of rapid-fire Spanish curses. Her ears singed, she at long last kept quiet. After a few weighty moments, though, she placed a tentative and calming hand on his arm, meant to relay friendly support.

He expelled a harsh breath and patted the back of her hand. "Forgive my temper. And I wasn't pouting. I've got a lot on my mind. It's got to do with — My brother is in trouble." Rafe gave a thumbnail sketch of his half brother's fight for human rights, yet she suspected he left quite a bit out. "The Federales are after Xzobal."

"I'd think your brother would have the Delgado family, if not the church, behind him," she said. "Forgive me for being personal, but don't the Delgados stick up for each other?"

"We aren't like you McLoughlins. And he is not a Delgado." Rafe explained his mother had remarried after his father, Venustiano Delgado, had suffered an untimely death. "My brother and late sister were fathered by Agustín Paz."

"I see."

Margaret tried to conjure up his family, unsuccessfully. She started to ask him about his uncle; he moved to sit up. She placed a hand on his shoulder. Her fingers trailed to his neck, and she felt the surge of his pulse, yet he lay all too still, as if he purposely wouldn't move a muscle to acknowledge her touch.

Believing his brother had fouled Rafe's mood, she said, "Everything will be okay. Once you put me and mine on a ship out of Tampico, you can do something to help him. Think how fortunate you are to be in Mexico already."

"That's one way to look at it." Rafe rolled to his side, giving her his back. "Good night."

"Good night?"

"Yes." He wiggled and settled in. "Good night."

Her mouth dropped; his cold shoulder made her downright indignant. "Rafe, I understand you're upset about your brother, but is this all I get? A simple good night?" He didn't answer. "Pardon me," she said, "but I thought you had different ideas for the rest of tonight."

"Go to sleep."

Never one to leave well enough alone, she crabbed,

"When *my* brother was out of pocket, you expected me to go about my merry and cheery way. When it comes to *your* brother—"

"You've never been merry or cheery."

His turning hot then cold had all the makings of a cruel game, yet this mean turn shouldn't come as a surprise. He was a man hurting from the conflicts of life. But she did her own share of hurting. She'd had a winter's worth of his cold shoulder between Juarez and here, and she wouldn't roll over and feign sleep. "Don't you know your legions of adoring lady friends would be shocked to see you now. Rafael the First, king of *la cópula espléndida,* fails at his specialty."

Rafe angled his taut body to gather her upper arm in his harsh and ruthless grip. His breath, tainted with lingering cigar smoke, spilled over her face. The heat of his annoyance was a scorching thing. "You're a smart woman, so don't act ignorant. I *can* make love to you. What I have been trying to tell you is, I don't *want* to!"

She went numb. Determined to gather some shred of her pride, she became like her mother: she made excuses. "You've been under a strain. We'll talk about it another time."

"There's not going to be another time. I've decided to—"

"Just a dad gum minute. You were doing everything in your power to seduce me. Whether it's because you were smitten, or just because I'm a female of the human race, or maybe because I have some resemblance to Olga, I don't know or care." She slapped at a tear that threatened to fall. "But what does concern me is . . . you've broken a gentleman's agreement."

"What?" Incredulous described him. "You thought we'd formed some sort of proper pact?"

"Of course, I did."

"Margarita, don't you know the man is supposed to take the aggressive role?"

"Blow me down. Knock me over with a feather. I'm poleaxed." She got to a sitting position. "Why am I surprised that Rafael Delgado, master stud, wants to do all the wooing? After all, he found a certain butter-doesn't-melt-in-her-mouth Spanish countess attractive. So much so that his libido overtook any sort of sensible or practical consideration, when he raped her!"

"I thought we settled that. Anything I ever got from your sister was given freely."

"How do you explain torn clothes and a bruised lip?"

"I can't explain something I know nothing about."

"A likely excuse." Margaret flipped to her side, giving him her own version of the back treatment. "Why should I believe a has-been rabble-rouser over my esteemed sister?"

"*Jesucristo,* you are a shrew."

The soft mattress became an uncomfortable place. And she saw the picture of Margaret McLoughlin clearly. *You are a shrew.* A shrew and a desperate old maid, spread out on Pancho Villa's bed in nothing more than pantaloons and camisole, willing to go to any lengths for a few crumbs from a sexy Mexican.

The same moment that she made up her mind to gather herself and her clothes and make an exit, it happened. Happened as it had happened thousands of times over the past five years. Her lungs began to close, her throat to constrict. *Not now! Not now!* But the cough grabbed hold. Wracking, wracking, wheezing. Breath — she battled for a draft of it. Fought in vain. With a resounding thud, she tumbled to the floor.

" 'Rita? Aw, damn. Oh, *ca-ca!* You'll be okay. You'll be okay. You'll be okay." Rafe bent over her, fanning her face with his hand. "I'll get some water."

"No," she choked. "Elixir. In valise."

Minutes passed. Pulled together, thanks to the sedating syrup and sheer will, Margaret sat on the earthen floor, her back against the mattress edge. Rafe hovered. She wiped her face with the cloth he'd wet in the pitcher on the washstand.

Concerned, he sniffed from the bottle's neck. "What is this stuff? Laudanum?"

"No. It has an alcohol base."

While she had refused opiates during her illness, she now had a wretched thought: if she could get her hands on something to dull her senses, she would. The alcohol helped. Something fuzzy began to expand her veins.

"Lie down." Rafe crouched next to her. "You need rest."

Rest? How could he know her need? But her coughing spell pointed out the reason she'd gone this far with Rafe. Without pride, without dignity, without anything except the desire for experience, she leaned toward him, a lock of her hair falling forward. "Rest isn't what I'm wanting," she said huskily, the elixir giving full effect. "It's you I want."

"I wish you wouldn't gaze at me like that." Shaking his head, he looked downward. "I can't fight the witch-

197

ery of your big blue eyes."

"You toy with me. Is that fair?"

" 'Rita, accept that we weren't fated to be lovers. My mind is elsewhere."

How plain did he have to make it? But . . . well, gosh! In one last bid — she wasn't certain if she begged for Rafe or for what — she confessed, "Be it known, Mr. Fickle Pickle, I want you *only* because I think you'll be my last chance. Margaret the Sickly Old Maid needs a man. I don't want to die a virgin."

She thought he'd laugh. Or at least defend himself against the fickle-pickle insult. Yanking her to him, he clamped her in a grip that sent pain through her arms. "Don't degrade yourself. You are Margaret. Daughter of riches, sister to royalty and the famous. Margaret, the scholar and author. Margaret, the bravest woman I know. Margaret the Glorious."

Gallant praise, unbelievable yet sweet in the ear. "Watch out, Rafe. Or I'll take your words as a compliment."

"You should."

Her wish was to leave him so satisfied that he'd never notice her faults, weaknesses, and failings. Later, when she tried to recall this evening, she couldn't be quite sure when the intensity shifted. Likely, it occurred when the tip of her forefinger brushed the corner of his mouth, and she asked, "It must have hurt, the getting of this scar. Did you cry?"

Disbelieving, he didn't move, then a grin lifted that whitened slash. "No."

"Why not?"

His brutish grip turned to a caress of her wrist. "Men don't cry."

"Men are humans." *Believe it or not!* "It's okay to cry."

"I have enough against me without turning into a crybaby."

"I cry," she admitted. "I cry a lot. I'm no crybaby."

"I know." His fingers closed around her hand, and he brought the center of her palm to his lips, to touch it with the tip of his tongue. The molten metal of his eyes plated to hers. "You deserve better than a coupling in some *bandido's* hovel with an hombre like me. That's what I've been trying to tell you all evening. I'm no good for you."

She leaned to drink in the warmth of his body and the reluctant passion of his gaze. "Let me be the judge of that."

Was his a laugh or a cry? While she knew his height would top hers by no more than two inches, were they to stand in stocking feet, he had the grace of a cougar and the strength of Hercules, as he lifted her into his arms and brought himself to a standing position. At the same moment the lantern flickered out, he murmured, "I wonder if I'll ever win an argument with you?"

"Not a chance."

Laughing once more—moonlight slanting over his shoulder—Rafe lay Margaret on the bed. He knelt by the bed, bracing an elbow on it, and lifted her hair to twine a strand around his wrist. Rubbing the lock against his cheek, he said tenderly, "I've never met anyone like you. You are one of a kind."

"I could say the same about you."

"Could you now." He straightened. Unbuttoned his

britches. Sliding his fingers behind the waistband, he pushed the denim down his legs.

"Good gracious," she marveled. "No wonder they call you magnificent."

He winked. "Undress for me, brazen virgin."

Suddenly reminded of her painful thinness, she crossed her arms over her camisole-covered bosom. "I'm too thin," she said, hating herself for sounding as though she fished for a compliment. "I wish I were different."

"You are too skinny, but it all comes together nicely. And I like you skinny." He slid under the sheets and nuzzled her nose. "I would also like you fat as a little barnyard sow."

In light of his behavior just minutes ago, she wouldn't delude herself into believing him. She chuckled nonetheless. "I thought you were supposed to have the tongue of a flatterer. Little sow doesn't measure up."

"Then I'll tell you exactly how I feel." He was all seriousness. "I've wanted you so much, I've thought of almost nothing but you. And having you under me. I would beg for you. I would crawl across brambles to have one taste of your lips. If you turned away from me right now, I would humiliate myself with tears of pleading."

What loving lies, how easily they flowed over and into her. So mad for him was she, that nothing mattered save for the moment. She inched closer, until he singed her with the furnace of his flesh. "No need for pleading."

"Thank God. I'm no good at it." He nipped at her earlobe. "You need to be ravished and often, vamp."

She smiled.

Layering his body half atop hers, he took both of her hands in one of his, and maneuvered them above her head. His mouth dipped to her throat. She squirmed as he alternated kisses and nips all the way to her temple, then retraced his journey.

"You are a learned woman, but there is only so much that books can teach." He gripped the back of her knee, drawing her leg over his thigh. "Do you realize what will happen to you?"

"It's like the corrida. You will progress to the *suerte de picar* . . . the lancing stage." The feel of him, naked . . . sublimely naked . . . caused her heart to race and her pulse to soar even higher than before. "In the bullrings of Ronda and Madrid, I've seen the great swordsmen of Spain. I have heard you are the greatest of . . . swordsmen. In all arenas."

He growled lowly. "I *am* the greatest of swordsmen."

He kissed her deeply, masterfully, his tongue plunging again and again. It was as if his hot tongue—and even hotter hands—were everywhere, exploring her every curve, igniting her to flames of impatient desire. Her hands did their own venturing, and every nerve in her body tingled as she contemplated their differences—hard and soft, manly and womanly. Lancer and mark.

At some point—it could have been seconds, more likely minutes—he whispered against her throat, "I am a wretched satyr. I have no control over my need to know all of you."

"Then, Sir Satyr, do get on with the lancing."

He laughed. A deep and beautiful sound. A thousand sensations buzzed through her when he kissed and caressed her once more. She barely noticed as he got her out of her clothes, so experienced were his disrobing skills.

"Touch me." His fingers kneaded her breast. "Touch me as you would have in Juarez. But promise—no crazy questions."

"I promise."

She started with a kiss. Her fingers smoothed down his chest and moved around his ribs to the sinew and levels of his back. Oh, how delightful it was to explore him like this, like she'd fantasized about so many times. Getting acquainted with the firm mound of a buttock, she hummed approval; he pivoted his hip. Her hand moved to the tumid member that began to throb against her fingers. He was like a knife set to the flame.

Once more she heard a growl, but this one was more of a groan. When she let go of his lips, he settled atop her, straddling her hips, his hirsute body abrading her flesh. Inhaling, she felt the rigid length of him against her belly. Her curiosities many, she managed to quell them, even before his splayed fingers channeled through her hair. Going on instinct, she tilted her pelvis forward. Feverish shiver after feverish shiver went through her, when manly angles found the feminine ones of hers.

"Hot little virgin." He twisted his fingers in her hair. "I never had a taste for virgins. Until now. Heaven help me."

She didn't speak. His tongue made kindling tracks on her nose, her eyelids, her temple. It circled her earlobe, dipping into her ear. She ached to beg for more. For exactly what, she wasn't certain, but Rafe could and would provide it.

All the while he moved against her, exciting her, exciting himself. He growled his favor over and again. "You're quite a woman. Ah, yes, touch me, *querida*. Touch me like that."

He didn't leave her wanting. With each sweep of his hand, she sailed higher and higher into sensual awakening. Then he leaned to the side, his mouth fastening over her nipple, his tongue flicking. Her eyes rolled as he suckled with all his might. She went crazy with the wonder of it! It was an urge she didn't quite know what to do about, save for obeying her instincts. Her hunger to envelop him into herself grew more voracious with each passing second. She lost herself in him.

His pace slowing, he combed his fingers through the dark curls at the top of her thighs, his hand cupping her womanhood. He rubbed, tickled, crooned, finding a region more sensitive than any other. A rush went through her.

"I want to feel more of you," he admitted and traced her lips with his. A finger slid inside her, the heel of his palm still at her special place. "You're so tight. So wet. Never in all my days in the arena, did I ever want the conquest as much as I want it from you."

Overwhelming were his admissions. He knew how to bring a woman to dizzying heights, and Margaret couldn't get enough of his finger and palm. Suddenly, a tremor went through her. And all the while, he chanted his elation along with encouragements.

"In the language of Hugo," she said, sometime after she'd begun the descent to rational thought, "this is called the little death. If this is dying, I have nothing to fear."

"The lovely dying has only begun." He moved his hand to her hip, sliding over the flesh, fastening on the curve of it. "May the Lady of Guadalupe strike me dead, but I've wanted to be your first lover. And your last."

"You well may be." . . . *the last*. She chopped off melancholy thoughts. Tomorrow was tomorrow, tonight was tonight, and who on this earth had a guarantee for the rocking chair and stewed prunes? "You have taunted me enough, *mi espada*. Do plunge your great knife into me."

He nudged her knees apart to site himself between her legs. She sighed at all that waited impatiently at her womanly gate. Bit by bit, he eased inside. While he did, he murmured the sweet nothings of sex. Yet he hesitated at breeching her.

"I hate to hurt you. I hate it, 'Rita . . . but I must."

"If you don't give me relief, I'm going to scream." On a fierce groan, he lunged. The membrane tore and she screamed, as she had threatened, but not for that reason. Despite the agony of her torn flesh, she felt an immense thrill at the same time. Impaled on the huge and thick blade of the grand *espadachín*, she curled her fingers into the hair on his chest, then moaned for more of all he had to give.

And he gave it.

Fifteen

"I'm proud of myself." Margaret cuddled in Rafe's arms. In the aftermath of lovemaking, in the aftermath of such a tide of shared satisfaction that she — and he — remained rocked to the core, joking seemed a natural and sequential happening. "Did you notice, Rafe? I didn't ask, not once, how anything worked."

He disengaged himself from the tangle that was them. "Are you pleased with my servicing, Margarita?"

Not having any experience with this sort of situation, she supposed it was a natural thing for a man to ask questions. Instinctively, though, she wasn't quite convinced such a bald query was apropos. "What do you mean?"

"I want to make certain you got what you wanted." He withdrew from bed and reached down for his discarded britches. "In this case, rid of your maidenhead."

Surely he didn't — He wouldn't — Was she caught in a nightmare? *No! This is reality.* "I didn't expect this reaction from you. Do you always behave this way after bedding a virgin?"

"I told you. I prefer a more seasoned woman. You're

my first virgin in a good while. As for your fishwife-hectoring, don't forget . . . you begged."

Speechless, wounded, she tried to assimilate the message he sent. Unless other women expected a lot less than this, Margaret couldn't understand how he claimed title to his venerated and rampant reputation as a great lover.

"Don't huddle like a wounded sparrow, Margaret."

He hadn't called her Margarita or 'Rita. While he reached for his shirt, moonlight splashed across the muscles of his back, the play of them showing off the superb physique that had just moments ago been so close, yet evidently so far, from her. Slowly, hesitantly, she asked, "What are you doing?"

"Going outside for a smoke."

"Oh. I see. I guess." She yearned to say something — anything! — to recapture the beauty of what they had shared, but her voice deserted her. *He's leaving for more than a smoke.* Ridiculous. He wasn't going anywhere but outside.

He pushed a foot into a boot, then tugged on its pull straps, and set to work on the other. He began to gather bits and pieces of this and this, then stuffed them in his britches pockets. In nothing flat he was at the door.

Hoping she read signs that weren't there, she asked in a voice an octave higher than normal, "What did I do? I know I didn't have any experience in giving pleasure, but I'd hoped to please you."

"Have you ever noticed, all you think about is the world as it relates to Miss Margaret McLoughlin?"

His cold words chilled her heart. Maybe, possibly, she had behaved selfishly. Charity, during their most recent visit, last summer, had accused her of becoming too insular. Of course, Charity was gregarious and unstoppable, having never met a stranger or an unworthy cause.

It didn't take much for Margaret to recall very real problems, not hers. "Forgive me if I seem heartless," she said. "I am concerned about you, Rafe. I'd like to know how you feel, returning to Mexico after so many years. Returning to . . . to all you have returned to."

"I don't feel. I do."

Until now, she wouldn't have believed him an unfeeling person. "Pancho Villa told me about the trouble you're having with your uncle. He said Arturo Delgado accuses you of murder."

"Pancho Villa talks too much."

"You didn't do it, did you, kill your cousin?"

"I . . . I don't know." Rafe strapped on a spur, unnecessary equipment for *smoking*. "There were a lot of bullets flying. It could have been mine." He wiped a hand down his face. "It may have been mine."

"Oh, dear." Into the weighty quiet that fell, she asked, "Is the law looking for you?"

"The law that is Arturo Delgado."

"He's why you didn't come back to Mexico, isn't he?"

"No, Margarita. Neither Hernándo nor his father was the reason I stayed in Texas."

He said no more, an answer in itself. Rafe didn't wish to discuss his reasons for becoming an expatriate. She ought not to press him on the subject. Ought not to. However, she'd traveled with a man who'd just admitted to a possible murder. She just gave him her virginity, her aching bottom reminded her. What in the world had she done? What in the world should she do next? It might be better to let him have his smoke, *carte blanche*.

That was the cowardly way. She swallowed. "Did it — Did your staying have to do with a woman?"

"If you *must* know, yes."

"Olga?"

"I don't kiss and tell." He combed his hair.

It was better, his silence on that more important woman. Margaret convinced her heart his special woman wasn't her sister. It hurt less that way. "What are you planning to do?" she asked. "About your brother, I mean."

"I haven't decided."

Feeling a certain kinship, she said, "So . . . we both have brothers to worry over."

"I meant to tell you, Tex is fine," Rafe said in a dismissive tone. "He rode up a few minutes before I left Villa outside. Everything is taken care of, he said. He was half-asleep, so Pedro gave up his bedroll. Tex said he'd see you in the morning."

Seeing a light in the awful abyss, she exclaimed, "Thank heavens! I tried to tell myself he was okay, but I've been dying a thousand deaths."

"I know the thousand deaths," Rafe commented dryly. "Xzobal will be shot. If he's captured."

"Is he safe for now?"

"For now."

"Don't you think that's a good sign?" She made every effort to infuse a chipper note.

"Margarita, I am *not* in the mood for this conversation."

"What are you in the mood for?" she asked hesitantly.

"A smoke."

Out of patience, weary of his hot and cold, and just

plain tired from an eventful day and an even more eventful evening, she turned her back, yanking the sheet over her shoulder.

Her expectation was to hear the door closing behind him. She heard him exhale. She heard him turn. He retraced his footsteps. Leaning across her, he guided her to face him, combed his fingers through her hair, and pressed his thumb just below her earlobe. "I can't leave here, uh, can't *go outside* without telling you . . . Thank you, *bruja de dulce*. It fills me with pride that you gave me the glorious gift of your virginity."

What in the dickens was she supposed to say to that? She kept her silence for a change.

"You are too good for me, my beautiful blue-eyed 'Rita. I am all the dirty names you called me in the past. And more. You were unwise to trust me."

"But—"

"Shhh." He pressed a fingertip to her lips. "Please remember something, 'Rita. Odd as it may seem, and no matter what happens, I didn't set out to hurt you. But I did as I've always done. I took without planning to give anything real in return." He paused. "I have nothing of myself to give back."

"I don't expect anything from you," she said. "But I think you're wrong when you say you have nothing to give back. You have much to give. And your great skill as a lover is but a small part of what you have to give . . . *El Aguila*."

"Remember that when times get bad."

Rafe quit the *casita* and made a beeline for Villa. "Draw me a map. I want to know exactly where Xzobal is hiding. And—by the ghost of Father Hidalgo—I don't want any trouble out of you. *¿Comprende?*"

Villa waved his hands in understanding and compliance. "When will you leave?"

"Now."

"You disappoint me, *El Aguila*. Since before my first shave, I thought you were a rebel through and through. When you headed outside just now, I assumed your rebellious streak hadn't been lost, that we'd ride together against the skunk of Santa Alicia."

"You assumed wrong. I thought we settled that earlier."

Villa glanced at his house, then at Rafe. "You have left the pretty toothpick. You cannot sleep. You are troubled."

Troubled? He was more than troubled. But he needed to work this situation to its best and safest advantage. "All right, Villa, I'll join you. *After* I've seen my brother to safety."

"That's all I ask. The robbery will wait for you." The bandit paused. "But what about your wife? What will you do with the toothpick, while you are saving Father Xzobal?"

What about Margarita? Rafe squeezed the bridge of his nose before exhaling. He'd been hard-hearted on purpose. When he'd gone to her bed, he'd tried to make her furious enough to toss him on his ear. Afterward— after her unabashed, rejoicing loving—he'd tried to make it easy for her to hate him. Why? His were the ways of a scoundrel. The epithet fit him like the silk stockings of a matador. Yet, in hindsight, he knew he shouldn't have entered that *casita*. He shouldn't have disrobed. He shouldn't have made love to her. His lusts had been his undoing.

Just minutes ago, he'd driven himself into her, time after time, each time with more force, a man possessed with the wonders of the virginal Margarita. He ached — plain *hurt!* — for another taste of her lips, for another opportunity to thrust himself mercilessly into the hot glove of her.

Sweat popped on his upper lip. Even in her innocence, she was fifty times the lover her sister had been. Except for that one special and spontaneous night in the shadow of the Alamo.

Despite being wrong — or was it naive? — in her political sympathies, Margarita was more woman than any hombre ought to have a right to. *You had no right to her.* Would that he could have the chance to set her straight. But it was too late for could's and would's and chances-were. The only thing left was to leave her.

Villa repeated his question.

"Her brother will attend her from here." Rafe took a menacing step forward and bared his teeth. "If you should cross her path, keep your hands to yourself. Make sure your *niños* stay away. If I find you've betrayed me, I will *kill you,* Francisco Villa."

"There will be no need for murder." Villa gave a half nod. "But if not for her ties to you, *El Aguila,* I would want the pretty toothpick for my own. For retraining purposes," he added with a snicker, "if nothing else."

"Just draw the map."

Villa went to his saddlebag and removed writing tools. Within a few minutes, he handed the sketch over. "Take the pinto. It is a good gelding. *Vaya con Dios,* amigo."

Rafe whipped around, making for Margarita's

brother and shaking his shoulder. "Wake up, McLoughlin. I've got to talk to you."

"Huh? What? Me? Oh, yeah." He rubbed his eyes. "What can I do for ya, Rafe ole buddy?"

"Saddle up. Give me ten minutes, then collect your sister. Strike out for the city of Chihuahua. It's not far—"

"I been there already. And—"

"Don't interrupt. Just listen. Don't let Margarita out of your sight. When you hit town, find the Avenida de los Niños Sacrificio. Call on the Naked Rooster cantina. Ask for an hombre named Hector Flores. He'll show you the way to Eden Roc."

"You mean you're not going with us? But you promised my sister—You're welshing on the deal, Rafe. I figured you was a better feller than that."

"I've got to do what I've got to do. And that is help someone in dire straits." Sternly, like a father, Rafe asked, "Now—will you promise me you'll not let 'Rita out of your sight?"

" 'Course I'll take care of her. But I—"

"I figured you would. You're a good hombre, Tex McLoughlin. I hope you find your Natalie again someday."

"Boy howdy, so do I."

Rafe saddled the borrowed pinto, put his booted foot in the stirrup, and swung into the saddle. Now to Xzobal. *Rapido.* He didn't look back. He wouldn't allow himself a glance. *But you'll never see her again.* A stab of pain—like iced heat—pierced his chest, as he had lanced between her legs. He knew that if he saw Margarita, or got a look at no more than the *casita* where they had made love, he wouldn't be able to ride

212

out of here.

He put a spur to the gelding's flank.

In the wee hours of a cold and damp night in the District of Columbia, Maisie McLoughlin shivered. She shivered despite the roaring fire in the hearth of her grandson's library, and the many layers of woolen night clothes she had gotten her nearly century-old body into. She shivered at what seemed to be happening to her family.

Insomnia had brought her downstairs for a cup of brandy-laced cocoa. Curiosity carried her to this Boston rocker that she now set in motion. Something kept The Honorable Gil McLoughlin awake, as well.

Fastening a look of disapproval on the Secretary of State, she waited for him to 'fess up. Any confession had nothing to do with the fraud that was her grandson. He claimed to hate cats, yet Deniece and Denephew lolled on his desk like fat characters from the funny papers, their loose hair a duo of coronas in the gaslight.

Cats had nothing to do with it.

For weeks Maisie had carried the terrible suspicion that her silver-haired Gilliegorm, who scratched an ink pen across paper, was keeping something from her. "Lad, did ye or did ye not, have some *other* reason for sending our Margaret to Mexico?"

He dipped into the ink pot. "I told you. I want Lisette back with me, and I knew I could depend on our daughter."

"Ye coulda gone after yer wife all by yerself."

"Maisie, America is on the verge of war," he said tiredly and rubbed his eyes. "You know I can't leave the

213

capital. Not for any reason. Not even for a footloose wife."

Footloose wife. Hmm. Maisie fell in love with the patient and serene Lisette on that first day she'd laid eyes on the blonde, in Kansas, in September of '69. Sometimes she feared she loved the German girl more than Gilliegorm himself loved his wife. He tended to be tense, overzealous in his undertakings, too earnest and serious in the making of money or peace. Too neglectful of family. He assumed—and expected—they would understand him and all the things he held in high regard. Personally, Maisie figured him for a jackanapes.

And for all the lass's strength, Lisette was as soft as a marshmallow on the inside. It hurt her to play second fiddle.

It wasn't Maisie's intention to quiz him about the couple's relationship—that would be seeking more trouble than Charles Stuart got at Culloden Moor—but this centenarian *would* get to the bottom of her concerns, or she'd be buried alive in this confounded uncomfortable rocker. *Devil a bit! 'Tis no good for a coffin.*

"Did she leave ye?"

He gripped the pen until India ink sprayed on his letter. "Why don't you go back to bed?"

"Canna sleep."

"I'll fix you a hot toddy."

"Nay. Ye doona have t' answer me in so many words."

She knew the answer. And it hurt. It hurt, like when she'd lost her Sandy. And their sons. And their other grandchildren. And the great-grandson also known as Gilliegorm. Having her family out of her control—having them where she couldn't make everything

214

right — well, what was the use in living a hundred years?

Her gnarled hands gripped the rocker arms as if they were a mooring device. "I willna be bothering ye about our darlin' Lisette again. But I will be telling ye — Ye were a selfish lad, sending our Margaret off t' Mexico at a time like this." Maisie sucked her teeth. "Ye know how she was needing t' get ready t' take on that job at Brandington College. And ye know she ain't fit o' body. That sawbones Woodward said —"

"Goddamn it, Maisie, leave go with your nagging." He slammed the pen to his desktop. "I know my own daughter's problems, thank you very much."

"I think ye sent the lass t' . . ." Maisie felt the gullies of her face spreading as she smiled. "T' match our lass up with that nice lad Rafael."

Gilliegorm patted Deniece's head; she purred. "Rafe Delgado is a good man, for a Casanova. Needs some direction, but if Margaret can't get him directed, no one can."

The tension easing, Gil and his grandmother shared a laugh, for Margaret was the consummate in bossiness.

"If she and Delgado do make a match," her father said, Deniece rousing, "I won't be offended. Little Maggie needs a husband. And ole Rafe, well, he's strong enough to match — and conquer — her hardheadedness. The way I call it, they'd complement each other."

"Ye always did like him. Would that be why ye gave him horses and cattle for his ranch?"

The Persian pussycat's tail brushed Gilliegorm's nose; she extended a back leg in a feline stretch; he sneezed before replying, "Don't push me on the subject."

"Doona ye be telling yer granny what t' do." Maisie

hunched her shoulders. "Why did ye renege on yer promise t' send him back t' Mexico with guns and ammunition?"

"He got paid. With the stock you mentioned."

"What made ye think he would be wanting cows instead of war supplies?" Uh, oh. Maisie didn't like the look on her grandson's face. Not one bit. "Ye dinna believe the mad rumor about the lad and our Olga, did ye?"

"It wasn't a rumor." Gil stroked the pussycat's white fur. "Olga wrote me. Asked if I'd help Rafe get started."

"How do ye think our Olga would feel if she found out ye set the lad up with her sister?"

"If you must know, it was her idea. She asked me to keep tabs on Rafe. She's concerned he'll never settle down. And it goes without saying she's worried about Maggie. Olga knows her triplet was infatuated with him." He leveled a look at his grandmother. "If Maggie and Rafe are thrown together, nature will take its course."

"Are ye as blind as our Olga? He willna be settling for our delicate Margaret."

"How do you know he won't?"

"I doona like this. Not at all. That Rafe has an eye for the pretty lasses." Secondly, goodwill didn't sound like Olga. Sympathizing with her loss of sight, her father couldn't see her flaws. Besides, there was more here than met Gilliegorm McLoughlin's eye. "Olga isna the main reason ye got them together."

"You're right." Gil pushed his chair back and lurched to stand, pacing back and forth. "I fear Olga will want Rafe. Again. I fear she'll leave Leonardo. Maisie, there is trouble in the House of Granada. I wouldn't be

216

surprised if she divorces her husband. It wouldn't come as a shock if she travels to San Antonio. To be with Rafe." Gil rubbed his forehead. "That's why I had to get him out of the country."

"Olga? Travel? Have ye lost yer marbles? She's blind as a bat. She willna be traveling anywhere wit'out her husband."

"Are you forgetting that she sprang from her indomitable mother? That she sprang from determined stock, both Scottish and Teutonic? Are you forgetting Olga is *your* great-granddaughter?"

"Ye dinna have t' put it that bluntly, lad." Maisie, fretful, reached for her cane and pushed the bag of bones that was herself off the seat, to join her grandson in his pacing.

"Maisie . . ."

"Aye?"

"That's not the worst of it."

Rafe had requested a ten-minute head start. It took a whole day for Margaret and her brother to leave the Villa encampment and to repair their disabled wagon, thanks to more wheel trouble. After Rafe dumped her with Villa, *et al,* Margaret cried. And cried. And cried. But she refused to shed those tears. She wouldn't allow outsiders to witness how much the humiliation hurt.

It was only after she and Tex had taken their leave in the patched up wagon that she let go her tears. Buckets of tears couldn't wash away the pain, though.

How cruel, life. How many times had Rafe ordered her to keep quiet? He should have taken his own advice. Did he know it was sadistic to praise so lavishly, then do as he'd done? Did he even care? Whatever the case, he had well and truly left for more than a smoke.

Somewhere along the path to the city of Chihuahua, Margaret became aware of a bitter irony. Bullfights were fought in three stages. The lancing was but the first. The second part had to do with planting the darts. That's what Rafe had done to her when he'd dressed to flee — planted hurting, subduing darts. His leaving had been the coup de grâce. The *suerte de matár*. The slaughter.

"Sis, honey, you've got to think about something else," Tex suggested softly, when they were riding into the outskirts of the city of Chihuahua.

Anything would beat thinking about Rafe's desertion or their last night together. She looked around. Rafe, during their trip to Pancho Villa, had told her about the prosperous and bustling town, a center for cattle and mining. As for the natural beauty, he'd been expansive. "He did brag on this place."

"It looks like a right nice town."

"He said the sky is as big as the heavens." She couldn't help lacing her words with references to Rafe. " 'It rains sunshine over the plaza.' " Not as arid as its neighbor to the north, El Paso, Chihuahua city in some ways resembled Juarez, but not really. This place was much nicer, much more genteel. "Rafe said palaces line the avenues near the aqueduct. He said the cathedral is lovely and grand with its golden chandeliers."

"I reckon he knew what he was talking about," Tex said, as he drove toward the Naked Rooster grogshop. "Don't reckon he was yarning."

"Not in regard to the town." Margaret wiped more tears and blew her nose on a rag — she'd boo-hoo'd into the last clean hankie this morning. Rafe had lied when he'd told her how much he'd wanted their . . . their—What did one call lovemaking without the love?

Sex.

Fornication.

Heavenly days.

The wagon veered as Tex drove around a small object that darted into the road. "Damn lil ole dog!"

The strange tiny *canis familiaris,* similar to Rafe's own Frita, made the opposite side of the street, and put up a large fuss. It was joined by a half dozen of its kind, each acting as if he would tear the wagon apart, single-pawed. Dynamite did come in tiny packages. They were enough to make a tormented woman chuckle.

"What was it ole Rafe said about them lil ole dogs?"

" 'Ever since the Apaches who raised them as pets were forced from the *apacheria* and were driven into Arizona Territory, the *perritos chihuahuenses* have roamed wild and free. Chihuahua dogs make pests of themselves, yapping, snapping, and getting in the way of wheels and ankles.' Or something on that order."

"He weren't lying."

Chihuahua city *was* a place all its own. "It's where he said he'd take me, in late '89."

And in late '97.

She never dreamed she'd see the town without Rafe at her side. Oh, Lord, how it hurt, losing him. This must be how it felt to have a heart yanked from a chest. Daft described her, because she wanted more of Rafe. She couldn't imagine why.

Sapped of strength for the tough journey of life, Margaret felt every one of her years. Plus a few more.

Sixteen

In the days following Rafe's abandonment, Margaret vacillated between anger and indignation. He'd forsaken her as well as the mission she paid him *five thousand dollars* to complete.

More problems surfaced. The journey progressed much slower than she'd anticipated. One more stumbling block, and her professorship could be in jeopardy. Then where would she be? Unlucky in love, unlucky in life. *That's me.* She had a word with herself not to sound like Charity.

Charity. How she missed her sister all of a sudden. And Olga. She missed her, too. In establishing the Wild West show, Charity, luckily, had found an outlet for her outgoing personality, had become wildly famous on three continents. Olga, too, had found her own brand of peace.

As youngsters, the triplets had fought like cats and dogs, but wasn't that the way with sisters? Margaret tried not to think about it, but if the truth were known, she felt as if a part of her was missing, when Olga and Charity weren't within reach.

Dang!

At times, here in the city of Chihuahua, Margaret got snide, like when she refused to eat a taco her brother had bought at the Naked Rooster while they awaited one Hector Flores, guide. They had been becalmed in the city for three days. It was now the evening of the fourth day.

January loomed closer and closer.

"Maggie, honey, you ought to eat. You're getting more drawed. And your cough . . ."

"No tacos for me." She jerked up her nose. "I've heard Mexicans are such barbarians they grind up those pesky little dogs for the meat filling."

"Did you hear that from ole Rafe?"

"No."

"I bet it ain't true."

"Oh?" She gave a superior look around the less-than-respectable-looking tavern. "I wonder why they don't have any dogs sniffing around in here?"

Tex put his own taco back on the table. Uneaten.

She didn't feel the least bit proud of herself. All she felt was awful. But she managed to hold back on another bucket of tears until late that night, after she and Tex had gone to their rooms in the lovely hotel that presented a marvelous view of the distant Santa Alicia Mountain.

The village of Santa Alicia—Rafe's hometown—hugged the side of that jagged mountain. She damned herself for wanting it, and knew the reason ridiculous, but she itched to visit the sight of his flying from his "golden bassinet" to "rain wheat on the hungry villages."

Margaret didn't visit Santa Alicia.

221

Amazingly, Santa Alicia came to her the next evening, in a manner of speaking. Tall, handsome, and with hair of steel gray, Soledad Delgado Paz de Aguilar called at the hotel room. Her bearing spoke pride and sharp brown eyes.

The question was: what did Rafe's mother want?

A photograph in her skirt pocket, Soledad Paz followed the wraithlike *gringa* to a cluster of burgundy-velvet chairs in a suite at the Hotel Chihuahua. The Countess of Granada showed no surprise upon reading the name of her lover's mother on a calling card. Pleasantly cordial, she offered chocolates and laurel tea, but Soledad disliked her anyway. Which had nothing to do with the woman having aged mightily since sitting for the photograph.

What did Rafito see in her? While her features had nothing out of kilter, drawn and pinched fit her; dark crescents lay beneath large and fatigued blue eyes. Rafito appreciated the buxom. Buxom blondes. *But she was lovely, once upon a time, when she hurt my Rafito.* Hurt him to the core. If not for this hag, Rafito would have come home.

But he is in Mexico. I know he is. But where? And she is here. What does all this mean? Upon receiving her son's coded message, Soledad had made a beeline to the Naked Rooster and the mysterious woman who'd spread the cryptic message. It had taken several minutes of wide-eyed staring through the window, before she'd realized this woman was Rafito's cherished Olga.

It took Soledad another day or so to come to grips with her son's poor choice in women.

The *gringa's* face going pale, she grabbed a handkerchief, turned away, and began to cough. When the racking spasm had spent itself—even though the handkerchief got shoved away quickly—Soledad didn't fail to notice the crimson stains.

"Please excuse me." Pink spots suffused the chalky cheeks. "Little touch of *el resfriado,* it seems."

A simple cold? Soledad thought not, and made the holy cross. As a mother who had lost her daughter, she knew the signs. It would take a more hard-hearted person than Soledad Paz not to feel sorry for the doomed Olga.

With shaking hand the dying woman reached to a table littered with brown apothecary bottles and poured some sort of syrup into a glass, swallowing the contents. Collected, she asked, "Did someone send you to call on me?"

"I was told you seek Hector Flores."

"Yes, I do. He was supposed to be at the Naked Rooster cantina, but hasn't been. Do you know where I can find him?"

The teacup set aside, Rafe's mother replied, "Señor Flores died last month. He died in the dungeon of this town. You see, the late señor dared to stand up to Arturo Delgado for what he thought right."

"My God." The *gringa* shuddered. "What is wrong with this country that a man cannot speak his mind?"

"Liberty has never been our privilege." Soledad leaned to plug the stopper into the bottle. "May I be blunt? By your asking after Hector Flores, my Rafito has sent a message. I—"

"A message? And what would that be?"

"That he is in Mexico."

"I—I see."

What a peculiar reaction. Soledad studied the other woman. "You seem surprised."

"If I am the bearer of messages, I am surprised."

Once more, Rafito had, it appeared, used a woman. More than likely, this was his way of repaying the hurt she'd wreaked on him. Oh, how he hurt when the truth won out, that the countess wouldn't be returning to him.

That aside, he would expect his *madrecita* to look out for this woman, for old time's sake, if for no other reason. "Tell me, are you in need?" Soledad asked. "Perhaps I can help you."

"Only if you know a good guide. My brother and I are on our way to a retreat called Eden Roc, near the Eye of the Canyon."

"I may be able to help. But I would advise you to stay away from *El Ojo*. Some of the slaves from the Santa Alicia silver mine have escaped, have taken refuge with the Tarahumara Indians. Arturo has set the Federales on them. There could be trouble."

The shaking hand took on more of a palsy; the waxy face lost any semblance of color. "My, my m-mother. She's there."

"She will be fine, as long as she doesn't leave the confines of Eden Roc."

The *gringa* stood, scoured her elbows with her fingers, then hugged her arms. Slowly, she began to pace the room. If she had been this concerned for Rafito, he wouldn't have wasted his life in Texas.

Soledad spoke. "The question remains, where is my son?"

The noblewoman opened her mouth, but clamped it.

224

MORE PASSION AND ADVENTURE AWAIT... YOUR TRIP TO A BIG ADVENTUROUS WORLD BEGINS WHEN YOU ACCEPT YOUR FIRST 4 NOVELS ABSOLUTELY *FREE* (AN $18.00 VALUE)

Accept your Free gift and start to experience more of the passion and adventure you like in a historical romance novel. Each Zebra novel is filled with proud men, spirited women and tempestuous love that you'll remember long after you turn the last page.

Zebra Historical Romances are the finest novels of their kind. They are written by authors who really know how to weave tales of romance and adventure in the historical settings you love. You'll feel like you've actually gone back in time with the thrilling stories that each Zebra novel offers.

GET YOUR FREE GIFT WITH THE START OF YOUR HOME SUBSCRIPTION

Our readers tell us that these books sell out very fast in book stores and often they miss the newest titles. So Zebra has made arrangements for you to receive the four newest novels published each month.

You'll be guaranteed that you'll never miss a title, and home delivery is so convenient. And to show you just how easy it is to get Zebra Historical Romances, we'll send you your first 4 books absolutely FREE! Our gift to you just for trying our home subscription service.

BIG SAVINGS AND FREE HOME DELIVERY

Each month, you'll receive the four newest titles as soon as they are published. You'll probably receive them even before the bookstores do. What's more, you may preview these exciting novels free for 10 days. If you like them as much as we think you will, just pay the low preferred subscriber's price of just $3.75 each. *You'll save $3.00 each month off the publisher's price.* AND, your savings are even greater because there are never any shipping, handling or other hidden charges—FREE Home Delivery. Of course you can return any shipment within 10 days for full credit, no questions asked. There is no minimum number of books you must buy.

Taking a seat once more, she picked a piece of lint from the chair's arm. "He, uh, he's . . . I understand he seeks his brother."

Xzobal. Poor Xzobal. Fated for an early death, like this Lady of Granada. Fated like Rafito. Fated like María Carmen. *What I would give to see my boys one last time!* Though resigned to losing all her children, Soledad mourned them nonetheless.

Curious about many things, she asked, "May I be so bold as to ask, what happened to your husband?"

"I don't have a husband."

"Did he die, Condesa?"

"Condesa?" A pained looked appearing to have no relation to physical discomfort crossed the ravaged face. "You mistake me for my sister. I am Margaret. Margaret McLoughlin of New York City."

Confused, Soledad pulled the photograph from her pocket. "This is not you? Several years ago."

"No. That is my sister."

Relieved, yet not quite certain how she should feel, Soledad buried the photograph in its hiding place, and wondered why *this* sister had traveled to Mexico.

"How did you come to have a picture of Lady Hapsburg?" asked the sister.

"I insisted my son give it to me when I visited San Antonio. That must have been four or five years ago." Soledad leaned toward Margaret, taking the cold and bony hand in her fleshy one. She smiled, now finding no reason to dislike this *gringa*. And, strangely, wishing she could give the gift of health. "Forgive me for mistaking you."

"What did . . . What did Rafe tell you about my sister?"

225

"That he stayed in Texas because she promised to leave her husband and join him there. He put together a *vacáda* for their future. The photograph was a too-sad reminder of what was not to be."

"How nice for her, to be so loved."

What did she say in that remark? Then Soledad knew. From the facial expression, from the set of Margaret's frail body, she knew. *Madre de Dios*. She'd made a grave error in being blunt, for Soledad now saw the truth. This woman, this poor unfortunate loved her son. She begged the Blessed Virgin's mercy on Margaret McLoughlin. In health and in love, she was fated to hopeless punishment.

"Take heed of loving Rafito too much," Soledad warned. "If you trust his word, you will be hurt."

The *gringa* wilted on the chair, her knuckles whitened on the velvet-covered arms.

"All the women love *El Aguila Magnífico*. He waits for but one special lady. He loves none but the Countess of Granada. Go back to Texas or New York or wherever you came from. Go back before it's too late."

He'd even given Olga's picture to his mama.

"Can you believe it, Tex? Rafe abandoned me—us— and that Hector Flores business served no one but himself!—but he was profoundly sentimental when it came to a married woman. I should have expected nothing more from someone who wouldn't even protect himself, much less a lady."

Less than an hour after Soledad Paz had taken her leave, Margaret lay abed, spent. It had taken a storehouse of energy to be angry, furious, and embittered, and those grievous feelings still raged. Soledad Paz had reinforced what she'd known already: He was Olga's man.

"May all the demons in perdition dance on his soul!"

"Honey, settle down." Tex bathed her forehead with a cool cloth. "We always knew he weren't no upstanding feller."

"If that's meant to make me feel better, you didn't."

"I'm just trying to make you see both sides of the story. What all he's done, well, they be awful things, but—"

"Angus Jones McLoughlin, you studied grammar. You attended fine boarding schools. You know better than to say 'they be' !" Margaret rolled to her side and yanked the cover over her shoulder. "I thought you'd take to arms, hearing about the rogue and our sister. Damn him. Not only did he insult me—us—he didn't even have the courtesy to visit his own mama." Margaret shook a fist. "I hope his whacker falls off!"

"Sis, you oughtn'ta be talking nasty."

"Nasty? I heard you use the word in front of some cowboys at the Four Aces."

"That's man-talk." Tex shuffled his feet. "Sis, honey, talking about ole Rafe ain't gonna help us outta the pickle we be, uh, we *are* in. With that Hector feller dead, what are we gonna do about getting to Mutti?"

Shame stilled Margaret's purple snit. "You're right. I've been thinking of myself; it's Mother we need to worry about."

"Maggie, we oughtn'ta borrow trouble. Mutti, why she's a strong lady. She knows how to take care of herself."

"True. But we aren't in Mexico to sit on our behinds

227

in a Chihuahua hotel." Margaret pushed the covers away, got to unsteady feet, and began to organize her belongings. "We must pack. And make Eden Roc in all haste."

"How we gonna find our way?"

"We'll find our way." She certainly wouldn't depend on Rafe's mother to find them a guide. "Our mother needs us."

As Margaret and Tex descended the curving staircase to the hotel lobby, it was the hour of the day when Mexicans stirred from siesta. A man with an overlong face and large ears cut across their path. Instantly Margaret recognized something—she didn't know what—about him.

She said to her brother, "That man—doesn't he look familiar?"

"Nope."

"But he . . . well, I don't suppose you would know him, now that I think about it. But I swear he looks like Felipe Apodaca of Granada. He's one of Leonardo's aides."

"You're seeing things, Sis."

"Maybe you're right. What would Señor Apodaca be doing in Chihuahua?"

From the street entrance, a mustachioed man of about fifty shuffled toward Margaret and Tex. His clothes could have accommodated another person or two, it seemed. He had mousy hair streaked with gray; he had little of it. So gaunt was he, Margaret thought of Ichabod Crane.

"Are you Señorita McLoughlin?" he asked. When

she nodded, he turned a hat around in his hands. "I am Luis Rivera. Señora Paz sent me."

Margaret whispered in English to her brother, "Apparently the females in Rafe's family are the more trustworthy."

"You want to go to *El Ojo de la Barranca?* Luis, he will take you there." Luis tapped a finger against his chest. Smiling an uneven smile, he said, "Señora Paz, she says you know *El Aguila*."

"Señor Rivera, if you're interested in earning money, you'll not mention his name to me. How quickly can you be ready? We must leave at our soonest."

Luis's eyes glazed. "What I would give to see the Eagle again."

Didn't he hear her? "Let me set you straight, Señor Rivera. You're lucky you haven't. I, for one, suffered from being in his company. He stole my money and left me stranded in this foreign country."

Luis shook his head. "No, señorita, he did not strand you. His *madrecita* put you in Luis's hands. And that is as good as his own. I will take very good care of you and your brother."

He made no sense at all. Who did, when it came to a certain blackguard of healthy bank account? "Señor Rivera, let's discuss finances. I won't be cheated again. Thus, I'll pay you nary a *centavo* until we reach the port of Tampico."

"I have a little wife and ten little children." He grabbed his belly. "They will be so hun-gree if I cannot feed them."

"All right. I'll pay half."

"Sis, you okay? I never knew you to be too generous."

"Hush." ·

Many times she'd cut cardboard liners for her shoes rather than pay the highway robbery of cobblers. And now she would advance money as if it were fool's gold? *You've spent too much time around that spendthrift Rafael Delgado.* Getting down to business, she inquired of the Chihuahueño guide, "How long do you think it will take to reach the Eye of the Canyon?"

Lifting his palms, Luis shrugged. "In a wagon? A week. Maybe ten days."

In Margaret's ear, this had a nice ring. Soon the journey home would begin.

Luis took a forward step. "The great Eagle . . . how is he, señorita? Do you know if he will ever return to his people?"

Margaret had an uneasy feeling about Luis Rivera. She said, "May I make my position glaringly clear? I do *not* want to spend seven minutes, much less seven days in the company of Señor Delgado's adoring fan."

"But, señorita, the great Eagle is my friend. I—"

"If you are going to guide me and my brother, no more mention will be made of the man. Is that agreeable?"

He nodded.

She snapped her fingers to catch a bellboy's attention; he didn't respond. *Welcome to Mexico.* And then she got a look at her guide. The expression on his face? What a pitiable woman not to appreciate the great Eagle.

Luis dug into his shirt pocket and produced a frayed photograph. Olga didn't simper from this one. "My lady, has *El Aguila Magnífico* changed since—?"

"That does it." Margaret swung around. "Your services will *not* be required, Señor Rivera."

230

She ground to a halt, guilt drenching good sense. Ten children. Ten little upturned beaks. Hungry nestlings. "Tex, take him to the market. Buy him some groceries."

Three days. Three days! Three long days Margaret spent looking for a guide. No one accepted the assignment. No one of any worth, to be specific. On the morning of the fourth day, she told her brother that they had to take the situation into their own hands.

"We need to travel light," she said, as Tex finished his breakfast and hers. Margaret considered the soda drinks, the various clothes for all sorts of weather changes, and the paraphernalia to make the trip easier. She had a sizable investment tied up in those trunks. "I'm donating the wagon and its contents to the Cathedral of St. Francis of Assisi. Provided the priest assures me the proceeds will go to needy children."

The priest, ten minutes later, gave all his assurances.

She felt good for her benevolence. And anyway, who was hungry? Well, Tex, of course. But he'd eat old shoe leather, if need be.

Next she found a street vendor and outfitted herself in the shirt and britches of a boy. "For riding astride," she told Tex, who picked out fine Mexican saddles and a pair of excellent mounts, a chestnut mare and sorrel gelding. She took nothing but a single valise filled mostly with elixirs, hooking it to the saddlehorn.

Another couple days passed, though, before they could take their leave, for Margaret fainted again. The doctor summoned by the hotel management gave a strong lecture on taking care of herself. "If you wish to live, señorita, you must protect yourself."

231

Thus, she spent two days in bed.

Becalmed—she'd had lots of experience with be-calmed—Margaret tried to be stoical about the course her life had taken. She couldn't and wouldn't blame Rafe for the loss of her virginity. That, she gave away. And she shouldn't be surprised he'd left her. After all, he'd made her no promises; until lately, he'd never shown an interest in her or made promises, except for *one*. Special didn't describe her.

It wasn't long before she was furious.

He'd taken her money.

Same as stole it.

How dare Rafe Delgado cheat her out of all that cash! If she ever saw him again—and she hoped she wouldn't—she intended to demand redress, either in currency or in his hide. And she expected full value for her dollar.

Seventeen

"Sis, we're lost."

Margaret McLoughlin refused to acknowledge her brother's statement. She refused to acknowledge her fears, though they were many. She sat high in Penny's saddle and kept her outward composure.

Yesterday, she and her brother had set out for Eden Roc. They had gotten hopelessly lost by the afternoon. They spent a cold and miserable night in a gulch, treated to a coyote serenade. Breakfast the next morning was no celebration. The urge to scream and cry and pout and stomp her foot had to be reckoned with.

"Let's follow the sun," she suggested as they saddled up.

"If we can get back to Chihuahua, Sis, let's stay put —"

"Until we hire a guide," she finished for Tex, having heard these words several times since dawn. "Let's follow the sun back to Chihuahua."

Their path, by afternoon, brought them to a recognizable sight. In the distance was the village of Santa Alicia. Margaret stuck her tongue out in a symbolic gesture.

The sun at three o'clock, she caught sight of some-

233

thing. That something was a someone. Actually, two people wearing sombreros. Two men. Riding on tall black stallions and seemingly in a hurry, they were headed east. Soon they would pass Margaret and Tex. And one of those men was Rafe Delgado.

"Sis . . . now, don't get riled. You ain't been outta bed—"

"Enough!" Her teeth ground together before she spat bullets. "I'm going after my money!"

She dug a heel into Penny's flank and took off in the miscreant's direction. It wouldn't have been surprising if he dodged her—he'd ducked out in El Paso, hadn't he?

Her hair flying loose from the hairpins, she stood in the stirrups and leaned over the mare's neck. Margaret McLoughlin might be rich and spoiled and frail—and she'd spent years in a sanatorium as well as the sanitarium of a big city—but she could still ride as if a posse were after her. It took less than five minutes to corral Rafe Delgado and his companion between a bluff and her mount. It was no dumb derringer she aimed at the cigar-smoking, black-attired villain. She steadied five pounds of Colt Percussion Revolver at the point between his eyes.

"¿Ay, Margarita, como esta?"

Como esta. He had a nerve, addressing her with the lazy, easy familiarity of a friend. Her chest heaving, her pulse surging in her ears, she steadied all twelve inches of the revolver's barrel and willed herself not to cough. "If you had a brain in your head, you'd have a fair idea how I am."

"Heyyy, when did a swarm of wasps bite you?" Flipping his sombrero behind his head and letting it dangle down his back on its string-moorings, Rafe rested his wrist on the saddlehorn. His eyes half-lidded, he rolled the cheroot to the other side of his mouth. A grin jacked up the scarred side of his mouth. Insolence could be his middle name. "I thought I told you not to point things at me."

"Unless you come up with five grand, preferably in gold and *right away,* you're going to get worse than pointed at. Starting with"—she adjusted her aim downward, and caught his squirm—"the origin of your dubious fame."

"Settle down, 'Rita. Just calm down. We'll get this worked out. Can't you see I don't carry big stacks of money on me?" He jerked his thumb to the right. "Let me introduce you to my brother. Xzobal Paz. Father Xzobal."

"I don't mean to be rude," she said snidely and kept her eyes on Rafe, "but I didn't catch you for the social graces. Since you are without recompense, I demand you guide me and Tex to Eden Roc."

"Can't. I've got to take care of my brother."

"May God have mercy on the poor soul," she said.

His brother chuckled softly. She dared a glance at Xzobal Paz. Gentle eyes in a tanned face met her wary gaze. His attire was not that of a man of God. Slim and handsome, he wore the straw sombrero, loose shirt, and trousers of a peasant. Leather sandals strapped very dirty feet. He had a placidity that went with his calling. While there was a slight resemblance between the half brothers, they were very different. The holy and the holy hell.

"Good day, my child," Father Xzobal smiled serenely. "My brother has spoken well of you."

"Spoken well of his fattened bank account, you

mean."

"Where is Hector?" The reins in one hand, the ever-present cigar in the other, the majestic black anxious to be gone, Rafe looked past her to the approaching rider, asking Tex, "Didn't you look for him, McLoughlin?"

She did the answering. "Your man is dead."

Rafe took the cigar from his mouth; his lips moved silently. Smoke waved from side to side as he made the ageless sign of his faith. *What a hypocrite.*

The Colt kept growing heavier and heavier; it was almost a relief when Tex took it and suggested a sensible talk between the aggrieved and the offender. "Let's be kind to all this good horseflesh we got, people. They look like they could use some water and a few blades of grass."

Tex and the priest fell to the chore of hostler, once Margaret and Rafe handed over their mounts.

As if negotiating with a mere acquaintance — and never once offering any sort of apology for stranding two foreigners, one an *intimate* acquaintance — Rafe tried to talk Margaret into letting him and Xzobal go on for Texas without any trouble.

Over and again, she replied, "Fine. As long as five thousand dollars is in my hand."

" 'Rita, I'll get your money to you, in San Antonio."

"Not good enough."

On and on they argued, until it degenerated to a shouting match. Once — once! — she'd found arguments attractive. No more. Feeling faint, she inched over to a boulder and sat down, bracing an elbow on a knee. She set to the business of breathing.

Rafe took a step in her direction. "Is the cough coming on? I'd better get — Where's your medicine?"

236

"Don't need . . . any. Leave . . . me alone."

Rafe retreated, went over to his brother.

Thankfully she didn't cough.

Tex rushed up. "Maggie, honey, you've gotta stop this stuff. You're looking foolish, yapping at ole Rafe like he was—well, tell me something. How many times have ya sworn ya didn't wanna see that ole boy again?"

"More times than Rafe Delgado has tumbled women."

Tex clicked his teeth. "You know, Sis, that Xzobal, he's a right nice feller. Drew me a map." He showed it off. "And he done give me names of some people we can call on along the way. There's these folks at Rancho Gato—"

"It would be nice if my own brother were on my side."

The backs of her eyes burned. She shook with the injustice of Rafe. The most hurtful part of all this? His lasting affections and unfulfilled wishes in regard to Olga. The morning after the supposed rape, he'd shown up at the Menger Hotel, begging an audience. *Begging* to see Leonardo's wife! From Margaret the only thing he'd begged was relief. All the while he'd been saving Olga's picture and pining for her return.

Yet Margaret couldn't stay away. Why? *Accept it.* Her present demand for money had excuse written in it. It was a bald cover for what she really wanted. She yearned for Rafe to do an about-face—and beg *her* forgiveness.

No more than a quarter furlong away, he and Xzobal chatted. Rafe stood with an elbow parked on his saddle, one foot crossed over the other, a booted heel propped up. She heard his laugh. The rogue! The wild and annoying rogue! Hurt and mad, she tried to grab her Colt from Tex, unsuccessfully. From between gritted teeth, she demanded, "Give me my gun."

"Maggie, honey, ease up. If you don't settle down,

you're gonna be a laughingstock. What's it gonna take to get through to you? Where's your pride?"

Laughingstock. She had made a joke of herself, demanding attention. Gooseflesh rose on her arm; she dropped her chin. She straightened her spine and shoulders, pulling her head up. "Let's ride for Eden Roc."

Covertly, Rafe watched Margarita swing into the saddle. *Mother of God, I've missed that girl.*

At least a thousand times since leaving her at Pancho Villa's, he'd thought about his *gringa* supreme. At least five hundred times he'd been tempted to forego duty, find her, beg forgiveness, then do anything it took to crawl between her legs.

And those legs, at the moment, were encased in britches. *Her legs are sure long. Long Texas legs. Long Texas legs wrapped around an hombre's behind*—Rafe cleared his throat and shifted his weight to the other foot. An hombre had to hand it to a *mujer* who never said die. No coy, simpering virgin, she. She'd wanted to write a book, then did it. Always willing to help her family, she'd sacrificed her time to go after her mother. Never did she shuffle her feet in indecision. And she could not only ride down a man, she didn't hesitate to lift a whole lot of Colt at him.

"Damn, she's great."

"What did you say, Brother Rafael?"

"Nothing."

Margarita. A woman. A warrior. Half Teutonic, half goddess. One of those Valkyries that he'd read about when he'd been looking up Teutonic gods.

He started toward her, but stopped.

He hadn't played disinterested to ruin it all now.

238

She was a sickly woman, not some wild-haired Brunhild carrying Siegfried off to Valhalla.

Thus, it had taken all Rafe's willpower not to make a fool of himself when he had realized she rode the chestnut. Furthermore, he worried for her. Outside of those long Texas legs, she looked bad, as if she hadn't slept in days. And whatever weight she put on between Juarez and Pancho Villa had vanished. The pain he'd seen radiating from her blue eyes—

You are a real bastard, Delgado. You know you hurt her. You know you owe her, and it's more than any five thousand dollars. You should see her back to Chihuahua, make certain she's put into good hands.

What would he do with Xzobal, while playing a hero straight from fables of old?

Margaret rode up. Dispassion in her eyes and voice, she said, "We'll let you men be on your way."

"Margarita, I'm going to take you to Chihuahua."

Evidently she didn't hear him. Having turned the chestnut mare in the opposite direction, she called over her shoulder, drowning his words, "Oh, by the way, I don't know if you're really interested, but your man Hector Flores stood up to your uncle. Flores died in the dungeon of Chihuahua city."

No!

"And be warned, Rafe. The Federales are looking for your brother. They know he's left Pancho Villa's house in Santa Eulalia." She kicked the mare's flank and took off, her brother in her dusty trail.

¡Merdo!

Rafe let her get away. He knew he could catch up. The most pressing matter, deciding what to do next, had to be addressed, because his plans to take the shortest route to

Texas, by way of Piedras Negras, must be scrapped.

"How many times do I have to tell you, Xzobal? It will work. I promise you it will." Rafe knew what they had to do, and he'd spent the past ten minutes trying to convince his brother. "I don't have a doubt that the Federales are thick to the east of us—Piedras Negras, Juarez, Tampico, and all their surrounds. South to Mexico City, too, I imagine. They won't expect us to head west. We have no choice except escape by the Gulf of California."

"The sea route to Texas is like sailing to the other side of the earth," Xzobal pointed out. "The Straits of Magellan—"

"Let me explain something to you," Rafe said, forcing an even tone. "We have few choices. And I've decided—" Actually, he'd thought, *What would 'Rita do in my boots?* "It's sail from Topolobampo, or we might as well surrender."

"Perhaps that is God's will."

Rafe chose not to listen. "We will pass by the Eye of the Canyon on our way to the Gulf. We'll take sanctuary in Eden Roc. For a while. Until everything dies down."

"The señorita will not help us." Xzobal shook his head. "You have hurt her. Her pride won't let her help us."

"Por Dios, you've gotten as bad as an old woman, with your fretting." A slow smile spread across Rafe's face. "And you're wrong. 'Rita will help us."

"What will you say to the señorita?" Xzobal asked. "I think you have much to make up for, big brother."

"Just leave her to me." While he boasted, the dark of his grim heart beat a tattoo against his breastbone; Rafe admitted, "I lie. I don't have any idea what to say."

"You were never at a loss with the ladies, not as I recall."

"I'd never met a woman quite like 'Rita." His gaze took the path she'd taken. "If Mexico had more of her courage and spunk, our country could become a finer place."

"You love her," Xzobal stated.

"Love her? No, no. Not that. I loved her sister. It's something else I feel for Margarita."

What something else? Rafe turned away to saddle his mount again. *What something else?* This particular Valkyrie, this very delicate one, didn't bore him. He admired and respected her. He was wild for her lovemaking, and he couldn't get his mind off all that was her. *I love her!* I do. *I love the sweet and sour witch, the warrior-woman, the nymph of a hundred dreams!*

"What plans do you have for her, Brother Rafael?"

He might have had a long list of noble answers, the most prominent having to do with her safety and well-being, if not in relation to two pairs of bent knees at the altar. But Rafael Delgado never claimed honor and integrity in affairs of the heart. He wanted to celebrate his newfound state by making love to her until she could scream her pleasure no more, and was forced to cuddle sweetly in the crook of his arm. Then recover to ride at his side as they slew the demon of Santa Alicia.

"Is she of our faith?" Xzobal asked. "You've known her, Brother Rafael. Known her as the Bible describes. And I believe you feel more for her than any woman besides your Olga. Will you marry Margarita McLoughlin?"

"You don't put an apron on Brunhild."

241

Eighteen

You'd think a woman could depend on her very own and only brother. You'd think a brother would have his sister's best interests at heart, especially after he, himself, had advised her to leave a certain scoundrel be. You'd think so. But what did Angus Jones McLoughlin do—not an hour after she'd made her grand exit from the pond algae called Eagle?

"Well, shore, Rafe ole buddy, you and Father Xzobal can ride along with us."

If not for recalling "laughingstock," she would have had a whole lot to say.

The Chihuahueño brothers closed ranks. Riding alongside her mount, Rafe leaned toward her to say, "Hello, *amorcito*. I didn't get the opportunity to tell you . . . I've missed you."

He wants something. "If I had a riding crop, I'd show you exactly how much I've missed you."

He chuckled, picked up the black stallion's reins, and let Margaret guide Penny ahead of him. Ten minutes later, Señor Despicable disgorged with yet another request to Tex. "Amigo, I've got an idea. Let's circle back to Santa Alicia."

Oh, yes, certainly. Let's do ride into the mouth of the beast. Yes, indeed. Margaret didn't know how much longer she could keep quiet, but surely Tex would see a detour as dangerous.

He said, "Ain't that where that uncle of yourn has got that silver mine?"

"It is."

Why don't you just surrender? Why don't you print broadsides? "Here I am, Uncle. Take me. I'm yours. And you'll get the priest thrown in for good measure." She shouldn't worry about Rafe's fate, but for the same reason she hadn't let loose in front of Soledad Paz, Margaret had the wholly unreasonable need to protect him. *He doesn't need cosseting.*

"Tex, you and Xzobal ride on to my old hacienda, El Aguilera Real," he said. "Margarita and I will meet you there. Before sunrise. She and I will go into town now. Together."

What a nerve!

And what did her very own and only brother do? He asked why they would visit the village, got a vague answer, and he rode off with the outlaw priest, leaving his sister to the man who'd done her wrong.

Stranded as she was in alien surroundings, what could she do but follow Rafe? Well, she could have gone after Tex and Xzobal, but she somehow knew Rafe wouldn't allow it. As he led her toward the village, she realized this was all too strange for reason. Obviously he didn't want to take up where they had left off in Villa's bed, because his were not the actions of a man in need of a woman, though he did, again and again, turn in the saddle and ask after her well-being. Or was he checking

243

to see if she planned to shoot him in the back?

Margaret being Margaret, she could keep mum for only so long. Once she succumbed to her nature, she and Penny caught up with Rafe and the black, then rode in front of them. "I prefer — I order — we go on to Eden Roc, forthwith."

"After we have visited my village."

"Think twice. You ask for trouble."

"Not to worry. My *vacáda* — my old one, that is — is too obvious. No one will search there." He settled the sombrero on his head, shoving it low on his brow. "The Arturianos will never think to look for Xzobal at Hacienda del Aguilera Real. Not right away."

"For a man who beggared his way into my company, you're playing fast and loose with my time."

He chuckled and addressed the sky. "Ah, yes. My 'Rita gets back to her old form."

"This is no time for joking. This is the first of November. January approaches. And it is a long, long journey between here and New York City."

"Correct. It is the first of November. *El Dia de los Muertos.*" Reins held high, he halted the black. "I will pay my respects to my father and sister . . . and to my cousin . . . on this Day of the Dead."

Well, what was one more day of delay?

The hardest part would be keeping a stiff upper lip. Laughingstock, she would not be. Somehow. Someway. In some form or fashion, her dignity wouldn't suffer. This in mind, she followed him to Santa Alicia.

She had expected people — unlike Rafe, who'd made no comment — to stare and point at seeing a woman dressed in the garb of a male. No one looked askance at her. But they couldn't believe their eyes, all right. The

244

Eagle had returned.

As Rafe rode through these busy streets, the shocked citizenry at first stared as if they had seen the dead. A hush fell. Then a roar of approval intermingled with wails of tears. Old women with black scarves wound around their heads offered him rosaries. Young women extended fake flowers. A small girl with a solemn look on her dirty face tendered a watermelon carved into the image of a goblin.

Rafe leaned to accept the gift. His hand patted the girlish cheek. *"Muchas gracias, muchacha."*

She dropped her lashes in acknowledgment, then backed away, still solemn as a judge.

Margaret rolled her eyes and turned her sharp eye to the surroundings, to look for uniformed men. She saw none. She drew a few more conclusions. This was a lovely little village, built into the foothill. The streets were cobbled, the whitewashed houses compact and well kept. The people showed more energy than she'd witnessed to this point in Mexico; they all moved with purpose. That purpose, she discovered, was fiesta, and not only in the plaza area.

Though converted to Catholicism in the previous centuries, these Indians along with those of mixed blood, the mestizos, turned All Saints Day into a celebration of their primitive roots. Music played. Libations flowed freely. The bakery buzzed with activity, patrons leaving with loaf after loaf of *pan de muerto,* death bread.

Margaret saw nary a uniformed official.

She led the mare abreast of the black. "Rafe, if you're so worried about your uncle, you shouldn't make your presence imminently well known."

"Arturo won't come to the village. He may be the

patrón, but he doesn't have the people's loyalty. They are my people. No one would call him into town."

Was this bravery? Or bald foolishness?

"Magnificent Eagle—is that you?" came a youthful male voice as they rode past the church. Hitching up the rope that served as belt for his pajamalike trousers, the boy of about fifteen asked in broken Spanish, "Where have you been? We of Santa Alicia have missed you."

Rafe answered in some strange dialect, Indian no doubt. He alit the saddle, handed the reins to the boy, then moved to help Margaret to the ground. "Carlos will watch our mounts. It's just a short walk to the cemetery. And it's better to go on foot." His eyes darkened. Tucking the watermelon under his arm, he took her elbows. "Shall I carry you, *amorcito?*"

"Absolutely not."

It became apparent why he wanted to be afoot. It made handling his tributes easier. Soon Margaret's arms brimmed with straw flowers, her fingers with tiny tinsel-eyed skeletons called *calacas.* Marigolds obscured the watermelon in Rafe's hands. He explained, "The strong odor of the flowers is the smell of death."

"Strange, if you ask me. I smelled death in the sanatorium, and I promise you, it doesn't smell like marigolds." Moving with her best effort at no-nonsense strides, she marched on. But stopped. "Rafe, it's getting dark. I think we should meet up with your brother and mine."

"Later. We haven't been to the cemetery."

"I am *not* going to some graveyard at dusk."

"Why? Do you think the ghouls will get you?" he teased.

"I think I have the shivers."

"Don't. In Mexico this is a day to rejoice. And to

grieve," he added with a shrug. "There is no need to be frightened of the cemetery." He laughed gently. "We might as well get used to them. If our bones aren't left to the buzzards, we will both end up in one someday."

"Believe me, I've given it some thought." She lifted the flowers to bat at a fly. "Dying doesn't scare me."

"What does scare you?"

Dying without experiencing life to its fullest. And here she was, already weary from a short walk. "I'd rather not get into a philosophical conversation with you."

She glanced over her shoulder. Behind them was a procession of silently weeping elderly women, carrying effigies of Christ and the Madonna as well as caldrons of chicken molé. "The traditional food to be eaten," Rafe further explained. "The leftovers are left for the spirits to enjoy in the wee hours of tomorrow. All Souls Day."

"That's rather Egyptian, you know." Caught up in the traditions, she allowed her guard to give. "They packed food into the pyramids for their dead, so that the deceased would be provisioned for the journey into the afterlife."

"You smiled. You don't do that often enough, *cariño.*"

They turned a corner. A cobbled path, somewhat crooked, led up the hill to the cemetery. The sight of it took Margaret's breath away, and that had nothing to do with her weak lungs. An orange glow lit the twilight with a surreal quality; it was the glow of a thousand candles sitting atop the numerous headstones.

Masks with ghoulish visages were much in evidence. Whole families picnicked around the remains of their loved ones. The scent of incense wound around and through, cloying and too sweet. *Calacas* danced from nimble fingers. And bottle after bottle of the milky-colored pulque tipped to eager lips. She couldn't help becoming enthused. It felt as if she'd been transplanted to some other place in time, to an era having nothing to do with the modern Gay Nineties.

The curious customs of this country—there were many. Margaret didn't find them loathsome. They intrigued her as she hadn't been fascinated since deciding to research the Great Discovery and its implications to Spain.

Rafe stopped at a well-tended grave. "María Carmen." Laying the watermelon and a bouquet of marigolds on the clipped grass, he leaned to kiss his sister's grave stone. He straightened, his lips moving in prayer as he crossed himself.

After shifting to a more conspicuous part of the cemetery, he opened the gate to a wrought iron fence, waited for Margaret's entrance as well as that of an old woman who left a covered basket and a pot of chicken molé, then gave likewise respect to the crypt of the late Venustiano Delgado, who had died in his thirty-ninth year. Rafe's present age.

"You were very young when you lost your father," she said. "How awful it must have been, growing up without him."

"I had plenty of attention."

"From whom?"

He bent to pluck a weed from the grave. "From Tío Arturo."

Rafe's expression told a sad story. But how could she not feel sorry for the youth who had lost his father, for the adult who became estranged from the uncle he cared more for than he would admit?

"Let's move on." Rafe passed the marble statue of a

248

crying angel separating two crypts. He knelt in prayer.

Margaret silently translated the Spanish inscription. "Hernán Venustiano Delgado Ybarra. August 28, 1864—December 14, 1889. Beloved son. Murdered by the bandit who was his cousin."

Margaret's eyes flew to Rafe. And his gaze was on her already. "He died as he would have wished, in battle. We are a people who've long believed violent death an honorable one."

Tongue-tied for the right thing to say, she informed, "I read that goes back to the games of the Mayas, where the victor had the honor of being sacrificed."

"Could be, *querida*. Could be." Rafe stared at the purple-streaked clouds of twilight. When he continued, his voice bore a ragged edge. "I lied to you about Hernándo, 'Rita. I kill him. It was . . . my bullet."

"Oh, Rafe," was all she could say. She went to him and put a comforting hand on his shoulder, and he covered her fingers with his palm. The look they exchanged sent apologies as well as comfort to the other. She knew pain; he knew suffering. The business of living had been difficult for both of them.

" 'Rita, *querida,* I'm sorry for all that has happened. I wish it could have been different. Mostly I'm sorry for disappointing you. You are all the wonderful entities of this earth. I'd like to have your respect," he said. "I know I'll have to earn it."

"But—"

"That you give me the chance is all I ask." He broke the maudlin mood by levering to his feet and reaching for the basket. "Our dinner grows cold."

Worried anew about the outside world, she replied, "I won't dine in a cemetery. Besides, don't you think your uncle might show up to eat molé and say a rosary over his son?"

"I've been told Tío Arturo isn't in the vicinity."

"You could have told me."

"I'm telling you now. He sent a telegram to Hacienda Delgado. He's on his way to the city of Mexico." Rafe spooned chicken onto a plate. "Even if he were in the vicinity, he wouldn't celebrate *El Dia de los Muertos*. This is an Indian tradition. My uncle is not Indian."

"Are you?"

"Some," he replied proudly. "The mother of my mother is half Aztec."

"I met your mother. She came to see me in Chihuahua."

"And what did Madrecita have to say?"

"Not much." Margaret didn't have the strength to fight over Olga or that cryptic-message business. And she didn't want to. Accepting the offered plate, she took a bite of the delicious chicken with unsweetened-chocolate sauce. "I suppose being part native is the reason you've such zeal for revolution."

"Indian blood isn't necessary." Rafe lit a candle and situated it on Hernán's headstone. "You just need to be a Mexican. Tomorrow . . . There's a place I would like to show you." He filled a plate for himself. "It's on our way to the Eye of the Canyon and your mother. I would like you to see the people my cousin died for."

Observing the look in his eye, she shivered. Many times she'd seen this sort of look in another man's eyes. Those of her father. No two men were ever more different from each other than the has-been matador and Secretary of State McLoughlin, but she saw a frightening similarity.

250

Politics fueled both men. If there was anything Margaret would fault her father on, it was his fervor in the arena of state. The family had many times suffered for his devotion. He was even too busy to reclaim his wife.

Maybe you're wrong about Rafe. Don't forget he spent eight years doing nothing but raising a few bulls and romancing quite a few ladies.

"Will you go with me to my uncle's silver mine?" he asked.

How could she tell him the truth? To go calling sounded as strenuous as a trek across the sands of the Sahara. Already she felt weak as a kitten. "We shouldn't tarry hereabouts." She related his mother's story about the escaped slaves taking refuge with the Tarahumara Indians, and how the Federales had gone after them. "I'm worried for my mother's safety."

"You needn't be. The trouble is over." He squinted at the sky, then lowered his distressed gaze at Margaret. "The runaways were caught last Friday. Caught and executed."

Dismay dropped through her. "Those poor men."

Rafe made no comment, and she couldn't keep mum. "I'm wondering—I'm thinking . . . Eden Roc isn't a good idea for you. And if you're planning to visit your uncle's silver mine, you should change your plans. Shouldn't you and your brother try to get on to Texas?"

"No, 'Rita." He put his plate down. "I've had days to think on this. And visiting Hernándo's grave has helped me see what I must do. I am never going back to Texas. I am returned. Forever. I will see Xzobal to the sea at Topolobampo, but I won't leave with him. Mexico is my destiny."

"You can't mean that."

251

"Rest assured, I mean it."

She retreated, until the back of her knees touched the fence. "Rafe, you court disaster. It will find you."

"Yes, I believe it will."

"You live under a death wish."

"If it takes my life, so be it. I don't know the full price, and I don't know if there's any turning back, but I will rid Mexico of Arturo Delgado. This is something I must do."

Either crazed or courageous, he had guts of iron. She thought of another obsessed man who'd plunged into the unknown without any assurances that there was a turning back. Columbus. Disgusted yet just a little bit envious of Rafe's courage, she said, "I would do anything for half a chance at grandchildren and the rocking chair. While you tempt death *sans souci*."

"What does it mean, *sans souci?*"

"Without a care."

"Well, I told you. Violent death is an honorable one."

Margaret didn't know whether to laugh or to cry or to try to argue some sense into Rafe. What did one do with a man who held his life in so little value that he would gamble it away?

Nineteen

Having left the Federal District thirty-six hours before, at midnight on Halloween, the train steamed north to the city of Chihuahua. On orders it wasted no time, careening around bends in the Sierra Madres, taking curves which would have arrested the breath of most mortals. Arturo Delgado, incensed and obsessed, was like an old salt of the sea in a hurricane. He rode the furies. Why? He would not rest until his fingers choked the life from Natalie Nash. She'd sent him chasing off to the capital city. Chasing air. The devious bitch.

Instinctively he knew where to find her. The state of Chihuahua. Most likely at Eden Roc. She always returned to Eden Roc. And the closer Arturo got to her, the more restless he became.

She's probably spreading her legs for Rafito at this minute. Whether or not they were tumbling each other, it went without saying that Arturo Delgado had murder in mind for her *and* for his treacherous nephew. "He will die." Arturo's fingers squeezed, his nails digging into his palms. "I'm going to kill Natalie. They will pay. Each in his own way has double-crossed me."

This was no idle threat. A fierce ripping—the sound of red velvet as he tore it from the window of his private railroad car—fought with the steady clip of steel wheels. The drapery gap exposed fierce rays of sunlight; they pierced the irises of Mexico's richest and most powerful man—*El Grandero Rico.*

Arturo, aggravated at the pain poking at the back of his eyeballs, slapped at the light, as if he had control over sunshine, then stomped over to the sideboard and downed two fingers of 1878-distilled Scotch whiskey.

"Enjoying your breakfast?"

Arturo swung around and forced himself not to scowl.

His arm resting across the back of a divan, the Count of Granada sat with a knee crossed over the other, scowling. "Why don't we get back to our discussion?"

Conversing on the subject of Spanish spies—tiresome. Tiresome engulfed the count, period. If not for Arturo's determination to take a titled bride, a daughter of Spain—oh, what he'd give for one of the *infantas,* were the princesses out of leading strings!—he would have tossed Leonardo de Hapsburg y Borbón from the train and onto the steep grade. And he would laugh upon seeing the body topple over and over, until it crashed and gashed on the rocks. Such would not be wise.

Being *El Grandero Rico* of Mexico; owning factories aplenty and millions of square miles of land along with a dozen mines that catacombed the mountains of northern Mexico; having pure Spanish bloodlines in the Americas reaching back to the Conquest. These meant little to royalty. Unless an upstart used his head.

Arturo eyed the count, who sipped tea and waited expectantly for an answer. Hapsburg had all the right connections in Madrid, as well as purple blood in his veins—he counted most of the crowned heads of Europe as cousin—so Arturo had been pleased to find him in Porfirio Díaz's company, and even more anxious to offer transport back to Chihuahua. Anything to ingratiate himself, even abiding the snide bastard.

Rubbing shoulders with this living proof that cousins shouldn't marry had helped Arturo keep his mind off how close he had come to giving in and taking that baggage Natalie for his bride. *She's not a good idea.*

A well-designed marriage to a well-bred bride—and subsequent children—would smother the demons of gossip. Always, they whispered thorn-sharp truths, that for Hernán, he'd stolen the domain from his father's rightful heir, and had done nothing to pay homage to that vast inheritance, even after his son became ashes and dust. A titled bride and progeny—and Rafito in his grave!—would give absolute legitimacy to Arturo's claim.

Though his patience verged on cracking, he made a magnanimous gesture. "Do go on, Lord Hapsburg."

"As I told you before we left the Presidential Palace, I received a distressing telegram. Felipe Apodaca has been arrested in Chihuahua city. He must be assassinated before he talks."

"That will be taken care of."

"Thank you. And . . . need I explain? It is but a matter of time before my country goes to war with the *norteamericanos*. We must keep abreast of the U.S. Army's movements. Furthermore, our operatives need reinforcements, if not replacements, especially in Nuevo Laredo and Chihuahua city. Will you permit me a free hand?"

"Yes. Yes, of course." The train took a sharp curve to

the left. Grabbing a golden handrail, Arturo added, "Anything for you and Her Royal Highness."

"Thank you." Lord Hapsburg lit a cigarette, inhaled. "You'll not regret aiding María Cristina, Alfonso XIII, and all of great and grand Spain."

"When will you return there? I wish to travel in your entourage."

"Actually, my countess and I have plans for Mexico." The count paused, as if to wait for a heralding trumpet. His answer being train wheels rumbling up the track, he picked up a silver ashtray (molded from Santa Alicia silver, .925 purity). He ground out his cigarette. "I've been recommended as ambassador to Mexico. Your president has kindly accepted my credentials."

"Congratulations."

Arturo didn't care for this turn. That mestizo Porfirio Díaz—who did he think he was, keeping such an appointment secret? And whose mad idea was it to flaunt a Hapsburg? The peasantry hadn't forgotten the last Mexican emperor, Maximilian of the same family.

Forget politics. Think of yourself. Without the count's help, it might take years to get a foot in the door of the Palacio Real. The sands of time were sifting away. No one had proof of how long Eden Roc's rejuvenating properties lasted. Arturo might not have years to waste!

Refilling his glass, he said, "I will go to Madrid on my own. I shall expect your letter of introduction forthwith."

"That seems so . . . tawdry. Cheap. Common, if you will. Without a proper introduction, María Cristina would never grant the sort of audience you solicit." The count reached for his teacup, sipped. "At any rate, you are in no position to travel to the Continent. Not with

256

disenchanted rabble disrupting the workings of your mines. How distasteful, having your slaves executed. And there is the no-small-business of avenging your son's murder."

Arturo's anger rose. Currying favor grew four times as tedious as Hapsburg himself. *I hate this condescending bastard.* The most powerful man in Mexico drew the line on any more fawning. He'd show this Spaniard some New World manners.

With a thumb and forefinger on the handle, he extracted Hapsburg's teacup to hold it aloft. Arturo hurled the cup across the car. As it crashed in many pieces against the mahogany paneling, the Count of Granada jumped as if struck.

Recovering, he looked down his too-thin nose. "You provincials can be so crude."

"Crude?" Arturo pointed downward. "The teacup— did you notice? But how would you have known? The gold rim was 24-karat, from the Delgado mines of Sonora. The porcelain was a Limoges special firing, part of a service for one hundred and twenty-eight. It commemorated my grandparents' marriage. The Delgados of the north with the Calderóns of the south. Did you know the King of Spain crossed the Ocean Sea to attend the wedding?"

"You were then New Spain. We owe Mexico nothing."

"Not even repayment for favors?" Arturo kicked a stray piece of porcelain. "Let's talk about how you think I ought to conduct my business, *expert* at commerce that nobility tends to be." He bent low to Hapsburg's face. "Don't second-guess me, you snot-dripping son-of-a-Moor. And don't address me as if I were a peon too stupid to find his *pene* to piss."

257

"I — I, uh, you shouldn't be so quick to take offense."

"I'm not offended. You can't offend a crude provincial. I've been called worse than gauche." An evil smile melted across Arturo's face; he loved being in his element. "Señor Ambassador, you are not the only man with informants in Mexico. *My* spies in Eden Roc tell me your lady has been fractious of late. I've been told she's locked you out of your *casita*. After you forced yourself on her. Shame on you. You know you love her. You will do anything to return to her good graces."

"I don't see how —"

"It is whispered you spend much time at the whorehouse of Areponapuchi."

Hapsburg blanched.

"Interesting place, isn't it? So near Eden Roc, yet altogether different. The Tarahumaras named the village, and some respectable people live there, but its infamous den of iniquity fits the name Areponapuchi." Arturo's upper lip quivered as he added, "Snake pit."

His manhood stirred as he recalled debauchery and lewd rituals. He held a crystal decanter up to the light gaping through the window, before pouring a stiff Scotch for the not-so-arrogant-now Hapsburg, then sat down in the rich embrace of cordovan leather. "The lovely Queen Regent . . . I think she'd be shocked to know such a place exists. If she were to learn you had sampled the bill of fare, I should imagine she'd be outraged."

Near to choking, the count tugged at his collar stays.

"The lovely Lady of Granada knows nothing of Areponapuchi, I'm sure." Again, Arturo flashed a smile. "You, I assume, wish to keep it that way. With both ladies."

Lord Hapsburg lurched to his feet and started toward his own private car. "I'll see to your introduction."

"In person? And soon?"

"Yes."

"I'm pleased we're in agreement."

That settled, Arturo got back to his plans for revenge against Rafito and Natalie. First, though, the avenger had to take care of the business of the Santa Alicia.

"So many times I have wondered if I would ever see my property again." By morning light, after an evening sitting vigil at the cemetery of Santa Alicia (Margarita had retreated to the church to sleep within an hour of sundown), Rafe and his delicate Valkyrie halted their mounts at the entrance to Hacienda del Aguilera Real. "So many times I've wondered how my ranch has fared."

"How does it measure up?" she inquired.

"The soul is no more."

"What a pity. It must have been a grand estate," Margarita commented, "once upon a time."

Rafe, gulping down a lump in his throat, took the reins he'd wound around the saddlehorn, kneed the black stallion he called Diablo, and rode through the rock archway leading into his former *vacáda*. The great herds of breeding cattle and fine horses had been taken away, or perhaps slaughtered. He didn't even see the odd goat or two. Outbuildings had fallen to disrepair, if not in on themselves. And when he and Margarita approached the house of twenty-five rooms and two stories, where he had lived in a more innocent and idealistic time, he saw more decay.

Many of the weathered shutters were missing, some

hung from rusted hinges. The hacienda house had been constructed of adobe with a red-tile roof, in the Colonial style with all rooms opening onto the patio and its fountain. The white facade had faded to the most dismal shade of depressing gray; the tiles were the hue of burnt sienna. Rafe said, "The spoils of the corrida built this house. Only fifteen years ago. It appears more like fifty."

"It's a pity." The words were trite, but her tone held sincerity.

"I wonder what my hacienda will be like fifteen years from now. In 1912." On a flash of insight, Rafe saw the bandit Pancho Villa as mature and venerated, and an upstart named Madero ascending the grand staircase of the Presidential Palace. He also saw Margarita, a streak of silver hair flaring from her temple. He smiled. He liked what he saw.

"Rafe? Rafe, are you all right? *Rafe*. Snap out of it."

He shook his head, smiled.

Margarita leaned to pat the neck of the chestnut she'd dubbed Penny. "Why won't you answer me? It's a simple enough question. Where does your uncle live?"

"On many haciendas. And there's the *palacio* in the Federal District. But the true Delgado family seat isn't far from here."

"How far from here?"

"It's between Santa Alicia and *El Ojo de la Barranca*."

"The idea of passing his property makes my skin crawl." She shuddered. "Explain something. This 'his' property. Why did you, a Delgado, have to buy your own land? You weren't disowned until later, I thought. I assumed you fell heir to Delgado property. I gathered Arturo was a younger son, and—"

"Arturo took it all for himself."

"How can that be? Surely there are laws of inheritance."

"My grandfather's will stipulated that no Delgado of mixed blood could inherit. That left Arturo and Hernán." Rafe directed Diablo alongside Penny. "It was just as well. I didn't want the responsibilities that went along with the fortune. Not until I realized, too late, that Delgado resources could have been used for the common good."

"I don't doubt your benevolent heart, but I wonder if you speak from both sides of your mouth. You could've given money to the poor instead of buying *this* hacienda."

He threw back his head and laughed, both loving and hating her forthrightness. "There is no way to fool you, is there, my 'Rita?"

"There is no way to fool me."

Rafe swung a leg over the saddle, wrapped the reins around a hitching post, then helped her to the ground. Of course, his hands lingered on her ribs. Of course, his fingers trailed up the sides of her breasts. Naturally he brushed her forehead with his lips. He needed and wanted another round of lovemaking with his warrior-woman. And he was eager to express his undying devotion.

But she took a wary step backwards. "Tell me, Rafe, why did you buy this ranch?"

The distance she put between them was measured in more than a couple of feet. *She's still like water for chocolate.* He couldn't blame her for being mad about his running out on her, but he would do his best to make up for it.

At last he answered her question. "I bought the property for a place to breed bulls for the ring. And for the quiet, to develop plans for the revolution that is yet to be."

"My father said your hacienda was a nest of activity, with so many toadies surrounding you, it took days of waiting to gain a ten-minute audience."

"Is he usually so talkative? What else did he say?"

"That you'd assembled an army of misfits. That the little dogs swarmed by the hundreds. That"—her expressive eyes clouded—"beautiful women waited with bated breaths to see to your every whim."

His hands going to his hips, Rafe laughed heartily. "All true, *mi soldadita*. All true."

"Why do you call me little soldier?"

"Would you rather I call you witch?"

"Little warrior will be fine."

She turned as if to look for their brothers, and lifted the hair from her nape, shaking it. Somewhere along the way, she'd lost hair paraphernalia, leaving her unable to fashion a severe chignon. *Thank you, sweet lady of Guadalupe*. Margarita's hair flowed long, dark, and free down her back. It softened her appearance, made her seem younger to Rafe. Younger or older didn't matter. To him, she was the most beautiful woman in the world.

"Yip! Yip, yip, ruff!"

Rafe turned to the racket. Something black and minuscule darted from behind a clay flowerpot. "By the ghost of Hidalgo, what have we here?" A sentimental tug in his chest, he stooped to pick up a palmful of half-eared, eager-for-kisses Chihuahua stud. "Look at you. Aren't you a mess? Where did you get these gray hairs on this muzzle? Only *old* hombres have gray hair. Hello, Caballo."

Margarita clapped her hands with the enthusiasm of a girl. "My goodness! What a day! An old friend to welcome you home." She scratched behind Caballo's mangled ear. "But how do you know this is *Horse?*"

"I recognize the ear." Rafe accepted a slobbering kiss to the wrist. "He's Frita's son." Holding Caballo up for inspection, Rafe turned him one way and then another, receiving yips and ruffs and blatant bids for cuddling. "If man were endowed in proportion to these *perritos,* the ladies of this earth would know heaven on earth."

"I don't know about that. Your endowment is — Well, goodness."

"Yes, goodness." The erotic energy that had pulsated between them in the past went into full power. Rafe absorbed her blue eyes, the lustrous hair, the tiny bead of moisture illuminating her lower lip, and his heart skipped a beat for the want of his willowy Margarita.

To break the spell, she lifted a finger to the scar at his mouth. "How did this come about? From a bull?"

"No *toro* got the better of me, ever. Tío Arturo did it."

"Why?" she asked, horror in her expression.

He didn't want to talk about it. He wanted to make love. Well, he'd grant her *some* time. "There were rumors I should have inherited from my grandfather. I told you about the stipulation in his will. Everyone said Constanzo Delgado wouldn't discriminate against me. I felt the same. My *abuelo* and I were close. Anyway, I called Tío on the document. I think he produced a forgery for the courts."

"He is treacherous," she commented.

"Yes, he is greedy. But you asked about this mark. My uncle tried to break my neck with a whip. He succeeded in splitting my mouth."

Rafe watched as gooseflesh trailed up and down her arms.

"Enough morose talk," he demanded. "Let's discuss you and me. Let's get comfortable, shall we?"

"Um, isn't it delightful, Caballo recognizing you?" She talked fast. "Pets are such precious joys. And shame on me. I haven't thought of my Deniece or Denephew in days."

Rafe didn't like to think of his warrior-woman going back to New York. Not at all. What was Attila without the Hun? "What have you thought about?" He got closer to her, close enough to remind her of a few pertinent things. "Shame, shame, Mamacita, if you haven't recalled the two of us together, as man and woman were meant to be joined."

"There's nothing wrong with my memory."

"Or mine." And there was nothing wrong with his *pene*. It was eager to frolic.

Margaret wasn't so eager for the frolic. She inched away. "I can't forget you abandoned me."

He lessened the gap between them. "Will you forgive me?"

"I—I don't know. There are other things . . ."

And if they got into them, there would be no loving tonight, Rafe figured. He offered the black mite. "Would you like to hold Caballo? He's shaking from nerves and needs warmth. Unfasten your shirt a button or two, Mamacita. Make him a nest."

"I will not. That is . . . That's warped."

"You overreact. A little dog seeks comfort. And it's a nice warm place at your breast." Rafe fastened an interested leer on the place of mention. "I remember quite well the joy of it."

264

She blushed but reached for Caballo anyway. Tucking him into the semblance of a cleft of breasts, she cupped her hand under Caballo's chambray-covered hind legs. "Don't get any ideas from this, Rafe."

"Oh, I won't," he lied and envied the dog. A mouthful of . . . Nuzzling his nose against . . . Pressing hard flesh to soft and womanly places . . . Clearing his throat, he motioned toward the house and enticed her into his web. "Shall we find our brothers?"

"We do need to hit the trail—Oh, Rafe, what will you do with Caballo?" She cuddled the dog tighter. "You can't leave him here."

"He's survived alone for eight years."

"But he's *shaking.*"

"All right. We'll take him along. But only to find him a good home."

"I'll take him home with me. He'll love New York."

Rafe doubted that. No Mexican hombre would fit into that city, he knew. He'd been there. He didn't see New York in the future for either Caballo or Margarita. "We'll see."

She walked toward the front door, but stopped by a yucca plant and looked down into the snake hole beside it. She leveled a mischievous gaze at him. "Hmm, this reminds me . . ."

"¿Como?"

"It's been said, back in the old days, that you caught rattlesnakes for pagan enjoyment."

"Ridiculous." Which it was. But Rafe got uncomfortable. Areponapuchi, he would not explain. "A lot of things have been said about me. The rattlesnake story is a, uh, a fable."

"Did you know Charity began to solve the mystery of

265

your identity through the rattlesnake story?" A pause. "I've heard other things about you. Charity's friend, María Sara, she—Well, she said you took her to bed."

"Surely you aren't wanting details."

"She said there was another man in bed with the two of you."

"I never touched him, and he never touched me. We were there for the little lady's pleasure."

Margarita exhaled a puff of relieved breath. "Thank heavens. Well, anyway, all that seems so very, very long ago."

He wanted no reminders of those long-ago days. Today was for the present, for him and the woman he loved. As of yet, he hadn't mentioned his feelings. Tonight would be the night. Here at his old home. In his bed, if it still stood in his bedroom. If not, he would improvise. He had plans for several soft places . . . "If the wine cellar hasn't been ransacked, shall we share a bottle of wine?"

"I'd rather get going as soon as possible. And you did want me to see the Santa Alicia mine."

"Sometimes you are too practical, my darling." Rafe led her into the grand *sala*. A closed-up, dusty smell hit him. The furniture, most of it, had been removed. A few pieces remained with canvas drapes over them.

"Tex," she called out as they stepped onto the patio. "Tex! Father Xzobal! Where are you?"

"Shhh." Rafe put his fingertips to her lips. "My brother left a coded message. They won't return until nightfall."

"You sons of Soledad Paz are well-versed in coded messages"—her mouth got pinched—"I'm beginning to understand."

266

Rafe didn't care for the edge that had wormed into her tone, nor for the distrust moving into her eyes. He started to quiz her on the source, but decided against it. This was not the afternoon to ask for trouble. He offered an elbow, saying, "May I have the honor of escorting you on a tour?"

Straightaway, Rafe led her to his old bedroom. To his delight and relief, the bed was there. So were the accoutrements of a matador; faded and dull they had become, though he could have cared less for these remembrances. The corrida might have been in another lifetime.

Margarita walked over to a cape that hung from a peg. Running her fingers along the material, she said, "I would have liked to have seen you, back then."

"No, Margarita. We weren't ready for each other, back then." He closed the door and rested his shoulders against it. "But now . . . come to me. I'm weary and you are, too. Let's take a short siesta, hmm?"

"I — I don't think so." She started easing toward the other door, the one that led to the patio. "Not interested."

"Oh, 'Rita, my queen, my warrior-woman, my darling love, I think you protest too much." He went to her, drawing her and Caballo close. "Let's make love."

Passion spooled in her eyes, urging her to yield, cautioning her not to do it. The expert took over. Rafe took Caballo from the nest-shirt; his hand dipped to the soft breasts. A nipple hardened when he grazed it with his finger. Rafe had a hardening of his own.

"I want you, my love." He blew a warm stream of breath into her ear, receiving the shiver he sought. The scents of the church — beeswax candles and incense — clung to her, as well as bits of Caballo and

Penny. But the womanly scent that was Margarita eclipsed the others. "It seems as if a year has passed since we made love."

He knew she was weakening. He saw it in her face.

Yet she gave him her profile, and retreated anew. "You insult me, bringing me to this room where you have had your wicked way with scores of women."

"*You* insult, presuming the worst. Many women have visited El Aguilera Real. Many women have lived on the premises. But you're wrong about scores of women. I have had my wicked way with hundreds at this hacienda, not scores. But never—ever—in this bedroom. This I swear is true. On the graves of my sister and father and cousin, I swear it."

Her eyes, winsome and wide, looked into his expectant ones. An imp's grin tickling her lips, she moistened those lips with the tip of her tongue. "Why didn't you?"

"A bedchamber is the most private of places in a residence. I have bathed here, and dressed here. It is here that I have dreamed and have experienced nightmares. This is where I retreated to think, and to strum my guitar and dream of the special woman who would change me for the better. To be in this room is to see a window into my soul."

Margarita had been scratching Caballo's brisket. Her fingers stilled. Those eyes, so blue, like the sky outside, glistened when he said, "I want you in my soul."

As if embarrassed, she perused the room before turning her attention to the capes, the caps, the silk stockings. The jeweled bolero jackets. The empty bandoliers, the vests and britches, and a leather floor-length duster. Her scrutiny moved to the shelves of dust-coated black slippers and the boots of a vaquero. Matching shelves held swords and darts, a bullwhip. Guitars. Many guitars.

Caballo whimpered, then scratched her foot.

"Rafe, I can't"—she blushed—"I won't make love with a dog in the room."

He put the dog out.

Twenty

"Will you have your wicked way with me, 'Rita? Right here, right now . . . in my bed."

She laughed at his audacity and cockiness. Many names described *El Aguila Magnífico,* few of them beautiful. Liar, lover, betrayer. Matador, revolutionist, deserter. Murderer. And he loved her sister. She ought to run screaming. Ought to. *"My* wicked way? Isn't it the other way around?"

"Don't split hairs, *soldadita.*"

In the memoir-festooned room where he had gone about the business of living in years past, Rafe pulled her even closer. He smelled of grass, horse, fiesta marigolds. And she caught a more seductive aroma, the slightly salty, slightly sweaty scent particular to Rafe. It might be crazy, foolish, and stupid, but Margaret wanted her wicked way with him, wanted it with every fiber of her being. She didn't understand this complicated man and didn't know if she needed to, but she wanted his body.

Just don't trust him. Don't trust anything he says or does. Even his own mother knows he's a glib-tongued charmer.

He took Margaret's hand, leading her to the massive bed. The style reminiscent of an earlier time, it might have appealed to *El Cid* or to bygone kings of Castile or Aragon. The bed was all man, all mighty man. He removed the dust cover, and red—lots of red decadence—flashed before her eyes, for a satin bedcover gleamed in the waning light of afternoon.

Red satin.

He brought her hands behind his waist, his lips to her eyebrow, and the gentle rush of his breath caressed her right eye, as he said, "Will a simple siesta be enough for you?"

She shivered, enthralled. Bending back from the waist, she watched his reaction as she replied, "Rest is my last desire. You are my first."

A smile—wide, bright, and enthusiastic—split his face, and his whoop of delight might have reached the Sea of Cortez and the Gulf of Mexico. Never had she seen such unabashed joy in his expression. Never had she considered his blatant good looks "handsome," but at this moment, he was the handsomest man ever to draw a breath.

"Are we going to stand here all afternoon?" she joked.

"*Generalissima.* That's what you are, the general, giving orders to her foot soldier." He sat down, his muscular legs spread wide at the edge of the bed. He pulled her into the *V.* His silver gaze lifting slowly, he cupped his hands over the fullness of her hips. "Warrior-woman, how will you have us start our lovemaking?"

"The veteran asks the recruit for strategy?" Her soft

271

scold went along with touching the tip of his nose; he played like he'd bite her finger. "Should I remind you of our train trip? You ordered me to respect your authority. And now you back down. I'm disappointed."

"You are, are you?" Caressing her behind, he countered, "Then listen closely to the sergeant of the corps. If you do not listen, you'll be punished severely. With a thousand kisses."

"Put that way . . ." She laughed. "Maybe I should desert."

"Oh, no, you will not. A good leader stays put." Rafe's hands moved to pick and pluck at her clothes. "Look at you. You are worse than our friend Caballo. He's let gray into his muzzle. And you wear too many clothes."

Brassy as a monkey, she asked, "What would happen if you took them off me?"

"Let's find out." He peeled her blouse away, his fingers lingering on her shoulders. *"Dios.* Your skin is so smooth and soft. I love the feel of you."

The feeling being mutual—except for smooth and soft being solid and fit in his case—she lifted her hand to his mouth and traced the rich outline of his lips, stopping at the scar.

"Señorita Generalissima, do you like fraternizing with an underling?" he teased.

"I could get used to it."

They kissed, and she couldn't decide who initiated it, but it was hot and challenging and as luscious as a big piece of chocolate fudge. What was it about a simple tongue, long and lean and flexible, that made it so handy for more than communicating or for passing food and drink to the gullet? The Creator had done a marvelous job, especially with Rafe's, for he was a master at South of the Border versions of French kisses. By the time this particular kiss ended, her knees were spongy and her insides heavy with desire.

He moved a finger to the top button of her britches. "When you step out of these, I want you to lay your arms on my shoulders, where my mouth can reach you . . . right here."

If not for the hold she took of his athletic shoulders, she would have collapsed from the luscious tricks his mouth played on her breasts.

His silver eyes conveying an age-old message, he wrapped his fingers around hers. "Would you, sweet 'Rita, brush me *here* when you reach down to toss your britches aside?"

He groaned when she did more than brush the hot, hard, denim-covered extension of him. They both shook from the next moment's promise. "Unbutton my shirt," he ordered, and pulled her hand to his chest. "And my britches. I'd like it if your hand lingered awhile."

"For how long?"

"Until I am very long."

She giggled. Her fingers lingered. And it pleased him.

Afterward, in her glow at seeing the stark magnificence of him once more, he said, "I'll finish undressing you now. Slowly. Soon you'll be naked on all this red satin. I want your legs spread, your arms wide for me. I want to kiss each inch of you."

His fingers captured the binding of her unmentionables, then drew them down her legs. He smiled at the naked sight of her, his hands stroking her legs and belly, before his fingers moved to the inside of her knees and smoothed all the way upward.

"You, oh my, Rafe . . . something . . . what about kissing?"

"And you had the nerve to call me a satyr." He chuckled wickedly. "It's time you felt the silk in the red satin."

One arm slipped around her back, the other braced her knees, and he lifted her to the bed. He stood above, watching as she squirmed on the cover and savored the cool slick feel of the lustrous material. But she craved the heat of Rafe, and opened her arms. He eased onto the satin, slipping his hand under and up her back; his hard, hot presence evoked "mmmmm."

"I love the decadence of this fabric," she admitted in a husky whisper. She'd never known anyone to use such a coverlet. "Wherever did it come from?"

"From the same bolt a seamstress cut the cape I wore during my greatest triumph in the ring. That was the afternoon I became *Magnífico* instead of plain *El Aguila.*"

"Oh, I'll bet you were never considered *plain.*"

"Whatever the case, I'm glad you approve of the way the satin feels on your skin." His big toe massaging her calf, he promised, "I'm going to kiss your face and your lips and your throat and your breasts and your tummy and your legs and your foot. And then I'm going to kiss your other leg . . . before I touch my tongue in the place where I'm touching" — he gentled his forefinger against her most sensitive area — "right now."

It was magic, his prelude. Dazed at the thousand

tingles in her blood, at the hundred thousand urges and surges of herself, she thrashed about, disturbing wads of satin. If this was a sin, she loved being a sinner.

"Ah, yes, my ravenous little soldier. Buck against my hand. Ah, yes." He blew a gentle stream of breath into her ear. "My lips need your kiss. Kiss me."

She obliged, happily and without hesitation.

But he took the aggressive role anew. His tongue moved past her teeth, tangling with hers. When he plowed his fingers into the hair at her temple, his thumbs pressed into the soft flesh beneath her ear. "Are you ready for more kisses?"

"Oh, yes. Please."

"Don't move a muscle. Just enjoy."

His lips, hot and warm, and his tongue, talented and steady, began the promised assault. She reveled in each and every emotion, each and every spasm that shook her body. *Rafe, praise be to you! You've shown me a little bit of heaven.*

Or was it hell?

Or was it heaven!

Somewhat after she'd screamed in ecstasy, Rafe slid up her body. His lips brushed the corner of hers, and a tangy scent filtered to her nose.

"Did you enjoy that?" He picked a strand of long hair that had tangled into her mouth, moved it over her shoulder. "Or must I start again?"

"No! Don't start again. It would be torture. Splendid torture. I want *you.*"

Adroitly he rolled over, taking her with him, until she lay sprawled atop him. Squirming against his erection, she held tight to the dense black hairs under his arms, asking, "What do you mean to do?"

"It's what you will do, that's the subject. Would you like to ride your workhorse, my general?"

She grinned and blushed. "You silly. You're no workhorse."

"Believe me, I will work like a horse to satisfy you."

The idea had much appeal. Yet, recalling how she'd loved having the weight of him on and above her, she replied, "What if I'm not tired of the old way?"

"Then I shall" — he nuzzled her throat — "work like a horse" — he licked her ear — "to bore you with monotony. For now I'm wanting you whatever way I can get you. But you will ride me before we leave this room. I *will* be had that way."

All the while he teased and taunted and aroused his Margarita, Rafe knew he'd never grow bored with her. Once more he turned her, until he had her beneath him. Her legs — those long and lovely legs! — lifted and wrapped around his buttocks. His rod found its way to the place it yearned to be, and he surged forward, deeply, waiting for her reaction. She gasped. And he marveled, Dios mio, *she's tight and sweet.*

His hands slid under her behind. He tilted his hips into hers, loving the heat that clasped him. All sincerity flooded his words when he confessed, "All my life I've looked for you."

Pangs of pleasure spiraled in his lower back when her legs tightened. And he might have died, he so loved the milkmaid sauciness of the learned Margarita. It beat at him, the yearning to pound her until there was no him or her, until they were one, until he was a part of her that could never be torn asunder.

Don't forget. She's still new to this. Knowing he must find her rhythm, he forced himself to take it slow and easy. He knew when to wait, to tease, to dare, and he knew she liked his considerations. He loved her trembling responses, the husky way she moaned, then the wordless entreaties signaling she needed more.

Her fingernails dug into his back, and he smiled. With all his might he plunged. Again and again, he pounded his darling love. And she responded with all the vivacity he remembered from last time. Wildly and without reserve, they mated until she had reached her peak time after time, and he was on the verge of spilling his seed into her hot hold.

He held back. He could wait. He had been trained to hold back. When he'd satisfied his mind that her needs were fulfilled, he released into her. *So good . . .* Never had he felt such calm in completion.

In his floating state, he slid his hands beneath her shoulders and brought her face to his. "I love you, *querida,* love you so much it hurts. I love you until death do us part. I'll love you for a thousand eternities. Stay with me, 'Rita. Stay here in Mexico. Be at my side, no matter what happens."

Her dark hair a fan across red satin, she squirmed beneath him. "Let's don't clutter this with avowals of love."

What? Taken aback, he lay stock-still. Never in his life had he confessed love, and *this* was his reward? The euphoric spell broken, he slid free and rolled to his side. "A woman isn't supposed to say things like that."

"In whose book?"

"It's just not done."

She met his glare. "Until now."

"You've always been the exception to rules."

Offended—hurt!—that she hadn't backed down from her ornery stand, he vowed she'd admit to undying love. Soon. In the meantime, why should he argue with the things he loved about her? If he'd wanted acquiescence, there were a million women of that persuasion. *But you should take care in your wishes, lest they come true.*

Kicking her legs over the bedside, she pushed to stand, then reached for her clothes. He stopped her. His hand fastened on her knee. His kiss centered on the side of her thigh. "My book says you mustn't rush from all that is glorious."

"But I'm *starving*. Do you think we might find something edible in your larder?"

It had been a long time since they'd eaten, yet he pulled her back into bed. "I'll do the looking."

Hair still mussed from their lovemaking, he returned with his arms filled with cans. "Canned figs and strings of jerky," he said. Crawling into bed, he leaned against the prop of pillows Margaret had made for him.

"Mmmm." Her stomach growled for the delights he popped into her mouth. One after another, he fed her. "Who would have thought those figs would last so long? Aren't you going to eat any? Oh, no. No more!" She raised a hand to ward off shavings of jerked beef. "That stuff looks horrid."

"How about this?" He kissed her.

"Very wicked."

He chuckled and she gawked at him, really took her fill of her lover. He was nicely formed, amazingly free of scars, all muscles and sinew. His skin held the brown patina of sun and almost forty years of living, though the elasticity remained. His face held her spellbound, for she loved the sight of black, black stubble against the sun-cured skin of his face. Caballo and his master had something in common. Rafe, too, had sprouted silver hairs, his at the temples.

"Do you like what you see?" he murmured and ran his thumb across her bottom lip.

"Yes, I like what I see."

"Do you *love* it?"

"Who wouldn't?"

"Well, I guess that's better than nothing," he muttered in a low voice.

And they made love again.

Their brothers, bearing venison and beans, arrived at the Eagle's Nest a couple hours after sundown. Being a soft touch for dogs, Tex took Caballo under his wing. Xzobal didn't have much to say, but Margaret suspected he knew what was what with her and Rafe, and he disapproved. *Through his eyes, we are sinners.* But she wasn't going to let a priest bother her, even if he was Rafe's brother.

After Tex and Xzobal retired to rooms on the opposite side of the house, Rafe led her back to his bed. Once more he proved his reputation as an unflagging lover. They got just enough sleep to refresh their bodies.

* * *

Streaks of dawn shot through the bedroom windows; Rafe buttoned Margaret's britches. "I've been thinking, Mexico needs women of your courage. I want you with me when I face down my uncle."

"Don't talk craziness." Forced airiness emitted from her. "You scare me with windmill-chasing talk, Señor Quixote."

"What would you like to do, 'Rita?" He pulled her onto his naked lap, then he pressed her hand to the part of him that was swelling anew for her. "Besides this, of course."

"What not this?" She trailed her fingernail along the head of his shaft.

"You'll get another go, don't worry about that. But I'm talking about something outside the bedroom. If not chasing windmills with me, what do you want for yourself?"

She turned her face. "I'm not certain I have the option to—"

"Nothing is certain in this life," he replied. "But no naysaying in this chat, all right? Now, tell me. Will you ever write another book? Isn't there anything here in Mexico that piques your interest or imagination? Do you feel you must teach? You know, children in this country need an education. There are so many ways you could help my country. Before long you'll be thinking of it as your country."

"Rafe, I am *not* a Mexican. And I have no desire— absolutely no desire—to stay here."

He had that resolute look in his face. "At the cemetery you mentioned grandchildren. If you're thinking the normal life is for you, my *soldadita,* don't. You aren't meant for it."

"That's not for you to say." It hurt, his cavalier taunting. "How do you know what is good for me? How do you know anything about me? You mock me and act as if you don't know it. You don't even . . . You don't even seem to know I'm dying."

"What silly talk. I'm the one with the death wish."

Aggravated at his insensitivity, she left his lap to flounce across the room, but he grabbed her hand. Her withering glare should have given him pause. "Margarita, you aren't going to die. You'll live forever."

She shook off his fingers and went through the motions of dressing.

"Do I have the wrong impression of you? Are you wanting children?" He paled under a thoughtful expression. "Damn, why didn't I think about . . . ? Margarita, you may get one whether you want it or not. If we continue to lay together, my babe will grow within you."

A baby? She hadn't given such a possibility a thought. Not that the idea — *Don't even think it*.

"If we're to protect you, I, well, I must visit the *curandera* of Areponapuchi." He thrust one leg, then the next into his britches. "The healer-woman has potions and herbs to prevent a babe."

She wasn't believing her ears, though she had no trouble imagining his recurring need for such measures in the past. "Just a minute. Just a damned minute. You presume quite a lot, Rafael Delgado. Soon, you'll have seen the last of me. I have a career in New York. Even if I didn't, I am an American. My sympathies are with the United States. And with Spain. My family calls Porfirio Díaz friend."

281

"That will change."

"There must have been peyote in that jar you ate from. The very idea of riding against the legal and peaceable government of Mexico defies all my beliefs. I can't think of a worse fate than spending the rest of my life—"

"Shall we send for the cats?"

The backs of her knuckles parking on her hips, she shouted, "Cats? Send for the *cats?* Have you not listened to one word I've said?"

"I've heard each syllable of every one of them. New York is your past. You'll never see it again, except, perhaps, for a visit. Mexico is your destiny. If you want your Deniece and Denephew, I'll arrange for their transport. But let me warn you, our plans don't include coddling pets. You are here. You are here forever. You will change this country."

"You are mad. You mistake me for Charity. She's the adventurous one."

"Your crazy sister is a circus performer, not a Valkyrie of the battlefield."

He continued his deranged praise, stressing her stout heart and invincibility; Margaret backed away. "What has possessed you to think such things?" she asked.

"It's the Aztec in me."

Twenty-one

The entrance to the silver mine of Santa Alicia stood halfway up the mountain, the office a stone's throw away. Gray dust shrouded everything. Margaret had expected a buzz of activity, with ore cars on rail lines going in and out of the gaping hole. She'd carried several misconceptions. Even from outside, the Santa Alicia could be compared only to Dante's levels of hell and purgatory.

"Women are forbidden—bad luck," Rafe explained in the late morning, after they'd quarreled over his deranged visions.

She had no desire to press *her* luck. All it took was one glance at the ashen-faced, skeletal workers as they held fast to the pulleys to ascend the vertical mine—great sacks of ore on their backs—and Margaret almost lost her breakfast.

A trail of cadaverous workers wearing little more than a few rags wrapped around their middles trudged by, on their way to hell's gate. Slave drivers with long whips made certain they didn't fall out of step. And when one worker stumbled, the lash bit into his back. Over and over. He didn't even, it seemed, have the energy to cry out.

"My God, how can this cruelty be allowed?" Margaret whispered, crying for him, and fell to her knees. "Those men are more dead than alive."

"This happens all over Mexico." Rafe, hunkering back on his booted heels, wiped her face with his finger. "They aren't men. They're slaves. Yaqui Indians, for the most part. When the Federales overwhelmed them in their home state of Sonora, your family friend Señor Porfirio Díaz gave them to Tío Arturo."

"My father fought a war to end slavery. And now I understand why." Trembling, she whispered hoarsely, "I never imagined it could be this horrible."

Her gaze going to Rafe's tense face, she slid her arms around his waist and leaned in to him, needing his strength. In the hours since he'd revealed his visions to her, he'd repeated his sentiments over and over, until she'd begun to believe in her own invincibility. But even the strong needed the strength of others, at times.

"Face those pitiful wretches, Margarita. See and remember what goes on here."

She forced herself to turn to the awful reality, shuddering anew when the whipped slave, runnels of red flowing into his ragged loincloth, grabbed a pick and an empty sack, then took hold of the rope pulley and disappeared straight down into the hole.

"Charity's husband inherited mines on the Eastern seaboard." Margaret shuddered. "The way the workers were exploited sickened Hawk. But nothing—nothing!—he's ever said prepared me for *this*."

"You haven't seen the half of it. *Now* do you understand why conditions must change?"

"I understand quite a lot."

She understood what had driven Rafe to rebellion. Injustice. She understood why the Mexican people moved with such lethargy. Despair. And she understood what motivated the likes of Arturo Delgado. Greed. One way or another, he had to be stopped!

For the first time in years, the excitement of a challenge set in. It was like when she'd first decided to study Columbus and the Catholic kings. It was like when she scrawled The End on her treatise, then finally seen it in print, even if the name Mortimer screamed from the copyright. Suddenly the idea of teaching history at Brandington College paled in comparison to being a part of history.

As if he could read her mind, Rafe took her hand. "Will you help us? Can I count on you?"

Yes was on the tip of her tongue. Yet her giddy, heady enthusiasm got dashed when the voice of good sense shouted the impulse down. Haring off in the name of social change took intestinal fortitude and rosy-cheeked stamina. She didn't doubt she had the guts for battle, but a good estate of body?

"I'll do what I can," she replied at last.

"At least you didn't say no." Winking, he tweaked her nose, then pulled her to him and kissed the tip of that nose. "I can accept one concession at a time."

She started to say that pleased her, but a curse issued from him.

"Merdo." His grip on her shoulders tightened, then loosened. "Trouble." He stood. "We've got trouble." He helped her to her feet. "My uncle and his men."

Six riders climbed the hill.

Six against two.

Six guns against one.

Why, oh why, hadn't she brought her firearm along? Just because it was five pounds of dead steel was no excuse!

Her heart knocked at the wall of her chest. *Tex, where are you when we need you!* A good two or three miles away, her brother—a sharpshooter *par excellence*—waited with Xzobal and the little dog. The horses were out of sight, tethered in a hiding place down the hill. On the other side of the riders. She prayed her strength wouldn't fail, that she wouldn't put Rafe in danger by holding him back.

"Let's go," he ordered.

They feinted to the right, dodging the approaching Arturo and his *pistoleros* to make for Penny and Diablo.

"The criminal has returned to the scene of his crime," Arturo Delgado said to his most trusted lieutenant, Diego Cantú.

His cadre of hired guns in company, Arturo led them onward, toward his murderer-nephew and his lover. The elder Delgado wasn't surprised to see them at the Santa Alicia. His spies in Chihuahua and Santa Eulalia, as well as his one good source of information in the village of Santa Alicia—the boy Carlos—had had much to say. Rafito had fallen in with Gil McLoughlin's daughter, the pair en route to Eden Roc. "I knew Rafito wouldn't be able to stay away from here."

Glowering, Arturo watched his brother's miserable spawn and the *gringa* try to escape. The McLoughlin daughter, slim as a boy, wore a shirt and pants. Her long dark hair, as well as her arms, swung from side to side as she ran. Arturo knew Rafito could run like a *jaguar,* but his strides were slow, were in pace with his new woman's.

"What is wrong with the girl?" Arturo said to Cantú. "Why would she settle for a black sheep?"

Those lucky—or was it crafty?—McLoughlins knew the art of marrying up, since one of the daughters had snared the Count of Granada himself, not that he'd be any prize if his titles were stripped.

The head of the family—Arturo had met him in Washington a few years back. They had gotten to a first-name basis, though Arturo disliked being addressed as "Artie old boy." Gil McLoughlin wielded power north of the Bravo, almost as much as Arturo wielded to the south. Tangling with McLoughlin could be costly. But so was tangling with a Delgado.

Cantú spoke. *"Patrón,* we await your orders."

"I want to see some dancing."

"Then?"

"Kill them."

Cantú and the other Arturianos put spurs to horse-flesh, firing at will toward the fleeing figures. Arturo headed the stallion Noche Negro down the incline, and drew his own revolver.

Gunfire exploded around the chased pair, in the air, on the ground, but they didn't dance around it. They kept to a steady course. Then Rafito turned. He lifted his arm, aiming at Arturo, yet he swung the revolver to the right, obviously unable to fire. Cantú shot the weapon out of his hand.

The prey froze for a split second; the six-shooter came apart, sending up a shower of shrapnel. The girl screamed. The shrapnel sprayed her arm, his neck.

"Let's go!" he shouted.

They took off in another near-torpid run. Arturo's slur "Fools!" got muffled by blasts of pistol fire. Bullets slammed into a tree trunk to the left of the couple, at their feet, and Arturo frowned. He kept seeing Rafito turning his aim away. *May the devil take the cur bastard.* Arturo ordered, "No more dancing. The hombre is mine."

The reins in one hand, Arturo steadied his aim on his mestizo nephew. *In a moment he'll be dead.* Revenge tasted sweet, sweet, sweet. Yet, for some unexplainable reason, Arturo's hand began to shake. Dropping the reins, he lifted his left palm under the right wrist. Still, his hand quaked. *You can't do it! You woman! You can't kill him yourself.*

Arturo ground his teeth together. What was wrong with him that he couldn't mete out punishment? Rafito had slaughtered his fair-haired son and heir. His only child. His reason for doctoring Constanzo Delgado's will. Arturo's wife, the late Yolanda, had insisted he do it. He had worshipped the domineering Yolanda, had never been able to deny the full-figured blonde anything. Had never wanted to.

But who said it hadn't troubled him, going to such lengths against the nephew he once loved and protected? After Yolanda had passed away, he had called his son to the office that lamentable day to ask Hernán to act as peacemaker. *Execute his murderer!*

"Diego and the *niños* will do it."

Arturo holstered his revolver, watching as the girl began to slow her pace, began to sway. Rafito's arm shot out to steady her. One, two. Pop, pop. He'd taken two bullets, one in the shoulder, one in the leg, both scattering flesh and blood, clothing and gunpowder.

He toppled to the ground.

The girl, her screams piercing the air, seemed oblivious to the bullets whizzing over her head. She bent over Rafito and lifted his shoulders from the rocks.

The Arturianos held their fire momentarily, each man looking to *el patrón* for instructions. He held up a hand. His men backed their mounts, turned them, returned to Arturo's side. "Go on," he ordered. "Go to my office. I'll meet you there. I'll handle this matter."

Cantú and the others did as ordered. With morbid interest Arturo walked Noche Negro forward, and watched his nephew and the girl. She worked tirelessly. With no regard to her own injury, or to the cough that wracked her thin body.

She jerked her blue shirt from her arms, leaving her torso in a camisole. She ripped the chambray into strips. She then tore Rafito's trousers above the wound and lifted his injured leg, and wrapped the bandages with the speed of a vaquero as he hog-tied a calf. Next she addressed her efforts to the wound at his shoulder and neck.

And all the while Rafito was arguing with her, shouting for her to "get out of here."

She paid no mind. Once the bandages were in place, she steadied her breath. She looked up. And never had Arturo Delgado seen as much defiance and loathing in a woman's eyes. They weren't a woman's eyes. They were the eyes of a tigress.

Arturo found himself respecting her courage.

She got to her feet. "If you want us dead, all you have to do is pull the trigger. If you don't, Arturo Delgado, be warned. You haven't seen the last of us. And next time we'll be better armed."

She reached down and helped Rafito to stand, though he slipped twice. The wounds looked bad, probably mortal. Winding his arm around her shoulder, she led him down the gravel path. Arturo followed, watching as she made for the horses tied behind the mining engineer's work shack. For a slender woman, she had the strength of five tigresses.

Arturo got a hardening in his loins from simply gazing upon the challenge of her. "You need a real man," he called after her.

She ignored him.

"*Tonta,* don't waste your time with trash such as Rafael Delgado. If he lives, he'll drag you down with him."

She kept to her path. And once they reached their mounts, Rafito made a puny effort to put his foot in the stirrup. Leaning down, she helped him. Afterward, she gave a mighty shove that helped him to the saddle; he slumped over it.

Rafito reared up to brush her jaw with his wavering hand. He said something. For a moment she leaned against his uninjured leg. Turning her face—and it was a beautiful face!—up to him, she shouted, "*¡Viva los ciudadanos! ¡Viva Mexico!*"

Long live the people. Long live Mexico.

Arturo didn't care much for her Spanish. But he knew at that moment he must have his way with her. He licked his chops, contemplating the taming of a tigress.

"Go on to Eden Roc," he said, knowing she didn't hear him. "Let it work its magic on you."

He turned his mount. A smirk accompanied his thought, *Yes, I'll give Eden Roc some time. Then I will deal with the tigress.*

290

Part 2

Eden Roc

"I compare it to Homer's Elysian Fields.
It is a blessed and happy harbor secluded at
world's end.
Here a select few favored by myself
will enjoy the earthly paradise where
life is easiest for man."

— Isaiah Nash in a letter
to his daughter Natalie, 1872.

"Please say your Mexican heaven doesn't include
carrots or prune juice."

— Natalie's reply.

Twenty-two

December 1, 1897
At the walled retreat known as
Eden Roc

"Lisette, Netoc has found your children."

Relief flooding, Lisette McLoughlin stepped toward Natalie Nash, who had translated for the gray-haired Tarahumara Indian. Netoc, wearing the pajamalike *huipils* that seemed to be uniform for the masses, turned to warm his hands in front of the great room's fireplace, and Natalie took Lisette's cold hands in her slender ones.

Lisette McLoughlin might have never known that her offspring, along with Rafe Delgado, were on their way to Eden Roc, if dear Natalie hadn't arrived at the beginning of November. Several times she'd wondered why her sickly daughter had linked up with the man she openly hated, but considering the situation, Lisette refused to borrow trouble. She'd had enough, worrying about their whereabouts.

Two weeks ago Netoc — belying his advanced age, an

untiring long-distance runner like many of his strange and reclusive tribesmen—had left in search of the missing threesome. This had been the worst month of Lisette's life.

"Angus, Gretchen," she said in a quivering voice, using the German diminutive for Margaret, "where are they?"

Natalie hesitated before answering, "At a ranch not far from the village of Santa Alicia."

"Tell me everything. Don't hold anything back."

Taking a sidestep, Natalie finger-combed a strawberry blond curl behind her ear. "Rafael Delgado was shot and nearly died, I understand. And—oh, Lisette, I'm sorry to tell you—but your daughter's been ill. Don't despair, though. A kindly rancher and his wife took them in. Apparently they're recovering and plan to be here soon."

Now that she knew her children weren't dead, Lisette said a prayer of appreciation and thanksgiving, then let curiosity flow. "My daughter. What's wrong with her? Is it her lungs?"

"Yes."

Dying the thousand deaths of a mother for her hapless child, Lisette sank onto a chair. *Be strong!* She'd had years to adjust to Gretchen's consumption; thus, she knew all the little devices of keeping her sanity. Using the best one, the change of subject, she asked, "Who shot Rafe?"

"Netoc doesn't know."

"Why didn't Angus ride ahead to let me know . . . ?"

"I would imagine they saw no reason to send word.

It would've done nothing but worry you. For all they knew, you thought they were still in the United States."

"That's reasonable."

"Something else — They have Señor Delgado's brother with them. Evidently he is a priest."

Strange. She asked a foolish question, hoping her fears were ill conceived, "Does Netoc know if my husband sent them?"

Turning to the Indian who was brushing the sole of a crusty foot, Natalie posed the question. It didn't take a translator for Lisette to understand he had no idea. *Don't be a Tropf.* As surely as the sun rose in the east, she knew Gil McLoughlin had sent his children — when he was the one who ought to be on his way to Eden Roc.

Gil, shame on you! You know poor Gretchen is not well. And she's had a relapse evidently. What if the caravan didn't make it here? If they did make it here, could Gretchen hold up to the return trip? Lisette choked back her fury. *Damn you, Gilliegorm McLoughlin, don't you love me enough to come after me yourself?*

She had a word with her rage. *Well, he's busy and he'll be here in person, eventually.* Enough! Since February of 1869 she'd been making excuses for her husband. She would be making no more excuses for Gil McLoughlin.

Natalie watched Lisette — her fair head bent, her lovely face a mixture of relief, joy, and pain — leave the great room of Eden Roc.

It was no accident that Natalie had been making overtures of friendship. Lisette was, after all, Tex's mother, and Natalie's plans for the McLoughlin heir remained many. Amazingly, being friends with the German woman had proved easier than Natalie could have imagined. Hence, she'd suffered along with Lisette during the awful days of not knowing what to expect, and not for totally selfish reasons, either.

As for her friend's daughter, the Countess of Granada, Natalie equated the blind and pregnant Olga with royalty all right. She was a royal pain in the ass.

"Did you tell your lady about *el grandero rico?*" Netoc asked in his curious mixture of Tarahumara and Spanish.

"No. I saved Arturo for her children to explain."

"You still love him." Netoc, the lines of his face deepening, stepped to her. "He's hurt you, yet you would take him back."

"The question isn't whether I'll take him back. The question is — what is he going to do, should he get his hands on me?"

"I won't let him touch you." His straight gray hair swung from side to side, brushing his shoulders, as Netoc promised, "You must trust me, Natalie. My love will protect you."

"Oh, Netoc, whatever am I going to do with you?"

His dark eyes snapped. "Make love with me?"

"No." She turned to place another log on the fire. "No more of that."

From behind, he pushed her hair out of the way to kiss her neck. His hands trailed to her breasts. She felt his hips grinding against her buttocks. Her fingers found and caressed his flaccid manhood. For all her adventures both in Mexico and abroad, for all the love she'd given Arturo, for all her wild and woolly romps with several leading swains of the stage and with many strangers in various locales, no one excited her as much as Netoc.

If only he were enough . . .

"I was your first man. You were my first woman. You are my only woman." His tongue flicked against her ear. "Remember when we were both young? Remember when we made love under the waterfall? Go with me to the waterfall, my beloved."

She turned in his arms. "I can't make it all the way out there. Take me. Here. Now."

And he tried.

Afterward, she cried in her heart. Running her fingers across his aged face, she kissed him and promised him it was all right, and she railed against this horrid Eden Roc, this piece of hell on earth, that made the young out of the old—except for the Tarahumaras. To them this awful place sapped their life force.

Isaiah held a different opinion. "The Fountain has nothing to do with it. They swill too much of their corn beer and then run their legs off, that's what sends them to early deaths," was what her father claimed. "Amazing little buggers, they could run all the way to hell. And probably do."

Netoc had gotten to be an old man, though he could still run like the gazelles of Africa. He'd yet to have his thirty-fifth birthday. He, an elder in his tribe, was more than five years Natalie Nash's junior.

"Young man. Young man!"

Alongside the locked gates to Eden Roc, a tow-headed youth slept soundly in the gate house's wicker chair, a blanket tucked around his legs.

Cranky Margaret, the Chihuahua dog riding shot-gun, secured the buckboard's hand brake. Tied to the rear of the wagon were Penny and Diablo. A crisp dry twilight approached in the Sierra Madres, as Margaret stood to shout, "Don't just sit there snoozing!"

" 'Rita, I don't need help."

"Behave!" The term "terrible patient" must have been coined in Rafe's honor, she complained to herself. Left to his own devices, despite the plaster-of-paris cast that came clear up to his hip, he might give the Mexican hat dance a try. "You said you need to relieve yourself, and—"

"If you wouldn't get embarrassed, I could hang—"

"Rafe Delgado, we've got to get through the gate anyway. And I'm trying to get help. So you just sit tight."

Once more, now that they had arrived at the health retreat, Margaret wondered why her brother was never around when she needed him. Tex and Xzobal, on horseback, had taken a small detour for the Texan to get a first look from the piney precipice to the canyon floor. Margaret had yet to see it. The whole area, she supposed, held a distinct beauty, though she was too tired to appreciate it.

Addressing herself to a more pressing situation—the sway of the wagon, thanks to movements from its bed—she begged the passenger who was shoving his pile of blankets aside, "Please lie still, Rafe, please!" Then insisted to the sleeper, "Wake up, laggard! We need help. Señor Delgado mustn't climb out on his own."

"Oh, yes, I can."

"Don't move a muscle, or you'll tempt the fates all over again!" Margaret made certain he sat tight by pointing her Colt percussion at his forehead. His was not the face of a happy traveler. "Rafe, this hurts me more than it does you."

"Rather doubtful."

"You've forced me into this." The little dog, for a better vantage point, put his front paws on the lower slat of the wagon seat and his nose between the slats. Margaret glanced furtively at the gate house, seeing that the sleeper still snoozed. She wilted on the seat again and twisted around to face Rafe. "The doctor warned me if you overdo it, the consequences will be—"

"You weren't too worried about consequences last night." A lopsided grin pulled at Rafe's haggard face, as he alluded to the lovemaking they had at long last been able to complete. He managed to wiggle into a seated position. His voice a whisker that tickled her insides, he lifted a hand to her shirt-clad arm. "Do you need me to remind you of our evening?"

He slipped his fingers into the crook of her elbow; her gaze slipped to his telltale bulge. She got a rush from recalling what they had shared under the moonlight and those blankets. In spite of the grave state of their collective health, she'd learned something. Stroking him *there* brought her almost as much pleasure as it gave him.

Sir Colt shook like a leaf. She placed the .44 on the seat next to Caballo, then took another look at Rafe. "I don't need reminders of how well-suited we are in the man-woman way."

"Would you like a *refresher?*"

"After we've caught our breaths." In her case, literally. She, too, had been on the verge of death, when they were taken in by the kindly folks at Rancho Gato. "Need I remind you that without a storehouse of strength, we can neither fight your uncle, nor see my vagabond mother to the port of Tampico?"

Near worship described the expression slipping into his eyes. "My adventurous warrior-woman aches for our escapades."

She got a gummy feeling. Where were their escapades headed? It was suicidal for him to seek Arturo Delgado's undoing, unless Rafe could bring himself to fire on that murderer of slaves and the human spirit. She understood why he couldn't. He hadn't recovered from shooting Hernán.

Beyond the showdown that might or might not come to pass, where were *they* headed? From Rancho Gato she'd sent word to Dean Acykbourn at Brandington College, telling him not to expect her in January. It had been a very rash move.

Never had Rafe so much as whispered about wanting her for ever-after. And he scoffed at her hints that she might yearn for more than a desperado's life, and his reasoning had little—if anything—to do with her health. She'd discovered a traditional streak in herself. It was daft to expect a complicated man like Rafe to adjust to tradition, but she wouldn't ride at his side without being more than the last in a long line of women.

You'll never be more. You're no longer young or beautiful or healthy, and he can have his pick of women. Once his strength returns, you'll be somewhere in the middle of the queue.

He pulled her fingers toward him. "Climb back here, *amorcito*. Let me kiss and caress you. Let's sip from the saucer of sin one more time."

"If you'd like to discuss excitement, I'm pleased to oblige. I'm thinking about how exciting these past five and a half weeks have been. Since you took two bullets, one right through your thighbone." Expanding on the more serious wound, she didn't mention the hole beneath his collarbone that had festered. "I'm recalling what the doctor said. That if you don't give yourself time to heal, you could be crippled for life. Now. If you don't behave"—again she secured Sir Colt in her hands—"I'll open another plug in your leg."

She'd never put it this bluntly; Rafe paled. "To think I said you were sweet—I must have been out of my head last night," he groused.

"I was sweet."

"Sweet as the inside of a lemon," he shouted.

"Hush, or that boy will hear you."

Rafe got a peeved look. "You're always giving orders. I'm tired of being laid up, at the mercy of a knuckle-wrapping schoolmarm. I want out of this wagon. I need to pee."

How childish. He'd mastered the art of backsliding. Lately he'd much too often equated her with teaching, which he believed didn't do justice to her abilities.

A chilled wind lifted her hair, reminding her that night would fall soon. She shouted in two languages, "Boy, do you make a habit of sleeping on the job?"

At last he opened his eyes. "Welcome to Eden Roc." The youth, now yawning and patting his mouth, walked toward the wagon. "I am—"

"Lazy." And an American, she decided. No doubt life had spoiled him, thanks to his sublime beauty. "Give us a hand and be quick about it. Then open that gate."

"Hipólito! *¡Andele, rapido!*" The gatekeeper glanced this way and that, looking past pines and oaks and quaking aspens. A rabbit dashed from a hiding place at his voice; Caballo didn't fail to bark at the bunny. "Hipólito, where are you? Come back, little fellow. We need your strong arms."

"Lazybones," she contended while Caballo growled, "you ought to be reported for pawning off your work."

"Why, you must be Miss Margaret McLoughlin."

From the wagon came a nasty snigger. "Has your reputation preceded you, *querida?* Do you suppose he recognized you from your tone alone?"

She imparted a quelling look.

"All of us at Eden Roc have been awaiting your arrival," the gatekeeper was saying. "Netoc said you were on your way."

The Indian who'd snooped around their temporary refuge, Rancho Gato, must have been Netoc. At the time Margaret had advised against confiding in a possible Arturiano spy, but Rafe had insisted on Tarahumaran integrity.

302

"See, 'Rita, didn't I tell you we could trust him?"

Ignoring Señor Told You So, she said to the boy, "I assume Mrs. McLoughlin is still on the premises."

"Oh, yes, the lovely Lisette is with us. But aren't you missing a couple of men?"

What cheek, calling a guest by her given name. How many times had she heard her great-grandmother gripe about hired help? Each of those complaints had been met with a mental "oh, please," but right now she better understood Maisie, who would have been fighting mad, were she to witness this youth in action.

He approached the wagon; Caballo let him have it with protective barks. *"Bienvenidos.* Rafael Delgado. We heard you are infirm. Let me give you a hand."

"I don't need any help. I can make it."

"Like this morning? When you *fell on your face?"*

"¡Basta!" Rafe shouted; she knew she had said enough, too much. "All right, *muchacho,* give me a hand."

When the offered hand reached into the wagon, she restrained Caballo, lest he try for a chunk the size of an Alsatian's bite out of the intruder's leg.

"Buenos tardes."

All heads turned to the man who offered good afternoon. A funny little chap with bow legs, a missing upper tooth, and a shock of coarse gray hair, he bounced toward them, sloshing beer from a pail as he moved.

"Hipólito, little monkey, lend a hand."

Watching the three men struggle with the cast, Margaret rubbed her tired brow. Caballo took advantage of her loosened grip. In the tradition of many small men gone before him, he leapt like a flying fish from the wagon to challenge the giants. He had the hem of Hipólito's *huipils* between his jaws in no time.

A harsh reprimand from Rafe stopped the attack. Caballo backed off. Amazingly, he didn't try to bite the gatekeeper; he licked the hand that patted his head. "Dogs are good judges of character," Maisie had said. Perhaps the youth had more to him than Margaret's first impression. Maisie's advice said something about the benign-appearing native, though, didn't it?

Caballo, meanwhile, abused the situation. He gave yapping supervision and canine criticism as his master was helped from the wagon, then nearly toppled to the ground.

Poor Rafe. The crutches under his arms, and the faithful little dog at his heels, he moved slowly and clumsily, favoring his injured shoulder, toward the privacy of a stand of ponderosa pines. With his freedom of movement gone, along with his natural grace, he in no way resembled the celebrated matador of days gone by. He looked his age. And more.

Watching his ungainly efforts, Margaret swallowed a lump in her throat. Poor Rafe. While she'd grown accustomed to being infirm, he didn't handle it well. No better than he handled his advancing age. If the rumors about this place were true, good. He needed a new lease on life.

The youth spoke. "Not to worry. A few days at Eden Roc, and your swain will be fine. You too. I have just the regimen to put the peaches back into a sallow complexion."

He had more than *cheek,* this one.

304

"Let me help you down, ma'am," he said, offering a hand. "Have you gotten a look at the canyon? It is spectacular. The view changes every hour of the day. You should see it at dawn! The walls look like they've been sprinkled with copper and gold. Did you know the Aztec people traveled here from central Mexico because they knew the barrancas have mystical powers?"

Rafe had mentioned its beauty as well as the legends, time and again. Oh, how he loved the Sierras! He might be miserable now, but he must have been terribly miserable, all those years in exile from his native land.

"May I tell you about the Tarahumara Indians?"

Normally, she would have been enchanted, getting a history lesson, but . . . "Young man, how far is it to headquarters?"

"No more than a couple of furlongs."

"Good. Señor Delgado can walk from here—if you or Hipólito will assist him. We are tired, the sun is setting, and I'd appreciate your opening the gate and being quick about it." He patted a yawn; she added, "Sleep after we're on our way."

"Be assured, I don't make a habit of greeting my guests while taking a siesta." He laughed at himself. "My man Hipólito went down to the caves to purchase that pail of *tesgüino*." He gestured to the foam-crowned bucket. "The local beer. I keep myself and my guests to a healthy diet and to a set routine of exercise and swimming, but an occasional slip with the *tesgüino* is good for the disposition."

She and Rafe could use a gallon or two of the stuff, she thought. That aside, she considered what was

305

happening here. The gatekeeper didn't speak as a cal-low youth. And once she'd brushed the sleeves of her woolen shirt, she took a hard look. This young man had soft brown eyes of the sort often seen in biblical illustrations, a halo of thick and wavy blond hair, and some ancestor of his must have posed for medieval stained-glass artists, when they needed to conjure up the image of an archangel.

"Do you not know me?" he asked in answer to her quizzical stare. "May I introduce myself? I am Isaiah. Isaiah Nash."

"I didn't know . . . I know your sister Natalie, but I had no idea Mr. Nash had a son of the same name."

"You mistake me. My daughter is Natalie."

Confused, Margaret said, "There's something wrong here. My father has known Mr. Nash for many years, ever since they discussed investing in Mexican mining interests. Back in Benito Juarez's era." *Gosh, Papa, am I glad you didn't get involved in that!* She wasn't above flattery, but she meant it upon saying, "You aren't old enough to be Natalie Nash's father."

A halcyon smile feathered across his face. "I was born in the year of Our Lord eighteen hundred and seventeen. I celebrated my eightieth birthday last June."

"Preposterous."

"No, my dear. Most people don't see such dramatic results, but my repeated exposure to the magical water-falls keeps the aging process from returning."

"Do you mean insult, lad? Or is this a boyish prank?"

"The truth is, the Fountain of Youth is mine."

306

It wasn't until after they had entered the well-tended complex — consisting of outbuildings, cottages, sporting fields, and a palatial edifice to crown it all — and it was after Margaret had gotten an eyeful of her mother, before she gave any credence whatsoever to his absurd claim, though Lisette, back home, had passed the rumor to the family. Margaret gaped at her mother.

She could barely remember when her mother hadn't carried extra weight at her middle. Ever since triplet Charity had nearly been lynched, Lisette had sprouted silver hairs among the gold. Her face had begun to line and sag. Not anymore.

Trim, slim, willowy, golden-haired. Smooth-cheeked. Lisette resembled the painting that hung in Papa's office in Washington. Lisette McLoughlin had sat for it in 1870.

Twenty-three

"What do I think? I think it's strange to have my mother looking younger than myself."

This made up the entirety of Margaret's verbal reaction.

Having said that, she asked to be put to bed, barely noticing the arrival of Tex and Xzobal, much less the environs. She did nod and smile at Rafe, who sat propped up and pouting in the great room's overstuffed chair. *We both need to sleep it off.*

As if from another planet, she heard her brother say to the vision of loveliness floating toward him, "I'll be danged. It's you. Natalie. Oh, Miss Natalie, I've been praying you'd be here."

Margaret smiled. It sapped the last of her strength.

A staff member showed her to one of several cozy cottages, called *casitas* or little houses, several hundred yards from the main dwelling, where she spent the next sixty hours sleeping, resting, reclaiming lost vitality.

She awoke to news more startling than a rejuvenated mother, and the alarming part wasn't recalling she and Rafe had slept separately for the first time since the second of November. Her triplet Olga, along with the Count of Granada, was in residence in Eden Roc.

"I knew they were traveling," she blustered to their mother, who'd brought a tray of breakfast to the guest house, "but I had no idea that meant to *Mexico!*"

Lisette stopped arranging the peculiar-looking food. "I'd written her about my plans, but it came as a pleasant surprise to me, too, when she and Leonardo appeared one fine morn." She sighed. "Pleasant but trying. *Liebchen,* I'm sorry to tell you, but Olga's sight is now completely gone."

A terrible wrenching went through Margaret. For the greater part of twenty-eight years, Margaret Janet Jean Campbell McLoughlin II (named after Maisie) had called Olga, namesake of their maternal aunt and grandmother, every scornful name in the book. Nevertheless, if someone else had used ninny or simpleton or dithering in relation to Olga in front of Margaret, that person—even Charity—would have paid on a corporal level. Funny thing it was, being a third of a mismatched set. Charity was the wild one; Olga was the vulnerable one; Margaret was supposed to have a good head on her shoulders. While they had alternated accusing the other, "You love her more than you do me," in truth they were the Three Musketeers. All for one and one for all. *Triplet, if I could give you my eyes, I would!*

"Shhh, *meine Liebchen,* hush those tears." Lisette sat on the bed's edge and gentled her fingers over

Margaret's weeping face. "We've known for so long about the glaucoma. I promise you, it doesn't hold her back. And—oh, Gretchen, you're going to love this. I do have good news. Two pieces of marvelous news! First off, Olga is with child. After all these years, she's going to be a mother."

"That's wonderful. She'll make a good and kind one."

Margaret meant the platitudes, yet she didn't know how to feel. It seemed as if too much was coming at her at once. A jealous question emerged. What would Rafe feel for Olga, now that they were in close proximity?

I shouldn't have left him with my bossiness ringing in his ear. She searched the walls for a mirror to tidy herself, but didn't find one. Just as well. She couldn't compare to Olga, sighted or not, and needed no reminders. "How . . . how is Rafe? How is his leg?"

"We haven't seen much of him. He stays in his *casita,* but I understand he's doing fine. Isaiah intends to get him started in a fitness program today."

"That's good." Margaret paused. How much did her mother know about Olga and Rafe? For most of that fateful period in San Antonio, Lisette had been in residence at the Four Aces Ranch. "Has, uh, um, has Olga gone by to visit him?"

"Not yet. She's waiting until he's on his feet again."

At least Olga wasn't rushing to him. What was she thinking, doing? While Margaret had quit believing the rape story, what *had* gone on between her sister and Rafe? It hurt to think that he had practiced his

310

specialty on her very own sister. But then, would Olga think the same?

"Mother, you mentioned two pieces of news."

"Oh, *ja*. Leonardo has accepted the post of Ambassador to Mexico."

Margaret hadn't even begun to reconcile having Olga blind and in their midst, and now this? "You must be joking."

"Gretchen, I don't lie. And you know it."

"Yes, I know." After adjusting the sheet under her armpits, she reached for the food tray's water glass. "Oooh, this stuff tastes awful. Sulfurous. Never mind, that's not important right now. Mother, listen closely. You can't mean a *Hapsburg* means to represent the Spanish crown. That is the most insane thing I've ever heard in my life. Spaniards aren't liked all that much. And Hapsburgs aren't welcome in this country. At all."

"Now, *Liebchen,* Leonardo isn't his cousin Maximilian. And all that nasty business with the emperor happened over thirty years ago. I'm sure most people have forgotten it."

"If there's anything I've learned, it's that Mexicans do *not* forget anything. There could be trouble. Speaking of trouble—When can you be ready to travel?"

But what about Xzobal? There was no simple answer that would protect both him and Lisette.

"Papa needs you. Another thing, I've heard reports the situation worsens in Cuba. Rafe and I believe you'll be safe sailing from Tampico, but it's in your best interest if you sail no farther than New Orleans. Then take a train to Washington."

"You and Rafe are in no condition to travel."

"A couple days' rest, and we'll be fine."

"You push yourselves." Lisette nibbled an oatcake. "Why are you here with Rafe? I thought you abhorred him."

She's being evasive. "When can you be ready to leave?"

"Like I said, you're in no shape to travel. Neither is Rafe."

"Mother," Margaret said, stretching each letter in that age-old tone hardheaded daughters were prone to using with their softhearted parent. It usually got results. Usually.

"You know I don't like ships."

True. *How did I manage to forget that?* When Lisette the young girl had crossed the Atlantic from the German states, the journey had been horrible. The first Olga died in the ship's dank hold. "All right. We'll beat for Texas, over land. We'll take any route that pleases you."

Lisette licked her lips. "I won't be returning to the States. I've decided to move with Olga and Leonardo to the city of Mexico. She needs me."

Shocked speechless, Margaret gaped. Her mother, calm as a summer morning, sat down in a straight chair, adjusted her skirts around her knees, and smiled her brilliant girlish smile.

Somehow Margaret found her voice. "Does this mean you're never going home?"

"I'm afraid it may come to that."

"You don't love us anymore? What about poor Papa? Does he know what you've done!"

"Gil knows." A shadow fell over the bright blue

eyes. "And don't ever think I don't love you. You know my family is the most important part of my heart and soul."

"Then why in the name of heaven are you doing this to us?"

"I love your father. I've loved your father through the good, the bad, and the best and the worst of our many years of marriage. He was my friend and my foe. And always my lover." She blushed. "My love grew with each passing year. But he took a mistress. The new love—"

"Papa wouldn't do that to you. He's never even glanced at another woman. He loves you as much as you loved him."

"His new love has his attention. I became the old gray mare. That's why, when I dined alone on my fiftieth birthday, I decided to leave home. Possibly for good. The mistress of politics stole my husband."

I should have suspected, should have known. Papa ate, slept, and lived politics, and anyone who wanted his attention summoned disappointment. Margaret got out of bed, her head swimming, and started toward her mother. Lisette stood. Their arms wound round each other. There would be no more arguing about a return.

"If Gil wants me," Lisette whispered, "he knows where I am."

Margaret wouldn't say anything, but she knew her father and his frame of mind, at least as of the end of last September. He wouldn't be leaving the district along the Potomac.

Where did that leave his family? Margaret wouldn't leave her mother in Mexico, either at this health retreat or in the hands of a member of the hated Hapsburg family. The irony of it all came down on her, and she suppressed a snort of hysterical laughter. Nothing would ever be the same for the threesome that had set out from San Antonio; their worlds have been turned upside down as they undertook this peculiar odyssey of goodwill. They shouldn't, couldn't, wouldn't leave empty-handed.

As well, they couldn't leave until she and Rafe were more fit to travel. *It will take more than a couple of days.*

"Up. Up, up. Up and at 'em! I'll abide no lying about at Eden Roc. Reveille, reveille!"

From the *casita's* porch, the voice boomed like thunder on the mountains, and a series of knocks on the wooden door sounded as if those mountains were crashing to rubble. Rafe jumped. His bed partner roused, dashed with sharp claws across the master's collarbone — right in the same spot where the Arturiano's second bullet had caught him, of course — and shot across the room to shove his nose to the crack beneath the door. All the while, Caballo barked.

"Eagle. Eagle, wake up. We have a regimen to commence!"

What? Rafe shook his head to clear it. Rubbing the sleep from his eyes, he realized that Isaiah Nash had some sort of plans. Why couldn't it have been Margarita with the wake-up call? Thanks to his injuries and her poor health, they were way behind with lovemaking. A few gropes and licks had their appeal, but he was anxious for more of what they had finally gotten around to, the night before arriving at Eden Roc.

"I say in there, I must insist you look alive!"

"Insist" from the hombre who'd been sleeping like a big dog in front of a Christmas fire, just three days ago? "Be right there."

If Rafe had a muscle that didn't ache, it had the size of Caballo's dewclaw. After yet another night without Margarita to comfort him, after one more night of not being able to roll and tumble to prevent kinks—not to mention Caballo proving to be a bed hog that, barring eviction from the *casita,* couldn't be kept off the bed—Rafe was in no mood for annoyances.

He longed to fall asleep again and return to his interrupted dream, where his beautiful Valkyrie had carried him from a battlefield to the Valhalla of her loving arms and seeking lips. *Forget dreams. Go after the real thing.*

He lumbered to stand, wrapped the sheet around his naked middle, and reached for the crutches. The door burst open. And there stood the proprietor, a bugle in hand. Nash brought the instrument to his mouth, and blew the horrid tune that had plagued many an Army man. Caballo was not amused.

Neither was Rafe. "Gabriel, go blow your horn somewhere else. I'm sick."

Nash freed his mouth. "How did you know my first name is Gabriel? My parents, God rest their souls, christened me Gabriel Isaiah Nash." He inspected the bugle, turning it up and down. "During the final days of my misspent youth, I served as

315

bugle boy for old Sam Houston up in Texas. Got me in the habit of rising early." He reached down and tucked the now tail-wagging Chihuahua in the crook of his arm. "Good habit to be in."

"I'm tickled pink for you."

"Yes, yes. Now, we must get down to business. You've got ten minutes to dress and stand attention at the exercise field. We'll start with an easy workout, then—"

"My leg is broken."

"You can move your arms, can't you? And you have but one injured leg. A bit of stretching, some steam, a massage. Did you know we have a resident masseuse? Big Swedish girl, Helga. Great hands. And she can suck the brass off a doorknob."

Once upon a time, big, blond, and specially talented would have piqued Rafe's interest.

"Watch her, Eagle. Best not to let Helga get the upper hand. She's one of those gals who like to do the bossing." Nash tossed his hand up. "At any rate, we must set you up for a visit to the magical waterfall. Don't worry, we have a winch rigged to lower the infirm to the canyon floor, and up again." Nash eyed the cast. "Don't imagine you'd better get that wet, though. We'll get you in the waters as soon as possible." He set Caballo to four paws, dusted his hands, then smiled. "Let us set to our designs. Then afterward, a bite of breakfast."

Rafe took a good look at the rosy-cheeked host. While the temperature outside had a bracing edge, Nash had dressed in cotton *huipils*. The legs and sleeves were cropped. Years ago, rumors of this health fanatic had circulated within the Tarahumara

316

tribe, had been retold to Rafe, but he'd never for a moment believed those stories. *They're true.*

Rafe started to tell the man, "Count me out," but when he caught his reflection in the mirror, he dropped a crutch. He jumped with fright. *That old hombre can't be me!* Just over two months had passed since he'd pulled that first gray hair from his scalp. If he went to yanking them now, he'd end up bald. And his face—he resembled three-week-old cow dung.

Washed-up, old, crippled. How had it all happened, and so quickly?

What a temptation, giving this crackpot's ideas a try, but the voice of Rafe's conscience shouted. His purpose wasn't to peel his years away. He had an uncle to subdue and conquer. He had a warrior-woman to deal with. To stay here and indulge in rejuvenation would be the nth degree of hypocrisy, for it condoned the pampered rich.

You've got more than yourself to consider. Margarita's health. At Rancho Gato he had spent several nights pouring elixir and bathing her sweaty brow. It scared the living daylights out of him, the thought that he might lose her.

"What about my *mujer?*" he asked the embodiment of youth and enthusiasm. "Is she included in the regimen?"

"Soon, my boy. Soon. Passed her and her mama not ten minutes ago, on their way to the dining hall. I must say the young lady didn't look nearly as peaked as she did upon arrival."

If this Eden Roc place might do Margaret some good, Rafe conceded they should give it a try.

317

"What's for breakfast?"

"Alfalfa sprouts, pine nuts, and yogurt. A big glass of prune juice kissed with fish-liver oil." One hand on the door latch, Nash clipped a salute. "In no time, my boy, your legs will be moving as fast as a Tarahumara."

"That's not all, I don't doubt."

Twenty-four

"Mother, that man is a nut. A bona fide lunatic. How can he expect people to get well eating grass and fermented milk, and drinking juices?"

"The proof surrounds you. Right here in the dining room." Seated at a table for two in the spacious dining hall, Lisette spread her arms to indicate the handful of devotees likewise seated. "A healthy diet, though, is only one aspect of Isaiah's rejuvenation program."

Hocus-pocus. Really? Some cursory reading on the mind's power of suggestion, done at the sanatorium, had given Margaret a basis for believing that anything was possible, if a person had enough faith. She figured it had more to do with how much a person was willing to devote to any program to enhance one's self. After all, rest and relaxation had saved her life. "But Dr. Woodward would be appalled. We ate diets rich in protein."

"Well, here you eat a diet rich in vitamins. And you'll get plenty of what you need from the yogurt and so forth." Lisette smiled proudly, as if she were the purveyor of good health. "Don't forget — it's all you can eat."

Oh, please. "Mother, where is Olga?" It hurt, not having her triplet rush to greet her. "I thought she'd have come by my *casita*. And where is Leonardo?"

"Leonardo's away from the compound — business, you understand. And Olga, well, I imagine she's resting. She tires so easily nowadays."

"Then I shall call on her *casita* — she does have a *casita,* doesn't she? — just as soon as I've seen to Rafe's well-being."

"Don't forget the stretching class at ten bells. Right afterward, Isaiah has arranged for Helga to give you a massage. Then it's a nap for you." Lisette nibbled something green and fresh. "He'll show you the waterfalls after siesta time."

With a nod, Margaret noticed the other diners were leaving. "I suppose it won't hurt anything. But it seems rather Alpine around here."

Alpine. Oh, to go back to Alpine, Texas. But would she have done anything differently? For all the awful things that had befallen them, Rafe was the greatest adventure of her life.

"Gretchen?"

"Oh, um, yes. Isn't it a bit chilly for bathing outdoors?"

"It's much warmer and drier on the canyon floor. It never gets cold down there. It's still the Chihuahuan desert, in the lower elevations." A moment passed. "Margaret" — Lisette addressed her in this fashion only at the gravest of times — "what is going on with you and Rafe?"

Margaret took a tiny sip of juice. Her line of

sight catching on a *retablo*—a painted panel representing the Virgin of Guadalupe, Mexico's patron saint—Margaret was reminded of a vow she'd made to God. Her mother needed to know about it. "I'm going to join the Catholic church."

"I, um, I can't criticize you for changing religions—I switched from Martin Luther's teachings to those of Calvin and Knox. And your sister converted in order to marry Leonardo. But why are you adopting papistry? For marriage?"

"No, not for anything like that. When it looked like Rafe was dying, I made a bargain with God. If He would let him live, I'd embrace Catholicism."

"You must . . . you must love Rafe very much."

Margaret gave a shrug conveying more nonchalance than she felt. "I'm not certain how I feel. I know I'm obsessed with him. Whatever my true feelings, they scare me."

"Is he courting you?"

"I'd say it's much more than courting. We're having an affair." Margaret might have blushed, but she'd always been open and honest with her mother. Besides, she knew Lisette's feet were once made of clay. The mean streets of life and love had given her strength and sagacity; judgmental wasn't Lisette's way.

Despite being the paradigm for parenthood, she took on an unhappy expression. "You're not happy—a mother knows these things. You're willing to settle for an affair—why? And you know he's a Romeo. What about the future? What about his future? *Gott in Himmel*, if you don't love Rafael Delgado—"

"I think I love him. He's helped me see that the life I chose for myself isn't the path I want to take. If I'm given the chance for a path. I don't know about the future—I'm not sure I have one. Mother, my tuberculosis has returned."

"If your health is all that holds you back from giving your heart, don't worry, my darling Gretchen." The serenity in Lisette's face and manner had a calming effect. "You've come to the right place. The falls will take care of you."

"What good has it done Olga?"

"That's different. Nothing can heal her eyes."

"As soon as your bathing costumes are sewn, Margaret," said the owner of Eden Roc, the afternoon sun shining on his hatless head, "you're to take the waters twice a day."

"Yes, Isaiah," she replied, conforming to his rule of first-names-only.

She'd learned much from him on the trek to the canyon floor. The natives lived in caves; the flora and fauna were much the same as in other arid sections of Chihuahua; he feared rumors of a railway to traverse the barrancas would come to fruition.

"Did you enjoy the massage and the fruit drink?"

"The massage was nice."

Margaret giggled, recalling buxom Helga. Forceful fit her, to say the least. She talked to everyone as if they were little children. Straight out of a Wagnerian opera, the masseuse had the strength of ten men in her large hands, and the roar of a cage of lions in her voice. All she lacked was a horned helmet, and she'd fit the popular image of a Valkyrie.

Valkyrie.

Rafe.

Best not to think about him and his whereabouts.

Margaret honed in on the Fountain of Youth. It seemed to spring from nowhere. Sounding and looking as if it would give great balm to the weary and the feeble, the waterfall cascaded from a height of about a hundred feet, plunging down a great pile of boulders to collect in a pool and to work its wizardry on Isaiah Nash's select few guests.

With the exception of Lisette McLoughlin, plus her titled daughter and son-in-law being on the premises for months, the guests were limited to a two-week stay that eased the lines from their mouths and put a new lift in their step. (Could have been all that prune juice.)

"Everyone!" Isaiah motioned them out of the pool. "Everyone, gather round. I want to make proper introductions."

They assembled. The ladies wore bathing pantalette-dresses of serge, ribbons, and bows; bathing caps covered their hair. The men had donned all-in-ones, some in stripes, others in solid navy blue. No one seemed concerned about ladies bathing with gentlemen.

There was the socialite Mrs. Hannibal Preston of Philadelphia; J. William Fisk, a one-eyed attorney from California; Mr. and Mrs. Abraham Watson and their spinster daughter Beatrice of the Netherlands Antilles, Edna Watson being Isaiah's third cousin; and Sean Moynihan, Irishman. All appeared hale and hearty.

Noticeably absent were *El Aguila Magnífico* and the Lady of Granada.

Now that the introductions were over, the devotees took to the pool afresh. Margaret had her doubts about a couple of angles, neither having anything to do with bathing costumes or social mores. Where were Rafe and Olga?

Don't create your own problems, for heaven's sake.

She stopped alongside the water's edge to ask, "Isaiah, how do you get your guests to leave at the end of two weeks?"

"I invite only the crème de la crème. It would be bad form to overstay one's welcome, and persons of refinement know it."

"Why are you letting Olga and her husband stay longer?"

"Because they belong to Lisette."

Suspicious of his motives toward her gorgeous and vulnerable mother, Margaret inquired, "Why do you allow *her* to linger?"

Much to her relief, he replied, "I think of Lisette as a second daughter. My father's heart has gone out to her. How could Gil ignore such a precious flower? As for why she's allowed to stay, I humor her as I do Natalie. Lisette believes her husband will fulfill her romantic illusions, will charge in on a magnificent steed to sweep her into his arms."

Margaret considered her single-minded papa. "I trust she's not counting too much on that."

"I hope not, too."

She glanced at the elfin Irishman; he gamboled in the water spray with the homely, athletic Beatrice Watson. "And from what list of crème de la crème does Mr. Moynihan, er, I mean *Sean* hail?"

"He's a mining engineer. An incredible mining engineer. Best man I had in my mines, when I had mines. We've kept in touch over the years. He's a widower, no children. Sean has been like a son to me. My late wife Alberta and I wanted a brood of children; alas, Natalie is the one and only, and she came in Alberta's Indian summer. Would that I could have found this Fountain before it was too late for my precious Alberta."

Remembrances saddened Isaiah's angelic face, but he never allowed himself to suffer the doldrums. "Melancholy saps energy needed for organic reconstruction. In any event, you asked about Sean. His ruddy grins and good humor filled the gap at many of our holiday and Sunday tables. He'd make a lady a good catch. Interested?"

"No, thank you," she answered, recalling the horrors of the Santa Alicia mine. "I would, however, be interested in an intellectual chat about the workings of mines."

At Rancho Gato, Rafe had come up with the harebrained idea to blow up the Santa Alicia. What end would such a ruthless act gain? Innocent people might get hurt. Though Arturo behaved in a manner typical of the all-too-greedy, the idea of using violence to subdue him had a nasty taste to it, worse than alfalfa sprouts and prune juice.

Disinterested in getting into the subject of retaliation with Isaiah Nash, she asked, "How do you get

325

everyone, once they leave, to keep quiet about the Fountain's healing properties?"

"It's never been a problem," he replied. "But I do fret, truth be known. If word is bandied about, the complex could be overrun by a bad element. That's why I insist each guest swear to secrecy."

"You haven't sworn me to secrecy."

Isaiah smiled. "If you must brag on Eden Roc, please consider employing the procedure that has worked well with my guests whose lips have loosened to the ears of pushy undesirables."

"Care to elaborate?"

"Tell the nosy that dysentery runs rampant from the water supply. No one can *stomach* more than a couple of weeks."

She laughed, so did the octogenarian. She was beginning to understand why her mother so loved Eden Roc. Dear, kind, and considerate fit Isaiah Nash. And his beloved utopia was the paradise of his vision. But Margaret wondered if he didn't trust too easily. For all his veneration of Lisette, she'd told several in the family about this place. Of course, no one gave it much credence. That, Margaret supposed, was another beauty to Eden Roc. It was too incredible for credibility.

Looking over at Isaiah, she said, "Here, a person can forget the outside world exists." She paused. "This piteous world of slavery and hunger and ignorance and inhumanity."

He nodded, then placed a comforting hand on her shoulder. "What troubles you, my dear?"

"Have you heard of Arturo Delgado?"

"But of course. He's been my guest on several

occasions."

"Then you have allowed the monstrous into your midst."

"I, well, I'm aware of his vices. But for so many years, he was Natalie's choice as a suitor. What was a father to do? I didn't want to lose my daughter."

Suspicious and worried, Margaret asked, "Is she still friendly with him?"

"Oh, no. Their link dissolved when she left for the theaters of the United States. Can't say I'm sorry."

She took comfort, yet . . . "Rafe assured me it isn't possible, but can Arturo Delgado gain entrance to Eden Roc?"

"No. Netoc would kill him first."

Well, thank God for Netoc.

"Maggie!"

She turned to her brother's voice. Waving, smiling, and garbed in a jersey all-in-one, he strutted toward her. Natalie, as much a vision of loveliness as she'd been on the train in Texas, had laid her palm across his proffered forearm. She, too, had dressed for the waterfall.

Father Xzobal, wearing a golden cross as well as the ecclesiastical soutane he'd been forced to abandon all the way to Eden Roc, followed behind them. A skull cap now covered his freshly shaved tonsure. Natalie kept turning to him.

"Sis, ain't this a great place?"

"Yes, Tex."

It turned sour within seconds of Margaret's reply. A loud squeaking rent the air, as the winch lowered a seat bucket. The basket seat's occupants? Rafe and Olga.

Laughing and chatting, he had an arm around her shoulders. The girlish-looking Olga—who'd been too tired, supposedly, to call on the triplet she hadn't visited in ages—fluttered her hand in the air, then leaned her cheek against Rafe's shoulder, which just happened to be the same one that had taken the bullet.

Any time Margaret had so much as touched it, he'd yelped like a stuck pig. *Face it. It's not your picture his mother is passing around.* If that meant she shouldn't feel the knife that stabbed her heart, then she was in trouble. *I'm in trouble, period.*

Twenty-five

If someone had asked Rafe Delgado to comment on his state of mind when Olga approached the mule-driven elevator system, his reply would have been, "Sour."

La Condesa had hurt him too deeply for a friendly reunion, replete with open arms. When she'd caught him as he climbed into the basket seat, he'd tried to ignore her and the tap, tap, tap of her white cane.

"Rafael? Rafael, is it you?"

Taking hesitant steps in his direction, she stubbed the toe of her shoe on a rock. She cried out. What could he do but rush over and keep her from falling? He was amazed to discover that he felt nothing from having her in his arms again.

Her fingertips feathered up his chest, moved up his throat to his mouth. "This is the way I see nowadays. With my fingers. It's nice to see you again, Rafael."

"Don't do too much looking. I'm in love with your sister, and I wouldn't want her walking up and getting the wrong idea."

"In love with Maggie? I'm so pleased. I've many times prayed you both would find happiness." Olga smiled brightly. "She's such a remarkable person."

Rafe studied Olga. She wasn't the least upset that he'd fallen in love with another woman, her own sister. What did that say about her feelings for him in bygone days? *Her empty promises should have told the story, Delgado.* He said, "Margarita is remarkable. She's all I've ever wanted in a lady."

"You're so very fortunate." Olga moistened her lips. "Are you on your way to the waterfall? May I join you? I fear Isaiah forbids me from taking the natural stairway."

What was Rafe to say? No? He helped her into the basket seat, then got aboard and hugged his side of the compact contraption.

She asked him to put his arm around her shoulders, when the basket had begun to lower. "I'm scared," she said in her little girl voice. "This seat makes for an uneven ride, wouldn't you agree? Without my sight, it seems as if we're falling. Tell me, please, Rafael. Tell me what it looks like."

Rafe didn't want to discuss the magnificent view, not unless he shared it with Margarita. *My delicate warrior-woman, where will we go from here?* Yes, she'd agreed to be part of his fight, but as cranky as she'd been of late, he'd begun to believe she had second thoughts where he was concerned.

"Why won't you answer?"

"Oh, uh. You wanted to know about the view." Rafe took a look at Olga. As usual, she was dressed primly. He couldn't help pitying her vacant stare,

330

yet . . . "It's a beautiful place. The very essence of beauty."

He saw an oval face, lips generous and sensuous, black winged brows, and a wealth of wavy hair the rich brown of Veracruzano coffee beans. The bloom of health brightened a flawless complexion, and filled out a body obviously not racked by terrible hacking fits nor strength-sapping night sweats. He saw Margarita at twenty, as she'd been when he'd first seen her in the Bexar County Courthouse.

¡Maldicion! It wasn't fair to Margarita that she'd aged at such a galloping rate, while her identical triplet sister never changed. His eyes burning for his beloved, he forced his gaze to the canyon. Its beauty engulfed him. And his memories . . . He loved the Sierras. It was home.

But he wouldn't share so much of himself with Olga. He replied, "It's big. It's deep. It's intimidating."

"Have you ever been to the Arizona Territory? I've been told there is a great canyon up there, but the Copper Canyon is bigger and deeper."

"I'll take your word for it."

Silence fell, punctuated by the creak of the pulley mechanism, and the wail of wind as it tumbled through the great chasm of the Sierra Madre Tarahumara. As far as Rafe was concerned, no talking suited him fine.

"Tell me about yourself, Rafael. I understand you own a ranch near San Antonio. You raise bulls and export them to Mexico for the bullring, Mutti says."

"I bought the ranch for me and you. I even took your papá's charity to stock it. I had a word with

331

my pride. I told myself it would benefit his daughter. And her . . . children. I should have been telling myself the truth." That truth choked him; it took a mighty effort to admit, "I traded guns and ammunition—and my principles—for a few head of cattle."

Olga moved her cane. "I always thought you'd return to Chihuahua and become a matador again."

That was how little she knew him. Never for a moment in the past had he intimated any desire to return to the corrida. Olga rattled and prattled on. Hate wasn't what he felt for her. Pleased didn't describe him, either. Beautiful she might be, but she hadn't changed in all these years. He didn't know how he'd ever preferred her to Margarita.

"Why, Rafael Delgado, I don't believe you've heard a word I've said."

"Guilty. Tell me again."

"I'm sorry I didn't write."

"Why didn't you? Write or come back."

"Goodness gracious, I was so very busy. Then Leonardo refused to give me a divorce. The royals and their Church are funny that way."

"He knows about us?" By nodding, she confirmed what Rafe suspected already, and he asked, "How much does he know? And did you lie to him, like you lied to your sister? Did you tell him I raped you?"

She blushed and chewed her bottom lip. "That was easier to explain than the truth. Which was just too, too shameful to confess. Oh, Rafael, you won't tell on me, will you? I would die of embarrassment if my mother or brother or sister—" She flailed around to take his hand and squeeze his fingers.

"Promise you won't tell!"

"Olga, what we had together was by mutual consent. I didn't force myself on you, ever. You were willing enough." Granted she'd lain in the dark like a limp rag most of the time, begging him not to touch her here, there, and most everywhere else. "My intentions were honorable all the way. But what did I get? Betrayal. Then you ruined my reputation."

"Oh, pish-posh." Her manner took a vinegary switch. "You never had a reputation to ruin. Plus, anyway, you're making it sound much worse than it was. The only ones I told were Maggie and Leonardo. Maggie, so she wouldn't think ill of me for sleeping with you. As for Leonardo —"

"Is it necessary to pepper every reference with his name?"

"Please don't yell at me." Her chin quivered. "I have enough trouble as is. I can't take anymore upsets. It's not good for us." Her palm pressed against the mound of her belly. "A gentleman wouldn't ask a lady to recant her story."

"I'm not a gentleman."

"Maybe not, but don't you feel an obligation to the past?"

He did. He had, after all, made a sinner out of a prim countess. "All right. I promise not to say anything."

She sighed. "Oh, thank you. That's so sweet of you. You were always so sweet. I have missed you so terribly, Rafael. You made me feel like a queen."

"Countess isn't good enough for you?" He wasn't proud of his sarcastic tone, but couldn't stop himself. Eyeing her stomach, he asked, "How many babies does this make for you? After all these years, it couldn't be your second."

"It . . . it is."

"What happened to the first? I seem to recall my child was the reason you wanted to come back to me."

Solemn moments passed before she replied, "I miscarried. Not long after I reached Granada."

"Merdo."

"It was my punishment for being an adulteress—I just know it was! And to think I didn't even enjoy sexual congress that much. Oh!" She covered her mouth with her fingers, blushing a scarlet red. "I—I didn't mean it like that. I—I d-didn't. I promise you."

He sat, numb. "Don't make excuses for honesty. If that's what you're being. I'll admit my touch seemed to revolt you, but what about the night before you told me goodbye? In the shadows of the Alamo. Are you saying you weren't enjoying the way I made love to you with my mouth and finger?"

"Finger? What finger? What Alamo? You've got me mixed up with one of your other ladies."

Her game didn't strike him as cute. "Shall I elaborate on the finger and—"

"Rafael, you're being indelicate."

"We got pretty damned indelicate, countess."

Her mouth flattened. "We never touched each other except behind locked doors, and when we did, I didn't allow you all those liberties you wanted. And you know it."

"Your memory may have faded." Which was no

compliment to his already bruised ego. "It was the night before you told me you had to go back to Spain, to tell your husband you wanted a divorce."

"Rafael, I remember that night. I called on old friends that evening, to bid them adios. I stayed until well past midnight, then the host escorted me back to the Menger Hotel."

Was he getting the old man's disease of memory loss? No. So much fire had been out of Olga's character; she endured sex; he should have questioned a change in behavior at the time.

Margarita was different. She savored and celebrated the act of mating, her spontaneity the substance of wonder.

You stupid fool. How could you have been so dumb? All these years he'd been longing for the wrong sister! All along *Margarita* had filled his hopes and dreams. He could have laughed and cried. And he could have choked her. Why did she do such a thing?

"What about me?" Olga asked quietly. "Are you mad? Please don't be mad, Rafael. I can't stand the thought . . ."

"Don't worry. What's done is done."

"Thank you. You were always so dear."

He took a long look at Olga. She might not have been his Alamo lover, yet he couldn't disregard all the times Olga had been Olga. Even though the overture had come from her, she'd been a woman unhappy and unfulfilled in her marriage, searching for something better than her lot—such was only human. And Rafe could have said no.

He'd been weak, had overlooked their sins against

her husband. And God. Rafe had introduced her to adultery, and he'd impregnated her. He owed her something. The extent of his debt, he couldn't reckon. He didn't wish to ruminate it.

"Rafael . . . were you teasing me about that finger business?"

"Yes," he replied, not wanting her to realize who had met him in the Alamo shadows. Thank the Holy Virgin, Olga was no genius. "It was all a joke."

He itched to get to the truth of that evening by the Alamo. On one hand he was thrilled to know Margarita had been the one to make him dream of settling down. On the other he could have strangled her for deceiving him all these years. Wasted years! Years they could have been laughing and loving—together.

You weren't ready for all that, back then, not with the girl who intimidated the Eagle. He ignored the whispers in his head.

"Can we be friends?" Olga asked him.

Hesitating to answer, Rafe squinted at the sky. *This is a mess.* He wanted no part of a friendship with her. He wanted her sister and no one to bother them.

While he didn't quite see the beauty in making Margarita his bride right now, he realized his aggravation would pass. If—when!—they were wed, trouble could be in the offing, should this dilemma with Olga not be settled. After all, she and her count would become kin.

Merdo.

Rafe turned to his beloved's sister. "As you wish.

We can be friends."

"Thank you."

The basket seat reached the ground, and his eager fingers unfastened the leather latch. He hopped out, grabbed his crutches, then noticed the gap-toothed attendant Hipólito wasn't at the moorage.

Something about the absent jack-of-all-trades had struck Rafe as peculiar, but he scoffed away his intuition. Hipólito was a benign little hombre.

"Hello, Triplet."

That wasn't Olga's whiney, little-girl voice, though she did say, "Why, Sissy, I'd know you anywhere. Did you have a nice trip? I'm so happy you're here."

Rafe twisted to the left. Margarita, the hurt of the world in her eyes and face, stood a few feet down the incline from the elevator. He saw that she had jumped to the wrong conclusion.

"We need to talk," he said to her. "I've been looking for you—"

"Spare me." Margarita raised a palm to ward off his words. "I'd rather not hear flimsy excuses." She whirled around, marched off.

" 'Rita, wait!" He tried to get the crutches going, but they seemed to get tangled in the unwieldy cast. " 'Rita! Hear me out!"

She didn't.

"Thanks for the insult," he said through gritted teeth.

Just like always, she hadn't given him the benefit of a doubt. What kind of team did they have, with her feeling so little for him? Damn her to hell. Where was her trust? Where was her faith in him, and their love?

"Sissy? Sissy, where are you? Rafael, where did she go? Rafael, please help me. Please! You've always been so strong. How I depend on your strength. I'm scared! I can't get out of this seat on my own. I shall fall if no one helps me. Rafael—You won't let me down, will you?"

" 'Rita!" Her name echoed through the canyon. She kept walking.

All right, fine.

Good.

Let her go. It was better this way. If she'd stayed, no telling what he would have done. It wouldn't have been pleasant. He was pissed-off from being pissed upon. In the past. And today. He needed time to cool his temper.

Rafe hopped around to help her triplet.

Twenty-six

Chin up. Shoulders square. Smile. Keep moving. This was how Margaret took leave of Rafe and Olga at the curious elevator. This was how she behaved all afternoon. It even worked at dinner, the highlights of which were muskmelon, goat cheese, and oat bread of heavy texture. The low part? Sitting at the table with a subdued Rafe and a chatty Olga.

Margaret could never recall if anyone else had occupied that dining room.

It hurt to witness what she'd always suspected. At first opportunity, Rafe—a rogue and a rambling man—had turned to Olga. Confirming her suspicions didn't make the pain go away. After that one blatant show of emotion at the falls, though, she was, nonetheless, proud of herself for not showing how much it hurt.

An hour after bedtime that night, she heard him tapping on her cottage door. She kept silent, fearing he'd break down the door. He didn't. The next day she immersed herself in the business of getting well, taking each and every one of Isaiah's suggestions.

Cornering Sean Moynihan, she addressed her brain to vertical mines.

"How do they work?"

Sean smiled his freckled smile. "A learned colleen ye are, but would not ye be bored with technicality?"

Rather than insult his profession by admitting she'd just as soon study the sleeping habits of the blind mole rat, she said, "Rafe and I have had some trouble with Arturo Delgado. We may need to get into the Santa Alicia silver mine at some point."

"Arturo Delgado? A sly beastie is he." Sean's elfin features turned dark. "Tell me, bonny colleen, what is it that ye wanna be doin' to Arturo Delgado?"

"Make him free his slaves. Rafe thinks that can only be done by some sort of armed confrontation, and to tell the truth, I fear it may come to that."

On a nod, Sean commented, " 'Twould seem the case, knowing the beastie as I do. But would ye be telling me where I fit into yer scheme?"

"Rafe has ideas to sabotage the Delgado mines. Starting with the Santa Alicia."

Interest danced in Sean's bottle-green eyes. "Ah . . . what a grand idea is yours! Ye do know that Irishmen love a fight, don't ye? How can this son o' Eire be o' help?"

"As I said before, teach me about mines."

For a while, as Sean explained the rudiments of his profession, she actually didn't think about Rafe. Well, no more than ten or twelve times.

She spent that night in her mother's *casita*. And

the next and the next.

Amazingly, her strength began to return.

Somewhere in between all that, Isaiah sawed off Rafe's cast. "To get air to the wound," the host revealed to her after wrapping his lips around a repast of carrots and watermelon juice. "That cast has been on long enough, anyway, and he needs the magical water—which he couldn't get all trussed up."

Isaiah knew what he was talking about. Who could fail to notice Rafe's immediate and marked improvement?

While she kidded herself into thinking she had no interest in his activities, her ears were peeled to any mention of him. He spent most of his time outdoors, had even started riding Diablo again. The Countess of Granada, still able to ride despite her impediment, went along with him. They both had many rhapsodic comments about the wonders of the surrounds.

Through it all, Margaret comported herself with civility toward Rafe and his constant companion, who ignored her triplet but clung to their lover as if he were a lifeline.

It seemed he hadn't forgotten her, though. One morning, when Helga was busy rearranging Margaret's muscles, the masseuse said, "There is a package for you. Do not forget it." And it turned out to be a package of herbs along with a sheet of instructions penned by Rafe. The birth control herbs from Areponapuchi. The nerve of him! Margaret could have strangled the gallant-come-lately.

341

She tossed part and parcel into the pot-bellied stove in her cottage. As soon as they went up in smoke, she had second thoughts. There might be an odd chance that she'd need them in the future.

When they had been at Eden Roc for a tennight, Margaret let it be known—a stage whisper did have its uses at times—she would return to her own cottage. But he didn't come calling. This made a fresh gash in her already damaged heart, since as long as he tapped on her door, she wasn't without hope.

"What should I do?" she whispered in the dark.

She couldn't ignore him forever. They had much to discuss; she wasn't sure he even knew that her mother had no intention of leaving. Of course, he could have asked. Obviously he was in no rush to get away from the more amiable Olga.

"That's unfair, Margaret McLoughlin," she scolded herself. "He was so very, very sick. He has a right to recuperate."

She turned her face into the pillow, trying to block the images of that worst time at Rancho Gato. The rancher and his wife had helped her bathe his face with wet cloths and tend the dreadful wounds, as Xzobal said prayer after prayer. A fat little old lady, the *curandera,* arrived with her pots of herbal remedies and the quackery that made up her witchcraft. Margaret demanded a doctor—a real doctor. But when the mustachioed young man arrived, the prognosis wasn't good.

"His only chance is if we take the leg."

"No." Fear tightened her windpipe. "He doesn't want that. You've got to try to save him and the limb."

Dr. Benavides worked diligently. Two nights later the doctor called Xzobal aside, then put his arm around Margaret's shoulder. "I've done all I can."

Panicked and frantic, she rushed to Rafe's bedside and fell to her knees. Already the rancher and his wife were there. So were Tex and Xzobal. And the priest, with his crucifix and holy water and lowly intoned Latin sacraments, administered extreme unction.

She cried for Rafe, her tears falling down her cheeks and off her chin. Somehow he moved his hand and placed it on her jaw. She leaned over him, pressing her lips to his fevered ones. "You mustn't give up. We have much to do, *compadre*."

"Yes . . . much."

"If he lives," she whispered to Xzobal Paz, "I'll take his religion."

Xzobal's gentle face filled with compassion. "Don't bargain with the devil."

"This is no bargain with the devil. This is a promise to your God and mine. If He in His grace will save Rafe, and if He allows me to have a little longer here on earth, I will repay Him the kind favor."

"Only a woman very in love would make such an offer."

She didn't answer. She didn't have an answer.

Before the next dawn, Rafe's fever broke. Three days later the doctor was able to set the leg. And three weeks later, she and Rafe, along with their brothers, set out for Eden Roc. She didn't forget her vow, once they had arrived, and several times Xzo-bal had questioned her on it.

"I intend to make good on my promise," she said to herself, here in this lonely *casita*. Throwing off the covers as well as her recollections, she got out of bed. "I need to do *something*. Rafe and I can't go on ignoring each other."

They needed to make plans for leaving, as well as for his Uncle Arturo. These were good enough intentions to call on a lover losing interest, weren't they?

She went to his *casita*. He wasn't there.

"You bastard," Margaret muttered. "You heartless callous rutting bastard. Why am I not surprised?"

From her vantage point a couple dozen footsteps away—she'd been passing by on her return from his empty bungalow—she watched Rafe close the door to Olga's *casita,* step onto the porch and into the clement air of midnight. His walking stick in one hand, he put a comb to his mussed hair.

She let him get into the pathway connecting the cottages before she marched up to him. "Fancy meeting you here. Out for a night's stroll?"

"I, uh, I was on my way to you."

Just like that afternoon at the elevator mooring, Rafe's excuse sounded hollow. "What a relief," she said cattily. "Out of the arms of one triplet and straight to the other. A scenario to warm the cockles of my heart."

He settled the crook of the cane over his forearm,

exhaling as if he'd never been more fatigued by a subject. "Let me explain—"

"No! I've heard enough."

She grabbed that stupid cane, swinging her arm high with all her might, meaning to toss it into the branch of a nearby pine tree. But the walking stick snapped on the side of Rafe's miserable disgusting head.

Her palm covered her mouth in horror.

He yelped, clutched his pate—which wasn't bleeding, thank heavens!—then grabbed her retreating arm. "Damn you to hell. You could've killed me."

"Impossible. Only the good die young, you narcissistic louse, you lothario of the lowest form. You, who abandoned a defenseless woman to Chihuahua's answer to Robin Hood and his merry men."

"You've never been defenseless." He yanked her to him. His voice as raspy as sandpaper, his eyes piercing hers under the full moon, he shook her shoulders. "What gives you the right to strike me?"

"Anger!"

He took a deep breath, obviously to calm himself. "You might try listening to reason, then you wouldn't need to work yourself into a lather."

"Reason? Where's the reason in your leaving a married woman's cottage? Where's the reason to make love with your lover's sister? But then, you've been doing that ever since that night in Pancho Villa's house. I'm just second in line." *And now you've gone back to the more important one, the beautiful one.* "You have the morals of a cat."

His fingers bit cruelly into her upper arm. When

345

he replied, ice cracked his tone. "Careful of passing judgments. You're no pillar of virtue yourself. I've been meaning to speak to you about—Ouch! Watch what you're doing. You kicked my hurt leg."

"If you were any kind of a man, you'd have shot those Arturiano dastards before they got the drop on you."

"If you were a man"—he got in her face—"I'd punch you for your remarks."

She peeled his fingers from her arm. "If you were a gentleman, I wouldn't have need to make them."

"You don't own me, Margarita."

"That's right. I don't." She stepped back, her face burning with anger, her limbs shaking with it. "And you don't own my sister. You might have taken up where you left off, but keep something in mind. She's married. And her husband isn't across the ocean this time."

"Let's hope this Eden Roc place heals your head as well as your body."

Margaret whirled away, walking as fast as her legs could carry her, yet she slowed down on the far side of Beatrice Watson's cottage.

Beatrice's voice floated through the open window. "Of course, Seanie, I'd love to see you again. Do come to Curacao and visit. Yes, I do regret that Mother and Father and I will leave on the morrow. Oh, I agree. A relationship must have openness and honesty, if it is to succeed."

Closing her ears to any more eavesdropping, Margaret couldn't help but think about what she'd overheard. *Why didn't you at least listen to what Rafe*

346

had to say? She turned. Hobbling and limping, he headed toward his quarters. He didn't take even the slightest glance to the rear.

She didn't go after him. If he'd cared anything about her, he wouldn't have let her flit away. His passions would have been so strong that wild horses couldn't have held him back.

Lies, eyes, and spies.

Women.

Margarita.

"Merdo."

Rafe, his leg hurting like a son-of-a-bitch, hobbled toward his quarters, muttering curses and berating life in general, Margarita in particular. *"La Bruja* is pushing me to an early grave."

He wouldn't think about the eyes and spies just now.

Cursing her self-righteousness, he let himself in the cottage, shoved a welcoming Caballo from the bed, then fell upon the mattress. A knife of agony carved its way through the marrow of his leg bone, sawing a path through every cell making up the whole of Rafael Delgado.

"Damn her to hell."

You should've let her have it out there. You should have confronted her with her cursed lie. The witch had turned his life inside out, to where he couldn't tell up or down, or right from wrong.

A whimper. A pant. A wet lick on Rafe's ear, along with a claw scratching in sympathy.

"Jesucristo, por el amor de Dios, get off this bed." Rafe swept his arm across the mattress.

The Chihuahua went flying to the floor, but he returned to the bosom of his master. Quickly. "Uumf?"

"All right, you can stay." Rafe, nonetheless, maneuvered to his side, putting Caballo at his back. "Just go to sleep, amigo."

About as obedient as Margarita, the dog sailed to the end of the bed and Rafe's booted feet, then, like a ship rounding the Horn, began the next leg of his journey, dropping the anchor of his chin on the inside of Rafe's crooked elbow. "Uumf?"

If Caballo wanted to hear his troubles, okay. "I've had it to the gills with the McLoughlin sisters. I read about Weird Sisters like them. In Teutonic mythology. I can't recall the Norns' names. But one of them was old, old, old—she's Olga." For all her beauty and youthful appearance, Olga might as well have been a centenarian, so sad was she. "Margarita, she's the image of another Weird Sister. She takes offense to any and every real or imagined slight."

Caballo squirmed. "Uumf?"

Rafe scratched that mangled canine ear. "I should have slammed the door in Margarita's face, when she showed up at my *vacáda*. But, damn, my little friend, can you imagine all I would have missed, if she weren't around?"

Harping. Nagging. Fault-finding.

To her credit, she'd done something he hadn't been able to do. She'd gotten him to Mexico. And here he was, sprawling on a rich man's bed and partaking of a routine allowed only to the most privileged. No telling how long he'd be here. Olga had been informative, where Margarita should have been. Their mother had no intention of going back to her *viejo,* and her most exasperating daughter—whose name started with an *M*—had ideas to escort her back across the Chihuahuan Desert. Naturally, she hadn't mentioned any of this to Rafe.

The witch.

And she'd conveniently forgotten, it seemed, about Xzobal. Did she propose they traipse all over Mexico with a hunted priest in the entourage?

What happened to her promises for the revolution? "Down a sinkhole." He uttered the most basic and vulgar curse in the ensemble of his vocabulary, both in English and Spanish.

If there was anything good going on, it was that Arturo had been lying low. But how long would that last?

Caballo whimpered, then bestowed another kiss.

Rafe cringed. *"Sabe Dios*—God knows—if it weren't for *her,* I wouldn't have to put up with you."

A whimper of injured canine dignity placed guilt where it ought to be. "You're a good *niño.* I'm glad you're with us. When I send for 'Rita's cats—heyyyy, you're gonna love chasing those cats—I'm gonna send for Frita. Remember your mamá?"

Merdo. What was he doing, thinking about collecting a menagerie? Margarita wasn't a settling-down lady, and Rafe had several scores to settle. The first? Having a few words with Margarita about switching places with her sister.

Rafe had gotten his aching body off the bed, had

somehow dragged that aching body to the door, before he had second thoughts. If she loved him — and she'd never once said it, not even in the throes of passion — she would have made mention of her shameless rotten lie, where they could chuckle over it. Or made love in its honor. Eventually.

But no.

He got back in bed and pulled man's best friend close to his chest. "While I'm getting my strength back, I'll stay away from her. I've got other things to keep me occupied. Like with eyes and spies. And Xzobal."

tormented dreams of that aching body to the door
before his wicked practices. She had loved him
when ... his tenderness ... even in the throes

Twenty-seven

"Leonardo, must you be insistent? Why aren't you thankful I've let you back in this *casita?*"

Actually, Olga hadn't let him in. Her husband had gotten a key from one of the easily corruptible minions, probably that lecherous Hipólito. Every time she had the misfortune to pass the churl, he crooned, "Ay, *mamacita.*"

Thankfully Rafael had taken his leave of her quarters before the count arrived. She didn't wish any trouble on the only man who'd made her want nasty things.

A disgusting hand pawed at her. "Please let me, Olgita, my little Olga. *Por favor.*"

"Go to sleep. It's very late."

"I've been gone for two months, yet you still hold yourself away from me. Oh, I know. You're still upset about . . . about, well, you know to what I refer. My temper—I'm sorry for it."

Upset? She hated him. And it had nothing to do with the rape he'd perpetrated on her, which had happened just before he left to perform the wicked business of spying. Two months ago. No, she didn't hate him for violating her person as well as the womb that sheltered her child. Her hatred had been building for years.

His hot breath on her shoulder, she felt his nasty poker drilling at her thigh. He smelled sweetly sweaty, traces of tobacco smoke and the animal stench of fornication clinging to his skin. Attar of roses combined with those other ghastly odors. *He's been to that awful Areponapuchi place.*

Too bad he hadn't gotten his fill there, because Olga had no interest in helping him out. The only man she'd consider was Rafael, yet he'd shown no interest in being naughty with her. He claimed to love Maggie; Olga feared it was true.

Wasn't this what she'd set out to accomplish, a match of her beloveds? She'd been noble enough in Granada, at the Alhambra.

Leonardo had never allowed her to return to Texas on her own, even when she had her eyesight, but after everything had fallen into place for their voyage to Mexico and ensuing stay here at Eden Roc, she'd schemed to get Rafael here. Just to be near him, she'd told herself.

It wasn't until her fingers had touched him that the truth climbed up to grab her throat. She wanted him for Olga. That's why she'd begged his silence about her lie. She wanted to keep the peace, while working on winning his love again. *A hopeless plan, I'm coming to believe.*

A slobbering kiss drew her attention as well as a shiver of revulsion.

"Was your trip successful?" she asked her husband, aspiring to a subject that would sidetrack his doggedness and her tortured truths. "Did Arturo Delgado allow you to do your will with the spies?"

"Don't say spies. It's such a vulgar word."

She found it vulgar that he would spy against his wife's country, but what did she know? Being a commoner in the courts of Europe had given her an education. While those in trade were scorned upon, those whose fathers had built their fortunes on pushing cows from Texas to Kansas were considered even less desirable than the garbage pickers of Delhi. Their Imperial and Royal Majesties treated her as if she were refuse on their jeweled slippers. Which hurt her pride. She wanted so desperately to please those around her. She basked in the sunshine of favor.

There'll be more than a mere scandal, once Leonardo's activities come to light. She had passed a secret to Rafael that could and probably would do her husband in. So be it. It would be the first step in his final payment . . .

His debt had begun years ago, when she'd returned to the shores of Iberia. Leonardo had refused her pleas for a divorce, so she had concocted the rape story. Why? To keep him from venting his fury on her and the—

Her recollections were interrupted as eager fingers started gathering her nightgown up her leg. "My beautiful countess . . ."

"I'm very tired. And my eyes hurt." Rafael had been advising her to go ahead with surgery to ease her discomfort. *Don't think about him. Or about losing your eyeballs.* "The pain has been very bad."

"Would you like some of your sleeping powder?"

How he lied with his attentive tone. That was the Count of Granada, nothing but a lie. Immune to punishment, thanks to his rank. And he put on such a good show as devoted husband and prospective father.

She cringed, imagining his eyes on her. "Leave me alone. Go to sleep."

Once, kindness and patience were your way. That was before Leonardo, in one of his dreadful fits of temper, had yanked Rafael Delgado's beautiful girl-child from her crib, then dunked the wailing babe's face in a golden chalice filled with wine. He held her until she cried no more.

The pit of darkness was Olga's world, yet she saw all the vivid colors, all the shades and shadows, as if her vision were perfect. *Oh, my little girl. If only I could have saved you!*

Leonardo thought he was so, so clever, thought that Olga knew nothing of his crime. Outside the window of the Alhambra, his mother and brother had gagged her, had pinned her arms, had chloroformed her, lest she save her bantling.

The dowager countess had justified it all by saying, "Leonardo loves and reveres you. Yet you sinned against him! You forced my son into putting your bastard out of her misery."

Her baby hadn't deserved punishment for her mother's sin! Olga damned her in-laws. And she laughed when a carriage overturned the next month, mortally injuring both the Dowager and her younger son. Even before their deaths, Olga had vowed to make her murdering husband pay—and pay with the greatest amount of suffering—for saying he'd rear the babe as his own, then killing her instead. *He's been paying. And he will continue to pay.*

It was this lust for vengeance that had kept her from returning to Rafael in 1890. She'd spent these years making Leonardo wish he'd never been born. Soon, her plans and schemes would come to a great and grand conclusion. Soon, the Mexican people would know that yet another devious Hapsburg was using their country to further his Spanish causes. *Like mad dogs, the Mexican peasantry will chew the Count of Granada to shreds.*

She snickered.

Her biggest regret in being sightless? That she couldn't see Leonardo's face when he tumbled into the kennel of his own corruption.

"Olgita . . ." Her husband moved away to sit on the edge of the bed and light a cigarette. The smell of smoldering tobacco nauseated Olga. His breath rushed out as he said, "I'm not taking the ambassadorship."

"Why?"

"I think we should return to Madrid. So my son will be born on Spanish soil. I've arranged for us to leave. Oh, by the way, Arturo Delgado will be accompanying us."

She couldn't see, but her other senses were more sharply defined, and visions of his fear came to her. "Arturo Delgado? You can barely abide the man."

355

She waited a moment. "What is he blackmailing you with?"

"Blackmail? Crudity from my own wife? Have you learned nothing from being in the company of royalty?"

Who was the blind one here? "Leonardo, you may not believe it, but I never knew intrigue, backbiting, and treachery until I married you."

She wormed her way to the far side of the bed, presenting her back and praying for the peace of sleep. She dozed, but came awake with a start when he shook her shoulder.

Leonardo spoke, a strange inflection in his voice. "I thought you said the other guests departed today."

"All but the Watsons and Sean Moynihan. The Watsons leave tomorrow. I don't know about the Irishman."

"They aren't the only guests, it appears." Dead silence fell before Leonardo insisted, "What . . . what is this? Olga—*what is this!*"

"What are you talking about?" She heard something, something that sounded like the links of a small chain pinging together. *Oh, no!* When she'd reached out to Rafe, the chain had broken and then—

"This crucifix," her husband demanded. "Who does it belong to?"

"I have no idea. One of the maids must have dropped it."

A moment passed. "I don't think so. Unless Rafael Delgado has taken to cleaning chambers."

"Really, Leonardo, you're being silly."

"Am I? It's engraved right here on the back. 'To my brother Rafael Delgado from María Carmen.'" Leonardo grabbed her wrist, yanking her across the bed. "He's here. You've enticed your Texas lover to Eden Roc. I will kill him. With my bare hands."

Enjoying his anguish, she tossed his favorite expression back at him. "Leonardo, that is so vulgar."

In the wee hours of morning, as the Tarahumara natives began to beat their drums to beg the sun to rise, the voice of reason had a stern talk with Margaret McLoughlin.

Just because he hadn't fallen to her level of yelling and screaming, who was to say Rafe had no passion for her? She had a roaring passion for him, yet she'd backed off, so who could say his thirsts for her had been slaked? Considering the lovemaking they had shared . . . Considering the ties that went beyond making love . . . Considering their cumulative state of physical dysfunction . . . she couldn't be that wrong about Rafe.

She jumped from bed to collect herself and the tools of peacemaking.

As dawn broke, she found him in a small clearing behind the calisthenics pavilion. The other guests had finished exercising, had gone on to the falls. Rafe lingered. He wore cropped white *huipils* that contrasted to his olive complexion and dark hair. Sitting on the ground with his hairy legs stretched out in front of him, he bent toward one foot, then another. Each movement etched agony and popped sweat on his face. When he caught sight of her, he leaned back on his elbows and took a series of restorative breaths.

His crucifix was missing, she noticed, and wondered why.

One eye squinted, he hoisted his gaze. "About last night . . ."

"I apologize for it. I've been awful. I hope Eden Roc can heal my head as well as my body. Further, I'm sorry for breaking your walking stick." She brought her hand from behind her back, extending a crude cypress cane. "It's not fancy, but maybe it will do until I can get you a proper one."

He took it, rubbed the sweat from his brow, and smiled. "I'll put it to good use. Where did you get it?"

"I, uh" — she shrugged — "my father taught me to whittle."

"Is there anything you can't do?" he asked, awed.

"I'm not very good at conducting a love affair."

"Come here." He winked and crooked a finger at her. "Come sit beside me."

Facing him, she knelt and rested her palms on her thighs. Loam, grass, and perspiration mingled in her nose, as she offered, "Let me rub your leg."

"Which one?" he returned, innuendo in his voice.

"The one that took the bullet." She glanced at the angry red scar. He'd always have a limp, but the outcome could have been much, much worse. Hoping he'd be able to cope with his handicap, she touched the prickly hair of his shin. "I'll grant I'm

358

not as good as Helga at this sort of thing." Her blue eyes met the silver of his. "But I do have enthusiasm on my side."

"No. You wouldn't be as good as Helga. You'd be better than that big blond cow. Much better." His fingers on Margaret's jaw, he rubbed his thumb on her chin, then up to her mouth, and slid it behind her lips to stroke her teeth. "It's not a rubdown I want from you, *querida*. I want to get some honesty between us."

She nodded.

"We can't stay here forever. As soon as we're patched up, we've got to move out. It appears we have a conflict, though. You want to take your mother to Texas, I want to see my brother to Topolobampo. I won't bend, Margarita. Your mother must put her pretty butt on a ship out of Topolobampo. They can sail up to California, then she can take a train from there."

"I don't think she'll agree."

"Then we'll have to leave her. Arturo's got a spy inside Eden Roc. I think it may be Netoc. We tempt the devil, if we don't get out of here forthwith."

"Rafe, I refuse to leave Mama here. I promised my father, and—" She searched his expression. "Rafe, why do I think this has nothing to do with 'honesty'?"

"Doesn't it?" He rearranged his legs, wincing. "I went to your sister's cottage, yes. She lured me there by appealing to my sympathies over her blindness and loveless marriage." He rushed on. "I didn't stay but a couple of minutes. But I won't lie to you, I had some thoughts about refreshing my memory in certain areas with Olga."

Margaret cringed, but tried to hide it. Hurt clogged her throat. "It . . . it's to be expected. You've loved her for forever and a day."

"You're good at jumping to a conclusion."

"What do you mean?" She stared at him, aghast. "Are you saying you don't love her?"

"I'm saying you've been lying for years."

She studied the flint of his gaze. "What do you mean?"

"If I had a bullet for every time I agonized over you, I could arm a revolution."

He took hold of her wrist and pulled her fingers to his hot groin. A surge of desire went through her, yet no passion was building in him. He lay slack beneath her fingers. And the razor's edge of hostility scored his expression.

"*¿Como fue?* How was it . . . the first time a man touched you here?" He put his thumb on her breast. "Were you in love? Is that why you would've spread your thighs for him? Or were you so desperate for *la cópula,* that any overheated hombre would do?"

"What in the devil are you talking about?" Surely he didn't know—but why wouldn't he? Olga probably set him straight. If he'd kept a distance between then, then just how had their conversation turned to intimate talk?

"You could have saved us both a lot of heartache if you'd—" He thrust her hand away. "Tell me something, Margarita. Would you have gone through

360

with it, that first night? I'm not talking about Juarez. I'm talking about San Antonio. San Antonio, Texas. Alongside the Alamo." He bared his teeth as he grabbed her face between his strong hands, squeezing . . . pressing. "Damn you, why didn't you tell me it was *you* that night?"

He knew. Oh, Lord! How long had he known? The shame of her deception washed over her, her blood rushing to her toes. "Wh-when did Olga tell you—"

"Give me credit for some sense, lax though it may be. I figured you out for myself. When Olga and I were riding the elevator. But what difference does it make? You . . . damn you! You played games with me for years, claiming to despise me, treating me as if I were dirt, insulting me at every turn." His thumbs dug into her throat before he released his hold, jerking his arms away. "When all you wanted was a good scr—"

"So what if I did? I'm no different from a thousand other women, I imagine. I—I . . . the first time I saw you, I went as loony as all the rest of your admirers. And when you said you'd steal me away to Chihuahua, I wanted to go. But you ignored me." She dropped her chin. "When you fell in love with my sister, I couldn't go back to my old life without . . . without having a taste of yours." Her gaze moving to weld to his, she continued. "Through all the years I told myself I hated you, I didn't understand the fine line between love and hate. I believed the worst in you, because it made it easier to accept that you didn't want *me*."

He pulled her back to his arms. "Oh, 'Rita . . ."

"I'm sorry I deceived you." Her face burrowing into the cotton of his shirt and the heated strength of Rafe, she put her arm around him. "It was a dirty trick to play on you and Olga. You were so much in love. I'm sorry, so ashamed."

Spent, she wilted against him, hoping and praying that he would understand or at least forgive her.

"My foolish, foolish 'Rita. Haven't you listened to me? I never loved her. I'm telling you it is *you*—" They eased to the ground, the gentle waft of his breath on her cheek. "I've been loving *you* all these years."

"Me? You've loved me?"

"Yes, *amorcito,* you. I have spent all this time remembering you. Wanting to give *you* all of this. Needing to spend the rest of my life with you." He guided her hand back to him, and this time he was quite aroused. "I want you. I want you now. I want to thrust into you so far, that you aren't able to let me go."

A shadow moved over them. Gold winked in the aurora. A chain. A broken chain. The interloper dropped it to the ground beside Rafe's head. "Is this yours?"

Twenty-eight

What?

What was going on?

Rafe's brow quirked. Who was this intruding hombre?

Shock and surprise bleached Margarita's face as the golden serpent—symbolic of original sin—slithered to the grass beside them. *Merdo*. Rafe's fingers slammed to his breastbone, searching. In vain. That was his chain. *The cross. Where is it?* It might be gone from its linkage, but he knew, without depending on second sight, who hovered above them.

"Leonardo," Margarita choked out, proving his conclusion.

"You keep bad company, sister-in-law."

She wiggled from under Rafe, then rose to stand as he pitched to his back, lunged upward to a sitting position, and ignored his protesting thighbone. He skewed an eye on the Count of Granada. Like everyone who spent a lot of time here, Olga's husband looked young. Young and strong and sly. A bellowing dislike roared within Rafe. On the same level with Tío Arturo, Hapsburg—Spain's master spy—exemplified evil.

Hapsburg stared downward, pointing to the coiled snake. "Did you not hear me, señor? I asked if this is yours."

"It's mine. Forgot it last night." Rafe, clasping the new cypress cane, got to unsteady feet. He put an arm around Margaret's shaking shoulders. *Please don't let her get the wrong idea here.* "Where's the cross?"

Hapsburg hoisted a closed fist; gold gleamed from between his fingers and palm. "Would you like it returned? I thought you would. Before I give it back, tell me—do you enjoy going from one sister to the other?"

Margaret gasped.

And Rafe had to force himself not to lunge for the bastard. "How about rephrasing that? Castilian Spanish coming to my Mexican ears—what you said got all mixed up. I know you couldn't have meant what it sounded like. No self-serving—I mean, self-respecting; patois problem, you know—no princely hombre would insult his lady and her sister."

"I am insulting the master of cuckoldry, a vile libertine, a cur even in this land of mongrels." Nostrils flared above the pencil-thin mustache. "You. Who raped my countess."

"I've known your wife. But I never touched her with force. Left the rough stuff to you. Want to discuss all I know?"

Margaret took Rafe's hand, in a show of support

364

and faith.

Hapsburg moved forward, crushing the golden chain beneath his shoe. "I've said everything I intend to say to you, Delgado. Except for—Stay away from my countess. And . . ." He opened his fingers to expose the cross. Then the symbol of love and faith and sacrifice dropped to the ground. "Be my guest."

Margarita bent to pick it up, but Rafe ordered, "No. Don't. Leave it. Go to your *casita*. Or better yet, to your sister. I'll be with you in a minute."

She straightened. "But, Rafe—"

"This is between me and your brother-in-law. Please do as I ask, my heart."

Turning to profile, she nodded and left.

"Rutting ram, how easily you make sheep of the women. But no more." Hapsburg sneered at Rafe, advanced. His hand reached into his coat pocket. For a gun. To level at Rafe.

From his years in the *plaza de toros,* Rafe knew how to get out of the way of fire-snorting anger, and when gunfire exploded, he had hopped to the right. He felt no pain from his old injury. All his anger at Hapsburg's evil-doing propelled him into action. In the blink of an eye, he feinted from another bullet, raised and swung the cypress cane, and knocked the pistol out of Hapsburg's hand.

As amazement burst in the highborn's countenance, Rafe made a back-sweep with the walking stick. The cane slammed against the nobleman's neck, and he cried, "Awwgh!" Rafe then went to fists.

With little effort he trounced, routed, defeated Hapsburg.

Standing over the battered and bloodied face, he said, "You're fortunate I don't carry a knife. Or I would gut you."

"I . . . I . . ." Starved for air, Hapsburg rolled into a fetal ball of misery. "I w-will see you laid out in lavender."

"Never. I will see *you* dead."

A thought occurred to Rafe. While he, like most Mexicans, had a fatalistic bent, he yearned to live many, many years. As long as Margarita was at his side.

People came running, and a man yelled, "Who fired that shot!"

"Is Hapsburg dead!"

"Rafe, ole buddy, are you all right?"

The Spaniard lifted his head. "Swine, you're not rid of me."

Leaning down, Rafe whispered in Hapsburg's ear. Words to keep him at bay. For a while, at least.

Rafe took hold of the gift cane, nudged Hapsburg's arm off the chain and cross, and picked up the last gift his sainted sister had given him. He turned from the circling crowd, heading for the magical fountain.

For the quiet of it.

After witnessing the tussle between Rafe and Leonardo—she'd turned back as soon as Leonardo had shouted at Rafe—Margaret went to her sister's quarters. She didn't bother to knock. Olga, propped up in bed, sipped something from a teacup.

Margaret slammed the door behind her, then marched over to the bed. "It's time you and I had a talk."

No reply.

She asked, "Didn't you hear gunfire? For heaven's sake, Olga, aren't you interested to know if someone's been hurt? Leonardo. Or Rafe. It could have been anyone!"

"Has someone been hurt?"

"Not fatally. But your husband took a battering."

She waited for her sister to comment. Olga said nothing, simply sat there in bed. If anything, she looked relieved.

Confused by Olga as well as by many things in this chaos called life, Margaret sighed. "I want to know something. And if you lie to me, I'll yank every hair from your head. Do you have designs on Rafe?"

"A woman doesn't cleave to her rapist."

"I'm not buying that. I know, you know, and Rafe knows he didn't rape you in Texas. Tell your husband the truth."

"He wouldn't believe me. Plus, anyway, he'd never think I would allow a man liberties."

"How do you know, if you haven't tried being honest?"

Setting the teacup on the tray that sat on the bed, to her right, Olga replied, "Maggie, you're probably not going to believe this, but I don't care what Leonardo thinks."

"I believe you." Margaret sat down on the edge of the bed. "What is wrong between the two of you? You should be so happy, with the baby on its way. Yet you allow men to act like dogs, fighting over you. Will you have more repeats of today?"

"Oh, Maggie, really. Boys will be boys. If they aren't fighting over me, they'd be fighting over something else."

"The something else couldn't be as serious as a husband wanting to defend his wife's honor. Rafe disarmed Leonardo, but your husband could very well hit his mark next time."

Olga straightened, her fingers walking to the table next to the bed. She donned a pair of spectacles, a nervous gesture, for the glasses might as well have been eye patches. "Why are you all the time trying to scare me? You always do that, Maggie. Besides, Leonardo has been threatening to kill Rafe for years. He won't. He doesn't pick on people his own size, or bigger."

"I want the misunderstanding cleared up."

"Don't be a worrywart. And where's your faith in your adored Rafe? He'll always get the better of Leonardo."

"My faith in him is what brought me to you." Margaret crossed the room, bending to sit at her sister's side. She took the dainty hand. "Olga, I love Rafe very much, and want to spend the rest of my days with him. Help me. Please call Leonardo off this vendetta!"

"How do you know Rafe didn't rape me?"

"He isn't drawn that way. Never in a million years

would I believe he would hurt a woman."

Still holding her sister's hand, Margaret lay her forehead on the mattress. Tentative fingers opened, the tips trailing up to an eye. "You're crying. Please don't cry, Maggie. Please don't. I — I'll do something to make it better. I promise."

"What? What will you do?" Raising her eyes, she gazed upon Olga's tormented face. "Will you clear Rafe's name, so that we may have peace in the family?"

"First . . . there's something I must say." Olga's lip trembled. "I concocted the rape story to save my child. Yes. My child."

She launched into a story so horrific that it sent spears of fury and grief and helplessness through Margaret. She opened her arms to her sister. Both women wept for Olga's dead baby.

Rafe's daughter.

How awful it must have been for the innocent infant, her last moments. Needing a mother and getting a murderer. *Leonardo must not get off scot-free!*

"My little girl," Olga divulged, once they had collected themselves, somewhat, "I called her Margarita. After you."

Touched and honored at the gesture, Margaret squeezed her sister's hand. "Does Rafe know about her?"

"No. It's better if he doesn't."

Margaret agreed. He would kill Leonardo. And Leonardo wasn't good enough for simple killing.

"Maggie . . . don't cry. There's something else I

must tell you. Something else about Leonardo. He plots against us. Us as an American nation. He's planted spies all over northern Mexico."

Once upon a time Margaret wouldn't have found his activities loathsome. This time spent in Mexico had changed her way of thinking, and she hoped Cuba would be liberated. *¡Cuba libre!* She prayed ill on Spain's heinous spy.

"Olga, you don't have to stay with Leonardo," she said. "You have a home. With your family who loves you. When we take Mama—"

"Mutti isn't going anywhere. And you know it."

"She'll have to leave. She can't stay here."

"Why not?"

"Because her family needs her. You need her. If she doesn't want to go back to Papa, then fine. You two can go back to the Four Aces together. Or anywhere you like—you can have my brownstone in Manhattan, if you please. I think you should settle somewhere that you can get good medical attention. You've got to think about your eyes. Surgery will ease your pain."

"My pain is my penitence for little Margarita."

"Balderdash. Straighten your back, take a deep breath, and grab your reins. You've got a new baby to think about, and if you drag your feet, you'll be too far along to travel."

"But, Maggie, if I leave, I'll miss my great revenge." She launched into explaining her plans for retribution. "I've waited too long to give up now."

"Balderdash. Let me be brutally honest. You can't see what happens anyway. Hearing about his fall will be just as satisfying."

Silence. Several moments later, Olga put the glasses away and straightened her shoulders. "Okay, you win. I'll leave him. Plus, anyway, Rafe has agreed to help spread the word that the Emperor Maximilian's cousin had designs on Mexico, so I don't have anything to worry about."

While visions of having a second Hapsburg dying by the will of the Mexican people had a generous appeal, Margaret froze. Surely Rafe wouldn't call trouble on Xzobal's sanctuary. Surely he wouldn't call trouble on the whole of Eden Roc! "Let's hope and pray that we all get out of here alive."

The Count of Granada fumed. He'd meant to bring down Delgado trash, but the tables were turned. Arturo's mestizo nephew—Olga's commoner lover!—controlled the situation.

Delgado knew about the spying and would use it against him. And he knew about Areponapuchi. Leonardo de Hapsburg y Borbón had sinned—murder heading the list—but he loved his wife. He wouldn't have his countess knowing his baseness.

He wouldn't have her knowing he'd lowered himself to debauchery, for Leonardo partook of any and all women willing to fornicate with him, even Helga the Dominatrix.

Olga must never know what a profligate I've become.

* * *

At dusk Rafe returned to his *casita*. He didn't return to an empty cottage. In the unlighted room, Margaret quit the chair and glided toward him.

Anticipation played tasty havoc with his senses.

After standing the gift cane against the doorjamb, he pulled her into his arms. Her lips met his. He took her hand, guiding her to his bed, where he turned down the covers and then turned his attentions to the buttons of her clothes. Uncertain what she would say about his fight with Leonardo, uncertain how she felt about marriage to a rogue from the Sierras, uncertain about the future in general, Rafe kept her too busy for any talk beyond the bills and coos of lovemaking.

Afterward they lay joined, Margarita resting on top of him, her fingers twining with his chest hair; he whispered, "Thank you for the cane. It's beautiful. Quite handy, too. In fisticuffs." He stroked her back. "I love you. For being you."

"I love you, too." Her tongue traced the scar at his lip. "But where have you been? I was looking for you. Olga. She told Leonardo that she lied about your relationship with her."

"What did he do?"

"He's taken himself off somewhere. To lick his wounds, I'd imagine."

"Good."

"Rafe . . . I know you know about Leonardo's clandestine activities. I trust you can appreciate what could happen here—we could be mobbed!—should word get out about Leonardo. Promise me . . ." She took his hand. "For the McLoughlins,

372

for your brother, for Isaiah and his people, for you and me, promise you'll keep mum."

"That's what I figured to do, all along. But it didn't stop me from threatening Hapsburg. It's all the ammunition we have to keep him at bay." Rafe fingercombed her hair. *"Querida,* enough talk about family. I want to talk about you and me."

"Excellent idea." She nodded. "Rafe, what about me and you? What about forever after? This morning, we didn't discuss what will happen, once we are shut of our duties."

"Do you want to go back to New York?"

"No."

He exhaled in relief. "Do you want to stay in Mexico with me?"

"I am so disposed."

Thrilled at her answer, he teased, "Shall I say 'I told you so'?"

"I would think you too noble for it."

He laughed. His manhood stirring within her, he kissed her with all enthusiasm. His hands flat against the sweet buttocks that had filled out nicely, he chided, "You neglected something. You haven't come right out and admitted *exactly* how you feel about me."

"An oversight." She smiled, her eyes dancing. "I love you, Rafe Delgado. Love you . . . love you . . . love you."

Those beautiful words—so long in coming—soaked through him like the sweet rains of May. With 'Rita's love, anything was possible. Again, he made love to her, showing all the gusto of a man besotted with love and adoration.

Later, though, he wondered what love meant to her. They had dozed, here in the dark of his room. Moonlight spilled across their awakening forms.

"Do you love me enough to be my wife?" he asked without preamble.

"For however long God gives me on this earth."

"Then we'll be together for a long, long time. But, 'Rita, my *querida*"—he buried his face in her hair—"are you willing to accept my way of life? The rebel's life."

"Yes." She cupped his face within her hands. "But you're wrong if you think I don't want children. Can we handle both at the same time?"

"Querida, you and I can do *anything!"*

Laughing and jubilant, they kissed and kissed and did more than kiss. They kicked at the linens, tossing them here and there as they celebrated the fusing of their souls. Their mating was even better than past ones, and Rafe would have never imagined that could be so. What sweet witchery was she.

Later, much later, they reveled in the afterglow. Meaning to feed her his cache of sugar-frosted oatcakes (bribed from the native cook) by candlelight, he lit a wick. Their images blinked from the looking glass hanging nearby.

He'd grown accustomed to seeing the years fall away from his visage, albeit salt remained in the pepper of his hair. Truth be known, he didn't hold his looks in quite as much importance as he used to. Margarita had fallen in love with him at his worst, and her opinion was all that mattered. Further, be-

374

cause it didn't bother her, it didn't even bother him that his left leg was shorter than the right.

Rafe smiled at her reflection. Margarita had gone still. On a quirk of brow, she leaned closer, her eyes rounding, her hand flopping to the mattress. "You have a mirror."

"Your cottage doesn't?"

"No. I haven't seen one anywhere on the premises." She cocked her head first one way, then another. Disoriented, confused, she said, "Who is that in bed with you? That can't be me."

"It is. You're beautiful. So beautiful. A face like a china doll. A body like—"

"My sister's." She made a funny face, then flinched. "It looks like my sister."

"It's not Olga. Or Charity."

He scooted around, where he held her on his lap, his fingers twined with hers. He saw the girl he loved, whether she was old, young, or in between. There was a cloud of wavy dark hair—lustrous and shining—framing a beautiful oval face unmarred by time or tragedy. Her dewy lips were the tint of ripe berries, her thick-lashed eyes the sky of summer. He touched a kiss to her shoulder, feeling her quiver, and he smiled at the flesh that was now healthy and rosy.

He smiled at her reflection again. "I love the way you look and feel. I *loved* the way you looked and *felt*. For all the days of our lives, I will love the way you are." He pulled her onto his lap and hugged her tightly. "You shouldn't be surprised at being so lovely, sweet witch. We are at the Fountain of

Youth."

Unimpressed with her great beauty renewed, she returned his hug. He felt her hot tears of joy on his shoulder.

"Oh, Rafe, do you know what this means? I haven't had a cough or a sweat in weeks. I've gained weight. I'm young again. *I'm going to live!*"

The next morning, after sleeping locked in each other's embrace, Rafe still held Margarita in his arms. It was time to get down to the nitty-gritty of their strategies. "You've been in Mexico long enough to know that, away from Eden Roc, it's no paradise," he said. "Even here has its problems. 'Rita, there's an enemy within these walls."

"I know. Leonardo. But he's off, pouting."

"I don't mean him. This spy is an Arturiano. Whoever he or she is, Tío Arturo is getting reports on our activities. And my uncle has been seen outside the walls."

She shuddered.

He continued. "We've got to get Xzobal to Topolobampo. And then there's your mother. What do we do about Lisette?"

Sighing and grimacing, Margarita shook her head. "She won't leave. I've asked her dozens of times. She doesn't admit it, but I know she's waiting for my father to rescue her."

"We can't wait a lifetime on the strength of her romantic dreams. This isn't a fairy tale—this is life! We've got to move. And we've got to move soon."

"Give me a few more days." Margarita sat up, brushed a lock of hair from her temple. "I'll do my best to talk her into leaving."

"For the Gulf of California?"

"I — I don't know."

Determined to find a solution, Rafe studied on the problem. *Ah, ha!* "Margarita, *querida,* why didn't we think of this before? We worry where we shouldn't. Let's ask your brother to see her home."

"Tex? You've got to be joking. He's so in thrall with Natalie, nothing outside of death will make him budge. Unless she goes along."

"She'll go along."

But, as it turned out, Natalie didn't go along with the plan.

Twenty-nine

Stars glittered like so many diamonds around the half moon. Crickets and locusts mingled with the cry of a faraway jaguar and the distant roar of the waterfalls. A native drummer spoke with his counterpart on the far side of *El Ojo de la Barranca*.

Looking up at the canyon walls, Natalie Nash murmured, "Fireflies. Look at them, Xzobal. Look at all the campfires up in the caves. They look like fireflies."

Natalie lay naked on a bed of leaves.

The priest, in full cassock, sat well away from her.

"Aren't you interested in fireflies?" She rolled to her side, drawing a knee up in yet another invitation. Nothing. What was the matter with him? "You're weary. You've spent all day fretting over your brother and giving Margaret religious instruction. You barely touched your dinner. Exhaustion contributes to sapping the life juices." *Good Lord, you sound like Isaiah!*

"This is a trying time for Rafael—for us all," the

priest replied. "And you make it hard for me, my child."

"Exactly my intention, making you hard." She took a long look at his long, long lines. "Remember tonight, between the yogurt soup and the bean paté? Did you enjoy it when I reached under the table and took hold of your big long . . . *rood?* I made it hard for you, didn't I? And I could tell you liked it."

"Natalie, get dressed. You'll catch your death."

"Do cover me up with something. Yourself." Holding a heavy breast in each hand, she pointed them at him. No man had been able to say no to this bid. Xzobal might be a priest, but he wasn't *dead,* for the love of Pete. She licked her lips and pinched her own nipple. "Why don't you come over here, and we'll see about saving my soul?"

He surged to stand. For a moment he hesitated, as if wrestling with the mortal and the spiritual. His fingers curled around the crucifix suspended from his neck, but not before the gold of it caught a ray of moonlight.

Turning on the ball of his foot, he retreated.

Natalie hissed an "oooh." A slave to her passions, she wanted all the men. Tex for his money and family influence; Arturo for old time's sake; Xzobal because of the lure of the forbidden. And, of course, Netoc, who couldn't.

If those McLoughlin sisters weren't fighting over Rafe, I'd corner him. He had eyes for Margaret and Margaret alone.

"Natalie Ann Nash, why don't you settle on one

and go after him?" she asked out loud.

There was no question as to the winner. She wanted to return to the United States, and Tex McLoughlin, the greenest and most gullible of all her choices, could help clear her name. Yes, Tex would be the man for her.

The next evening she invited him to the canyon floor.

He went willingly, enthusiastically. She made a lover out of a green fumbler that night, for he learned many lessons in the art of pleasing a woman. So in love he couldn't get enough of her, he proved a quick study. He ought to be enough. Young, handsome, rich, randy as a ram, hung like a horse.

But she needed more.

She needed Xzobal. And she had him the next night. Almost had him. In his excitement he spilled himself too early. Desperate for relief, she called on Hipólito and two of the other servants. They proved the least memorable assignations of her four decades of life. More than anyone, she realized, she had a hunger for Netoc.

"Do you have a minute?"

His voice made a vapor cloud. A breeze ruffling the hem of his sashed robes, the tonsured cleric stood on the porch of his brother's *casita*. Buttoning his britches, Rafe limped outside. The repaired crucifix again graced his bare chest.

"What the hell do you want at this hour of the

night?" he asked sourly.

"Who is it, Rafe? What is it? Is something wrong?"

Love for his *amante* obvious, Rafe turned to answer. "It's okay, *querida*. It's my brother."

"Oh, I'll get dressed."

Rafe pulled the door closed. *"¿Que pase?"*

"I'm going to leave Eden Roc."

Rafe exhaled a tired breath. "Please. We've discussed this over and over, and my answer is still the same. Don't."

"But I have prayed over my profane passions. And I know I can't stay away from Natalie. I want her, and the strength of my desire shames me."

Lighting a cheroot, Rafe pointed out, "You were a hotblooded hombre, before your papá talked you into the priesthood. Maybe you ought to give up the church, and—"

"I won't."

"Then don't. But you must be patient. Do whatever it takes to ignore Natalie."

"Could you ignore Margarita? If she were forbidden to you, would you be able to keep your hands to yourself?"

Rafe tossed the smoke off the porch. "We're not talking about me and 'Rita. We're getting married as soon as we can get to a church."

"When will we get to a church? When are we going to leave, Brother Rafe?"

"Soon."

Margarita, wearing a thick woolen wrapper, stepped onto the porch. "Hello, *Padre*."

"My child."

Xzobal admired this beautiful lady. She was good for his loco brother. And the priest looked forward to joining their hands in marriage. Soon. "How soon is soon?"

"As soon as we can talk sense into my mother," Margaret answered. "She keeps hoping for a miracle."

Xzobal pitied the beautiful Lisette. The German woman longed to recapture the love faded by time and politics. He hoped her miracle would happen. "Do you propose that Señora McLoughlin accompany us to Topolobampo and onward?"

Rafe replied, "She'll stay here until we can circle back for her. If she's not willing to sail out with you, that is. That is what holds us back, Xzobal. She's a stubborn woman, Margarita's mama. Just as stubborn as her smartest daughter."

Rafe kissed his woman's cheek. "This one won't leave Señora McLoughlin here. And Señora McLoughlin frets over Lady Hapsburg's advancing *embarazo*. Then there's the countess's husband—I don't need to explain him to you. Then there's Tex. He refuses to leave unless Natalie goes with him."

Natalie. So many of Xzobal's problems would go away, if she went east or he went west. Nonetheless, he shuddered at the thought of never seeing her again. Which way should he turn? He said to his older brother, "You don't need trouble from me."

"That says it all. I've got a plate full of problems without you heaping more on it." Rafe took his brother's shoulder and shook it gently. "Promise me

382

you won't leave without us."

Xzobal wouldn't make a promise he couldn't keep. He couldn't stay, he couldn't leave; he was a priest in a quandary. He considered all slants to the situation, and accepted that he would cause nothing but trouble for Rafael if he left. "I will stay."

He prayed—and prayed!—for the strength to stay away from those milk-white breasts, bee-sting red lips, and sinfully beautiful legs.

The power of prayer failed him.

Christmas came and went. The new year had just begun. Natalie began to assess her predicament. Tex was pressuring her to marry him, but she couldn't bring herself to take that step. Already she'd grown tired of Xzobal—he was too staid for any sort of variety. *He takes "missionary" seriously.*

And then there was her father. She was sick to death of being around him. All the time he nagged her to stay here at Eden Roc, not to leave. Except for the various and sundry McLoughlins—and Sean, of course—Isaiah was so obsessed with keeping his daughter at home, that he'd refused to take any more guests.

He was a lovesick puppy around Lisette, hoping and praying that Gil McLoughlin would keep his distance, which the husband was doing. As of yet, Isaiah wasn't privy to what Lisette had confided to Natalie tonight: Lisette had agreed to leave with her daughters. The party would make for the port of Topolobampo forthwith.

383

By their departure, Isaiah would become even more pathetic than usual, Natalie felt certain.

"I can't stay," she said to her reflection.

Youth and beauty stared back.

Natalie closed her eyes. Her mind's eye drew a picture. Netoc as a young man, like the day under the waterfall when they had lost their virginity. Another picture invaded her thoughts. The Netoc of 1898.

He grew more feeble each day. Fearing she'd live to the age of Methuselah, she saw herself screwing her way into the next millennium. And never having peace of mind or body.

A warm wrap draping her shoulders, she left her cottage as the clock on her dressing table struck midnight. Her feet carried her to Eden Roc's exit. When she opened the heavy creaking gate to the outside world, she saw that, as usual, as always, Netoc protected her.

A campfire hissed and popped near the gate house, where a group of old-looking men—she remembered most of them as children—were gathered, Netoc among them. They drank beer and laughed at someone's joke.

"Netoc . . ." Her voice carried sweetly across the crisp air of the Sierra. "Netoc."

When she approached, quiet fell over the group. The fire's orange flames lighting a cherished face, Netoc got to his feet. "My love," he murmured. "My love . . ."

Natalie extended her hand to him. "It is time."

He brought her fingers to his lips, feathering a

kiss on her knuckles. There were tears in his eyes. Or were they in her own?

She buried her face in his shoulder. "My native sweetheart. My Netoc." Her eyes met his. "We will be together now."

He nodded imperceptibly, then pulled her into the cloak of his arms. "It is time."

Thirty

The time grew near.

The woman was ready.

This was the new year.

Noche Negro skittish, Arturo Delgado and his Arturianos, the mountain breeze whipping their sombreros, looked down at the gate to Eden Roc. A native with a serape thrown over his shoulder, waited expectantly in front of their mounts.

For weeks Arturo had been waiting for the right moment. For his nephew to get back on his feet, so they could be shot from beneath him again. For Margaret to return to the flush of beauty. She was remitted. A sly grin pulled at Arturo's mouth. *I have seen you,* tigresa, *and soon I will tame you.*

"Tell me," Arturo demanded from the spy. "Tell me everything."

The skinny Indian stepped up to Noche Negro, then patted the stallion's sleek neck. His upturned palm lifted toward *El Grandero Rico.* Arturo tossed a silver coin — .925 from the Santa Alicia, of course — to the Tarahumara.

386

"There is much discord." Hipólito's smile accentuated a missing upper tooth. "The Lord Hapsburg lives in fear of the Magnificent Eagle. The servants gossip that it is over Areponapuchi."

Arturo laughed. "I'd like to see that *pene*-head Hapsburg on the run."

He'd grown less and less infatuated with the idea of accompanying the condescending Hapsburg to Madrid, since the more he thought about balling the McLoughlin girl, the more he wanted to savor her favors, so Arturo had stalled Hapsburg on leaving for the court of the boy king.

Hipólito carried on. "Señora McLoughlin, she is sad. Her tears fall. Every night she cries for her husband. But she has said she will go to Topolobampo with her family."

"What about the daughter Margarita?"

"She will marry the Magnificent Eagle."

"I don't think so," Arturo muttered under his breath.

"They are very pretty"—Hipólito grinned his gap-toothed grin—"the *niñas* of Señora McLoughlin."

Cantú laughed. So did the other Arturianos. The *patrón* didn't laugh. "Get them out of your mind. They are too far above you, you little worm, for you even to consider. Get on with the facts."

"*Sí. Señor Patrón.*" Hipólito shifted his weight from one leg to the other. "The young señor, Tex"—the hard *X* in Tex proved beyond the skill of the informer's tongue; the name sounded like *teh*—"he is unhappy. The Señorita Natalie, she has turned her eyes to Father Xzobal. But the *padre,* he wants to leave Eden Roc, because he is making" — Hipólito made a universal sign with two of his fingers — "with the hot tamale Natalie."

"What did I tell you about overstepping your bounds?"

"But, *patrón.* I have tasted the hot tamale myself. Many times." Lifting his shoulders as well as his palms, Hipólito grinned. "She is very hot."

Once upon a time Arturo would have shot a man for making a remark such as Hipólito's. No more. His lip quivered. So, Natalie had her sloe eyes on yet another lover, this time the loathsome priest who'd led last March's strike at the mine. They deserved each other.

His love for Natalie had died five years ago, when she left him. No, that wasn't so. His love didn't die until later, when he learned the truth. About how she had taken on all comers. On the very night he'd asked for her hand in marriage, she'd gone to Areponapuchi. She paid each of the whores to leave, to let her handle all the trade.

Sneering, Arturo told Hipólito, "Enjoy the tamale."

"*Gracias.*" The spy's grin widened. "Señor Isaiah, he says the magic of the falls will go away, if Natalie goes away."

"I don't give a fig about that old fool. What else?"

"The Magnificent Eagle has promised not to tell the peons that Lord Hapsburg is here."

Hapsburg needs another New World lesson. "Go

388

to the village. Tell the madam Pilar about Hapsburg. Tell her I said to spread the story . . . he'll be in Areponapuchi. Soon."

"Sí, Señor Patrón."

Cantú spoke next. "Do you want us to go in after your nephew and the McLoughlin woman?"

"Not yet. We've waited this long for them to recover—what's a few more days? I want to see what happens to Hapsburg. And when the time is right, we will flush the covey of quail from the bush."

"What about the other woman?"

Arturo turned the stallion, kneed him, and headed toward the village. Natalie could go to hell. She rode for a fall, anyway, so vast were her depravities. "She'll destroy herself." And if not, well . . .

Miracles do happen.

For months—for years!—Lisette McLoughlin had been yearning for this moment. Finally, her husband had shunned his mistress. In the seclusion of her cottage, as twilight fell, he stood before his wife—tall, silver-haired, hat in hand.

Never had Gil looked so handsome to these sore eyes of hers.

Thank you, mein Gott. *If my husband had arrived one day later, the children and I would have been gone.*

She opened her arms wide. "Hello, my precious *Liebster.*"

He dropped the Stetson and swooped her into his embrace. "I couldn't stand it. I couldn't stand being without you. Why didn't you tell me how much I depend on you?"

"You weren't listening."

"I'm listening now."

He carried her to her bed, stripped her clothes away, and made love to her with the intensity of their long-awaited reunion, mixed with love grown mature by age and experience.

Later, they sat nude in bed, shared a bottle of cognac, and caressed each other's various parts. Rearing back, Gil scrutinized his wife of almost thirty years. "You look different. Are my eyes playing tricks on me? I see you, well, like you were when we first married."

"I'm glad you noticed—I've been working on it. Oh, Gil, I have to tell you! I can't wait until you see Gretchen. It's like the hands of time have turned back." Lisette waxed enthusiastic. "She's a girl again."

"So are you. And I'm an old man."

"Nonsense. You're barely sixty years old."

"I don't like you looking all girlish." It had been years since Gil displayed the jealousy that he'd had to work at constantly to keep under control, but it snapped tonight. "Who did you pretty yourself up for?"

"For me."

"You're sure it had nothing to do with Isaiah Nash?"

"He had something to do with it, all right. If not

390

for his Eden Roc, I'd still be fat and flabby."

"I liked the way you looked." He poured her another cognac. And when he handed the glass over, his hand brushed her naked breast. The tip sprang under his fingers, and Lisette sucked in her breath. Gil groaned. "Aw, hell, honey. You look real damn good."

Saucy as a woman of eighteen, Lisette leaned toward him. "Is sixty too old for another round of lovemaking, Mr. McLoughlin?"

"Sixty is not too old."

"Satisfied? Sixty wasn't too old."

"Mmm, *ja, Liebster,* I know."

Sharing the fuzzy warmth of the moments after spectacular intimacy, Gil plumped the pillow and wiggled to sit up in his wife's bed. A scowl etched his face anew. "Are you ready to answer a question—with no hem-hawing around? What's going on around this place? And what in the name of blue blazes happened to turn you young?"

"Don't glower." The lovely spell was shattered, letting in the chaos of their family. But Lisette forced those thoughts aside. This was the moment for her and Gil, and for her and Gil alone. "You aren't pretty when you glower."

"I've never been pretty, goddammit. So tell me what you've done to yourself."

"It's Eden Roc. It makes the old young. And, Gil, I have the most splendid news." She had a lot of news, little of it good, yet Lisette launched into

391

a report webbed with the lace of enthusiasm. "What do you think about Gretchen marrying Rafe Delgado?"

"That was the point of sending her down here."

"I beg your pardon?" Lisette's brow quirked, while uneasiness tugged at her newfound peace of mind. "Was I suffering under a wrong impression? I, well, I thought she traveled down here to talk me into going home."

"She did." Gil rubbed his still-firm stomach. "But I figured—and Maisie agrees—those two will make a good match."

Amazed at her husband, Lisette smiled. "I never thought I'd live to see the day the big papa bear would match-make one of his cubs."

"There's a first time for everything."

Lisette rolled her eyes, then got to the rest of the news. "We're going to have a daughter-in-law. Of course, it's not finalized yet, but Angus wants to marry Isaiah's daughter."

"Isaiah's daughter? Don't you mean grand-daughter?"

"No. I mean daughter. Natalie."

"Wait a minute, honey. If I'm remembering correctly, Isaiah's only got one child." Gil blanched under his perpetual tan. "She's old enough to be our boy's *mother*."

"She's ten years younger than I am. You wouldn't know her age from looking at her."

"Haven't you learned by now? You can't go by looks."

Actually, Lisette had grave reservations about

392

Angus and Natalie. She loved Natalie. Forty or not, Natalie would be welcomed into the family. It was just — well, Lisette had heard some unpleasant downstairs gossip about Natalie and men. *I'd overlook those rumors, if I could believe she loves Angus.*

"Lisette . . . ? Is something wrong, honey?"

She shook her head. "You know me. If I don't have something to worry about, I worry about having nothing to worry about."

"Now that you mention problems, brace yourself, sweetheart." He blew out a puff of breath. "I know you don't want to hear this, but it's gotta be said. I've got a responsibility to our adopted country. The President counts on me. The American people count on me. And you know I don't like welshing on things I ought to do. I need to get back to the White House. As fast as possible."

Argue, she wouldn't. She'd gotten her message across. When push came to shove, her husband had chosen her over politics. That was what mattered, after all. She wasn't looking to change him completely — if she did, she would be renouncing all that she loved about the complicated and intense man who was Gilliegorm McLoughlin. "What are the plans?"

"A regiment of Federales waits not far from here to escort us away. The steamship *Atlantic Fire* is anchored in the port of Tampico. She's waiting to sail us to Washington."

"All right, *Liebster.* Let's assemble our children and leave."

The McLoughlin retinue left Eden Roc before the break of dawn, two mornings later. Margaret and Rafe refused to go along. If Tex left, he had informed his parents, it would be with his wife at his side.

With every intention of asking for Natalie's hand in marriage, Tex made one more trip to her *casita*. She hadn't returned. She hadn't been there all night. He hadn't seen her in a couple of days. Where was she?

He paced up and down the path fronting her little house. Her corn-colored hair in braids wound round her head, the buxom masseuse Helga clomped by and offered a vigorous good morning.

"Have you seen Natalie?" Tex asked.

"Young man, I do not make it my business to keep up with the young lady." Helga frowned and pointed to his feet. "Take care! Do not be kicking the dust. You are getting dirt on your boots. Someone should spank you—should blister your behind!" Glaze melted over her eyes, and a line of drool seeped down her chin. "If you don't behave . . ."

Tex groaned and turned away.

It was the worst kept secret at Eden Roc that Leonardo had been fooling around with that gal. Tex had even heard it said that his brother-in-law had let her put a diaper on him. And spanked him, while he sucked on a lollipop! Tex thought that downright odd—for sure worse than that old saw about Texas being where the men were men and the sheep knew it. Him playing a baby, no wonder Olga ran off and left ole Leo!

Leonardo walked up. Tex asked after Natalie. In a sour mood because his wife had left with her parents, Leonardo didn't bother to comment on Natalie. He disappeared into the woods, chasing after Helga.

The Irishman, Hipólito in his wake, strolled by. Neither man had seen Natalie. An hour or so after the breakfast hour, Margaret and Rafe — with a saddlebag thrown over his shoulder, the walking stick in his right hand — approached Tex.

"Last chance, hombre. We're leaving as soon as we can get Diablo and Penny saddled up."

"Do come with us," his sister appealed.

"I've gotta talk with Natalie. Got to." Fear clawed Tex's heart. "I'm worried. I'm afraid something's happened to her."

Rafe set their grips on the ground. "We can wait awhile, can't we, *querida?*"

"Absolutely."

Tex didn't know how long he could stall his sister and her man. He knew he shouldn't, period. They were on pins and needles to get Xzobal to a safe harbor. "Why don't y'all go on without me? I ain't gonna give up on Miss Natalie."

As soon as Tex finished speaking, Isaiah rounded the bend that led to the lift contraption.

Something was wrong.

"Oh, dear," Margaret murmured.

There were tears in Isaiah's angelic eyes. His

shoulders shook. His hand trembling, he put it on Tex's shoulder. The elderly man, who had always seemed so young, was now broken and sorrowful. "Come to the main house with me, Son. You and I need to talk."

"What's wrong?" Shards of ice shaved Tex's veins. "What's the matter? It's Natalie, isn't it?"

Rafe said, "Hombre, we—"

"What's wrong with Natalie!" the Texan demanded.

Margaret faced the path Isaiah had taken; she paled. Rafe captured her hand. She stepped toward her brother. "Oh, Tex, I'm so sorry."

Tex started to take a look, but with determined force, Isaiah shoved Tex in the opposite direction. "Let's get on back to the main house, Son. I've got some Tennessee sour mash—the good stuff, out of Lynchburg—hidden."

"I don't want nothing to drink. I want to know about Natalie!"

Isaiah gestured with his head to Rafe, who grabbed Tex's upper arm.

"Every once in a while," Isaiah said gravely, "a man needs a shot of good whiskey."

Tex jerked out of his bonds. He spun around, intent on finding out what Isaiah shielded him from. The elevator. It topped the canyon wall, swaying like a bottom-heavy bell as it came to rest at its berth. No passengers were visible in the basket seat. Tex ran toward it. A putrid smell rolled toward him, making him gag. And what he saw stayed with him all the days of his life.

Broken and bloody, two bodies covered the litter's floor.

That of the funny little Indian Netoc.

And that of Natalie Nash.

They had thrown themselves from the cliff.

Thirty-one

On the same brisk morning that the elevator deposited its gruesome burden at the crest of the canyon's eye—and in back of the heartsick young cowboy being delivered into the numbing embrace of Jack Daniel's Old No. 7—Isaiah Nash took to his bed.

Not a tear fell for his only child. But as each moment passed, as morning became afternoon and afternoon changed to the pale gray of twilight, his skin turned lax and gray, his hair the color of snow, and a haunted expression—like that of a traumatized soldier—settled in his eyes. His spirit gone, the magic of Eden Roc was no more for him.

When Margaret went to awaken him the next day, so that he could pay last respects to poor Natalie, he lay dead of a broken heart.

When the burials were complete, Tex McLoughlin went to his sister. His eyes bleak and red-rimmed, both from alcohol and mourning, he said, "According to Papa, the U.S. Navy has a ship anchored in Tampico. It's headed for Cuba. I think I'll get on outta here, join up."

Margaret didn't know what to say. She understood Tex's grief. She understood how hurt he'd been upon learning Natalie and the likable little Tarahumaran man had been in love for many, many years. What to say to her brother was beyond Margaret.

Frantically, her eyes implored Rafe; she hoped he had the answer.

"Do you know much about sailing?" he asked.

"Nope." Studying the floor, Tex buried his hands under his armpits. "I didn't know nothing about a broken heart, but I done come by experience quick enough."

There was no arguing his logic. Margaret hoped and prayed her brother would be all right. "If that's what you feel you must do, then Rafe and I support you. Don't we, Rafe?"

He tightened his hand on her shoulder. "We do."

She stepped away to throw her arms around her baby brother. Her tears scalded her eyes as she buried her face in his shoulder. "I love you, kid brother. Please don't let this be the last time we see you."

"I'll come back so's you can sign me a book."

What a strange remark. "*Christopher Columbus and the Catholic Kings* has been out of print for years. And you have a copy already, back home at the Four Aces."

"Maggie, I mean the new one. Sign the new one for me."

"What new one?"

"The one ole Rafe here says you're gonna write."

She turned a questioning gaze to the culprit, who had a deceptive innocence in his silver eyes. At last Rafe replied, "Mexico is every bit as interesting as Columbus or Isabella or her husband Fernando. We've got a rich history. Somebody smart needs to write our story."

"And when will I write a book?" She exhaled and shook her head at Tex, saying to him, "Why is it that everyone thinks a book just writes itself, when there's nothing better to do?"

"You can do it," said Rafe. "You can do anything."

His faith added to her height. "Yes, I think I can."

"Well, folks, I better hit the road. You, too."

Rafe clasped Tex's hand, but both men stopped in the middle of the handshake, then went into a brief back-patting hug. "Adios, young lion. Take care of yourself. *Vaya con Dios.*"

Tex departed.

More misery came to Eden Roc. It was time to leave for the western coast, but where was Xzobal Paz? Gone. Had he left of his own accord, or had Arturo Delgado—with no Netoc to protect the premises—breached the walls to capture one of the Santa Alicia's troublemakers?

And what had happened to the Count of Granada? When he surfaced from his sulk, day before yesterday, he had ranted and raved, making a nuisance of himself by berating his wife over her shortcomings, especially that of being a promiscuous commoner undeserving of her exalted station in life.

Everyone did their best to ignore him.

In the outcome of Olga leaving him, he continued to behave in a deranged manner, alternately justifying his own stance, shouting his innocence in her desertion, and not understanding how she could desert a member of European royalty. It all trailed into sobs of not knowing how to live without his Olgita.

Frankly, Margaret began to see the beauty in her sister's game of enjoying his suffering.

But where was he? Where had he gone?

In the stable Rafe groomed Diablo to ready the stallion for wherever the search for Xzobal would lead him and Margaret. When she questioned Rafe on both men's disappearance, he surmised, "I'll bet the count is chasing Olga."

"Oh, dear. I'd hoped she could get out of the country without trouble from him."

"Don't worry, *amorcito*," Rafe assured Margaret. "Your family's got a generous head start. Even if that wasn't so, their Federale escorts won't let him near her."

Margaret kicked some hay aside. "Let's hope so."

"Let's hope his absence and Xzobal's isn't tied in with Tío Arturo. Last thing Netoc told me, my uncle and his hombres have been lurking around the gate to Eden Roc."

"*Hola.*" Hipólito strolled into the stable and offered up information. "Your brother the priest, he is at Areponapuchi."

"He wouldn't go there," Rafe said.

"Areponapuchi. Where have I heard that name before? Areponapuchi. Snake pit!" Margaret shivered. "Hipólito, what makes you think he's there?"

Lifting shoulders as well as his upturned hands, the peculiar Indian replied, "The drums in the canyon say the Federales that come with the *gran señor* your papá, they find the *padre*. They arrest him. Take him to the jail in Areponapuchi."

"Rafe!" she exclaimed. "Whatever shall we do?"

"Pack light."

Now that the excitement had died down, Arturo Delgado needed to relax. A cigar stuck between his teeth and a nubile whore at work between his legs, he lay smiling in the warren of Señora Pilar's whorehouse. Hunting the foxes, Mexican style, had always fascinated him, and today's hunt set his heart to tripping. "Ah, yes. Ahhh, yes, señorita."

A voice from the doorway snatched his attention. Cantú. "It is done, *patrón*."

"My nephew and the McLoughlin girl have been flushed from their nest? Excellent." Arturo smiled with malice. "The yellowbelly will get his punishment. Soon."

Cantú got a strange look on his face. "You never called him a coward before."

"It's taken him all these years to brave a showdown with me. Form your own opinion."

Back in the old days, Arturo never would have imagined calling Rafito a disparaging name. Matter of fact, he used to wish that Hernán had had his cousin's backbone. "By *La Santisima Virgen*," Arturo murmured under his breath, "my son so loved his cousin."

A knot formed in *El Grandero Rico's* throat.

Suddenly restless with the smacking and sucking from his lower regions, he shouted, "Get off. I have business to take care of."

He thrust his knee into the naked girl's midsection. And, wailing, she flew across the room. The back of her hand brushed across her mouth as she scrambled away.

"Cantú?" Arturo called out. "Where are you?"

"Right here." He remained standing in the doorway.

"The other matter . . ." Brushing his hands, Arturo shot to his feet and gathered his discarded clothes. "Is he dead and buried?"

"He is."

"Excellent."

Hipólito on a burro to the rear of their mounts, Caballo's muzzle peeping from Margaret's saddlebag, she followed Rafe along the twisting, rocky mountain path. They reached Areponapuchi just before sundown. Until today she hadn't given this village much thought, but she remembered it with all clarity: this was where Rafe had called on the local *curandera*.

403

Margaret shivered.

Once, Rafe had asked if she'd used the quackery he'd sent to Areponapuchi for. She'd hedged answering. And now she was glad she hadn't taken it. No telling what went into the stuff.

It was a strange little village, this. An eerie air prevailed. The children appeared subdued. No dogs or cats or goats wandered the streets. The only light poured from a few scattered shacks. Sobs—the wails of many women—emitted from the little church. Margaret hoped against hope—*Please don't let them be grieving for Father Xzobal.*

She alit Penny as Rafe tied Diablo to a hitching post in front of a stucco cantina. Caballo jumped to the ground to relieve himself, then yipped to be put back in the saddle.

Rafe frowned. He'd been frowning for hours, ever since Hipólito relayed the rumor of Xzobal's capture. Peacemaker in hand, Rafe filled and spun the cylinder.

Margaret ached to go to him, to comfort him, to express the depth of her love and concern. But a warrior's job was to get in, get out, and be victorious with both. This was no time for hearts and flowers.

"See after the horses," Rafe ordered Hipólito, then limped toward the main plaza, *el zócalo.*

She followed. All five pounds of Sir Colt dragged from the gun belt at her waist.

A stooped—cowed?—middle-aged man, wearing a sombrero and a serape, shuffled past them. He didn't gaze upon Margaret. When he looked up at

404

Rafe, his eyes flashed with a mixture of surprise and uncertainty, the expression of a person faced with someone they think they might know.

"Hombre, halt," Rafe called to him. "I have a question."

The *mexicano* stopped, turned back on the toe of a sandaled foot. *"¿Que?"*

"The priest Xzobal Paz. Is he here?"

"Sí, señor." He pointed a timid finger. "Outside the cemetery. *El Grandero Rico,* he would not let the *padre* be buried in hallowed ground."

This was their worst fear come true.

Arturo had done Xzobal in.

Margaret's heart plunged.

Hope blighted, Rafe blanched and was swaying on his uneven legs.

She took his hand as he rationalized, "It couldn't be him. Not even Tío Arturo would work that fast."

"Let's find out."

In the fading light, they moved as fast as Rafe's legs would carry him. They turned the corner. The cemetery crowned the hill; Rafe and Margaret charged up it. This side of the gate, a tiny nun, rosary in hand, knelt in front of a fresh grave. Her prayers mingled with her wails.

Rafe froze, a garbled "No" rising from his throat.

Margaret looped one arm around his, and squeezed the other wrist. "We don't know that it's him. We have no proof."

Leaves crunched nearby. Then everything happened at once. Figures lunged from the shadows. Arturianos! The ones who'd chased her and Rafe at

405

the mine. The ones who'd shot him.

Margaret screamed. A strong arm grabbed her waist. Fingers grasped her throat. Another ruffian lent a hand to bind and gag her, then to snatch Sir Colt away.

Meanwhile, three men had lunged at Rafe; the one from behind had kicked the Peacemaker out of Rafe's hand. It landed a dozen feet away. Rafe fought with all his might, landing blow after blow, but the marauders prevailed by falling upon and knocking him to the ground. A noiseless scream vibrated in Margaret's throat, as one of the thugs pinned Rafe's arms behind him, while his accomplice hammered a pistol butt on Rafe's head.

He went unconscious.

Continuing to scream behind her gag, Margaret struggled to get away. She kicked. She grappled. No use. The assailants dragged her away from her fallen Eagle.

They took her to a place beyond horrible.

Shoving her into an odd and squat building of many rooms, she sprawled trussed on the dirty red carpet. The music of guitars, an accordion, and several mariachi singers beat through her ears. Red surrounded her. Chairs upholstered in red velvet. Draperies of heavy red material. Red-flocked wallpaper. Whereas the red satin coverlet of Rafe's bed at El Aguilera Real had sent her on a sensory magic-carpet ride, this place just looked tawdry and cheap.

And roses. Everywhere, roses, some of them real. The smell of too much attar of roses clung to the air, funereal and dank.

Margaret's stomach roiled.

A harlot walked through the beaded doorway. Red plumes that had seen better days topped her dark head. Rice powder and kohl caked her face, a fake mole dotting her cheek. She wore heeled shoes, and a red corset over some sort of abbreviated red silk pajamas. In her hand she carried a riding crop.

She minced over to Margaret, then unfastened the gag. A disgusting display of bosom jiggled as she worked. *"Hola, muchacha.* I am Pilar. Welcome to my house of many surprises."

"Proving that a house isn't always a home," Margaret, inhaling great lungsful of air, shot back, and got a slap from one of her assailants. "Let me go!"

Another slap.

"Stop that, *niños.*" Pilar scratched a flea. *"El Grandero Rico* won't want her bruised."

El Grandero Rico. Arturo Delgado. *What hell have I toppled into?* Margaret struggled with her fetters, but they seemed to tighten with each of her efforts.

Pilar motioned to the men. "Stand her up, Cantú, Martin. Up, up. There. That's better." She motioned toward the beaded doorway. "Take her to the fourth door on the right."

Margaret resorted to a different tack. "Let me go. Please, Pilar. Call off these dogs. I've done nothing to you. I've done nothing to them." *Where is Rafe? What have they done to him?* "Let me go!"

Pilar lifted a penciled brow; her pale amber eyes snapped. "I understand you are the mistress of *El*

407

Aguila Magnífico."

"What do you know of him?"

"Why, what an absurd question." The painted mouth bowed. "The master stud has been gracing my presence since he was but a yearling."

"I don't believe you."

"Oh? What about the time he called on me to get the herbs to prevent pregnancy? I assume they were for you."

Margaret slammed her eyes closed. What did she really know about him? What kind of man had she given her all to? *Damn you, Rafe Delgado!*

Her heart warned her head not to make too much of this vile creature's word. Rafe deserved her faith.

"Take her on to the room, *niños.*" The madam slapped the riding crop against her leg. "I will be with you in a minute, Señorita McLoughlin. I will strip you, make you ready. *El Grandero Rico* grows impatient."

Thirty-two

Fear. Anger. Sheer cowardice. All these emotions tumbled end over end in Margaret, when the duo of Arturianos dragged her down a lengthy and crooked hallway, toward Pilar's fourth room. She refused to give them an upper hand by displaying her terrors.

The older thug spoke. "Martín, do you think the señorita would enjoy a look around?"

"Why not?"

Glad that Pilar had removed the gag, Margaret jumped in. "I am perfectly capable of speaking for myself, and I don't —"

Cantú interrupted with, *"¡Basta!"* Stopping at the first doorway, his fingers cut into her wrist. "Take a look, pretty peach."

"No thank you."

From behind, she felt sturdy hands grip her head. "Watch," said a man, neither Cantú nor his conspirator.

With the fascination that ofttimes accompanies repugnance, Margaret saw a hooded man chained spread-eagle to manacles on the wall; he hadn't a stitch of clothes. Her back to the door, a big woman wearing a flowing black robe ran her hand along his thigh. He cried out. "Be quiet, young man! Or I will be forced to paddle you."

Good Lord, that's Helga!

"Ready for more?" asked the stranger.

Not waiting for her reply, Cantú shoved Margaret to the next room, where a bound and gagged woman moaned when an unclothed, aroused man snapped a bullwhip over her behind. Margaret made a face. *She ought to kick his privates, just as soon as he sets her loose.*

Next, Margaret was forced to witness—she had some private-kicking of her own to do, that she did!—a large arena with a row of men seated on ice-cream parlor chairs along one wall; smoke wound through the air, the smell redolent of hashish.

The men ogled a pair of roosters. Their feathers swirling like small tornadoes, the cocks battled amid coins that had been tossed near their sharp spurs. "You people ought to be shot for being cruel to those dumb roosters."

"Shhh," ordered Cantú.

"I will not. This is an awful place." One rooster prevailed as she said, "A sick circus with two rings, stinking to high heaven of animal, sweat, and decay. And dissipation!"

"*¡Ole!*" roared the crowd, and closed in to gather their cockfight winnings.

Hugging the second ring, cheering men observed a woman, wearing leather and little of it, circle a donkey while she scratched his ear and chanted to

410

him as she went.

"Do you know what she'll do with the donkey?" asked the stranger who held Margaret's head.

"I don't want to know."

Her eyelids slammed down, she closed a mental trapdoor on her ears. To think—Rafe had visited this den of iniquity, and lately. It disgusted her to picture him enjoying the attractions. *How bored he must get with my inexperienced—and basically conventional!—lovemaking.*

He'd had lots and lots of experience. Most of it with loose women and in dens such as Casa Pilar, if gossip was any barometer. The McLoughlins would never have known Rafe Delgado existed if he hadn't gotten drunk in a Nuevo Laredo whorehouse. Gotten drunk, then had gotten in one of those chains-and-shackles carousals with a couple of felonious Mexicans!

"Penny for your thoughts," spoken by the stranger, yanked her back to this house of harlotry and hell.

"Who are you?" she asked.

No answer. But his hands let go their vise.

The ruffians yanked her onward to the next doorway, then pushed her inside the dimly lit, windowless room. No furniture. Satin pillows littered the wooden floor. A tray of bottles and glasses sat in the middle, inviting entrance and indulgence. That unpleasant scent of roses lingered here. She knew that to her dying day, she would never again abide the smell of them.

From behind, the small sound of a door clicking

411

shut drew her attention.

Terrified at what might happen to her if she didn't escape, Margaret, nonetheless, squared her shoulders and schooled her voice. "Stay away from me, Pilar. I am not taking my clothes off."

"I am not the proprietress."

It was the man who had held her head. She suspected his identity. He wasn't a comforting thought. And she was trapped. Trapped! What should she do? Which way should she turn? *You'll have to bide your time, think through the situation, before you can get control.*

With as much hauteur as her shackles and circumstance would allow, she struggled to a sitting position, then turned her nose up toward the doorway. The light poor in that direction, Margaret tried to get a good look at the man who leaned back against the jamb, one ankle crossed over the other. He wore a white shirt and dark trousers.

She demanded, "Don't just stand there. Cut these bonds and be quick about it. I am quite uncomfortable."

He started to comply, but checked the instinct. "It seems, Miss McLoughlin, you are a young woman of your own mind."

"How do you know my name?"

"We've met before. Do you not remember?" He took a step into the faint stream of light. Crouching back on his heels, he rested a wrist on a knee and bent his face closer. His was a handsome visage, resembling Rafe's face. She recognized him way before he said, "I am Arturo Delgado. *El Grandero*

412

Rico. The uncle of your paramour."

The urge to spit in his eye got quelled. If she wanted the advantage, she had to fight fire with fire. At least she hoped this strategy would work.

She blew a stray lock of hair out of her eyes. "What took you so long? We've been expecting you for weeks."

His left eyebrow jerked up and down, twice. "The tigress doesn't back down. I like that."

"Where is Rafe?" *Please let him be all right!*

Arturo moved to the tray of drinks, crouching down to pour a snifterful, then sat back on his heels. "Evidently you don't know your man as well as a bride-to-be ought to."

"Whether that is so or it isn't, it's my business. And since he is my business, I demand you tell me where he is."

"He's next door. In room five. Don't bother to scream. He can neither hear nor help you." Arturo took a sip, then set the drink aside to plump a couple of pillows. He snuggled into the softness. "I should imagine Rafito is doing what he's done a hundred times in this emporium of variety. Oh, that's right. You wouldn't know . . . We never got to door number five."

"The last I saw him, your thugs—no doubt they are your thugs—had rendered him senseless."

"He's recovered." Arturo swirled the contents of his snifter, then held the rim to her nose to sniff the bouquet. "Tell me, beauty. What do you see in a worthless cripple like my nephew?"

"Anything bad, I equate with you."

413

He tipped the cognac to her lips. Rather than choke, she took some onto her tongue. "That's a good girl," he cooed.

"What are you about, *El Grandero Rico?*" By halves she didn't feel as bold and calm as portrayed in the content of her discourse or in the tone of her voice. "What game do you play that you would have your own flesh and blood shot down first, and now bludgeoned? And why did you stalk us to the Sierras in the first place?"

"You know the answer as well as I do. At least where Rafito is concerned."

Forcing the emotion from her voice, she replied, "You want to avenge your son's death. And you would like to get rid of any reminders of your stolen fortune."

"I stole nothing." His expression betrayed his denial.

"Ah. What does it matter? Anyway, no one could blame you for looking out for you and yours. That's one of mankind's most basic instincts, wouldn't you say?"

He grinned. And Margaret was taken aback at his handsomeness. His nephew really did favor him. Too bad so much beauty was spoiled by so much greed and insensitivity.

"Arturo—you don't mind if I call you by your given name, do you?—what was the point in killing Father Xzobal? He, a simple parish priest, couldn't have done much to hurt a man as powerful and as revered as *El Grandero Rico.*"

A chuckle, low and dry. "He isn't dead." Margaret hid her sigh of relief, and Arturo went on. "We only made it look like the rabble-rouser had died."

"Why should I believe you?"

"Did you not recognize the priest? The big Swede Helga wears his holy robes, and is as we speak"— Arturo sniggered, smacked his lips—"she is giving him a blessed sacrament."

Poor, sensitive Xzobal. First attacked by the piranha Natalie, and now to be violated by that ghastly Helga. Yet Margaret forced a laugh. "That Helga, isn't she amazing? A man of your stature, I should think you'd be attracted to a woman who can go heads up with you." Margaret paused. "Unless you prefer shrinking violets."

"I prefer fauna to flora."

Getting some ideas of his character, Margaret said, "Have you given Helga a go?"

"Never gave it much thought. But now that I do, yes, I find her interesting. She rather reminds me of my late wife. Yolanda enjoyed being in charge."

Uh, huh. *He does like to be bossed around.* "Pour me another splash of that cognac. And be quick about it."

Arturo hastened to oblige, then Margaret asked, "If Xzobal isn't dead, who is in that fresh grave? Or did you turn up dirt for show?"

"There's a proper corpse." Stretched out on his side, the side of his head cradled in one palm, Arturo reached for her hand with his free fingers. "The Count of Granada . . . what do you think of him?"

"Very little."

415

"Then we have something in common. I found him sly and patronizing." Arturo flashed a smile. "Your brother-in-law has gone to a greater reward. Or to his just deserts. Whichever way you prefer to look at it."

Leonardo. Dead. *There is a God!* Should she take everything Arturo said as fact, though? "What assurances do I have that you speak the truth? That grave could be anything or nothing. And what reason did you have for killing the count?"

"*I* didn't kill him. Nor did my minions." Indignation laced Arturo's words. "I don't regret his death, you can be assured. Actually, I find it amusing. A dozen peasants—several of them old enough to remember the first of his family in Mexico—clubbed Lord Hapsburg to death when he tried to enter this village, Helga at his side."

There was no playacting on Margaret's part when she uttered, "The earth has just become a more genteel place for the loss of Leonardo."

"Yes, yes." Arturo laughed. "We should hang a warning on posts in our ports. HAPSBURGS, ENTER AT YOUR OWN RISK."

Violence always lurked just beneath the surface of normalcy in this god-awful country, and it sickened Margaret to realize she'd gotten caught up in her own glee. Would Mexico sap all her honor and conscience?

This is the life you've committed to. Are you sure you can deal with it? New York City, after all, was a civil and respectable city. And it was home, home, home.

"Would you like another sip of cognac, tigress princess?"

"No." She shot him a stern look. "I want you to loosen these bindings. I want you to tell me where I can find Rafe. And don't hand me that fifth-door nonsense."

His eyes brightened. "All right. I'll be honest. He escaped. No more than five minutes before you arrived here at Casa Pilar."

"I don't believe you. He couldn't have recovered so quickly. He was unconscious at the cemetery, which wasn't that long ago."

She had to get out of here. On her own. Under her own steam. And rescue Rafe and his brother in the process. But how to escape? This for all intents and purposes was a cage. It was a long way to the entrance. *You'll have to outwit Arturo.*

He sipped cognac, his eyelids falling to half-mast. He lifted a hand to scrape his fingernail across her chambray-covered breast. "Would you like to know why I've brought you here?"

"The thought has crossed my mind."

"I want you for my mistress." His fingers moved to the front of his trousers; he ran his fingertip on the elongated outline. "I want to pound you until you cry for mercy."

When Rafe said these sort of things to her, they aroused her. When his uncle said them, they fell on deaf ears. *Don't show it, not if you want to get the best of him.* "This pounding. Do you intend to do it while my hands are tied behind my back?"

"Why not? At least until you get broken to my

417

saddle. I will take you to my hacienda . . . if you please me. I know you will. Tonight makes me certain of it. And if you bear me a boy-child, I shall make you my wife."

A child. A fist closed in her chest, a lump kept her from swallowing. For weeks she'd suspected but refused to acknowledge, not even to herself, that she'd soon be holding Rafe's child in her arms.

She'd blamed her faintness on her lungs; the Fountain had returned her strength, though. But her flow hadn't come since before leaving Texas. What else could it be, but the obvious?

Heaven help me, do I chance being honest with my child's own uncle . . . ?

She couldn't, shouldn't, and wouldn't. She would trust no one with Rafe's precious babe.

Though her hands were bound, she cuddled her abdominal muscles around the tiny precious life. "If you mean to make me your mistress, I must insist on my rights. I refuse to allow you to touch me when I am restrained."

"What a tigress."

He lunged for her, but she rolled away. Rolled to her knees. Recalling Yolanda and Helga along with her own conclusions, she gambled. "Did you not understand my Spanish? Must I repeat what I said? Or . . ." Her eyes welded to his hips; she widened her eyes, drawing in a deep breath of supposed interest. "Get up from there."

It was all she could do not to giggle. "You've been a bad, bad boy, having me tied up like this. When I get loose, I'm going to give you the spanking you so richly deserve."

He beamed. "Yolanda. You sound just like Yolanda."

Like a lad digging into a bowl of cherries, Arturo delved into untying the leather straps. Within thirty seconds Margaret had crowned him with the cognac decanter, rendered him insensate, and was rushing on tiptoes up the hallway. Just as she reached the last turn, she pulled up short.

"Rafe!"

She flew into his arms.

Behind him she caught sight of a clothed Father Xzobal. To his left, Sean Moynihan. And Pancho Villa. Pancho Villa! Plus his man Javier. The Villanista Pedro? Missing.

This was no time for a reunion or for questions about how Rafe and his brother had gotten free, or about how these men had come to help out. Rafe took her hand, and hopping along with his best effort, they burst into the red room where Pilar had been gagged already.

The contingent made a fast exit.

Pedro wasn't missing, she learned after they had gotten away from Areponapuchi. He would catch up with them, Rafe explained and rubbed his sore head. The group made camp near Eden Roc.

Pancho Villa had much to say, mainly to Margaret. Ready to raid the Santa Alicia, he'd followed Rafe's path to Eden Roc. One of the cooks had stopped her packing to send Villa to Areponapuchi. At the cemetery Villa and his men found a half-dazed Rafe, the Arturianos preparing to carry him to Casa Pilar.

Hipólito ran from the cemetery, Rafe said. Never to be seen again.

"I tossed the Eagle a gun," said Villa, "and he came out of his daze." The walrus mustache lifted in a smile. "The Magnificent Eagle shot the three criminals dead."

He put her beliefs to rest that Rafe wouldn't defend himself.

Villa carried on with the story. By the time they reached Pilar's house of whoredom, Xzobal had gotten free of Helga, who, he said, had done nothing more than touch his leg after the Arturianos had strung him up.

"She was reeling from the shock of seeing Lord Hapsburg drawn and quartered," Xzobal explained.

While Rafe serenaded the group with a guitar borrowed from Javier, Pedro returned. He brought news that Arturo's wound was superficial. Already, *El Grandero Rico* had started back for Santa Alicia, his remaining Arturianos in attendance.

Rafe, naturally, vowed to follow them. He and Pancho Villa made expansive plans to bring the Santa Alicia mine down. Actually, Villa wanted nothing more than the money in the office safe; he'd leave the do-gooder part to Rafe, Xzobal, and Sean.

"Why did you leave Arturo at Casa Pilar?" Margaret asked Rafe by the crackling and popping campfire, when the others had scattered for various and sundry chores and privacies. "Rafe, if you wanted your revenge, why didn't you take it before we left?"

"I had to get you out of there."

"Why? If your favorite playpen is good enough for you, why wouldn't it be good enough for me?"

A muscle in his jaw went rigid. "Pilar's establishment is not my favorite playpen."

"I do believe the madam begs to differ."

A thunderous look passing across his face, Rafe replied, "If you were looking for a man without a few sins to his name, you picked the wrong hombre. If you're looking for me to apologize for my past, you're in trouble. I can't change it. I won't make excuses for it. And that's that."

That's that. One of her hardheaded father's favorite expressions.

I can't deal with Rafe tonight.

Later, she heard him say to Villa, *et al,* "Too bad we're fettered by the need for rest. I'm burning to ride on to the Santa Alicia mine."

Seeing another man of zeal—her father—Margaret questioned a lot of things. She turned away and moved to the area where she and Rafe would sleep tonight. She spread a saddle blanket on the ground. She kept hearing Pilar call Rafe "master stud." She kept remembering how she'd smiled upon hearing of her brother-in-law's brutal death. She kept thinking about all the awful things that could happen when they sabotaged the Santa Alicia silver mine.

And she cried. Cried for herself and for Rafe. And for their baby.

Get a grip. You're tired. You're upset. Don't say something you'll regret later.

She took her own advice. She refused to discuss her feelings. It wasn't until they neared the village of San Antonio that the rumblings of her true nature reverberated.

The Delgado band planned to spend one night at Rancho Gato, the gate of which stood no more than two miles from San Antonio. Margaret decided, *Once we reach the Fuentes ranch, I'm going to call Rafe aside. We are going to get our house in order.*

Thirty-three

Rafe and Margaret, along with their followers, descended to the base of the Sierra Madres and reached Rancho Gato on a crisp January afternoon. The rancher and his wife greeted the returned visitors warmly. Vicente and Esther Vasquez welcomed Margaret with special warmth.

Without so much as a backward glance at Rafe, Margaret tucked Caballo in the crook of one arm, locked the other one with Esther's, and made for the adobe ranch house.

Margarita had been quiet, much too quiet since leaving Areponapuchi five nights ago, and her actions had Rafe concerned. Even her usual enthusiasm in lovemaking had been lacking.

He sighed as he led Diablo into the stable and unsaddled the fitful stallion. Something had to be wrong with Margarita — something very wrong — for her not to talk. It had to be more than jealousy over Casa Pilar.

Going in to their love affair, Margaret had known he was immoral and likely to stay that way. *Stay* that way? He'd never cuckold her. Never. But how was she to know that?

Damn.

Maldicion.

He glanced at Xzobal, who was running a curry-comb through his mount's mane. Rafe had the urge to say something to his brother, something on the order of, "I think Margarita has changed her mind about me." But Xzobal had enough worries without piling Rafe's on top.

Rafe patted Diablo's rump, then stepped to the adjacent stall. "Are you gonna be all right, *muchacho?*"

Xzobal rubbed his palm down the side of his britches. With the Federales still looking for him, he wore the clothes of a common vaquero. He turned to Rafe, and the fatigue of a thousand years dulled his brown eyes.

"You're not going back to the church, are you?" Rafe said.

"But I am. With more dedication than ever before. I'm going to join a monastery."

"You're going to be a *monk?* Have you lost your mind? You joined the priesthood just to please your father, you don't have a true calling."

"Not so." Xzobal gave a dry laugh. "If I didn't have a calling, I would have swept Natalie away the first time she flirted with me."

"Seems to me your heels got round. And quick. So don't hand me that line." Rafe saw he was getting nowhere. "Think on this. Those places would bore a mouse, much less an hombre who's sampled

424

a tasty morsel like that Natalie."

Scowling now, Xzobal yanked the currycomb down the gelding's neck, receiving a bite on his forearm for his roughness.

As the victim yelped and rubbed his abused flesh, Rafe smirked knowingly. "You're joshing me with that monk business. There hasn't been a monastery in Mexico for thirty-odd years."

"They still have them in Spain. And that's where I'm going."

Rafe grimaced, blew a stream of breath out his rigid mouth, and shook his head. "You'll live to regret taking off for there. You wait and see. It won't be anytime 'til you have such a craving for a mouthful of tit and a handful of hot woman, you'll be scaling the monastery walls."

Xzobal said nothing.

One last bit had to be said. "If you're leaving, fine. But you're not going until after you marry me and 'Rita."

"Who says we're going to be married?" came a feminine voice.

'Rita.

Rafe spun around.

She stood barefooted in the door of the stable, sunlight shooting through the dark hair that lay thick and wavy over her shoulders. Esther Vasquez must have loaned her some clothes, for Margarita wore a red skirt and a white peasant blouse, the drawstringed collar of the latter settling just below her shoulders. As usual, she looked sensational. Except for her expression.

"Xzobal," Rafe demanded, "leave us."

He did. Margarita entered the stable, stopped at Diablo's stall. When Rafe tried to take her in his arms, she backed away. Again they surfaced, his fears about her intentions.

She spoke. "I want you to back off this vendetta against Arturo."

"I beg your pardon?"

"Arturo isn't a totally unreasonable man. If you put your heart into it, I think you can reason with him. Actually, all you need to do is set forth *demands,* and he'll listen to you."

Was he hearing right? Margarita—Margarita the warrior-woman!—had turned coat? "He's duped you."

"I don't think so. I believe I understand him quite well. And after talking with him, I better understand myself. I realized that I was enjoying violence. Having a blood thirst scares me witless."

"You aren't obligated to go with us on the raid. Stay here 'til I return for you."

She shook her head. "What I'm trying to say is, I don't want *you* to jeopardize your life. You must give up this revenge bunk. I want us to leave for Texas at first light. If you want to marry me"—she plumbed her spine—"you'll have to accept that our home will be New York City."

His ears weren't working right. Or this was a dream that would fade when he awoke. But it wasn't a nightmare. And there was nothing wrong with his hearing. "Your terms are unacceptable."

"Then you and I are finished."

"Bullshit." His words gritted past his clenched teeth. "We've come all this way, fought so many odds, and you want us to retreat like cowed curs? Unacceptable."

"I find it unacceptable, the idea of a husband who's used for target practice."

Struck dumb by all she'd thrown at him, he tried to understand her reasoning. All this time, he'd believed her steady and true to their shared ideals. Obviously their ideals weren't shared. Had her promises been empty, too? "What is it you're wanting?" he asked sourly. "A rose garden?"

"Never a rose garden."

"A cottage in the glen? Quiet evenings, hearth-side. A passel of babies?"

She flinched. "We . . . we both agreed we wanted children. A while back you didn't think they were an impossibility. Have you changed your mind?"

"I want to father your children. But not *now*. We're on the eve of our greatest triumph."

Shaking with frustration, she shouted, "Triumph? Better call it tragedy. Don't you realize you could get killed in that mine!"

"Diablo could kick me right now, and I could die from it. We have no life guarantees."

"Oooh." Her hands made fists that she pounded against Rafe's chest. "Rafael Delgado, damn you to hell! You're too much like my father."

"How so?" He closed his fingers around her fists, holding them to his heart.

"He always made my mother second in his priori-ties. She deserved better than her constant hoping against hope that he'd wise up."

"He wised up."

"It took him almost thirty years to do it. You and I, we've lost the dew of youth, save for that which Eden Roc gave us. We don't have thirty years to waste."

Her arguments were getting to him. But if he went along with her, what would happen? He saw himself as what he would be: an hombre who'd done nothing to honor his sainted cousin.

He had to make Margarita understand. "I love you, *mi corazón*. I love you more than the stars in the heavens or the air that we breathe. You are the song in my heart. You are the light of my life. You've given me hope and happiness, and a reason to look forward to growing old. In return I will give you anything you want, anywhere you want it. You'll have it all . . . except for one thing. I won't surrender my principles." Blood surged in his ears. "Thirty years or thirty minutes or for whatever life I've got left, I have to live with my conscience—and do penance for my sins. I refuse to abandon my mission until the people of the Santa Alicia know a better life."

Tears welled and her chin trembled. "You thrive on violence."

"Not so." Trying to appease, he said, " 'Rita, *mi dulce,* once Arturo is routed, we'll have the rest of our lives for children and picket fences. I promise."

She yanked her hand from his heart, and backed away, almost stumbling. She grabbed hold of a support post. Taking a restorative breath, she stood to her full height. "You've forgotten something. You're forty years old. Already, you're old enough to be a grandfather, yet you aren't ready to be a father? Fine. That's your prerogative. But I'm not getting any younger. I want children. Your children. If you go face off with the Arturianos at the mine, you'll never see being a father."

He glared at her.

"You don't stand a chance"—she batted at a tear—"because there's a place in your heart that still beats for your uncle. Do you know why you can't kill him? Because you haven't quit loving him! Unless one of you gives in, though, you'll be carried out of that damned hole in the ground! Because his hired guns damned sure don't have any love for you."

"Are you through?"

"If I can't have you the way I want you, I might as well go back to my Persians."

He stomped around her, quitting the stable. Given his limp, she didn't have any trouble catching up, which she did, not twenty feet outside the stable. He ordered her off. She stopped.

He took another ten steps, then halted when she shouted to him, "I'm not through with you!"

Wheeling around, he started toward her but she withdrew. The distance separating them might as well have been a continent in length, when she said, "You would cut down your uncle in the chivalrous name of honor, yet it wasn't his bullet that struck Hernándo Delgado."

A bullet couldn't hurt any worse than the sting in

Rafe's chest. At that moment he hated Margaret McLoughlin. It was too bad she'd ever left those damned cats, because she damned sure didn't belong in Mexico.

Loathing in his tone, he said, "Congratulations. You've finally done what you set out to do, years ago. You've cut my nuts."

She'd made a mess of trying to reason with Rafe. He hated her, and she couldn't blame him. All she'd wanted was to open his eyes! No matter what she did, he wouldn't accept her apologies.

Not an hour after their pitched battle, he had collected his brother, the bandit Pancho Villa, and the rest of their party, and they had ridden away from Rancho Gato. Rafe, without a backward glance.

She knew his plans, and they scared her. Tomorrow, as soon as they could fetch the guns and ammunition Villa had stockpiled at his house in Santa Eulalia, Rafe and his partners would stand and deliver at the Delgado silver mine.

On second thought, Margaret decided she should have told Rafe about the baby. If he knew fatherhood wasn't just a concept — On third thought, she was glad she hadn't. She and their child didn't need him, if he had to be coerced into staying with them.

This was the longest night of Margaret's life.

She rolled and tossed and trembled. Then she cackled like an idiot at the irony of the situation. They had begun in San Antonio. And their love affair had ended in another San Antonio. Two towns a world apart. Just like Margaret and Rafe were worlds apart.

She did no more laughing, not when she drew mental images of all the terrible things that could happen to Rafe. Along with all these gruesome scenarios, she had terrible stomach cramps. The reason became apparent when she left the bed where she had spent that sleepless night. Her flow had begun.

Damn.

Double damn.

She wouldn't even have a child to remember Rafe by.

It was tempting, the urge to take to her borrowed bed and cry her eyes out. After all, she'd wanted Rafe to want her more than anything in the world. "It's better this way," she told herself. "He could be killed today, and where would I be?"

Rafe—killed!

Today.

And he would die with her hateful remarks ringing in his ears.

The trouble with issuing an ultimatum, Margaret had to live with the negative results. Going back to her cats held little appeal. *Oh, Lord, what am I going to do without Rafe?* She'd lived all these years without him, but the prospects of the future . . . Her stomach pulled into knots having nothing to do with monthly flow.

Wait a minute.

Without a baby, there was no reason why she couldn't ride after him.

431

Esther Vasquez, as she cooked breakfast and Margaret worked as assistant, took on the voice of her conscience. "But, *amiga,* you said you are sickened by the violence you've seen in Mexico."

"Leonardo was an awful man. A philanderer and a rapist and a murderer. He deserved to suffer." Margaret mixed tomatoes to chiles and onions to make *salsa.* "Rafe is a wonderful man."

"*Sí.*" Esther tossed a tortilla on the hot griddle. "The Eagle is a special man. But he is human. If he gave you another chance, could you accept him as he is? A rogue with a string of lovers."

Margaret stirred the *salsa.* Could she accept him? The romantic part of her heart said yes. The practical part of her brain had a positive thought: So what if he'd done this and that with who-knew-what, no telling how many times. Considering his mastery at lovemaking, she ought to be glad he was no green fumbler.

"I wouldn't want him if I could change him," she answered. "He wouldn't be appealing if he were timid and meek, or if I could henpeck him. I fell in love with Rafe for Rafe. He's brave and courageous and determined. And not bad-looking, either."

"Very true."

"Excuse me, Esther. I'm going to my man."

"What if he won't take you back?"

Anxiety spiraled. "I — I . . . I don't know if he'll forgive me. If he'll allow me, I'll stand by him through thick and thin, through revolution and times of peace, no matter the price."

Esther smiled. "*Andele, muchacha.* Hurry, girl.

Before it's too late."

After packing the bare necessities into her saddle-bags, Margaret rode hard for the Santa Alicia silver mine. *Don't let it be too late for us, Rafe, my darling!*

Thirty-four

The terrible ache of losing out on love twisted through Rafe to tie knots in his head and his muscles and his heart. When he'd been standing stalwart by his principles in the argument with Margarita, then had quit her as well as Rancho Gato, he'd neglected to consider the consequences of breaking up. He hadn't realized how much it could hurt.

A half-dozen times that day, he turned Diablo around. A half -dozen times he turned the stallion back around. Dying on the inside—dying without any help from the Arturianos!—Rafe persisted on his path to the Santa Alicia.

Anyway, it was too late to turn back.

He collected the armaments Villa had been stockpiling. He headed his band of men onward. They reached the foot of Santa Alicia Mountain just prior to the day shift leaving the mine. Already they knew Arturo had returned to the mine, thanks to a spy for Rafe's cause.

Rafe pulled in Diablo's reins. "Villa, my brother and I—Sean, too—will follow behind the slave drivers." Any minute now the overseers would escort the night crew to the mouth of the mine. "Villa, take your men and surround the office. Clean out the safe and be gone."

Villa waved, kneed his palomino, and pointed his men up the hill.

Rafe, his saddle creaking when he turned to the mining engineer, said, "Sean, you know what to do. Get into the mine and place the charges. But wait for my signal to set them."

As he and his brother waited for the line of workers, Rafe couldn't help getting maudlin. *You've lost her, you fool. She was the best thing that ever happened to you. And now you've turned your back.*

What if he quit right now? What if he begged forgiveness? He didn't expect her to be waiting, when he circled back to Rancho Gato. Probably—no doubt—she was long gone by now.

"I'll find her," he vowed to his brother. "I'll make it up to her. Once I get rid of Arturo, I'll do anything 'Rita wants. I'll even move to"—he gulped—"New York City."

"If you are alive to offer up the whole of yourself."

"You sound like 'Rita."

"Smart woman, your *gringa*. Wouldn't you agree?"

Rafe frowned. As if she rode next to him, he could hear her voice. *Tell your uncle what to do. He's not unreasonable. He's inclined to agree to demands.* Sure, and Porfirio Díaz would be sainted by the Mother Church! Despite his cynicism, Rafe swallowed and remembered the Tío of days gone by. He remembered his boyhood, when his uncle had been like a father to him. A fist clawed at his chest.

Xzobal glanced over Rafe's shoulder. "Here they come, the night shift."

Rafe alit the saddle, hobbled Diablo, then replied, "Hold the drivers back. I'm going in to talk with my uncle."

Fearing what she'd find on arrival at the Santa Alicia, Margaret put her spurs to Penny and rushed to the mine. She caught a glimpse of Father Xzobal as she started to climb the hill. A group of slaves sat on the ground, their overseers standing with arms raised in front of the clergyman's borrowed six-gun.

Margaret checked the open side of her saddlebag, making sure her passenger rode safely, then kicked Penny's flank. Pancho Villa and his men, bulging sacks thrown over their saddle horns, cheered as she approached.

Villa patted the sacks. "Ay, Señora Eagle. The poor will eat well tonight."

"Will they now?" Arturo Delgado's finances wouldn't be ruined by one spell of robbery. And the bandit would do honor to his spoils. "Good for you, Pancho Villa!"

"*Hasta luego*, pretty toothpick." Villa and his Villanistas carried on.

Darkness. A pit of darkness, stinking and reeking of dust, sweat, vomit. Making every effort not to add her own gorge, Margaret held tight to the pulley; it creaked as she descended to the inferno of Dante.

A single lantern lit the bottom, a cavern of wide dimensions. Three cages of canaries hung from hooks in the ceiling. Slaves huddled in one corner. A man—she recognized the slave driver—lay prone and hog-tied on

436

the rock floor. Cantú and Martín were also restrained.

A gash in his head, Sean Moynihan sat stunned, his back to a wall. Coils of detonator wire were stacked askance to his left. And Arturo had a pistol leveled on his nephew.

Likewise, Rafe had the Peacemaker trained on him.

Tension stretched even tighter in Margaret's nerves.

In the muted light she knew Rafe watched her from the corner of his eye. Those eyes demanded she leave. *I'm with you, Rafe. Come what may.*

"What are you doing here, lovely Margaret?" asked Arturo.

She couldn't say, "I'm here to prostrate myself to Rafe and his any decision." She couldn't fall to the ground and grab his ankle, kissing it over and over in remorse. Could she? This was a matter of pride.

"He forgot his dog."

She reached into her pocket and extracted a handful of black Chihuahua, who yipped.

Arturo laughed.

Rafe groaned.

"You braved this mine to deliver a dog?" the uncle asked. "What a woman. Too bad you love this rogue. I would have enjoyed having you as my own. Are you sure you won't change your mind about me?"

"I would love to love you. As an *uncle.*"

"Get out of here," Rafe ordered her. "Get back to your cats."

Her hopes plunged. What had she expected, though? A wet kiss, a wag of tail, and doleful eyes begging for a reconciliation?

She turned her attentions to the uncle. "Put down the gun. You can't shoot him. You can't shoot Rafe any more than he can shoot you. Thank God." She walked up to Arturo and put her hand on his free arm. "You love him. That's why it hurts so much, isn't it? Because you lost *two* sons that night eight years ago."

"Basta, mujer!"

"No, Arturo, I've not said enough. Stop this infernal feud. Stop it right now."

"I wouldn't listen to my nephew when he said these same things, why would I listen to you?"

Startled, she glanced at Rafe. *You went with my idea?* His telepathic reply: Yes. Her heart danced a jig of joy. A grin did the polka across her face. All wasn't lost!

If the Delgado men didn't shoot each other, that is.

Determined to keep at the elder Delgado, she pivoted around to face him. Caballo held to the right of her breast, she stepped up to Arturo. He held out his left hand to ward off the dog, but Caballo's long pink tongue darted out, laving the side of the human's hand.

"He likes you," Margaret commented. "And I've found him to be a fairly good judge of character. Would you like to hold him?"

"No."

She leaned toward Arturo's ear, whispering in a no-nonsense tone, "I am ashamed of you. Unwilling to bend with your nephew. And now you insult his little dog. I've had enough of the Delgado family feud. You *will* call it off. You *will* give Rafe his rightful legacy. And you *will* atone for your wrongs." She straightened and held out her palm. Her voice rose. "Hand me the gun. And I mean it!"

He placed the cold steel in her hand.

* * *

438

Neither Rafe nor his uncle had been able to fire on the other, and, as it were, neither man ever again leveled a firearm at another person.

It was difficult to believe that the horrors of the Santa Alicia would end, but end it did. After reconciling with his nephew, Arturo Delgado went to see his attorney. He renounced all claims to the estate of Constanzo Delgado.

"In Hernán's honor," he told Rafe and Margaret after signing the documents, "and yours, too."

The happy couple smiled at each other, Rafe snaking his arm around her waist. Once Arturo handed over the firearm, they had fallen into each other's arms.

It was Arturo who pleaded for mercy. He got it.

The Delgado family was once again whole. Even Soledad—who had hated her brother-in-law for as long as she'd known him—appeared at the fiesta Rafe organized for the people of Santa Alicia. The festivities were held on the thirteenth of February, 1898.

Yes, Arturo attended the fiesta.

Helga accompanied him.

With his personal fortune—he did have some money and property in his own right—Arturo Delgado promised to build a school for the children of Santa Alicia. He also promised to leave Mexico, to make a start in another country. Cuba might be the spot, he said. Already Cantú and Martín—both now recovered, as was Sean Moynihan—had offered to go with him to the West Indies.

Arturo hugged his nephew before he took his leave, then kissed Margaret's cheek. "Thank you, dear lady, for showing me the way."

"I imagine your son would be pleased to know how everything has turned out," she said.

Arturo's eyes glistened. "Yes, he would be pleased."

On the bedside table in the master suite at El Aguilera Real, sat a Spanish-language copy of *Christopher Columbus and the Catholic Kings*. Rafe had finished reading it an hour ago. It was the first book he'd ever finished. The author was pleased and proud, even before he had given her a left-handed compliment: "It's much better than most of the crap I've tried to read."

Later that night, atop the erotic red coverlet at El Aguilera Real, Rafe held his *enamorada* in his arms. Lodged high in her womanly place, they were joined as he'd always wished . . . to where she could never get away. It all seemed too good to be true, life.

"Xzobal leaves day after tomorrow for Spain." Rafe nibbled her neck, drawing shivers of excitement. "Are we, or are we not, going to ask him to marry us?"

Her fingertips drew invisible hearts into his thick mat of black chest hair, her toes making circles on the top of his feet. Oh, how she loved this man. *Thank you, Papa, for sending me to him!* "My darling rogue, you have the best ideas . . ." She licked the scar at his lip. "What a fabulous way to spend Valentine's Day."

They sealed it with a kiss.

Epilogue

It was an hour before the doors would open to the public.

Tall stacks of *The Tears of Cuauhtémoc* by Margarita Delgado de McLoughlin lined the Manhattan bookstore. This time the publisher hadn't insisted on a male pseudonym, thanks to the author's prominence as an expert on Mexico.

Nonetheless, a nervous Margaret stood at the back of the store, wringing her hands. "Our family is so scattered. Do you think everyone will get here on time?"

"They will be here, *querida*."

Rafe had such trust in family and friends—as well as in train and ship arrivals! How she loved this husband of hers. A crashing noise to the rear drew her attention. Both she and Rafe lunged for the sturdy lads—better known as The Stairsteps—who now wailed from the center of a dislodged stack of their mother's books.

Rafe took Hernándo into his arms; Margaret took charge of young Rafael. Angus, blond and blue-eyed like his namesake, got a stern word from his father; he stuck out his tongue and marched to Soledad Paz, who doted on him as well as her other grandsons.

A helpful store clerk righted the volumes.

The front door creaked open. Addressing the clerk who had just finished stacking those books, a familiar voice filled the air like rolling thunder on the Loch Ness. "Doona ye be standing there, ye jackanapes. The way ye loaf on the job, I would be thinking ye English."

"Actually, madam, I am."

"Weel, fine. I will be looking for the authoress. My great-granddaughter, ye see. She wrote yon book. How much is the treatise?"

"A dollar, madam."

"A whole *dollar?*"

"Yes, ma'am." He offered an arm. "May I escort you to your granddaughter?"

Rafe and Margaret rolled their eyes at each other. Maisie never changed. They handed the boys to their paternal uncle, who'd had second thoughts about Spain, once he had a taste of it.

Maisie, tartan cloth draping her shoulders, marched down the aisle, the lift in her step belying her age—105. "Ye've a nerve, missy, asking highway robbery for yer book. I'll be trusting ye did a good job. Ye always do. Did ye do right by the Mexican people? In yer book and on yer plantations?"

"Haciendas. We call them haciendas. And, no, we couldn't save everyone. But we've saved our own people. It's up to our friends like Villa and Zapata and *la cucaracha* Madera to handle the overall scheme of revolution. But it will happen. The whole of Mexico will change for the better."

"I trust ye willna leave yer wee lads—me very own great-great-grandbairns!—in the line of fire?" Family pride fought with concern in the centenarian's gullied visage.

"Believe me, we'll take care of our boys," Rafe replied.

Maisie turned to him. "Hello, lad. Ye get prettier every year."

Rafael Delgado Senior had made many strides in his years with Margaret, but his vanity remained fair. He preened like a peacock under his great-grand-mother-in-law's praise.

"Whatever happened t' that Eden Roc?" she asked.

A pang of sadness for the Nashes went through Margaret. "It's in ruin. All grown over in vines. The falls stopped flowing the day Isaiah died."

"'Tis a pity. I coulda used yon place."

More of the McLoughlin clan filed into the book-store. Gil and Lisette headed the list, she as lovely as ever. Recently, Gil had retired from government, and they had returned to the Four Aces Ranch. They were more in love than ever.

Again the front door opened. Fresh from Europe came the Hawk branch of the clan. The children, all spit and shine, bounced toward their aunt and uncle. There were the girl twins, Leslie and Sharon. And their younger brother, Narramore.

Hawk and Charity had much news to impart. The Osage nation had become wealthy beyond imagina-tion, thanks to oil being discovered on their reserva-tion. Charity crowed over Hawk's contribution to that good fortune. Years ago he worked diligently to retain those mineral rights for his people.

"And we're back in the States for good," the flamboyant Charity announced. "I've just signed a contract to perform in motion pictures!"

A hum of oohs and aahs coursed around the books and through the air. But today was for Margaret, and everyone praised her devotion to her adopted country. Her love and dedication to the Mexican people shone from each page of her story.

She almost didn't hear the door opening one more time.

"Sissy?"

Margaret turned. A beautiful dark-haired woman, cane in hand, hesitated at the entrance. Dark glasses covered her eyes. Margaret rushed up the aisle and hugged her. "I was scared your ship wouldn't dock in time. It's so good to see you. And you're looking more exquisite than ever."

"Pish-posh. I have sockets where my eyes used to be. But the pain is gone." The Dowager Countess of Granada beamed. "For that I am thankful."

"Where is your son?" Margaret asked.

"Outside. His Tío Arturo is showing him a display of ducks in a pet shop. They will be here in a few minutes."

"*Tío* Arturo? This wouldn't be *our* Arturo, would it?"

"One and the same. He and Helga sailed with me. They'd been on holiday at Biarritz, you see. What a great help they were. They so love little Vicente. You know how it is with childless couples."

"What about you? Are you happy?"

"Very." A serene smile tilted lovely lips. "I bring

444

good news. I am in love with an Englishman. A specialist who works with the visually impaired. We'll be married in the fall."

The sisters embraced. But Charity walked up to tap Margaret on the shoulder, and pout. "You always did love her more than you love me."

A trio of giggles bounced through the store. The triplets loved their old joke. There were no favorites. Their love for one another remained unequivocal. Margaret scanned the faces of all her loved ones. They were all here. All but Tex.

Tears burned the back of her eyes. He'd promised to return from Cuba, if for no other reason to get an autographed copy of the book now on the shelves.

She'd dedicated *The Tears of Cuauhtémoc* to Tex's memory. On the fifteenth of February, 1898, the day after she and Rafe had married, the McLoughlins' young lion went down with the *Maine*.

The bespectacled clerk approached, dragging her thoughts to the present. Thankfully.

"Would you mind taking your seat now, Mrs. Delgado? There seems to be a line at the door . . ."

She glanced to the entrance and saw Dean Ira Ayckbourn heading the queue. *My life would have been so different if I'd said no to Papa, and had started teaching at Brandington.* And then she caught sight of another familiar face. That of Frederick von Nimzhausen. She smiled. When Academic Press had announced the release of her study of the modern Mexican people, Frederick had been the first to send a letter of congratulations.

"Stranger things have happened," Rafe said at the time, and his wife agreed.

Rafe, his limp barely noticeable anymore, stepped forward to take her hand. "It's time to sit down, *querida*." He leaned to whisper, "I'm so proud of you, my love."

Her fingers lifted to his wondrous face, and her gaze welded to his. "Even if I fight my wars with a typewriter rather than with Sir Colt?"

"Don't ask ridiculous questions, woman." In front of her family, as well as a window filled with onlookers, her wild Sierra rogue swatted her behind.

A matron near the door said to her elderly companion, "As I live and breathe! What are these times coming to, when a man fondles a woman in public?"

"Good times."

Margaret quite agreed.

Author's Note

To everyone who's gotten in touch with me about the McLoughlin Clan series—first *Caress of Fire,* then *Lone Star Loving*—thank you for your kind words and interesting advice. I always love hearing from my readers, and I answer each one that includes a SASE. (As soon as I win the Texas Lottery, you won't need to send a stamped envelope!)

I hope you've enjoyed the McLoughlins. It feels strange, finishing with them. (I keep thinking about those kids of Margaret's, as well as Charity's . . . and then there's the young Count of Granada. Shucks!) The McLoughlins have become such a part of my life, it's hard to let go. In the triplets, I've seen my own splendid and obstinate daughters, Leslie Bird and Sharon Beights, as well as my numerous female Jamerson cousins. (We're a very loving yet volatile family!) And on April 29 of this year, our family aped the McLoughlins—we got our own triplets. But ours are all boys . . .

Maisie was easy to write. My aunt Lois Jamerson Atherton inspired the younger Maisie. I told you about Lisette and Gil at the finish of *Lone Star Loving* . . . As for their fictional characters, I couldn't imagine them all hearts and flowers from the end of *Caress of Fire*. They would have died of boredom, if never a word had crossed!

All these generations of McLoughlins — warts and all — wouldn't have been possible without the support of my editor, Alice Alfonsi. She allowed me to write about continuing generations with all their imperfections.

We've been together a good while, Alice and I, starting at Silhouette Books. A certain handsome boxer just *thinks* he's the greatest — Alice is!

Martha Hix
San Antonio, Texas
May, 1993